BORROWED TIME

Also by Robert Goddard

PAST CARING

IN PALE BATTALIONS

PAINTING THE DARKNESS

INTO THE BLUE

TAKE NO FAREWELL

HAND IN GLOVE

CLOSED CIRCLE

Robert Goddard

BORROWED TIME

BANTAM PRESS

LONDON · NEW YORK · TORONTO · SYDNEY · AUCKLAND

TRANSWORLD PUBLISHERS LTD
61–63 Uxbridge Road, London W5 5SA

TRANSWORLD PUBLISHERS (AUSTRALIA) PTY LTD
15–25 Helles Avenue, Moorebank, NSW 2170

TRANSWORLD PUBLISHERS (NZ) LTD
3 William Pickering Drive, Albany, Auckland

Published 1995 by Bantam Press
a division of Transworld Publishers Ltd

All of the characters in this book
are fictitious, and any resemblance
to actual persons, living or dead,
is purely coincidental.

A catalogue record for this book is available from the British Library
ISBN 0593 03587 9

Typeset in 11/12pt Times by
County Typesetters, Margate, Kent.

Printed in Great Britain by
Mackays of Chatham plc, Chatham, Kent.

For the Boys

ACKNOWLEDGEMENTS

For help and advice freely and generously given me during the planning and writing of this novel, I sincerely thank the following.

Jonathon and Susan Stoodley and their many friends in Brussels, notably Xavier Lewis and Nicholas Chan, without whom Robin Timariot's career as a *fonctionnaire titulaire de la Commission Européenne* would never have begun, but upon whom his disillusionments were in no way based; Alistair Brown of the Home Office Prison Department and Colin Symons, Assistant Governor of Albany Prison, who enabled me to imagine the life Shaun Naylor would have led inside; Nigel Pascoe, who proved a more enlightened judge than I would ever have been; and, last but by no means least, Malcolm McCarraher, who must sometimes have regretted offering to apply his expert mind to legal conundrums arising from the plot but never once complained.

I am also grateful to the Governor of Albany Prison for allowing me access to the institution; to Hugh Barty-King, author of *Quilt Winders and Pod Shavers*, a book which played a vital part in the literary genesis of Timariot & Small, cricket bat manufacturers of Petersfield, whose story this partly is; and to the late Edward Thomas, whose poems supplied a wonderfully evocative and eerily appropriate sub-text to many of the scenes I described. (Those specifically quoted from are, in order of reference, 'The Cherry Trees', 'After You Speak', 'It Was Upon', 'Celandine', 'The Unknown', 'What Shall I Give?', 'Like the Touch of Rain', 'The Other', 'When First' and 'Early One Morning'.)

PROLOGUE

It began more than three years ago, on a golden evening of high summer. You know that, of course. You know all the wheres and whens. But not the whys. Not yet, at any rate. I do. I understand the entire sequence of cause and effect leading from that day to this. I can encompass it like a bird of prey circling in the sky above the intervening landscape. I can see the whole winding length of the road I followed from then to now. There were no exits I could have taken, no junctions where I could have left the route. It was always bound to end like this. A future becomes inevitable the moment it touches the present.

You know it all, or think you do. And now you say you want to understand. Very well. Clearly, I must try to explain. Not to excuse; not to mitigate; not to exonerate. Merely to explain. Merely to tell the whole truth for the first time. As I will. As I have to. Then you will understand. For the same reason. You say you want the truth. Very well. You shall have it.

CHAPTER

One

It began [illegible]
[illegible]
[illegible]
[illegible] always [illegible]
since I had a great deal to think about at the time [illegible]
walk seemed one way of ensuring I thought [illegible] and [illegible]
[illegible]
[illegible]
[illegible] wanted [illegible]
[illegible]
[illegible]
[illegible] well [illegible]
[illegible] and [illegible]
[illegible] A day of [illegible]
[illegible]
[illegible]
[illegible] all [illegible] something [illegible]
night, seeing and knowing that [illegible]
I travelled up to [illegible] the [illegible]
previous day, happy to [illegible] away and [illegible]
brother Hugh had [illegible]
[illegible] it had been a shock [illegible]
[illegible] my mother. But Hugh [illegible]
[illegible]
[illegible]

CHAPTER

ONE

It began more than three years ago, on a golden evening of high summer. I'd started out from Knighton that morning on what was projected to be a six-day tramp along the southern half of Offa's Dyke. I've always found I think best when walking alone. And since I had a great deal to think about at the time, a really long walk seemed one way of ensuring I thought clearly and well. Decisions masquerading as choices were closing in around me. Middle age was beckoning, a fork in life's path looming ahead. Nothing was as simple as I wanted it to be, nor as certain. But up in the hills, there was the hope it might seem so.

It was Tuesday the seventeenth of July, 1990. A well-remembered date, well remembered and much recorded. A day of baking heat and unbroken sunshine, declining to a dusk of sultry langour. A day of solid walking and serious thinking for me, of bone-hard turf beneath my feet and hazy blue above my head. I saw no buzzards, as I'd hoped to, circling in the thermals, though maybe, after all, there was something hovering up there, out of sight, seeing and knowing what I was heading towards.

I'd travelled up to Knighton by train from Petersfield the previous day, happy to be away and alone at last. My eldest brother, Hugh, had died of a heart attack, aged forty-nine, five weeks before. It had been a shock, of course. A grievous one – especially for my mother. But Hugh and I had never been what you'd call close. Twelve years was just too big an age gap, I suppose. About the only time we'd really got to know each other as brothers was when we'd walked the Pennine Way together, in the summer of 1973. Since his death, the memory of those three distant weeks on the northern fells had become in my mind a sort of talisman of lost fraternity. My trip to the Welsh borders was partly a conscious act of mourning, partly a search for just a few of the pleasures and opportunities life had offered then.

Above all, however, the trip was intended to clear my mind and decide my future. My sister Jennifer and my other two brothers, Simon and Adrian, all worked in the family business, Timariot & Small, of which Hugh had been managing director. In that sense – and several others – I was the odd one out. I used to claim my career with the European Commission in Brussels gave me immunity from their parochial cares and perpetual squabbles. And so it did. Along with absolute security and relative prosperity. It had given me twelve years of that and could be relied on to give me at least another twenty. Followed by early retirement and an index-linked pension. Oh yes, the life of a Eurocrat has its undoubted rewards.

But it also exacts its penalties. And they'd begun to weigh me down of late. The Berlaymont, an X-shaped mountain of glass and concrete where I'd worked in one cramped office or another since arriving in Brussels, had become even more oppressive in my imagination than it was in reality. It's been closed since, following the discovery of carcinogenic asbestos dust in its every cavity. So, even if you shake the dust of the Berlaymont from your feet, it may still linger in your lungs, waiting patiently – for many decades, so the experts say – to claim its due. Well, there's nothing I can do about that now. And, at the time, it wasn't anything as tangible as asbestos that was choking me. It was the knowledge of all the kilometres of corridor I'd dutifully trudged, all the hectares of memoranda I'd solemnly paraphed, all the tonnes of institutional gravitas I'd played my small part in bearing – and would go on bearing, year after year, until kingdom or retirement or asbestosis come.

I would have done, of course. I'd have gone on for want of any alternative, becoming more cynical and disillusioned as the years passed, becoming more and more like those worn-down colleagues of mine in their mid-fifties, dreaming of Surrey bungalows and golfing days to come. It was already too late to avoid sharing their fate. It was already, as sometimes I realized in the bland Brussels night, over for me.

But then Hugh died. And it didn't have to be over after all. It gives me no pleasure to say this. God knows, I still wish it hadn't happened to him. But my life's turned around since he succumbed to his own punishing workload and slid slowly to the floor of his office just after nine o'clock one evening in June, 1990. I could never have believed what his death would lead me into. And perhaps that's just as well. I'd have fled back to my dull but secure existence in Brussels if I'd known even half of it. That's for certain. But, despite everything that's happened, I'm glad I didn't. I'm glad to have followed this road.

At first, it just seemed like a savage bolt from the blue, a nasty intimation of my own mortality. But the signs were there at the funeral, in the tension that wasn't just grief. For fifteen years, Hugh had *been* Timariot & Small, sustaining it as much by his energy and commitment as by any nurturing of commercial advantage. Now he was gone. And the question wasn't simply who would replace him, but whether the company could survive without his hand on the tiller. Even at the crematorium, Simon and Adrian were eyeing each other in preparation for the contest to come, while Reg Chignell, the production manager, was eyeing both of them and clearly wondering if either was up to the job.

Uncle Larry had come out of retirement to chair the board on a temporary basis. It was he and my mother who put a suggestion to me the day after the funeral which I was still mulling over a month later when I set out from Knighton. Though the youngest of us, Adrian had worked in the company the longest. He also had two sons, which was two more than the rest of us put together and by my uncle's quaint logic made him a fitting guardian of family tradition. Moreover, by virtue of some shares held in trust for the eldest of those sons, Adrian brought more voting power to the table than Simon, Jennifer or me. The managing directorship was properly his, they explained. With the support of Hugh's widow, Bella, who had inherited his shares, they proposed to offer Adrian the post. But they foresaw friction between him and Simon. Well, that hardly required a crystal ball. What was needed was a calming influence, somebody to succeed Adrian as works director and bring the cool good sense of a trained economist to the board's deliberations. What was needed, in short, was me.

Their case wasn't, to be honest, a strong one. I'd worked in the factory during university vacations and in the office during the eighteen months or so it had taken the European Commission to decide they wanted me. But that was all a long time ago and my background in economics was so much eyewash. What my mother really wanted was to lure me home and see me settled in Petersfield, ideally with a wife and children, before she died. Uncle Larry was more than willing to play along. And I was tempted to do the same – for reasons of my own.

I didn't tell them how eager I was to leave Brussels, of course. I didn't want them – and I especially didn't want my brothers or sister – to think they'd be doing me a bigger favour than I'd be doing them. I did my best to imply that for the sake of the family I might be prepared to give up my lucrative career – on the right terms. But there was the rub, as the Commission's conditions of service artfully ensured. The terms would never be good enough. Frustrated or not, as a *fonctionnaire* I was feather-bedded. With Timariot & Small, I was going to feel the draught.

Then there was the future of the company to consider. I wasn't absolutely sure it had one. A past, yes. In 1836, my great-grandfather Joseph Timariot went into partnership with John Small making cricket bats in a modest workshop in Sheep Street, Petersfield. With one change of site – to the present factory in Frenchman's Road – the business had grown since into something like the third largest manufacturer of cricket bats in the country. But that hardly made it General Motors. It employed about fifty people in a medium-sized Hampshire market town, using old-fashioned methods to turn out a handcrafted product in one branch of the sports industry where the Far East hadn't yet caught up with English traditions. The past it proudly possessed, in faded medal certificates from the Great Exhibition, in brown-edged letters of appreciation from Edwardian cricketers, in the sawdusty air of the workshop my father walked through in the footsteps of his father and his father before him. But the furture? Did that really hold a place for the likes of Timariot & Small?

The Timariot family, as I saw it, was in danger of putting all its eggs in one very old and increasingly frail basket. I don't think my father ever thought all five of his children would work for the company. Until his retirement, only Hugh had done so. Then Adrian went into the business straight from school. Uncle Larry retired a few years later and was succeeded as finance director by Jennifer, who until then had been working as an accountant for a supermarket chain. When my father died, Hugh became chairman in fact as well as name and promptly installed Simon as marketing director, rescuing him from some long and inglorious struggles as a photocopier salesman. Which left only me on the outside.

Where good sense suggested I should remain. But the offer of a directorship had been made. And, flushed with generosity following his move to the top of the table, Adrian was happy to confirm it. Simon and Jennifer, seeing me, I suspect, as some sort of check on Adrian's power, urged me to accept. I went back to Brussels promising to give them a decision during the fortnight's leave I'd booked for late July.

So, in a sense, the Rubicon rather than the Severn waited for me at the end of Offa's Dyke. But careworn was the last thing I felt when I stepped out of the George & Dragon in Knighton early that Tuesday morning. I took one glance up at the clock tower, then headed down Broad Street in the direction of the Dyke. My rucksack was full, but, strangely enough, my shoulders felt as light as if they'd just been relieved of some heavy burden. For six days I was free, incommunicado, unobtainable, gone away. For six days, I was my own man.

I walked south through the rolling East Radnor hills as the sun climbed burningly in the sky, shadeless ridges alternating with steep wooded valleys. At some point of the early afternoon I'd have been able to see Hergest Ridge ahead of me, if I'd troubled to look at my map and pick it out through the heat haze. But it was only one landmark among many to me then. Just a name and a place.

I spent the hottest hour and a half of the day in a pub off the route, then pressed on towards the next town on the Dyke: Kington. It waited below me as I rounded the eastern flank of Bradnor Hill: a compact huddle of slate-roofed houses dozing in the sunshine, with the Black Mountains rising beyond. It was a sleepy vision of rural England, with a picturesque touch of wild Wales thrown in.

My destination that night was Gladestry, a village about three miles west of Kington, where I'd booked a room at the Royal Oak Inn. The walk to it along Hergest Ridge was a pleasant one according to my guidebook, so I'd decided to leave it until the cool of the evening. I spent the late afternoon in Kington, pottering aimlessly round the shops until the pubs opened and I could slake my thirst. At a corner table of the Swan Inn, I eavesdropped happily on the local gossip while trying to do some of the thinking my week in the hills was supposed to facilitate. Giving up on the grounds that there were another five days for that sort of thing, I wrote a postcard to my mother instead. It was a muddy-coloured shot of Kington Market Hall circa 1960 and was the only depiction of the town I'd found in any of the newsagents' carousels. I dropped it into a pillar-box on my way back to the path.

The ascent to Hergest Ridge was a narrow tarmac lane called Ridgebourne Road, deteriorating after it had passed a few houses into a stony track. I started up it shortly after seven o'clock. The going was steep but steady. Midges were massing between the fern-banks to either side, the sunlight filtering warmly through the foliage. It was – I'd have said if anyone had asked me – a perfect summer's evening.

A five-bar gate separated the end of the track from the open moorland of the ridge. To the right of the gate, a car had been parked beneath the trees. It was a G-registered white Mercedes two-seater, gleaming from a recent clean. I glanced at it approvingly – even enviously – as I passed, thinking of the wretched little can-on-wheels I ran around Brussels. Some people, I reflected, had all the luck.

I went through the gate and out onto the ridge: a whale-backed expanse of grass and gorse, views to the north opening up as I gained height. Sheep were bleating everywhere, occasionally scattering as I came on them unawares. I passed two weary-looking walkers bound for Kington, who nodded in some kind of fellowship at the sight of my rucksack. Otherwise, my attention was reserved for the horizon of hill and forest, bathed in fading sunlight. As mornings bring expectation, so evenings, I suppose, are naturally peaceful. Certainly, I felt something very like peace descend on me as I gazed out at the loveliness of one portion of my homeland. Returning to the Berlaymont after this, I realized, was going to be like returning to prison.

It must have been near the mid-point of the ridge that I stopped simply to stare for a few minutes at the wide green world laid out before me. I sighed and shook my head and said aloud, for no particular reason: 'Heavenly.'

And a voice behind me said, 'Isn't it just?'

I started and looked round. A few yards away, a woman was sitting on a flat stone at the base of a ruined cairn. She was smiling, though whether at me or the scenery her dark glasses made it impossible to tell. Her blonde shoulder-length hair looked golden in the sunlight, though maybe there were some streaks of silver there as well. She wore a white blouse and tailored beige slacks, slender ankles showing above moccasin-style shoes. Her smile was beguiling, almost girlish, but my immediate impression was of somebody who was no longer young but somehow better for it, somebody who might once have been pretty but was now beautiful.

'I'm sorry if I startled you,' she continued, in a soft slightly husky voice.

'No, no. It . . . doesn't matter. I was . . .'

'Lost in thought?'

'Well . . .' I too smiled. 'You could say so, yes.'

'It's an ideal place for it. I quite understand.' Oddly, I felt she did. I felt she understood completely without needing to be told. She took off her glasses and gazed past me. 'Up here, everything's so . . . so very clear. Don't you think?'

'You . . . come here often?' I asked, wincing at the inanity of the question.

'Not as often as I'd like. But that may be about to change. What about you?'

'Never before. I live . . . a long way away.' Thinking of Brussels, I added: 'But that may be about to change as well.'

'Really?'

I shrugged. 'We'll see.'

'You're walking Offa's Dyke?'

'Part of it.'

I stepped across to the cairn, lowered my rucksack to the ground and sat down on a boulder beside her. She looked round at me, her smile fading into the gentlest of appraising frowns. Closer to, my earlier guess was confirmed. She was older than me, in her mid-forties perhaps, but younger in spirit. There was something graceful but also skittish about her, something elegantly unpredictable. Hers was the face you'd notice across a crowded room, the voice you'd strain to hear, the quiet air of mystery you'd long to breathe.

I glanced at her left hand where it rested on her knee. There was no ring on the third finger. But there was a pale band of untanned flesh where one had recently been. Some flicker of her blue-grey eyes suggested she knew I'd noticed. But she didn't withdraw her hand. I coughed to cover my embarrassment and said: 'Yours is the Mercedes parked in the lane?'

'Yes.' She laughed. 'Pathetic, isn't it? That it's so obvious, I mean.'

'It was the only car there. I—'

'Can we really change anything, do you think?' Her tone had become suddenly urgent. Her hand tightened on her knee. 'Can any of us ever stop being what we are and become something else?'

'Yes,' I said, taken aback by her intensity. 'Surely. If we want to.'

'You think it's as simple as that?'

'I think it is simple, yes. But not easy. I think the real problem is . . .' I hesitated. We were talking about each other's life without knowing what the other's life comprised. It made no sense. And yet it seemed to.

'What is the real problem?'

'*Knowing* what we want.'

'Deciding, you mean?'

'If you like.'

'But once we have decided?'

'Then . . . it's still not easy. But at least it's possible.'

'You believe that?'

She was staring at me intently, as if what I said – as if my exact choice of words – might make a real difference. For a fleeting instant, I was convinced she was asking me to make up her mind for her. What about I didn't know and didn't want to know. The freedom to choose a future mattered more than our separate pasts. That freedom was what she was silently urging me to assert. So I did – for my sake as well as hers. 'I believe it,' I said, with quiet emphasis.

She nodded in satisfaction and glanced down at her wristwatch, then back up at me. 'Where are you heading tonight?'

'Gladestry.'

'Then I should let you get on.'

'I'm in no hurry. But perhaps you . . .'

She chuckled faintly. 'I'm in no hurry either. But, still, I must be going.' She rose to her feet, leaning forward as she did so. I caught a lacy glimpse of bra – a cool hint of flesh – between the buttons of her blouse. Then I stood up as well and realized how much shorter she was than I'd thought, how much slighter and more vulnerable than her eyes and voice had implied. 'Yes, I really must be going,' she murmured, scanning the horizon. She turned to me with a broad smile. 'Can I offer you a lift to Gladestry? Or would that be cheating? I know what sticklers you hikers are.'

I was tempted to contradict her, to say no, on the contrary, a lift to Gladestry – perhaps a drink in the pub there – would be delightful. But somehow I knew she didn't want me to say that. The true value of a stranger lies in his never becoming anything else. 'I'll walk it, thanks.'

'Goodbye, then,' she said. 'And good luck.'

I grinned, thinking she was casting humorous doubt on my hiking abilities. 'You reckon I'll need it to reach Chepstow?'

'I'm sorry.' She blushed slightly and shook her head. 'I didn't mean that.'

'Never mind. I probably will. Good luck to you too.'

'Thank you.'

I found myself shaking her hand. One fleeting touch of palms and fingers. Then the same dazzling smile she'd greeted me with. Before she turned and walked away down the broad grass track towards Kington. I watched her for a minute or so, then, fearing she'd look back to find me staring dolefully after her, I too turned, heaved on my rucksack and started on my way. I glanced at my watch as I did so and noted the time. It was just after a quarter to eight. She would still have been in sight then. The future would still have been retrievable. But by the time I next stopped to look back, near the summit of the ridge, she'd vanished. And the future had taken its invisible shape.

I reached Gladestry at dusk. A cluster of stone cottages by a drought-sapped brook, complete with church, school, post office and pub. I lingered long enough in the bar of the Royal Oak to eat a hearty supper. Then I went up to my feather-mattressed bed and slept the log-like sleep of the long distance walker. Early next morning, I set out for Hay-on-Wye.

That day and the four following settled into a pattern of prompt starts, midday lay-ups to dodge the heat and evening arrivals at comfortable inns. The landscape varied from the bleak grandeur of the Black Mountains to the soothing beauties of the Wye Valley. On a conscious level, I thought of little beyond mileages and map references. But subconsciously, as I realized at the end of the walk, my mind was hardening itself against a return to the life I'd led in Brussels. I'd have to go back, of course, if only to resign, but I could never go back in the true sense. Somewhere behind me on the path, a bridge had been decisively burnt. If I'd had to specify where, I'd have opted for Hergest Ridge. The woman I'd met that first evening didn't fade from my memory. On the contrary, my encounter with her seemed to grow in significance as I went on. Not because of the words we'd exchanged so much as the suspicion that somehow, by letting her go so easily, I'd let some opportunity – sexual, psychological, altogether magical – slip from my grasp. I didn't know her name or where she lived. I knew nothing about her at all. And now I never would. It was a melancholic reflection, heightened by solitude. Yet it steeled my resolve. Whatever happened, I wasn't going back to the life I'd left behind.

During those six days on Offa's Dyke, I was effectively sealed off from the outside world. I read no newspapers, watched no television, heard no radio. My conversation was limited to trifling exchanges with publicans, shopkeepers and fellow hikers. I suppose it was a little like retreating to a monastery for a week. As a source of refreshment, it equalled the most ravishing scenery. Being out of touch came to seem a deliciously pleasant condition. I didn't want it to end. But it had to, of course. Every journey has a destination. And mine was the real world.

At sunset on Sunday the twenty-second of July, I stood on Sedbury Cliffs, at the very end of the Dyke, gazing across the Severn Estuary at the motorway suspension bridge, thick with traffic speeding back to London and the cares of the working week. I remember thinking at the time how pointless their haste was. With the perspective of six days walking behind me, I saw their ant-like bustle as stupendously futile. I felt momentarily superior to them all, detached from their petty struggles and enlightened beyond their power to imagine. Which was ironic, since most of them probably already knew. Had known, anyway, even if they'd subsequently forgotten. What I'd not yet found out. But very soon would.

I stayed overnight in Chepstow, at the George Hotel, and left late the following morning after treating myself to a long lie-in and a leisurely breakfast. The rail route back to Petersfield was time-consumingly indirect, though I can't say I much minded, dozing in sun-warmed carriages as various trains rattled me around South Wales and Wessex. With my mind made up, I was no longer in any hurry.

When my father retired from Timariot & Small, he and my mother sold the house in Petersfield where I'd been born and bought a bungalow in the nearby village of Steep. It was where I was heading that day: a thirties construction of tile and brick set on sloping ground near the foot of Stoner Hill, easily mistakable for an ancient cottage thanks to swags of wisteria, patches of lichen and a riotously fertile flower garden. Its name – Greenhayes – *was* ancient, belonging to a demolished dwelling whose stones had survived in a rockery. Steep's famous dead poet, Edward Thomas, is supposed to have mentioned Greenhayes in one of his prose pieces, though I've never bothered to track it down, so I don't know what he made of the original. As for its successor, it was looking at its best that late summer's afternoon when I climbed from the taxi. But I never forgot the mists that rolled down from the combes in winter and stayed for days, shortening, I maintained, my father's life. Greenhayes' welcome was for me always double-edged.

My mother, by contrast, loved the house without reservation. She'd filled it to the brim with the hotchpotch furnishings and bric-à-brac of the family home and had become an ever more demonic gardener as the years of her widowhood passed. She'd also acquired a yappy little cross-bred terrier called Brillo (on account of his strong resemblance to a wire scouring pad) who rendered a doorbell redundant. As usual, he alerted her to my arrival before I'd done much more than lift the latch on the front gate.

'Who's that, Brillo?' she called from out of sight as he growled at the scent of alien soil on my boots. Then she emerged round the side of the house, rubber-gloved and panting from some vigorous bout of weeding. She was in her gardening outfit of faded frock and broken-down shoes, bare-headed despite my gift to her two birthdays back of just the wide-brimmed straw hat she'd claimed to want. It had lain unused in a supermarket carrier bag on top of her wardrobe ever since and I'd stopped asking why she never wore it. 'Oh, it's Robin. How lovely to have you back, dear,' she said, advancing to give me an elderflower-perfumed hug. 'Nice walk?'

'Fine, thanks.' And so eighty miles of Offa's Dyke were somehow written off as no more than a stroll down the lane.

'You're just in time for tea.'

'I thought I might be.'

'And in need of it, by the look of you.' Stepping back to examine me, she frowned and said: 'You're getting too thin, dear. Really you are.' Actually, it was she not me who was growing thinner with the years. But any of her offspring who were less than two stones overweight were anorexic in her eyes. 'We'll have to feed him up, won't we, Brillo?' At which Brillo barked in what she took for agreement but I knew to be an automatic reaction to any mention of food.

I followed her into the house, scarcely listening as she described the difficulties she was having with her runner beans on account of the heat. I wondered when – if I said nothing – she'd ask what decision I'd made about joining the company. Around the time she offered me a third cup of tea and a second slice of cake – or earlier?

I dumped my rucksack at the foot of the stairs, pulled off my boots and ambled into the sitting-room. On the mantelpiece, propped between framed photographs of two of Adrian's children, was my postcard from Kington. But of the other two I'd sent – one from Hay-on-Wye, one from Monmouth – there was no sign.

'Only one card so far, Mother?' I shouted into the kitchen, where crockery was rattling and the kettle already sizzling.

'What, dear?'

'*There are two more cards on their way.*'

'Cards?' She bustled in with a cloth for the coffee table and pulled up beside me. 'It's there, look. Staring at you.' She nodded at the fuzzy shot of Kington Market Hall.

'Yes, but—'

'Which reminds me. Simon was here for lunch yesterday. He was peering at that card. Said what a coincidence it was.'

'Coincidence?'

'Said I was to ask you whether you'd seen anything. Police. Film crews. Journalists. I suppose the place was crawling with them.'

'Sorry?'

'Kington. Where you sent the card from.' She snatched it up and squinted at the postmark. 'The eighteenth. When was that?'

'Wednesday. But it was Tuesday when I—'

'Wednesday! There you are. That's when it was on the news.'

'What was?'

'The two people who were murdered. You must have heard about it. They've arrested somebody now, according to the papers. Haven't you seen today's?'

'No. Nor any—'

The kettle began to boil. 'It's there, by my chair.' Pointing vaguely at the crumpled wreckage of her *Daily Telegraph*, she hurried out. Puzzled, I grabbed up the paper and riffled my way to the front page. A single-column headline towards the bottom caught my eye. KINGTON MURDERS: MAN HELD. *Police investigating last week's brutal double murder in Kington yesterday confirmed that a man is helping them with their enquiries. They did not indicate whether charges were imminent, but the shocked population of the quiet Welsh borders market town will be hoping this brings an early end to the hunt for whoever was responsible for strangling internationally renowned artist Oscar Bantock and raping and strangling a woman since identified as Louise Paxton, wife of royal physician and society doctor Sir Keith Paxton, at Mr Bantock's home in Kington on the evening of July 17. The man, who has not been named, was arrested in London yesterday afternoon and taken to Worcester Police Headquarters for questioning. A spokesman for West Mercia C.I.D. said it was unlikely that—*

The evening of July 17. I'd left Kington at seven o'clock and walked along Hergest Ridge to Gladestry. And on the way I'd met— There was no reason why there should be any connection. There were lots of reasons, in fact, why there shouldn't be. But my hands were still shaking as I pulled the previous day's paper from the canterbury. It was Sunday's and therefore likely to have a feature on the case. I knelt over it on the floor and began turning the pages. Then I stopped. There was her face, gazing out of the black-and-white photograph as she'd once gazed past me at the sunset-gilded horizon. And the caption beneath the photograph read: *Rape and murder victim Louise Paxton.* I'd let her walk away from me that evening – to her death.

CHAPTER

TWO

My mother wasn't in the habit of throwing newspapers away; she had too many uses for them. When I scrabbled through the stack she kept in the scullery, I found a more or less complete set for the past week. Complete enough, at all events, to tell me as much as anybody else had been told of the Kington killings.

'I didn't know you'd be so interested, dear,' she said, as I spread them out on the kitchen table and tried to assemble a clear account of what had happened. 'There are people being murdered every day. Why don't you come into the sitting-room and have your tea?'

'You go ahead, Mother. I won't be long.' I wasn't ready to reveal my connection with the case. I couldn't help thinking it would be easier if I were a friend or relative of Louise Paxton. Then I'd have some genuine reaction to cling to. Instead, I was gripped by a sort of dislocated horror. She was a stranger to me. No more, no less, than she was to the two hikers I'd passed on my way up onto the ridge. They probably hadn't even noticed her. But I had. Or rather *she* had noticed *me*. Logically, it shouldn't have mattered. She could have died in a car crash that same night and I'd never have known. But she hadn't. And now I knew what had really happened to her, I was never going to be able to forget.

The murders had taken place at a house called Whistler's Cot. It stood at the far end of Butterbur Lane, a turning off Hergest Road, which led out of Kington on the southern side of

Hergest Ridge. Comparison of my Ordnance Survey map of the area with a town plan I'd picked up at the tourist information office in Kington enabled me to locate the spot precisely. It was scarcely a mile from where I'd met Louise Paxton, though getting there by car would have involved her driving back into Kington and out again. Butterbur Lane was narrow and winding, climbing steeply across the south-eastern flank of Hergest Ridge until it petered out in the woods and pastures of Haywood Common. The last residence in the lane was Whistler's Cot.

Its owner was a well-known artist I'd never heard of called Oscar Kentigern Bantock, aged sixty according to the police and fifty-eight according to his *Daily Telegraph* obituarist. Bantock had bought the place about ten years before and had a studio built onto the rear of what would otherwise have been a two-up-two-down cottage. He'd also added a garage for his notoriously noisy Triumph sports car. Despite his London roots and artistic temperament, Bantock was popular with his neighbours and the regulars of several Kington pubs. They knew little of his tattered reputation as a hero of English Expressionism. The obituarist referred to a brief vogue for his work in the sixties. Since then, by implication, his career had been anti-climactic. But a trickle of commissions and exhibitions, along with some sort of inheritance from an aunt, had kept him going. Until violent death called by to make him suddenly collectable.

At about half past ten on the morning of Wednesday 18 July, Derek Jones, a local postman, stopped his van outside Whistler's Cot. He normally pulled into the parking bay in front of Bantock's garage, but that was occupied by a car he didn't recognize: a white Mercedes two-seater. Jones got out, carrying a few letters, and made his way to the rear of the house. He was in the habit of cadging a mug of tea off the old boy at the end of his round and usually found him in his studio. He'd tap on the window and go into the kitchen, where they'd talk about motor racing – a shared enthusiasm. But as soon as he reached the studio window, Jones realized something was dreadfully wrong.

The room was in chaos, pictures and easels up-ended, paints and brushes littering the floor. And he could see the lower half of Bantock's body, protruding from under a bench. Jones rushed in through the kitchen, finding the door, as usual, closed but not locked. As soon as he saw Bantock's face, he knew he was dead. He'd been strangled. More accurately, as the police later discovered, he'd been garrotted with a short length of picture-hanging wire left embedded in his neck.

Jones tried the telephone in the kitchen, but it wasn't working. The lead had been ripped out of the socket. He then ran down to the next cottage in the lane and raised the alarm, waiting there until the police arrived. It was just one policeman at first, PC George Allen from the station in Kington. He questioned Jones, then entered Whistler's Cot, confirmed Bantock was dead and searched the rest of the house before summoning help.

Upstairs, in one of the two bedrooms, Allen found the second victim: a middle-aged woman, naked, face-down on a bed and strangled in identical fashion to Bantock. Subsequent examination showed she'd been sexually assaulted. This was Louise Paxton. And the time of her death was later put at between nine and ten o'clock the previous night, no more than two hours, in other words, after our meeting on Hergest Ridge.

A full-scale murder inquiry now swung into operation under Detective Chief Superintendent Walter Gough of West Mercia CID. Whistler's Cot was sealed off. Scene-of-crime officers set to work combing the house and garden for evidence. A Home Office pathologist, Dr Brian Robinson of Birmingham University, arrived by helicopter to inspect the bodies. The other residents of Butterbur Lane were questioned. A press conference was fixed for the afternoon. And frantic efforts to contact friends or relatives of the dead woman commenced.

The contents of a handbag in the house and computer records of the registration of the white Mercedes suggested she was Louise Jane Paxton of Holland Park, London. But her next of kin proved elusive and it was Friday morning before she was named in the press. It transpired that her husband, Sir Keith Paxton, was abroad and, of their two children, one, Sarah, was on a touring holiday in Scotland, while the other, Rowena, was at the family's country residence in Gloucestershire. Rowena had identified her mother's body on Wednesday night, but problems in contacting Sir Keith and the other daughter delayed an announcement.

Louise Paxton's identification heightened media interest in the case, elevating it to the front page. Sir Keith was a consultant gynaecologist who'd officiated in his time at several royal births, been given a knighthood as his reward and now dispensed advice to the infertile rich from brass-plaqued premises in Harley Street. It was explained on his behalf that his wife was a connoisseuse of Expressionist art. She owned several Bantock originals, had been trying to persuade Bantock to sell her another and had travelled to Kington on July 17 in response to a message from the artist indicating he was now prepared to accept her offer for the ominously named work *Black Widow*. There'd been hurtful gossip in Kington since the murders based on the time of death and Bantock's goatish reputation, but the police were as anxious as the Paxton family to quash it. There was a margin of error in Dr Robinson's estimate of the time of death, they pointed out. The pathologist also thought Bantock could have died up to an hour before Lady Paxton. Chief Superintendent Gough's theory was that she'd called at the house for the reason supplied by her husband, had surprised Bantock's killer, been forced by him to strip, then been raped and eventually strangled. The circumstances were horrific enough, even to a seasoned officer such as himself, without adding malicious tittle-tattle to the family's burden of grief.

Quite so. But I'd seen her ringless finger. I'd heard the tone of her voice. Whatever she'd been thinking about on Hergest Ridge, it wasn't the purchase of an oil painting. Not that her motives were relevant, of course. Only the motives of her killer mattered now.

And the police seemed at a loss. There were no signs of forcible entry at the house. But Jones – and several neighbours – confirmed that Bantock often left doors unlocked and windows open when he went out. And more than one of those neighbours thought they'd heard his Triumph driving down the lane in the early afternoon of July 17, then back up the lane some time between seven and eight o'clock that evening. He could easily have come upon an opportunist burglar and been strangled for his pains. Only for Lady Paxton to arrive before the murderer could beat a retreat. The timing – as I knew better than most – certainly made sense.

But something else didn't. What burglar turned so easily to rape and murder? Why not just leg it across the fields when he heard Bantock's car? And had he actually stolen anything? The police seemed coy on the point, suggesting that, since Bantock lived alone and in some disorder, it was hard to tell. They admitted, however, that Lady Paxton's credit cards and cheque book had been found in her handbag, along with more than a hundred pounds in cash. It seemed a strange oversight for a burglar.

Then there was the question of how he'd arrived and left. On foot, presumably, since nobody had heard a car leaving at the appropriate time. The police reckoned a car in such a narrow lane would have been too risky anyway. What they didn't rule out was that he'd driven up to spy out the land earlier in the day; perhaps spotted Whistler's Cot as a soft touch then. Several residents of Butterbur Lane mentioned strange cars coming and going, but they were different colours and makes at different times. Besides, dog-walkers and the like heading for the common always did come and go. Such sightings meant nothing.

And nothing was what the police seemed to have to go on. Until the bald announcement of an arrest in London. Till then, they'd been saying the culprit was probably local. Well, perhaps he'd fled to London after the event. Perhaps his flight was what aroused suspicion. There was no way for me to know.

But, arrest or no arrest, I couldn't ignore their appeals for information. They'd been trying to trace the last movements of the deceased with remarkably little success. Somebody thought they'd seen Bantock in Ludlow, twenty miles north-east of Kington, at about four o'clock on the afternoon of July 17. Somebody else thought he'd staged a reckless piece of overtaking on the Hereford to Abergavenny road, twenty miles *south* of Kington, around the same time. They might both be wrong, but they couldn't both be right. As for Lady Paxton, she'd had lunch with her daughter Rowena at their Cotswold home and set off for Kington at about three o'clock that afternoon. She'd declared her intention of taking *Black Widow*, if she bought it, to show off to an old schoolfriend in Shropshire who shared her taste. In that event, she wasn't to be expected back until some time the next day. The daughter had assumed that's exactly what she'd done.

So, from at least mid-afternoon onwards, both the deceased had vanished from sight. At least as far as the police were concerned. But I knew better. I knew precisely where one of them had been within two hours of their estimated time of death. As that fact emerged more and more clearly, so what I knew became not just important but disturbing. At first, I felt excited, intoxicated by the uniqueness of the information I possessed. Then it began to worry me. Would I be believed? Would I, perish the thought, be *suspected*? Somewhere, at the back of my mind, dwelt an old adage that the last person known to have seen a murder victim alive is the first person the police suspect of being the murderer. Then I dismissed the idea as paranoid nonsense. They already had their murderer. And I had an alibi. The landlord of the Royal Oak, Gladestry, wouldn't have forgotten me. Would he? Well, he might be vague enough about my time of arrival to be inconclusive, it was true. And for all I knew the man they'd arrested in London might by now have been eliminated from their inquiries. But, then again, there'd be fingerprints, wouldn't there? More than fingerprints if rape was involved. DNA analysis of sperm and blood meant they couldn't really get the wrong man these days. Could they?

I walked out into the garden and gazed up at the thickly wooded hills above Greenhayes, sun and shadow revealing the switchback succession of crest and combe beneath the trees, the bone of white chalk beneath the flesh of green leaves. I remembered Hergest Ridge and the world spread out in golden promise at our feet. Two strangers. One fleeting moment. It didn't mean anything. They had their man. Why confuse the issue? Why involve myself? Because there was nobody else, of course. Nobody else who knew where she'd been and what she'd said that evening.

Ah yes. *What she'd said.* Was I really going to reveal that? Every word? Every hint of a double meaning? Was I going to break her confidence? She'd trusted me as a stranger. Perhaps that's what I ought to remain. No, no. That was special pleading. That was the false logic part of me wanted to cling to. The other part dwelt on the horror of her death. Stripped. Raped. Strangled. What, as a matter of simple fact, could actually be worse? I shook my head, sickened by my inability – my unwillingness – to imagine. And sickened also by a memory. A single recollected pang of lust. Mine. With her as its object. It wasn't to be compared with what *he* had done to her. Of course it wasn't. But it was how it began. For him as well as me. A long way, a world, apart. Yes. But linked, like two distant dots on a graph. Connected, however faintly, by some tiny strand of sympathy.

I walked slowly back into the house and looked down at the pile of newspapers spread out on the kitchen table. The television was on in the sitting-room, the signature tune of an Australian soap fading vapidly away. My mother would be wondering what I was up to. And her curiosity, once aroused, was indefatigable. Only a vigorous display of normality was likely to hold it at bay. So, summoning a grin, I went in to join her.

'Where *have* you been, Robin?' she asked, glaring round at Brillo's warning yelp.

'Sorry. I was . . .' A phrase came unbidden to my mind. 'Lost in thought.'

'Didn't you do all the thinking you needed to on your walk? I was hoping you'd have made up your mind by now.'

'Don't worry. I have.'

'So you *will* be joining the company?'

'The company?' My frown must have puzzled her. For the moment, Timariot & Small, with or without me, seemed too trivial a subject to discuss. 'Well . . .' I hesitated, struggling to remember just what I *had* decided. 'Yes.'

'Oh, how wonderful.' She jumped up and kissed me. 'Your father would have been so pleased.'

'Would he?'

'I must phone Larry. He'll be delighted.' She bustled out into the hall, leaving me staring vacantly into space. By rights, I should be the one using the telephone. But to call the police, not Uncle Larry. I smiled ruefully. It would be quicker to drive to the police station in Petersfield than wait for my mother to come off the line. Still, at least she'd given me—

The newsreader's voice cut across my thoughts. *'West Mercia police have now charged the man they've been holding since yesterday with the murders of Louise Paxton and Oscar Bantock at Kington in Herefordshire last week. Shaun Andrew Naylor, a twenty-eight-year-old electrician from Bermondsey, south London, has also been charged with the rape of Lady Paxton. He will appear before Worcester magistrates tomorrow morning. Here's our Midlands crime correspondent, David Murray.'*

And there *was* David Murray, a sloppily dressed figure in front of Worcester police station, mouthing the customary platitudes at the fag end of what looked to have been a bad day. I hardly heard what he said. A name, an age, an occupation and an approximate address. That was all we were getting. And all we would get, until the trial. Unless we were looking for an excuse, of course. Like I was. They'd charged him. With rape as well as murder. They must have all the evidence they wanted. They didn't need my obscure little piece of the jigsaw. I'd just be wasting their time by telling them. Wouldn't I?

It seemed sensible, in the end, to sleep on the problem. Easier, anyway, than explaining it to my mother. But sleep wouldn't play along. My first idle day after six on the hoof left me alert and thoughtful long past midnight. I lay in my bed, listening to the owl-hoots and fox-barks that drifted in through the window, to the muffled fluttering of bats and the distant scurrying of other things I couldn't name.

Eventually, I realized there was only one thing for it. It was a solution that neatly spared me a cross-examination by my mother, while just as neatly salving my conscience. Getting out of bed as quietly as I could, I tiptoed down to the hall, carried the telephone into the sitting-room, closed the door over the trailing lead and dialled the number given in the paper for West Mercia CID's incident room. But the only answer was a recorded message, to which I responded with one of my own.

'My name is Robin Timariot. I've just returned home after walking Offa's Dyke and only now heard about the Kington killings. I believe I may have met Lady Paxton near Kington during the early evening of July seventeenth. If I can be of any assistance, please ring me on Petersfield 733984.'

I put the telephone down with a sensation of relief. The ball was in their court now. Perhaps they wouldn't call back. Perhaps they wouldn't even listen to the message. Then I'd be able to say I'd done my duty. If they chose to neglect theirs, I wouldn't be to blame. So I told myself, anyway, as I crept back up to bed.

Uncle Larry's reaction to my decision to accept the post of works director of Timariot & Small was to call an informal board meeting the following morning. Only executive directors were invited, which eliminated Bella as well as my mother. Having inherited Hugh's 20 per cent shareholding, Bella was potentially a power in the land, but so far she'd shown no sign of wishing to exert any influence. She'd given my appointment the sort of disdainful blessing those more credulous than me took for the numbed consent of a grieving widow. But I knew there was a hint of scorn behind the veil.

The meeting was fixed for eleven o'clock. Determined to start as I meant to go on, I was at the factory by nine thirty, ingratiating myself with the clerks and secretaries. Then I toured the workshops with Reg Chignell, sniffing the glue-flavoured air, shaking hands with the bat makers, listening to their words of cautious welcome. Ethel Langton, who'd been binding bat handles since Grace was a lad, reminded me of some scrapes I'd got into as a student labourer. And Barry Noakes, the misanthropic storekeeper, explained why the cricket bat industry was bound to go down the drain before he reached retirement. I tried to take it all in good part and found it surprisingly easy to do so. After twelve years at the so-called centre of Europe, I was eager to immerse myself in a world where people, profits and products had some obvious and tangible connection. Peripheral or not, Timariot & Small was suddenly where I wanted to be. I'd often talked at dinner parties in Brussels when the nostalgia flowed with the wine of how I missed the culture, language and countryside of my homeland. It was a simple and obvious sentiment, shared by many in the expatriate community. But, standing in the yard between the ramshackle sheds and patched-up Nissen huts that comprised my new and far from gleaming empire, I realized what I'd really missed all along. Just a place to belong. And this, for better or worse, was it.

The office block was a modern featureless structure of brick and glass. But the boardroom, thanks to subdued lighting, wood-panelled walls, gilt-framed photographs of the staff at twenty-year intervals and a presiding portrait of Joseph Timariot in mutton-chop whiskers and top hat, preserved a soothing air of tradition.

I arrived there a few minutes late, having been detained in the sanding shed by one of Dick Turner's rambling monologues. Uncle Larry was already in the chairman's place. He'd agreed to stay on until I – or whoever they'd have chosen if I'd turned the job down – was in post. Catching his keen-eyed glance and dimpled grin, I wished for a moment that he could remain as chairman. He was getting a little shaky, it was true, but there are many things worse than decrepitude. His mind was still razor-sharp. And, with him in the chair, we might at least have pretended to be loyal siblings.

My brother Adrian, managing director and chairman elect, sat at Uncle Larry's right hand. He seemed to look sleeker and slimmer every time I saw him, a smooth-talking tribute to the merits of fatherhood, fitness and low-alcohol lager. He'd turned himself, from unpromising beginnings, into a perfect simulacrum of the snappily dressed businessman. I couldn't help admiring his transformation from the sullen child I'd grown up with. In the process, he'd become just what he wanted to be. Head of the family business. And, by this latest manoeuvre, my boss. Which, if I cared to dwell on it, cast a disturbing light on his eagerness to recruit me.

Jennifer, who sat opposite him, seemed by contrast less and less ambitious as the years passed. With Hugh gone, she was, at forty-five, the oldest of us. She didn't look it, thanks to a stylish dress sense and a boyish haircut, but her impish humour was less in evidence than it used to be. An earnestness – a conservatism that would once have horrified her – was extending its stealthy grip. I hadn't forgotten her colourful youth. Her exotic taste in clothes and boyfriends, glamourized by never specified dabblings in the drugs scene, was a source of wonderment to me in my early teens. But if I'd mentioned any of that to her now, she'd probably have accused me of making it all up. And looking at the cautious smile playing across her face, I might even have believed I had.

Simon, however, who was sitting next to her, had remained loyal to his own reputation if to nothing else. He was in the lower sixth at Churcher's, the local grammar school, when I arrived as a callow first-former. During the next two years, he got himself expelled, reinstated and expelled again while proving he was the hell-raiser everybody thought, before earning short-lived celebrity in October 1967 as the first driver in Hampshire to be breathalysed. All this rebellious irresponsibility was supposed to have been laid to rest by marriage to the redoubtable Joan Henderson, but it didn't stay dormant for long and divorce soon followed, though not before the birth of a daughter, Laura. She was destined for an expensive upbringing and Joan dedicated many of her waking hours to ensuring Simon made a fair contribution to the cost. *Un*fair, to listen to him, of course. And certainly a drain on his natural ebullience these past seventeen years. The drink had also begun to catch up with him lately, his once handsome features acquiring a tell-tale flush. But he was, for all that, the first to shake my hand.

'Welcome back to the asylum, Rob,' he said with a conspiratorial wink.

And welcome, strangely enough, I felt. There was, I sensed, a general agreement that, come what may, it was good to have me aboard. Hugh's death had touched each of us in different ways, but for the moment those ways had drawn us together. The effect was temporary, of course. It was bound to be. The death of a close friend or relative reminds us of the brevity of life and the absurdity of every form of conflict and rancour. But, being human, we soon forget all over again. Those of us gathered at that table hadn't forgotten just yet. But in due course we would.

We talked about which office I'd have, which secretary, what kind of car the business might run to, how soon I could start. It was all briskly good-natured. I could see contentment spreading slowly across Uncle Larry's face. And I could feel the beginnings of it in myself. This was the right thing to do. For them as well as me.

We broke up around noon with an agreement that I'd sit in on the next production meeting, on Thursday, and go over my duties with Adrian in more detail afterwards. I told them I'd be handing in my resignation from the Commission as soon as I got back to Brussels: I was hoping to negotiate an early release, but would be with them by November at the latest. Everything sounded perfectly straightforward. And for the first time since seeing Louise Paxton's face in my mother's newspaper, I forgot about Hergest Ridge and the killings at Whistler's Cot altogether.

But I wasn't to be allowed to do so for long. Simon caught up with me in the corridor and invited me to an early lunch, by which he meant a two-hour soak at his favourite watering-hole, the Old Drum, in Chapel Street. Ordinarily, I'd have excused myself, not sharing his liking for thick-headed afternoons or caring much for the diatribes against Joan he usually embarked on when he'd had a few. But we were both indulging the long-lost brothers routine and I had nothing to get back to Greenhayes for, so I let him lead the way.

Only to be hijacked, before I'd swallowed my first mouthful of Burton bitter, by his hoarse whisper: 'Bit of a coinkidinky, you being in Kington when those murders were done.'

I tried to laugh it off. 'Any chance of an alibi?'

'Seriously, did you see anything?'

This was awkward. If the police never followed up my message, I didn't want to broadcast what I knew. But if they did contact me, Simon was going to remind me of any denial I uttered now. 'What sort of thing did you have in mind?' I prevaricated.

'I don't know. The local constabulary mob-handed. Flashing blue lights. That fluorescent red-and-white tape they rig up everywhere. Oh, and a helicopter. Didn't I read something about a helicopter?'

'Wrong day, Sime. I was on my way south and none the wiser when all that happened.'

'You didn't know about it?'

'Not until I got back to Greenhayes yesterday afternoon.'

He snorted in disappointment. 'Bang goes my chance of some gory details, then.'

'You wouldn't really want any, would you?'

'Maybe.'

'Sorry to let you down.'

'Oh, it's no surprise. You're the sort who'd have been on holiday in Texas in November sixty-three and left Dallas the day *before* Kennedy was shot.'

I shrugged. 'None of us can foretell the future.'

'No, thank Christ. Otherwise, I'd have topped myself the day I first met Joan.'

'You don't mean that.'

'Don't I?'

I sat back and looked at him and decided, on an impulse, to test just how predictable he thought I was. 'What would you say, Sime, if I told you I met the woman who was murdered – Lady Paxton – in Kington the day I was there – July seventeenth? What would you say if I told you she offered me a lift to the next village and I turned her down?'

'I'd say you were stark raving bonkers. According to the papers, she was driving a brand new Mercedes SL. Nobody would turn down a ride in that.'

'It *was* a nice car.'

He frowned. 'You're having me on.'

'No. It's the truth. I recognized her photograph in the *Sunday Telegraph*.'

'Bloody hell.'

'What do you think I should do? Tell the police?'

His reply was instant and instinctive. 'No, I bloody don't.'

'Why not?'

'Because you don't know what you'd be getting yourself into. *Have* you got an alibi?'

'I don't need one. I'm not even a witness.'

'We all need alibis, old son. Every step of the way.' He leant across the table and lowered his voice. 'You'll admit I've never been one for handing out brotherly advice?'

'True.'

'Well, I'm going to start now. If you can avoid getting mixed up in something like this, avoid it. Like the plague. There's no telling where it might end.'

'And if I can't avoid it?'

'Then don't say you weren't warned.'

Simon's concept of the responsible citizen had never coincided with mine. I didn't take his warning seriously. Nevertheless, I'd already decided that, if there was no response to my message, I wouldn't be sorry. I wasn't bothered about alibis – or the lack of them. But I was beginning to suspect that what little I knew was best forgotten. I couldn't properly have explained why, but something about my meeting with Louise Paxton had already become unreal, disturbingly elusive. I'd dreamt about her on several occasions without clearly being able to recollect what I was dreaming. And perhaps that was just as well. The dreams had begun before I knew of her death. But not before the fact of her death. My mind had begun looking for somebody who was no longer there to be found. And I wanted it to stop.

But I'd already given up the power to call a halt. When I reached Greenhayes that afternoon, my mother had a message for me.

'What's this all about, Robin? I've had the police on the phone. A Detective Sergeant Joyce. From Worcester. He wants you to ring him. Urgently.'

CHAPTER

THREE

Detective Sergeant David Joyce of West Mercia CID arrived at eleven o'clock the following morning. He was smartly dressed and well-spoken, with choirboy looks that made him seem even younger than he probably was. My mother took an instant and irritating shine to him, plying him with coffee and cake as if he were the new curate paying a courtesy call. Eventually, she left us to ourselves in the sitting-room.

I'd had the whole of a restless night to prepare what I was going to say. When it came to the point, however, I was tempted to be frank as well as factual. Why not tell him about Louise Paxton's elliptical remarks, her enigmatic glances to the horizon, her implications by word and gesture that she was about to take some significant step in her life? Because I didn't want to be responsible for throwing those particular pebbles into the pond, I suppose. Because I didn't want to share what she'd made exclusive to me: insight without understanding.

Accordingly, I stuck to a plain and simple version of events. We'd met on Hergest Ridge. We'd exchanged a few comments about the weather and scenery. She'd offered me a lift to Gladestry which I'd declined. And then we'd parted. A brief and inconsequential encounter which I'd forgotten all about until I'd seen her photograph in the paper.

'And the time, sir? You said on the telephone you could be specific about the time.'

'Seven forty-five, when we parted.'

'You're sure?'
'Absolutely.'
'It couldn't be later?'
'No. I looked at my watch as she walked away.'
It was a point he seemed anxious about, almost fretful, but he wouldn't say whether it had any bearing on the evidence they'd amassed against Shaun Naylor, whose blanket-draped figure I'd seen bustled out of a Worcester court on the television news the previous night. Clearly, however, the time and circumstances of our parting interested Joyce more than a little.
'This lift, sir. Why do you think she offered you one?'
'The sun was setting. I was probably looking pretty weary. It had been a hot day . . .'
'A friendly gesture, then?'
'Yes.'
'But Gladestry was out of her way, wasn't it, if she was going to Whistler's Cot?'
'I didn't know where she was going.'
'No, sir. Of course you didn't. But tell me, why did you turn the lift down?'
'Because the point of walking a long distance footpath is to walk all of it, not all of it bar two miles.'
'With you there, sir. I did it myself, a few years ago. Offa's Dyke, I mean. The whole way. Chepstow to Prestatyn.'
'Congratulations.'
'But you were only doing the southern half, weren't you? So, completeness doesn't really come into it, does it?'
I looked at him levelly. What was he driving at? 'I'm hoping to do the northern half next year.'
'Oh, I see. Right. And you wouldn't want to have to go back to Hergest Ridge.'
'No. I wouldn't.'
'So, that was the only reason for refusing the lift?'
'What other reason could there be?'
'Oh, I don't know. You might have decided to play safe. If you thought she was offering something more than a lift, I mean. If you and her . . . misunderstood each other.'
I felt a surge of anger at what he was implying. But I was determined not to show it. 'I at no point suspected – or had cause to suspect – that Lady Paxton was trying to pick me up.'
'No, sir. Of course not.'
'In the circumstances, the very idea seems positively offensive.'
'Oh, I agree, sir. But we have to consider offensive ideas in this

sort of case. If only to anticipate what the defence may come up with. They can be very inventive, you know.'

'This man Naylor's denying everything?'

'In a manner of speaking, sir. But I really can't discuss the matter. I've probably already taken up too much of your time. If I made the appropriate arrangements, could you call at the station in Petersfield, say this afternoon, and make out a formal statement of what you've told me?'

'Yes. Certainly.'

'Good. And the time, sir. Seven forty-five. You can swear to that?'

'I can. And will, if necessary.'

'Thank you, sir. That's just what I wanted to hear.'

I walked into Petersfield to dictate and sign the statement that afternoon. My mother had even more questions to ask me than Sergeant Joyce and I was keen to grasp any opportunity of being alone. It wasn't just that I was afraid of letting something slip. The fact was that my life in Brussels had become more and more solitary and this I'd grown rather to enjoy. Since a disastrous affair with an Italian *stagiaire*, I'd deliberately kept intimacy at bay. My bachelor flat in the rue Pascale had become a haven which I only now realized I was going to miss. Especially if my mother's hopes of my living with her at Greenhayes were fulfilled. Which naturally I was determined they wouldn't be.

I was at the police station nearly an hour. The statement I signed, when at last it had been typed, was as accurate yet uninformative as the account I'd given Joyce. It seemed at the time to answer all the different calls on my conscience, though none of them fully.

I can't remember what I was planning to do when I left the station. Perhaps I still hadn't decided by the time I reached the pavement. If not, my mind was soon made up for me. A car horn sounded and, looking round, I saw my sister-in-law Bella smiling at me from behind the wheel of her BMW convertible as it coasted to a halt beside me. 'Hop in,' she said. And, obediently, I did.

By the time I'd fastened my seat-belt, we'd accelerated away down the street. Bella turned onto the main road and headed south out of the town. Middle age and bereavement hadn't sapped her enthusiasm for speed and glamour; quite the reverse. But then I was confident nothing ever would. She'd always been larger than life. And not just metaphorically. Tall, red-haired and built like an Olympic skiing champion, she'd never been what you'd call beautiful. Her jaw and nose were too prominent, her shoulders too broad for that. What she had was a striking, almost intimidating, presence. The way she ate and drank, the way she walked and talked, were part of a physical message only slightly muted now the copper sheen came out of a bottle and the firm thighs courtesy of dedicated hours on an exercise bike. I knew why Hugh had fallen for her. I knew only too well. I understood exactly what drew men to her, formerly in droves, but lately still in appreciative numbers. She exuded sexual appeal like a musk, stronger than any perfume. Meeting her, it was always difficult not to imagine – or remember – the act she took such pleasure in. When would it fade, I sometimes wondered? This power she couldn't help exerting. And the only answer I could give was: not yet.

'Were you going back to Brussels without seeing me, Robin? That wouldn't have been very nice, would it?'

'I haven't been avoiding you, Bella. But . . . pressure of time . . .'

'And pressure of police inquiries? Hilda's told me all about it. That's how I knew where you were.'

'This isn't a chance meeting, then?'

'There's no such thing, is there?'

I couldn't help thinking of Hergest Ridge as I replied: 'I'm not sure.'

'I was hoping you'd come out for a drink with me. It's a lovely evening. The sunny garden of some country pub with an unattached lady for company. What more could you ask for?'

A decent sense of mourning, I was tempted to suggest. But what would have been the point? Bella had never made any secret of her indifference to Hugh. She'd never made a secret of very much at all, to tell the truth. Except what she really felt. About me. And the rest of my sex.

'Shocked not to find me in tears and widow's weeds, Robin?'

'No. Not shocked.'

'But disappointed?'

'No. Not even that.'

'You'll come, then?'

'Do I have a choice?'

'Oh yes. We all have a choice. And from what I hear, you've been making some pretty odd ones lately.'

We stopped at the Red Lion in Chalton and sat with our drinks in the garden. The sun was still hot, unnaturally so, as it had been all week, the sky cloudless, the air dry. Behind us, a gentle breeze rolled in slow blue waves across a field of linseed. I sensed unreality at the edge of my sight, significance close by but out of reach. As if there were symbols in everything I saw and said, but I couldn't find the key to read them by.

Bella closed her eyes and bent back her head, luxuriating in the heat. Her white shirt was knotted at the waist, exposing an inch or more of well-tanned midriff above her pale blue jeans. The bangles at her wrist glinted and rang as she lowered her arm to the table. Then I noticed: she too had abandoned her wedding ring. But the tan had hidden the mark. She must have cast it aside soon after the funeral. Or perhaps not so soon. It would only have taken a day or so in such burning sun to obliterate all trace. In which case—

'I'm no longer married,' she said suddenly. Her eyes were open and trained on mine. 'Why wear the chain of office?'

'Out of respect, I suppose.'

'Ah, but I never was respectful. Was I?'

'Not very. But enough to keep on wearing it while Hugh was alive.'

'I don't believe in throwing things in people's faces. Nor do you, as I recall.' She slid the tip of a finger down the condensation on the outside of her glass. 'Tell me about Lady Paxton.'

'Nothing to tell.'

'Liar.'

I couldn't help smiling as I sipped some beer. It was good to know something she didn't when it had so often been the other way around. 'You haven't congratulated me on the directorship,' I said, changing the subject, as I thought, adroitly.

'Congratulations aren't in order, Robin. You're making a big mistake.'

'You think so?'

'A tiny old-fashioned company making cricket bats? It's got no future, has it? In twenty years, all the kids will be playing baseball. And Timariot and Small will be history.'

'Maybe the European Community will be as well.'

'You know better than that.'

I shrugged. 'We'll see. Meanwhile, I'm throwing in my lot with history.'

'And coming home to Petersfield. I expected better of you, I really did. Hilda says you'll be moving in with her at Greenhayes.'

'Wishful thinking.'
'Where *will* you live, then?'
'I don't know.'
'There's plenty of room at The Hurdles.' That I could easily believe. The Hurdles was the uxoriously over-sized house Hugh had built for Bella at Hindhead in his first flush of possessive ardour. 'I feel quite lonely there these days. I miss Hugh, I suppose. The idea of him living there, I mean. The coming and going. I've even thought of taking a lodger. Just for the company. Perhaps . . .'
'I don't think so, do you?'
'No.' She treated me to a glance of withering assessment. 'Perhaps not.' She took out a cigarette and lit it, then offered me one. I shook my head. 'My, we are becoming ascetic, aren't we?'
'Just taking care of my health.'
'I'm glad to hear it. Is *that* what Offa's Dyke was all about?'
'Partly.'
'But you got more than you bargained for, didn't you?'
'Did I?'
'Well, getting mixed up in these murders.'
'I'm not mixed up in them. I just . . . happened to meet one of the victims.'
'The last person to see her, according to Hilda. Other than the murderer.'
'Apparently.'
She stroked her neck reflectively. 'Was it really rape, do you think? Or just some fun that got out of hand? Sex can, can't it? Sometimes.'
'It was rape. The woman I met wouldn't have . . .' I grimaced, aware of the expertise with which she'd drawn me out.
'There *is* something to tell, then?'
'No. Nothing at all.'
'The place where it happened. Whistler's . . . Whistler's . . .' Her wrist made a few jangling circles in the air.
'Cot.' Another grimace.
'Did you see it while you were in Kington?'
'No, Bella. I did not.'
She nodded and took a thoughtful sip of her spritzer, then grinned mischievously. 'Want to?'
'What do you mean?'
'Well, you must be interested. Just a little. If you had your car with you, I bet you'd drive up there and take a look before going back to Brussels. Too good a chance to miss. But you haven't,

have you? So, perhaps I could give you a lift. Come along for the ride, so to speak. Satisfy my curiosity as well as yours.'

I couldn't suppress a chuckle at her audacity. 'No. Definitely not.'

'Tomorrow?'

'No.'

'The day after?'

'No.'

'Think about it.'

'I won't.'

'You will.' She gave a throaty laugh. 'I know you will.'

My meeting with Adrian the following morning went as well as I could have hoped. He made it clear I'd be expected to pull my weight; the works directorship was no sinecure. If offering me the post was a favour, it was the only one he meant to do me. But that's how I wanted it as well, so we parted on good terms. Mercifully, he said nothing about the Kington killings. He probably considered it beneath his new-found dignity. Whatever the reason, I was grateful to be spared another round of explanations.

'When do you go back to Brussels?' he asked as I was leaving.

'Sunday.'

'So, you'd be free tomorrow? I've got three tickets for the Test Match. Debenture seats. Simon and I were going to make up a threesome with . . .' His face fell. 'Well, with . . .'

'Hugh?'

'Yeh.' The managerial mask had slipped for an instant. 'Hugh liked his cricket. Never missed a Lord's Test that I can remember.' Adrian had known Hugh better than me, probably better than Bella. He'd certainly respected him more. And now he missed him. All this show of confidence and control was really only over-compensation for the loss of his big brother – and mentor. 'Can you make it? It should be a good day. And it's been years since—'

'Sorry, but I can't. I'd really like to. But . . . I have to be somewhere else.'

Bella collected me from Greenhayes at nine o'clock on Friday morning and by midday we were in Kington. The cross-country route and heavy traffic should have delayed us, but Bella was so annoyed by the drizzle that forced her to keep the roof up that she drove even more aggressively than usual. She'd hoped for brilliant sunshine and a warm breeze to stir her hair. But instead the day was grey, still and sappingly humid.

Kington was exactly as I remembered it: a small unpretentious town busily attending to its own affairs. The media circus that had rolled in the week before had rolled out again, leaving the staleness of old news in its wake. Normality had so completely reasserted itself that I could have believed – as part of me wanted to – that nothing had happened there at all.

With some difficulty, I persuaded Bella to leave the car by the church at the western edge of the town and walk down Hergest Road to Butterbur Lane. On foot I thought we'd look less like sensation-seekers than townies out for a stroll, but Bella's idea of casual wear didn't preclude a conspicuous quantity of jewellery and an ostentatiously styled hat straight out of *Harper's & Queen*. We attracted several suspicious looks from occupants of wayside cottages who happened to be in their gardens. And the haughty stare which Bella treated them to in return probably convinced them we were a TV director and his secretary-cum-mistress researching locations for a fictionalized study of rape and murder in the Welsh borders.

Butterbur Lane itself was quieter, as if the residents were deliberately lying low. The cottages here were tucked away behind overgrown hedges and folds in the hillside, sheltered from prying eyes as well as winter winds. We climbed in silence towards a sharp bend which I knew from the map was about halfway to Whistler's Cot. Nothing but the knowledge of what had occurred there infected the scene with strangeness, the breathless air with expectancy. But even Bella sensed it.

'What a place for such a thing to happen,' she whispered to me. 'It's so . . . eerie.'

'You're imagining it.'

'I know. But that doesn't—'

Suddenly, a car burst round the bend ahead of us, the sound of its approach deadened till the moment it appeared by the banks and hedges to either side. It was a large maroon estate, travelling too fast for such a narrow lane. It slewed round the corner, peppering a garden fence with pebbles, then swung back to the crown of the road and headed straight for us. Instinctively, I grabbed Bella's arm and pulled her towards the ditch. Only for the driver to realize the danger and slam on the brakes. More pebbles showered up behind him, followed by a crunching skid and a cloud of dust. Far too late for comfort, he lurched to a halt.

And stared blankly at us through the open side window of the car. He was a man of fifty or sixty, with a thatch of silver-grey hair and a round sagging face. Loose skin hung beneath his jaw where once it might have sat confidently as a double chin. His cheeks were hollow, his eyebrows drooping. And he was crying. His eyes were red and brimming, the tear-tracks moist against his skin. For a second or two, he looked at me, as if trying to frame an apology. I saw him lick his lips. Then he mumbled, 'Sorry,' released the brake and coasted on down the lane.

'Stupid bugger,' hissed Bella. 'He could have killed us.' I heard him engage a gear and speed up, moderately this time, as if he'd been shocked back to reality. 'What did he think he was doing?'

'Probably didn't *think* at all. You know what it's like. Some old codger who's never passed a test or driven in town.'

'He wasn't *that* old.'

No. He wasn't. Nor did he fit the picture I'd painted in any other way. He hadn't looked remotely bucolic. The car was new and in good condition, for which we could be grateful. And he was disorientated by grief, not failing faculties. But I was reluctant to draw the obvious conclusion – that he'd been mourning one or both of the people killed at Whistler's Cot. Why I couldn't have explained. Unless it was the intensity of his grief, the glimpse it had given me of the passion such events could stir. Perhaps I wasn't ready to admit how deep it could run, how formidable it could be. Perhaps I just didn't want to understand.

We went on, both of us shaken but pretending not to be. The bend approached, then fell behind. The cottages thinned. Hints of field and heath appeared beyond the hedges. And then we were there. I recognized Whistler's Cot instantly from newspaper photographs: an old half-timbered dwelling facing the lane, with a modern brick wing running away behind and a garage to one side, set a little back from the line of the house. A gravelled path between led to the rear, without gate or hindrance. The garden looked neglected, the house likewise. Tiles slipping, paint peeling: money spent but never followed up, or never replenished. The name, Whistler's Cot, carved on a wooden sign in runic characters. And some weird sculpture by the front door, half cherub, half God knows what, crudely carved by design, one hand raised, as if to beckon or bar the way but uncertain which.

'Is this it?' asked Bella, a note of disappointment in her voice.

'Yes. This is all there is.' I glanced around. Several windows were open. When Bantock was alive, that wouldn't have meant much. Now it implied occupation. His family, perhaps? If so, I didn't want them to notice us. 'Shall we walk on?'

'Aren't we going to take a closer look?'

'I don't think so.'

'Well, I didn't drive a hundred and fifty miles just to *walk on*. Let's see if there's anybody in.' She started towards the door.

'Bella!'

But she wasn't to be deterred. Pausing only to stick out her tongue at the statue, she rapped the knocker. Then, when several silent seconds had passed and I'd begun to hope she might give up, she rapped it again, louder.

At which the garage door slowly swung up and a figure appeared beneath it, craning across the bonnet of an old Triumph sports car to operate the handle. He was a slightly built man in corduroy trousers and check shirt, a narrow squirrel-like face framed by tufts of ginger hair. He peered out at me with raised inquisitive eyebrows and all I seemed able to say was a weak 'Good morning.'

'It's afternoon, actually,' he replied. 'The afternoon of a long and trying day. I'd be grateful – enormously grateful – if you didn't make it any more trying than it already has been.'

'Sorry. I—'

'Was just nosing around the scene of the crime? Believe me, you're not the first. And it would be unreasonable of me to expect you to be the last, wouldn't it?'

'We *are* sorry,' said Bella, walking boldly across to him, hand outstretched. 'But we're not what you think.'

'No?' He sounded sceptical, but Bella's smile was hard to resist. His head twitched slightly, as if he were about to bow, even kiss her hand. Instead, he merely shook it. 'What then, might I ask?'

'My brother—' She glanced towards me, acknowledging the misrepresentation with a faint flick of the eyebrows. 'Knew Lady Paxton.'

'Really?' Doubt wrestled for a moment with susceptibility, then gave way. 'Well, pleased to meet you, Mr . . .'

'Timariot. Robin Timariot.'

'Henley Bantock.' We shook hands. 'Nephew and heir of Oscar Bantock.'

'My . . . er . . . sister, Bella . . . Timariot.'

'Delighted, I'm sure.'

'Lady Paxton's death came as a . . . a terrible shock. I . . . felt I had to . . .'

'That's quite all right. Why don't you both come inside?' He led the way and we fell in behind, Bella treating me to a triumphant smirk. 'I'm sorry if I was a little curt. This is the first day the police would allow me past the door and I've been attempting to sort things out. But the interruptions have been continual. Neighbours thinking I might be a squatter. Tradesmen flapping unpaid bills under my nose.' We were heading for the rear of the house, taking the same route the postman had that fateful morning. 'And, just before you came, a well-dressed middle-aged man weeping – yes, I do mean weeping – on the doorstep. He was in floods of tears. It was quite pitiful.'

'Who was he?' I asked.

'I really couldn't say. You might have known him. I'm surprised you didn't meet him in the lane.' The studio was in front of us now, commanding a broad view to the south, where the garden sloped away. It was an airy structure, lit by enough windows to resemble a conservatory. The blinds were half down, but, through the gaps beneath them, I could see disorderly piles of canvases, large and small, covered in aggressive swirls of colour; Oscar Bantock had been nothing if not prolific. 'As a result, I've made scant progress. Which is inconvenient, to say the least.' He opened the kitchen door and ushered us in. 'Call me superstitious if you like, but I've no intention of staying here overnight.'

And so we entered the house where two people had died – violently and recently. But their deaths had left no presence there, not one I could detect anyway. There were no bloodstains, of course, but, even if there had been, I'm not sure it would have helped me conjure up what had happened. The studio, bathed in sallow light, filled with half a lifetime's unappreciated work and its impedimenta: canvases, frames, brushes, paints, palettes, easels, rags, pots of varnish, bottles of turps and a spattered smock gathering dust in its folds. I'd never seen Oscar Bantock alive and I couldn't imagine him dead, a stark slumped form beneath one of the benches. There was no helpful chalk outline of the corpse to tell me where he'd been found and I hadn't the heart to ask his nephew. Not that Henley Bantock looked or sounded like a man gripped by grief. He stood between us in the kitchen, watching calmly as we stared through the open doorway into the room where his uncle had been choked to death with a noose of picture-hanging wire. Then he sighed heavily.

'It's going to be quite a task, shifting that lot. And cataloguing it, of course. I can't abide the stuff myself. I mean, why couldn't he have turned out tasteful landscapes? But it sets some people's pulses racing, so who am I to complain?'

'Lady Paxton liked his work,' I murmured.

'Yes. So I believe. You could say *she* died for *his* art.' Catching my eye, he added: 'I'm sorry. That was unfeeling of me.'

'The picture she wanted. *Black Widow*. Is it here?'

'Wrapped up in the lounge. I haven't moved it. Uncle Oscar must have had it ready for her, I suppose.'

'Could we see it?'

'Why not? Who knows, you might want to . . .' He frowned. 'Were you a close friend of Lady Paxton, Mr Timariot?'

'Not close, no.'

'A friend of the family, perhaps?'

'Not really.'

'Only one of her daughters is due to meet me here this afternoon. I wondered if . . .'

'We *would* like to see the painting,' put in Bella with a winning smile. 'If that's possible.'

'Certainly. Follow me.' He led us out of the kitchen, down a short passage and into a sitting-room. It was comfortably if untidily furnished. There were well-stocked bookshelves and several paintings by Bantock – or fellow Expressionists – lining the walls. A parcel stood on the only table, the wrappings folded open to reveal the back of a canvas, already hooked and strung with copper-coated wire. Henley lifted the picture out and propped it against the wall behind the table, then stepped back to let us admire it. 'The English Rouault, they said of him in the sixties. I think this one dates from that period. No better or worse than the rest, in my opinion. But, happily, *my* opinion counts for little.'

Black Widow measured about three feet by two foot six. It depicted a woman's face – or a young boy's – seen against a pale blue background. The hair and shoulders were splashes of black and purple, the face yellow tinged with red, the eyes nowhere save in the contrivance of dab and daub, their gaze – solemn, averted, downcast, defiant – a haunting mix of whatever you wanted to read there: the spider, the widow, the murderess, the victim. There was nothing pretty or comforting about it. Louise Paxton hadn't wanted this picture to brighten her wallpaper. But precisely why she'd wanted it we'd never know now.

I stepped back to view it from the doorway. As I did so, Bella moved closer to Henley, cocking her head to squint at the image before her. 'I'd have to agree with you, Mr Bantock,' she said with a chuckle. 'Not quite my idea of art.' I saw Henley glance appreciatively at the smooth T-shirted outline of her breasts beneath her linen jacket. His idea of art was fairly obvious: more Ingres than Rouault, I'd have guessed. 'Inheriting all this must have caused you quite a few problems.'

'It certainly has. The police. The press. You wouldn't believe it.'

'Have you travelled far today?'

'From London.'

'You must have made an early start, then.'

'Indeed I did.'

I edged out into the passage. There were the stairs, leading up to the room she'd died in. Why not go up and take a look? Henley would tell Bella his entire life story if she continued to encourage him. She was assessing him, of course. I knew that. Worth getting to know, or not? Not, I suspected. But clearly she hadn't yet reached that conclusion. And until she did . . .

I took the stairs two at a time, relieved not to set off a fusillade of creaks. The landing was small and narrow. There was a bathroom in front of me, built over the houseward half of the extension. Through a window I could see the shuttered skylights of the studio. The bedrooms were to left and right. The one on the left had been given over to storage: a desk and filing cabinet marooned in a sea of tea chests, packing cases and yet more canvases. From the one on the right came a faint draught. Henley must have opened the window, in an attempt to blow away the memory as well as the mustiness. I walked in, hurrying to forestall any sense that what I was doing was better not done.

But there was nothing to see. A bare room, with white walls and no paintings. One wardrobe, its doors closed. A large double bed, stripped to the mattress, its pillows, sheets and blankets all gone. Absurdly feminine flower-patterned curtains stirring languidly. And a huge gilt-framed mirror on the wall facing the bed, smashed in one corner, cracks radiating to all sides, fracturing the reflection of the room into random triangles. When had it been smashed? I wondered. At what moment? Before? Or after? I shivered and looked at the bed. It was impossible to imagine, too awful to want to imagine. The breath straining, the wire tearing, the flesh yielding. So much agony. So much revulsion. Too much of everything. And now, as its antithesis, a vacuum, a space waiting to be filled. The room was drained, as the house was drained, exhausted by the violence that had briefly filled it. The night of July 17 wasn't there any more. Even the impression it had left had been removed, on strips of tape and forensic slides, in sterile bags and sealed envelopes. In its place was an empty tomb.

By the time I returned to the sitting-room, Henley Bantock's general amiability had refined itself into a drooling eagerness for Bella's company: I knew the signs well enough. Forgetting his earlier determination to 'sort things out' and apparently oblivious of my brief absence, he proposed we go out to lunch together. Bella not yet having ceased to find him amusing, we went. To the Harp at Old Radnor, a hilltop hamlet a few miles north-west of Kington, just off the road to Gladestry. It was a charmingly well-preserved old inn, with picnic benches set up on a bank outside, where a vast panorama of Radnor Forest was added gratis to the menu.

Henley had gone there with his uncle several times, apparently, during periodic visits with his wife, Muriel. She hadn't been able to come this time and Henley was clearly enjoying being off the leash. They both worked as administrators for one of the London Boroughs. Havering, I think. Or Hounslow. Henley spoke so casually of Oscar that I couldn't help suspecting the visits had been designed more to safeguard his inheritance than check on the old boy's well-being. Muriel probably hadn't considered it necessary to accompany him now Whistler's Cot and an entire Expressionist *oeuvre* were in the bag. She might have changed her mind, of course, if she'd known her husband was going to spend half the day ogling my sister-in-law over a ploughman's lunch.

I listened distractedly to his autobiographical insights into the character of Oscar Bantock, which grew less and less complimentary as the shandy flowed. 'He might have looked like a cross between Santa Claus and Captain Bird's Eye but there was a streak of cruelty in him. Call it an artistic temperament if you like, but I saw it differently. He lived with us most of the time I was growing up and coping with him as well as a sick husband was what took my mother to an early grave in my opinion.' While he waxed resentful, my eyes drifted north to the hills I'd crossed ten days before on the path from Knighton. If I'd accepted Louise Paxton's offer of a lift that evening, we might have stopped here for a drink. Then, at the very least, she might have arrived at Whistler's Cot a crucial hour later. Life, in Henley Bantock's self-pitying account, wasn't fair. But death, it seemed, had an artistic temperament.

'What little he made from painting he spent twice over. Not on us, of course. Not even on anything as useful as brushes and canvases. Most of it went on whisky. Only the finest malts would do for Uncle Oscar. And then there were his women. He had a better eye for the ladies than for art, I can't deny. You'd certainly not have left Whistler's Cot in his day without a pinched bottom to remember him by at the very least, Miss Timariot, believe you me. But then, as I say, he did have good taste in that regard if in no other.'

This contrived compliment, risqué as Henley no doubt thought it, was followed by an outburst of chortling and the appearance in Bella's eyes of the steely boredom I'd often seen before. It seemed like the cue I'd been waiting for. 'You don't make your uncle sound like a natural candidate for burglary, Mr Bantock.'

'Oh, I don't know. He was probably splashing money around in some pub. Spending the price agreed for *Black Widow* before he'd actually been paid it. That would be his style. Some ne'er-do-well from London on a housebreaking tour of the provinces takes note and follows him home. Then things turn nasty. Uncle Oscar wouldn't have backed down from a fight, especially not with drink on board.'

'That's how you see it, is it?'

'That's how the police see it. So I understand, anyway. He must have been out when Lady Paxton first called. Probably forgot the time they'd fixed to meet. It would have been unlike him not to. That would explain why she left home at lunchtime. Set on buying the picture, she went back later, I suppose. And walked straight into . . . well, something quite frightful.'

'You think it's open and shut?'

'Presumably. The police must have had good reason to arrest this man Naylor. They seem certain he did it. I assume there's clinching forensic evidence. What more is there to say? Apart from the acute distress Lady Paxton's family must have suffered, of course. Identifying my uncle's body was upsetting enough for me. What it can have been like for Lady Paxton's daughter – a girl not yet out of her teens, I believe – to see her mother, well, in the state she must have been in, in a mortuary, in the middle of the night . . .' He shook his head, briefly sobered by the contemplation of such an experience.

'Is she the daughter you're seeing this afternoon?'

'No, no. The elder daughter's coming. Sarah, I think she said her name was. I'm not quite sure what she hopes to accomplish, but . . .' A point suddenly occurred to him. His nose quivered as it registered. 'Are you acquainted with the girls, Mr Timariot?'

'No. I only ever met their mother.'

'You knew her well?'

I could sense Bella watching me as I replied. 'I felt I did, yes. We . . . understood each other. So I thought.'

'You shared her interest in Expressionism?'

'We never discussed it.'

'Never?'

'We only met once, you see. Just once. Before the end.'

'But . . . I thought you said . . .' He frowned at me, his mouth forming a suspicious pout. 'When *exactly* did you meet her, Mr Timariot?'

'The early evening of July seventeenth.'

'When?'

'The day she died. Just a few hours before, as a matter of fact.'

'But . . . I understood you to say . . . you were a friend of hers.'

'No. I didn't say that. You assumed it.'

'You're splitting hairs. You let me think . . .' He glared round at Bella. 'You both let me think . . .'

Bella glanced irritably at me, then laid a calming hand on Henley's elbow and smiled sweetly at him. 'When's your appointment with Miss Paxton, Mr Bantock?'

'What? Oh, three o'clock. But—'

'We'd better get you back, then, hadn't we? We wouldn't want her to be stood up.'

It was half past two when we drove away from Whistler's Cot. I'd assured Henley that the police knew all about my meeting with Louise Paxton, but I still reckoned he'd be on the phone to them before we reached the bottom of the lane. His wasn't a trusting nature. Nor a grieving one, for that matter.

It would be different for the Paxton family, of course. Louise had left a husband and two daughters, rather than one ingrate nephew. They'd be mourning her now, in full and genuine measure. And one of those mourning her – Sarah Paxton – would be there, on the doorstep, within half an hour of our departure. I could easily have waited for her. Henley couldn't have prevented me, even if he'd wanted to. But I didn't. When it came to it, I was impatient to be gone, eager to avoid the encounter.

What it amounted to, I suppose, was fear. The fear that Sarah Paxton might resemble her mother too closely for me to fob her off with the account I'd given the police. But she wouldn't necessarily welcome the truth. Nor would anyone else who'd loved Louise Paxton. Because the truth made what had happened to her seem just a little too complicated for comfort. To enlighten might also be to antagonize. So I preferred to do neither.

There was another fear as well, running even deeper. The fear of what *I* might learn in the process. Who was Louise Paxton? What sort of woman was she? What sort of mother? What sort of wife? And what *had* she been trying to change, that evening on Hergest Ridge? I wasn't sure I wanted to know the answers. We'd met and parted as total strangers to each other. Perhaps that's what we ought to remain. If we could.

I flew back to Brussels on Sunday as planned. The following morning, I returned to my office at the Berlaymont and informed my head of unit that he would soon be losing my services. Around the same time, I read later, at a village churchyard in Gloucestershire, Louise Paxton was buried.

CHAPTER FOUR

Resignation isn't easy if you're a *fonctionnaire titulaire de la Commission Européenne*. In fact, it's next to impossible, because any attempt to resign is officially interpreted as a request for long-term leave of absence. When I handed in my notice to my gratifyingly dismayed head of unit that morning in July 1990, he treated it as an application for what we Eurocrats called a *congé de convenance personelle*. Unpaid leave, to put it less grandly. A sabbatical, if you like. A career on ice. For a year in the first instance, but automatically renewable for a second year and a third after that; conceivably, even longer. Opinion was divided over whether, theoretically, it could ever come to a conclusive end short of retirement.

But technicalities didn't interest me. I was leaving with no intention of coming back. My colleagues might be saying *au revoir*, but I'd be bidding them *adieu*. That evening, I took a few of them to Kitty O'Shea's, an Irish bar-cum-English pub near the Berlaymont that supplied an escapist haven for displaced Celts and Anglo-Saxons, to toast my departure. Taken aback by my generosity, they were clearly reluctant to say what they really thought. Poor old Timariot. Giving up an A6 post in the Directorate-General of Economic and Financial Affairs for – what was it? – cricket bats. Oh dear. Oh dear, oh dear, oh dear.

'Are you sure this is a good idea, Robin?' asked Ronnie Linklater in a soulful moment brought on by a third scotch and soda. 'I mean, *absolutely* sure?' I told him I was. But he obviously didn't believe me. It was true, though. I was certain I was doing the right thing.

My only frustration was that I couldn't do it immediately. Three months' notice loomed oppressively ahead. I tried persuading my head of unit that Timariot & Small were *in extremis* without me and he agreed to recommend an early release. But those whose approval was needed were away for the rest of the summer in their Tuscan villas and Provençal retreats. I would simply have to wait.

I was still waiting two weeks later when I returned to my flat in the rue Pascale one evening to find a letter waiting for me forwarded by my mother from Steep. It had originally been posted in Worcester, with my name and Petersfield address written in two different hands. I recognized neither. But one of them, it transpired, belonged to Sarah Paxton.

The Old Parsonage,
Sapperton,
Gloucestershire

5th August 1990

Dear Mr Timariot,
I have hesitated a long time before writing this. I learned of your existence from Henley Bantock. He did not know your address and the police, though very kind, said they could not release such information. But they did offer to forward this letter to you.

If it reaches you, I do hope you will agree to meet me. It is more important to me than I can properly explain to learn as much as possible of my mother's state of mind during the last day of her life. My sister saw her that afternoon, but I had not seen her in over a week. I am having particular difficulty coming to terms with that fact. I am not sure why. Something about not saying goodbye, I suppose. But you did say goodbye to her, in a sense. It really would help to talk to you about how she seemed and what she said. Could we meet, do you think? It need not be for long. And I will happily travel to wherever causes you least inconvenience.

If you are willing to meet, please ring me on Cirencester 855785, or write, if you prefer. Either way, I would be very glad to hear from you.

Yours sincerely,
Sarah Paxton.

The appeal was simple and direct. I could try to help her cope with her mother's death. Or I could ignore the request. She didn't know where I was. She had no way of tracing me if I didn't want to be found. I was safely out of reach. All I had to do was pretend I hadn't received the letter. Screw it up and throw it away. Burn it. Forget it. She'd cope without me. There was nothing we had to say to each other. That's what I kept telling myself, anyway. Until I picked up the telephone and dialled her number.

To my surprise, she insisted on coming to Brussels. I suggested she wait until my next visit to England. But, even if I'd been able to say when that would be, I doubt she'd have thought it soon enough. There was an urgency – a hint of desperation – in her voice that made me regret contacting her almost as soon as I'd done so. And there was a resemblance to her mother's voice that worried me even more. It wouldn't have taken much to imagine I was actually talking to Louise Paxton. As a result, in the days that passed between our conversation and her arrival in Brussels, I could only picture her in my mind's eye as a younger version of her mother: an idealized recreation of a dead woman.

That, I suppose, is what I set out apprehensively expecting to meet the following Friday night. She'd come for the weekend and was staying at the Hilton on boulevard Waterloo. We'd arranged to meet in the foyer at six o'clock. This turned out to be a bad choice. The place was filled with clacking quartets of jewel-draped women. I cast around amongst them, looking for one young face in the middle-aged crowd, still subconsciously expecting to recognize her. But there was nobody there who even remotely looked the part.

I was on the point of giving up and seeking help from the

concièrge when somebody said from close behind me: 'Robin Timariot?' I knew at once who it must be.

Sarah Paxton had her mother's slightness of build and much else about her that was immediately reminiscent of the woman I'd met on Hergest Ridge. Yet the differences seemed to amount to more than the similarities. Her hair was darker and cut much shorter. Her eyes too were darker, their gaze less open. She was clearly young – twenty-one or twenty-two I'd have guessed – but the freshness of youth was overlaid by something else. A hardness not of feature but of mind. An earnestness amounting almost to a warning. She wore little make-up and no jewellery bar a silver locket on a chain around her neck. Her dress was simple and practical: a plain blouse, loose calf-length skirt, flat-soled shoes; and unpretentious satchel-style handbag. She had enough of her mother's looks and bearing to turn heads if she wanted to. But her expression implied a wish to do no such thing. It could have been the visible effect of bereavement, of course, but somehow it seemed too entrenched – too permanent – for that. Her smile had a stiffness about it, her handshake a coolness, that mere shyness couldn't explain. Suspicion. Yes, that was it. A barely veiled scepticism about the world and the people she met in it. Me included.

'Shall we . . . er . . . find somewhere else?' I asked, gesturing around at the tableloads of Chanel and Silk Cut. 'There's a . . . bar I know nearby. It'll be quieter there.'

She agreed and we made for the exit. It was a sultry evening, sunlight lancing between the tower blocks to turn the traffic fumes into golden clouds. I felt tongue-tied and uncertain. Already, the meeting had enough signs of travesty about it to depress me. I was unable to find anything to say. And Sarah seemed disinclined to help me out.

Mercifully, the walk to the Copenhagen Tavern was a short one. The place wasn't too busy and the waitresses were as welcoming as ever. They knew me from many solitary evenings spent in its restful corners. But there was nothing restful about my latest visit.

Sarah ordered coffee and mineral water. I asked for my favourite beer, forgetting it was served in a novelty glass shaped like the bottom half of a kangaroo. I could see Sarah's gaze lingering incredulously on it as the beer was poured and considered making some sort of joke out of it. Then I reconsidered. Humour – even introductory small talk – seemed impossible. We were there to discuss one thing and one thing only. Its shadow stretched between us, drying my throat as I drank, threading doubt between my carefully laid plans. What *was* I to say?

'I . . . I'm sorry,' I ventured. 'I should have spared you the trouble of tracking me down. *I* should have written to *you*. To offer my condolences.'

'There was no reason for you to do that.' Her tone implied the idea might almost have been presumptuous. 'It's not as if you knew Mummy, is it? Or any of us.'

'No, but . . . the condolences would have been genuine, strangers or not. What happened was . . . awful. You have my sincere sympathy.'

'Thank you.' She looked away. 'It was. Like you say. Awful. The worst it could be, I suppose. What every mother's afraid might happen to her daughter. It's not supposed to be the other way round, is it?' Tears had been shed over such thoughts, I sensed. Many of them. And now there were none left. 'I can't stop wondering. Nor can my sister. We don't talk about it, but . . . what it must have been like weevils into your mind. You can't dislodge it. It just stays there, waiting for you to wake up or stop concentrating on something else. The wondering.' She shook her head. 'It's always there.'

'At least they've got the man who did it.'

'Oh yes. They've got him. And there's no real room for doubt. Not these days. I've become quite an expert on DNA analysis in recent weeks. I've read everything there is on the subject. As if my knowing all about it will somehow help. Silly, don't you think?'

'No. I don't.'

Her eyes moved slowly to meet mine. 'Tell me about . . . that evening on Hergest Ridge. I went up there. Same time. Same weather. I imagined her being there. I almost . . .' She sipped some coffee. 'Please tell me.'

So I did. I gave her the anodyne version of events I'd treated the police to, supplemented for her benefit with some remarks on how pleasant, how charming, her mother had been. She'd been beautiful too. But I didn't mention that. It smacked too much of the physical reality of what had happened to her. To describe the sunlight falling on her hair, the warm breeze moving the shadows of its strands across her face, the gleam of something forbidden but imminent in her eyes, would have led inexorably on. To the bedroom at Whistler's Cot. Sarah had been there and seen the broken mirror. She'd stared at its reflection of the room and imagined the writhing wrenching choking end. Just as I had. But we couldn't speak of it. Neither of us dared.

'She seemed happy?'

'Very.'

'Contented?'

'Yes.'

'At ease with herself?'

'That too.'

'Not . . . worried about anything?'

'No. But it was only a fleeting encounter. A few words. No more. I didn't think it was important . . . at the time.'

'Of course not.'

'I wish there was more I could tell you. More I could say. But there were no presentiments, Sarah. Nothing to show her – or me – what was about to happen. We met. And we parted. As strangers. I didn't even know her name. But for the photograph in the paper . . .'

'You'd never have known.'

'No. I wouldn't.'

'And now you know so much about her. Where she lived. Who she was married to. The sort of art she collected. The make of car she drove. Even her date of birth.' Her tone had become suddenly bitter, almost sarcastic. But at whose expense I couldn't tell. 'And one thing none of the papers has revealed. She wasn't wearing her wedding ring, was she, Robin? Don't pretend you didn't notice. Men do, don't they? They notice that sort of thing.'

I shrugged. 'All right. She wasn't. I didn't think anything of it.'

'You're the only one, then. The police didn't know what to make of it. But it certainly worried them. Not at first. At first, they thought *he'd* taken it. Because it was gold, I suppose. But then Rowena mentioned Mummy didn't have it on when she got home that morning. She'd lost it, apparently, the day before. On the beach. In Biarritz. We have a villa there. Mummy and Daddy spend . . .' Her face fell. 'They *used* to spend a lot of time there. Daddy's father bought it just after the war. My grandmother was French, you see. They retired there. Daddy thought he and Mummy would do the same one day.'

'So,' I said awkwardly, 'she simply lost it.'

'Apparently.'

'It doesn't mean anything, then, does it?'

'That depends.'

'On what?'

'On whether you believe she lost it.' Seeing me frown, she went on. 'Naylor denies the charges. All of them. He plans to plead not guilty. The police think he'll change his mind before the trial, but if he doesn't . . .'

'How can he plead not guilty? You said yourself. DNA fingerprinting. It's foolproof.'

'Not if he claims the sex was voluntary.'

'*Voluntary?* That's absurd. He murdered her, for God's sake.'

'Somebody murdered her. I'm not sure the police have any evidence to prove it was Naylor who actually strangled her. They haven't told us much, of course. I've pieced this together from the questions they've asked. And the ones they haven't asked. I'm actually studying to be a lawyer. It doesn't help a lot, but it gives me some idea what's going on. Naylor's going to say he met her at a pub near Kington. A place called the Harp, at Old Radnor.' She paused. 'You look as if you know it.'

'I had lunch there with Henley Bantock. The day we . . . just missed each other.'

'How did he know it?'

'Through his uncle.'

'Damn,' she said under her breath.

'What's wrong?'

'It's a connection, isn't it? With Mummy. It means she could have been there before.'

'I don't understand.'

'Old Radnor's the back of beyond. Naylor's story isn't credible if it's unlikely Mummy ever went there. But if she did go there . . .'

'With Oscar Bantock?'

'Maybe. She'd visited him in Kington before. And he liked a drink. It's possible, isn't it?'

'I suppose it is. But so what?'

'Naylor will say they met there by chance. She propositioned him. Or he propositioned her. It doesn't matter which. He'll say she took him to Whistler's Cot and they had what the law calls consensual sex. Then he left, with Mummy alive and Oscar Bantock nowhere to be seen. He'll say somebody else must have murdered them later.'

'Nobody will believe that.'

'No. But the defence will argue it as best they can. It's the only thing they can argue. And this business about the Harp makes it one degree less incredible. Plus the timing, of course. The police were disappointed when you said Mummy left Hergest Ridge at seven forty-five. It means Naylor's claim to have met her at the Harp between eight and eight thirty can't be ruled out.'

'But surely . . . if nobody saw them there . . .'

'It's still theoretically possible though, isn't it? Mummy offered you a lift. You said so yourself. The defence will try to make that sound like a pick-up line. They'll say it failed with you but worked with Naylor.'

'I won't let them get away with that.'

'It won't be easy to stop them. Once you're in court, you're on their territory.'

Court. There was the word. And there was the realization I'd somehow dodged. Making a guarded statement to the police wasn't the end of this. I was going to have to give evidence at Naylor's trial. To answer questions on oath. If Naylor persisted in his plea of innocence, it was virtually certain I'd be called as a witness by one side or the other.

'Naylor's guilty. But proving it could be messy. Mummy loses her wedding ring, flies to England and goes to see a man who lives alone on the Welsh borders. On the way, she offers a stranger a lift that would take her on a long detour if he accepted. Don't you see how it could all be made to sound?'

She'd come to find out what I meant to say. That was it, of course. I could tell by the hint of impatience in her tone. She didn't want my help in coping with her grief. What she wanted was my confirmation that there was nothing else still to emerge. A bundle of slender connections and stray coincidences was bad enough. But something concrete – something attributed to her mother by a disinterested witness – would be infinitely worse. She needed me to tell her it wasn't going to happen.

'Mummy was careless with possessions and tended to lose all sorts of things. She was keen enough on Expressionist art to break off a holiday simply to buy a coveted example. And she had a generous nature. She acted on impulse. Whim, you could call it. Like offering you a lift. There's no hidden meaning in any of it.'

'Of course there isn't.'

'But you have to have known her to understand that. The jury will be strangers. So will the judge and the barristers and the people in the public gallery and anybody who reads about the trial while it's going on. They won't understand her at all. But they'll think they do.'

'If I'm called, Sarah . . .' I leant forward to give emphasis to my words. 'I'll do my best to ensure there's no possibility of any misunderstanding. Your mother's reputation won't suffer at my hands.'

She looked at me intently for a moment, then said: 'I'm so glad to hear you say that.'

'I mean it.'

'Thank you.'

'There's no need to thank me. All I'll be doing is telling the truth.'

But that wasn't all, was it? And if my evidence was compromised, how could I be sure the explanations Sarah had given me for the loss of the ring and the impetuous flight from Biarritz weren't as well? In doing the decent thing, I was tacitly agreeing to play my part in a subtle editing of the facts: a damage limitation exercise on behalf of Louise Paxton's good name. And why not? It couldn't do any harm. Nobody lost by it. Not even Naylor. Since he was undoubtedly guilty. Wasn't he?

I wasn't sure whether Sarah expected to meet me again while she was in Brussels. When I showed her back to the Hilton, I asked – more out of politeness than anything else – if she wanted to see the sights. The city didn't boast many, to be honest, but it seemed the least I could do. To my surprise, her reaction was enthusiastic. I suppose a solitary weekend in a foreign country was the last thing she needed. I agreed to pick her up at ten o'clock the following morning.

Saturday dawned warm and bright. She was waiting for me when I reached the Hilton and we set off for a tour of what Brussels had to offer. The Grand Place and the Mannekin Pis on foot. Then out in my car to the Atomium – Belgium's answer to the Eiffel Tower. Lunch at a café near Square Montgomery. A stroll round the Parc du Cinquantenaire and a visit – at her insistence – to the Berlaymont. Followed by tea back at my flat in rue Pascale.

At first, we didn't talk about the trial – or even directly about her mother's death. Instead, I described the life of a Eurocrat and the alternative attractions of Timariot & Small, revealing more about myself in the process than I'd intended to. It turned out that Sarah's knowledge of the poems of Edward Thomas put mine to shame. She could quote them seemingly at will. And she could recite the names of the hangers above Steep even though she'd been there no more than once.

'Mummy drove me down to Steep one Sunday during my last year at school,' she recalled as we stood in the topmost ball of the Atomium, ostensibly admiring the view of the Parc de Laeken and the Château Royal but both picturing in our mind's eye the thickly wooded flanks of Stoner Hill. 'We were studying Thomas for A level and he'd become my favourite poet. Something to do with his melancholia, I suppose. Adolescents understand that condition better than most adults, don't you think?' Seeing me frown in a vain effort to recollect my state of mind at the age of eighteen, she took pity and went on: 'I wanted to see the places that had inspired his poems. And Mummy was keen to take me, though she must have regretted it later, driving round and round those winding lanes while I lapped up the scenery. We probably passed Greenhayes several times in the course of the afternoon. Without ever thinking that one day . . .'

'When would this have been?'

'Spring eighty-seven. May, I think.' She paused. When she resumed, I knew at once the words were no longer hers. '"The cherry trees bend over and are shedding, on the old road where all that passed are dead, their petals, strewing the grass as for a wedding, this early May morn when there is none to wed."' She gave a sad little smile. 'Strange, isn't it? I mean, our paths coming so close three years ago, but not crossing till now. I suppose fate just wasn't ready.'

'You believe in fate?'

'I'm not sure. Perhaps it helps if you do. If anything *can* help.' She took a long calming breath. 'The police offered to arrange counselling for us and Daddy persuaded Rowena to try it. She's seeing a trauma expert twice a week.'

'But you aren't?'

'I don't want counselling. I want justice.' The hardness was back in her voice now, the sentimental philosophizing brought abruptly to an end. 'I want Shaun Naylor put behind bars for the rest of his unnatural life.' Another smile, different now, self-aware, almost self-mocking. 'A trainee lawyer isn't supposed to talk like that, is she?'

'Maybe not. But I'm no lawyer, so I can say it. Any man who does what Naylor did has forfeited the right to live.'

She looked at me sharply. 'You really think so?'

'Yes. Don't you? I mean, when the platitudes – the social niceties – are swept aside. Don't we all fundamentally believe in an eye for an eye?'

She didn't answer. Her gaze moved past me to focus on some distant point beyond the horizon. And I felt suddenly embarrassed by my own vehemence, ashamed by the primitive instinct Louise Paxton's death had stirred in me – but that her daughter was capable of keeping in check. 'Let's go down,' she said softly. 'I've seen enough.'

* * *

Over lunch – and afterwards, as we sat on a shady bench in the Parc du Cinquantenaire – Sarah grew more forthcoming about herself and the Paxton family. Her grandfather, Dudley Paxton, had been in the Diplomatic Service, his career culminating in his appointment as British Ambassador to several former French African colonies just after their independence in the late fifties and early sixties. He and his Basque wife spent their retirement in Biarritz, close to *Grandmère*'s numerous relatives. Their villa, L'Hivernance, inherited by Sarah's father, was the scene of many of her happiest childhood memories. She and Rowena would spend days on end playing in the garden or building sandcastles on the world-famous beach, only a pebble's throw away, during long sun-drenched summers.

Sir Keith, meanwhile, was making a name for himself in the medical world. With royal patients and a knighthood came a lucrative private practice, a large town house in Holland Park, a homely weekend retreat in the Cotswolds and the best of everything for his wife and children. He was a doting and generous father, buying both daughters an expensive education, a succession of well-bred ponies, a skiing holiday every winter and a car for their eighteenth birthdays. As for Louise, who was fifteen years younger than him and looked more beautiful at forty than she had at thirty, there was nothing Sir Keith wasn't prepared to do. A dress allowance she couldn't spend. A luxury car she didn't want. And a gilded cage – I couldn't help suspecting – she wasn't prepared to remain in for ever.

Sir Keith didn't share Louise's interest in Expressionist art and, for all his lavishness in other directions, seemed to begrudge the money she spent on it. She and a schoolfriend, Sophie Marsden, began dabbling as collectors to see if they could make more than their husbands earned from sound and sober investments. They didn't, of course, but they enjoyed becoming expert amateurs and started trying to spot unrecognized talent before it acquired the price-tag to match. Oscar Bantock was more of a has-been than a might-be, but Louise did her best to make something of him, arranging exhibitions at small but select galleries where the right sort of people might realize what they were missing.

One such exhibition was held in Cambridge during Sarah's last year at King's College. Her presence at the private view was virtually mandatory and it was there she met Bantock for the first and last time. 'A short and stocky man with white hair and a bushy beard. A bit cantankerous, of course. A bit "Why am I dressed up like a dog's dinner sipping warm white wine with this rabble of Philistines?" But you could see he was trying to behave well for Mummy's sake. Which was ironic, since the event was supposed to be for *his* benefit, not hers. He was nice to me, probably for the same reason. Even to the man I'd brought with me, who made some pretty cringe-inducing remarks I remember. But old Oscar just grinned and twinkled his eyes at me. They were a quite startling blue. Pale yet bright at the same time. And he had this low rumbling *suppressed* voice. Like some operatic baritone singing a lullaby. You know? Power on a short leash. Energy waiting to be released. I can see him now so clearly. It's no more than five months ago. But in other ways it seems like five years.'

There it was. The same dead end we couldn't avoid coming back to. Take any path you liked through the maze. Admire any vista you pleased over the hedge en route. It was still waiting. If not round the next corner, then round the one after that.

'Why did he do it?' she asked later. 'I mean, if he was just a burglar, as they seem to think. Why murder? Why rape?'

'One thing leads to another, I suppose. Probably high as a kite on drugs. And your mother . . .'

'Yes?'

'Was a very beautiful woman.'

'You make that sound almost like an excuse.'

'It's not meant to be. Just an explanation. His type see something lovely and precious and want to destroy it. Looking – even touching – isn't good enough for them. What they can't have they smash.'

'Yes.' She nodded. 'And the rest of us are left to pick up the pieces.' She walked on down the tree-lined avenue of the park and I stood where I was, watching her for a few seconds, before following. Her head was bowed, her shoulders almost visibly sagging. She was doing her best to gather up the fragments of her life – and her sister's and her father's too. But there were so many. They were so widely scattered. And so sharp that those who touched them were bound to bleed.

I didn't analyse the assumptions and prejudices Sarah and I shared that weekend until much later. They were there, of course, underpinning everything we said and thought. Long before we knew all the facts, long before a court of law had weighed and tested the evidence, we were sure we knew exactly what had happened. Above all, we were sure Shaun Naylor was guilty.

According to Sarah, the police had only caught him thanks to a tip-off. From whom she didn't know. A wife. A girlfriend. A mate he'd boasted to. It didn't really matter who or why. The evidence must have piled up against him since. Otherwise he'd never have dreamt up such an implausible story. Would he?

I took Sarah out for dinner that night to my favourite Italian restaurant, Castello Banfi. She gave me a sharp lesson in her determination to be beholden to nobody by threatening a public scene if I didn't let her pay half the bill. But she did let me walk her back to the Hilton. There it could easily have been goodbye, since she was flying home the following afternoon and I'd been invited to Sunday lunch by some Eurocrat friends in Waterloo who were concerned for my sanity. But, unsure whether I wanted to face them anyway, I claimed to have no commitments and offered her a ride to the airport, which she accepted.

As I walked away from the hotel, I glanced across the boulevard at the frontage of the Toison d'Or cinema complex. One of the films whose illuminated titles glared back was the latest Harrison Ford thriller: *Presumed Innocent.* But I can honestly say that the irony registered with me for no more than an instant before I pressed on towards rue Pascale, devising an excuse for my friends in Waterloo as I went.

Something else I chose not to analyse was my reluctance to let Sarah Paxton vanish from my life so soon after entering it. Such analysis might have revealed whether the attraction I'd begun to feel was to her or the part of her that reminded me of her mother. Perhaps we always chase ghosts or tokens or chance resemblances. Perhaps everyone we're ever drawn to is really only a pallid version of the real thing we'll never meet. But, if so, it doesn't help to confront the fact.

It was only when I was sitting with Sarah in the airport coffee bar an hour before her flight, in fact, that I thought to ask what life – what immediate future – she was going back to in England. And only when I heard her answer did I realize that keeping in touch with her needn't be so difficult after all.

'A year at law college before I take articles. I'd thought of postponing, but . . . what would be the point? Life, so they tell me, must go on. So, I've enrolled to start at Guildford next month.'

'Guildford? But that's not far—'

'From Steep? No. Not a million miles. Actually, it's why I chose it. I didn't realize then, of course . . .'

'Will you commute from London?'

'Ideally, no. I really want somewhere local to stay during the week. But . . . it's been hard to concentrate on practicalities like that recently. By now, the best places will already have been snapped up.'

'If they have . . .' I hesitated, then decided it was just a suggestion she might find helpful. Nothing significant hung on whether she did or not. How could it? 'My sister-in-law – my brother's widow, that is – has a large house with plenty of room to spare in Hindhead. It can't be more than twelve miles from Guildford. And she's looking for a lodger. She told me so herself. You've both suffered a loss recently. Perhaps . . . Well, it might be worth considering.'

'Yes,' said Sarah thoughtfully. 'It might.'

When she left, ten minutes or so later, it was with Bella's address and telephone number recorded in her diary.

The following day, at Brussels' largest stockist of English language books, I bought a collection of Edward Thomas's verse. I soon found the poem Sarah had recited and others too to haunt me with their resonance of things half seen and understood but never grasped or named or known for precisely what they are. Whether because I'd ignored them before or simply not been ready for them, his poems came to me now with a sort of revelatory force. How could they fail to, when so much of my own experience seemed embedded in the verse? And how could I not think of Louise Paxton – or her daughter – when I read such lines as:

> After you speak
> And what you meant
> Is plain,
> My eyes
> Meet yours that mean,
> With your cheeks and hair,
> Something more wise,
> More dark,
> And far different.

Especially when Thomas seemed to have foreseen even our meeting on Hergest Ridge.

> It was upon a July evening.
> At a stile I stood looking along a path

Over the country by a second Spring
Drenched perfect green again. 'The lattermath
Will be a fine one.' So the stranger said.

But there he'd erred. Or the stranger had. Our lattermath wasn't to be a fine one.

A week or so later, I had a telephone call from Bella. She wanted to thank me for finding her a lodger. 'One of your better ideas, Robin,' she said. 'Sarah and I hit it off straightaway.' This I found hard to believe. But if Bella wanted to believe it, who was I to argue? 'I think we could turn out to be rather good for each other. Don't you?'

CHAPTER

FIVE

The powers that be couldn't in the end be persuaded to release me early. In fact, somewhat to my surprise, they didn't want me to go at all. Phrases like 'sadly missed' and 'hard to replace' were bandied about. It was rather like reading your obituary without actually being dead. Gratifying in one sense, but also frustrating. Not least because it meant I had to see out my notice to the bitter-sweet end: 31 October 1990. For me it turned out to be an anti-climactic date, since my farewell bash got tacked unsatisfactorily onto an office Hallowe'en party. I left uncertain whether my colleagues' gift to me – a Timariot & Small grade A cricket bat signed by them in the style of an England touring team – constituted trick or treat.

Either way, a chapter of my life had belatedly closed. I flew home to England and took up my post as works director of Timariot & Small the following Monday. Reminding my mother at regular intervals that it was only a temporary arrangement until I had time to find suitable accommodation of my own, I moved into Greenhayes. I meant what I said, even though the UK property market had risen way beyond my reach during the twelve years I'd been complacently renting bachelor apartments in Brussels. But, for the moment, there was so much to be mastered and assimilated at work that I was grateful to have Mother cooking and washing for me. Even at the expense of her remorseless chatter and Simon's satirical remarks. I promised myself I'd sort something out in the New Year.

By then, for all I knew, Shaun Naylor's trial would be upon us. While I was still in Brussels, I'd received a conditional witness order from the Crown Court stipulating that I might be required to appear at the trial, a date for which hadn't yet been fixed. The Kington killings had dropped out of the papers altogether, vanishing into the limbo of judicial delay. The thousands who'd read and speculated about them at the time had probably forgotten them altogether. But for those who couldn't forget – for the Paxton family – it must have been like waiting for Louise's funeral over again, on and on, as the months passed. A cathartic moment indefinitely postponed. As far as they or any of us knew, Naylor was still planning to plead not guilty. Eventually, he was bound to be given his moment in court.

I tried to contact Sarah on several occasions during my first few weeks back in England, but without success. If I was busy getting to know the workforce at Timariot & Small and imposing my authority as firmly but gently as I could, no doubt she was equally busy absorbing contract, tort and criminal law while trying not to brood on the experience she'd soon have of the real thing. I only ever seemed to get Bella on the telephone, which I couldn't risk doing too often without her putting two and two together and making five. And Sarah simply didn't return my calls. I began to suspect she might want to discourage my attention. I began to think how understandable it would be if she did. There'd be boyfriends on the scene. Half a dozen men closer to her own age and interests than me. Who exactly was I kidding? And why? The attraction I'd felt in Brussels wasn't really to her, was it?

My mother was certainly curious about the arrangement. Why had Bella taken a lodger? And why *that* lodger? But her attempts to engineer a meeting came to nothing. Even her curiosity faltered with so little to sustain it. And our contacts with Bella had become fewer as Hugh's death receded into the past. Events and emotions drifted. As they're bound to, I suppose. As they'd have gone on doing – but for the trial.

I got home earlier than usual one evening in the first week of December to find Brillo and my mother sharing the fireside at Greenhayes with Bella. Tea and cake were being consumed, the family photograph albums – all four of them – keenly examined. And Bella was giving a good impression of the indulgent daughter-in-law happy to take a stroll down memory lane. Which might have fooled Mother. But not me. Not for an instant. Bella wanted something. The question was: what?

I wasn't to be kept waiting long for the answer. As soon as Mother left the room to make fresh tea, Bella said to me: 'We've seen nothing of you since you came back, Robin. It's really not good enough.'

'We?'

'Sarah and me.'

'I *have* phoned. Several times.'

'Well, it *is* difficult, I admit. They keep Sarah so busy at that college. And she goes home every weekend. My life's been pretty hectic as well, of course.'

'I've had one or two things to do myself.'

'Do you know you sound just like Hugh when you adopt that sulky tone?'

'Really? Well, I—'

'Anyway, never mind. Sarah *isn't* going home this weekend. In fact, Keith's coming to see her with Rowena and—'

'Keith? You mean her father?'

'Yes. I've met him' – she tossed her hair enigmatically – 'oh, quite a few times now. He's really a very nice man. Genuine, you know? He hasn't grown hard and resentful, as so many men do.' Usually after exposure to women like Bella, I couldn't help thinking. Still, she was always infectiously optimistic. Fun – even when she was at her most infuriating. If Sir Keith Paxton had found her company a pleasant relief from his troubles, I couldn't entirely blame him. Nevertheless, I didn't like the sound of it. Bella might be exaggerating for effect with her casual dropping of his name minus the title. But, all the same, I felt resentment stir in me. 'He's suffered a great deal, of course. And he's far from over the worst. Rowena's a terrible worry to him. And to Sarah.'

'Why?'

'Hasn't Sarah told you?' She smiled. 'No, I suppose not. In that case, perhaps I oughtn't to . . .' She waited for me to rise to the bait, but I merely smiled back. 'Still, I suppose I ought to prepare you in some way.'

'Prepare me for what, Bella?'

'I was hoping – *we* were hoping – you'd come to lunch next Sunday. Meet Keith. And Rowena. He'll be bringing her along. You see— Oh, here's Hilda with your tea.' And that, a flashing glance told me, was all she could say for the moment. Like the actress I sometimes thought she ought to have been, she'd timed her curtain line to perfection.

The next act was delivered to me in the lounge bar of the

Cricketers, Steep's village inn, where Bella proposed a drink to see her on her way, knowing my mother wouldn't dream of accompanying us. Mother regarded pubs as places ladies should avoid, except for the occasional lunchtime snack, and then only under heavy escort. Bella, needless to say, didn't see them that way at all. But then Bella, as Mother sometimes pointed out, was no lady.

'I have to be careful what I say about Sarah's family, Robin. I'm sure you appreciate that.'

'Of course.' I also appreciated that nothing pleased Bella more than teasing other people with tit-bits of information she possessed but they didn't.

'I've only met Rowena once, but it was obvious to me she wasn't recovering from the loss of her mother as well as Sarah. She was supposed to be starting university this autumn, you know. But that's had to be postponed. She isn't really capable of taking on any kind of commitment – work *or* study – at the moment. The whole thing has quite shattered her.' Sarah had spoken in Brussels of 'picking up the pieces'. I wondered now if she'd been referring to her sister rather than herself all along. 'She's seeing a psychiatrist, though what help he is . . .'

'Sarah mentioned trauma counselling.'

'It's become rather more serious than counselling. Rowena doesn't have Sarah's strength of mind, her . . . resilience. She's really quite fragile. Doesn't look her age at all. More like fourteen than nineteen. On a personality like hers, well, you can imagine the effect this must have had. She had to identify her mother's body, you know. And she was the last to see Louise before . . .' Why did Bella's use of Louise Paxton's Christian name anger me? Why should I still care so much? 'Except she wasn't the last to see her, was she, Robin? Not quite.'

'Where's this leading, Bella?'

'To a possible way of helping her, that's all. It might make it easier for her to accept if you explained how carefree, how oblivious to what was going to happen, Louise was when you met her. Rowena seems to think . . . Well, her psychiatrist thinks . . . The girl believes her mother had something on her mind that day. Something . . . more than she's been told. Something . . . that could have amounted to a premonition.'

'What makes her think that?'

'Who knows? Guilt for not stopping her. An inability to take things at face value. Whatever it is, you might be able to rid her of the delusion where others have failed.'

'Why?'

'Because you know it's not true. You saw Louise that day. Like Rowena. But unlike anyone else.'

'I'm a stranger to Rowena. She won't trust me.'

'Maybe she'll trust you *because* you're a stranger.'

I wasn't going to refuse, of course. The argument made a kind of sense. And I wanted to scc Rowena now this hint had been dropped that she too had glimpsed the ambiguity – the mystery – in her mother's soul. But why was Bella the messenger? Why not Sarah – or Sir Keith? Why was my sister-in-law suddenly an insider while I remained a stranger? 'Who's idea was this, Bella? Yours?'

'I suggested it, yes. But Keith saw the sense of it at once. He agreed it was well worth trying – if you were prepared to cooperate.'

'Of course I'll cooperate. There's just one thing I don't understand.'

'Well?'

'What's in it for you?'

She arched her eyebrows. 'Does there have to be anything? I simply want to help.' But she must have read the disbelief in my eyes. It riled her. More than I'd have expected. 'You bloody Timariots. So suspicious. So sceptical. So . . . miserly with your high opinion. Have you considered that I might have met somebody who brings out the best in me, rather than the worst?'

'Unlike Hugh, you mean?'

'If you like. Hugh. Or his brother.'

I looked away and sighed without attempting to disguise the reaction. It was an old battle nobody was ever going to win. But some of the wounds still hadn't healed. 'This somebody is Sir Keith Paxton?'

'Maybe.'

'With his wife less than five months dead?'

'I'll leave the arithmetic to you.'

'Fine. What it adds up to is this. You want me to make you look concerned and sensitive for the widower knight's benefit.'

'It'd be for his daughter's benefit, actually. But if that's going to be your attitude, perhaps it would be better if—'

'No.' I held up my hand, in warning as well as truce. The sniping had gone on long enough. 'I'll come, Bella. I'll do what I can. I'll try to help. Not for your sake. Nor for mine. Just because it really is the least I can do. Good enough?'

She nodded and, after a moment's silent contemplation,

smiled. We understood each other. Better than most. Though not as well – not nearly as well – as I might have hoped to know another. Had she lived.

Sunday was a cold grey winter's day – raw, damp and stark. A polar opposite of the summer's day my mind dwelt on as I drove up to Hindhead. And of other days I didn't want to remember. But which my destination always evoked.

The Hurdles occupied a large and secluded site backing onto Hindhead golf course. It needed summer foliage to soften its harsh roof-line and faintly alien appearance. Without camouflage, it looked as if it might blend more happily with the landscape of southern California than the Home Counties. Like wedding photographs in which the guests are wearing the risible fashions of the day, The Hurdles stubbornly reflected aspirations that hadn't long outlasted its construction. For cosmopolitan boldness, as the architect had fatuously put it. For a loving but enlightened marriage, as Hugh had convinced himself he was to have. And for ownership of a definable future, which he should have realized was available only on the shortest of leases.

There was a Daimler parked beside Bella's BMW in the drive. Sir Keith, I assumed, had already arrived. When I rang the bell, Sarah opened the door. She'd had her hair cut even shorter since her visit to Brussels. And she'd lost a little weight too. It suited her, though it was also worrying. I doubted if counting calories was the cause.

'Good of you to come, Robin,' she said. 'I mean it. Really very kind.'

'Not at all.'

'I'm sorry we've not been able to get together since you . . .' She was nervous, though whether because of meeting me again or because of the reason for our meeting I couldn't tell. 'Well, we've both been busy, haven't we? Come on through.'

The others were in the drawing-room. Bella came forward as I entered and gave me a kiss on both cheeks. I suppose she reckoned that's how normal people would expect her to greet her brother-in-law, though it took me aback. Then she introduced me to Rowena and Sir Keith.

Rowena was even slimmer and slighter than her sister. She had long fair hair, almost exactly the shade of her mother's. It cascaded in waves down the back of her dress as far as her hips. Uncut since childhood, I assumed. And an arresting sight. But not quite as arresting as her aquamarine eyes. They gazed up at me as I shook her hand, solemn and unblinking, fixed momentarily on mine. And for that moment her concentration – her absorption – seemed total. As if we were alone together. As if nothing mattered except what we might be about to say to each other.

'Hello,' she said softly, frowning like some cautious but well-bred child. 'Sarah's told me about you, Mr Timariot. I'm very pleased to meet you.'

'And I you.' I wanted to offer her my condolences, but something stopped me. Then Sir Keith was beside us, sliding a fatherly arm round Rowena's shoulders while he treated me to a firm handshake and a formal smile. The chance was gone.

He was a big man, in manner as much as physique. Grey-haired, broadly built and handsomely weather-beaten. He met my glance with the brisk confidence of somebody whose profession it is to encounter a wide variety of people in difficult circumstances. But there was a diffidence there as well. Our roles were strangely reversed. I should have been the one offering consolation. But his breezy warmth seemed to forbid it. We could laugh or converse or share a drink, it implied. Anything more profound – anything remotely intimate – was territory best left unexplored. Which was only to be expected, I suppose. The ingrained reticence of a certain generation of Englishmen. Yet there was another layer to it, I felt. There was a suspicion of me. I was the last man to see his wife alive – apart from her murderer. I was the stranger who possessed a small piece of knowledge he might have craved. If he'd allowed himself to admit as much. But he wasn't going to. That was clear. Bereavement was to him an enemy you engaged and defeated, grief a weakness you never showed.

Lunch was one of the more uncomfortable experiences of my life. I sat next to Rowena and exchanged few words with her beyond an excruciating discussion of the weather and how best to cook broccoli. Every other subject that came into my head – Christmas, the Cotswolds, her plans, her pastimes, her present, her future – came back to her mother and what had happened to her. Precisely how to talk about that in a casual and reassuring manner over roast beef and burgundy with a girl who could hardly have looked and sounded less like the average nineteen-year-old sophisticate was a task I couldn't begin to tackle.

Not that my confusion seemed to communicate itself round the table. Sir Keith held awkward silences at bay with practised aplomb, discoursing on wine, medicine and the law with no particular need of an interlocutor. He even seemed to know something about cricket bats, provoking Bella to display greater familiarity with the history of Timariot & Small than I'd ever have credited her with. Well, I knew the game she was playing. And it looked as if Sir Keith did too. But it wasn't cricket.

I didn't disapprove. I was in no position to. You have to lose somebody you've been physically and mentally close to for more than twenty years before you know what it leaves you needing and yearning and seeking. Keith Paxton had my sympathy on several counts. He'd suffered what I could only imagine. A theft of something precious but also familiar. A deprivation as undeserved as it was unexpected. And in the face of all that, he'd held on.

As had one of his daughters. But not the other. Her voice wavered. Her hand trembled. Her mind froze. I could see and hear it happening. I could sense her grasp growing ever frailer. This very lunch – this cautious venture into limited society – was for her an ordeal. And a trial still lay ahead. Which I, incredibly, was expected to help her face.

How only became apparent after the meal. Bella went into the kitchen to clear up. Sarah went to help her. And Rowena excused herself. Leaving Sir Keith and me alone together in the lounge. Able at last to speak freely. Man to man.

'I gather Bella's put you in the picture, Robin.' He'd slipped readily into using my Christian name. 'About Rowena, I mean.'

'Yes. I was sorry to hear of her difficulties. But they're perfectly understandable. The loss of a mother must be hard enough for a daughter to come to terms with in any circumstances.'

'But these weren't just *any* circumstances. Quite so. They certainly weren't.' He sighed and for a moment looked all and more of his age. 'If I could get my hands on Naylor . . . But perhaps it's just as well I can't.' He sat forward and pressed his hands together, gazing at the carpet between us as if I were one of his patients he was about to inform of the progress of a terminal disease. 'Louise was . . . quite a lot younger than me. And beautiful. Well, you met her, so you'll know that. I suppose men in my position always half expect they'll be left in the end. Ditched for some gigolo or other. At the very least betrayed. Cuckolded. Made a fool of. And the worst kind of fool at that. An old one.'

'Are you saying—'

'No. That's the point, Robin. It didn't happen. Louise was loving *and* faithful. She'd have gone on being both till my dying day. I'm sure of it. More sure now than ever. But I lost her anyway, didn't I? She didn't desert me. She was taken from me. Which would be bad enough without . . . God, I can't describe how I felt when I heard. I'd been in Madrid for a few days. There was a conference I wanted to attend. When I got back to Biarritz she'd flown to England to buy one of Oscar Bantock's paintings. I wasn't surprised. She adored his work. And she was a creature of impulse. That was one of the things I most . . .' He broke off and smiled apologetically at the iceberg-tip of emotion he'd revealed.

'You don't have to tell me this,' I said. 'There's really no—'

'But there is. I have to explain, you see. The police phoned me with the news. Frightful. Awful. Unbelievable. But true. And worse – a hundred times worse – for Rowena. They'd been unable to contact me at first. And Sarah was in Scotland, exact whereabouts unknown. So they'd had to ask Rowena to identify her mother's body. Somehow, that seemed even more horrible to me than what had happened to Louise. You've seen what sort of girl Rowena is. It was asking too much of her to shrug off the experience. I only wish . . .' He spread his hands helplessly.

'Are you sure it'll do any good for me to talk to her about it?'

'No. Not sure at all. But her psychiatrist thinks Rowena feels responsible for Louise's death. Guilty for letting her drive to Kington that afternoon. Ridiculous, I know, but deeply rooted. She's invented signs, danger signals, she should have spotted. They weren't there to be spotted, of course. If Louise had foreseen what was going to happen to her in Kington, she wouldn't have gone there. That stands to reason.' Did it? I wondered. Could we be absolutely certain of that? 'I can't persuade her the signs didn't exist. I can't prove it to her. Nor can Sarah. Because we weren't there. We didn't see Louise that day. We didn't get the chance.'

'But I did.'

'Exactly. You met her. Later than Rowena. And there were no . . . signs . . . were there?'

'Of course not.'

'Well, maybe you can convince Rowena of that. At the very least, make her see this guilt she feels isn't exclusive to her. Others missed the same chance.' Was this an oblique accusation? I asked myself. Was this a glimpse he'd unwittingly given me of a grudge he couldn't help bearing, however irrationally? If so, he tried to brush it off at once. 'Not that there *was* a chance, of course. Not a real one.' He smiled. But the smile didn't completely reassure me. And then it broadened into something warm and genuine and unstinting. For behind me, in the doorway, Rowena had appeared. And Sir Keith blamed her at least for nothing.

It was Sarah, executing what I took to be a prearranged plan, who proposed a walk in the little daylight that remained to give us an appetite for tea. Rowena said at once she'd go with her. I had the impression her sister's company was vital to the equilibrium she was just about maintaining. I fell in with the idea, leaving Bella and Sir Keith to invent reasons for staying behind.

The girls donned their Barbours and wellingtons and I drove them the few miles to Frensham, where we joined the hardier set of Sunday afternooners strolling round the Great Pond. We'd nearly completed a circuit before Sarah tired of waiting for me to mention her mother and did so herself. At which Rowena cast me a lingering glance whose meaning was clear. The elaborate manoeuvres hadn't deceived her for a moment. She knew exactly why we'd been thrown together. The glance, with its flickering hint of sympathy, even implied I was to be pitied for playing my part. Especially since, in her opinion, it couldn't achieve a thing. Beneath the wide-eyed unworldliness, there was a determination I couldn't help admiring to mourn her mother in her own particular way.

'Would you like to go to Hergest Ridge one day, Ro? It's where Robin met Mummy.'

'I know where he met her. And when.'

'It was only a fleeting encounter,' I put in. 'We talked for a few minutes, hardly more.'

'And what did you talk about?' Rowena looked round at me as she asked the question.

'Nothing much. The weather. The scenery. The view was . . . magnificent.' I shivered, but not because of the cold. Her eyes wouldn't release me, wouldn't give up their hold. *Go on*, they implored me. *Tell me what she really said.* 'She seemed . . . very happy.'

'She often did. When she wasn't.'

'I don't think it was put on. Her happiness almost amounted to joy. You can't feign that.'

'No. But joy's different, isn't it? I haven't been happy since . . . the summer. But sometimes I have been joyful.'

'I'm not sure I—'

'Sarah says Mummy offered you a lift.'
'Yes. She did. It was kind of her.'
'Why didn't you accept?'
'I wanted to walk.'
'You didn't understand, then?'
I stopped. And she stopped too, her gaze fixed calmly on me. Sarah came to a halt a few yards further on along the sandy path. She turned and looked back at us, then said, almost on my behalf: 'What was there to understand, Ro?'
'She needed protection.'
'She can't have known that.'
'Besides,' I said, 'if she'd felt in danger, she only had to drive away. There was nothing to stop her.'
Still Rowena stared at me. 'Some things you can't drive away from. Or fly. Or run. Or even crawl. Some things have to be.'
What I said next wasn't provoked so much by irritation at the opacity of her reasoning as by fear of what she might be beginning to discern: that she and I had both seen – or been shown – some part of the truth about the events of that day. But we hadn't understood, hadn't recognized it for what it was; and we still didn't. *'Can we really change anything, do you think?'* Louise had asked me. *'Can any of us ever stop being what we are and become something else?' 'Yes,'* I'd replied. *'Surely. If we want to.'* And then I'd watched her walk away to her transformation. From life to death. From enigma to conundrum. 'If you're right, Rowena, what good would my protection have been?'
She smiled. And looked away at last. 'No good at all,' she murmured. 'None whatsoever.'
I caught the disappointment turning to anger in Sarah's face. This wasn't what she'd hoped I'd achieve. This wasn't what she'd expected of me. 'Your mother's death wasn't inevitable,' I went on. 'But it wasn't preventable either. Surely you can see that.'
Rowena gazed past me, past both of us, her eyes scanning the bleak heathland beyond the pond. Dusk was encroaching, gathering like some grey presence at our backs, advancing with the steady tread of something that doesn't need to hurry – because it's bound to happen. 'Soon it'll be too dark to see anything,' she said. 'I think I want to go home.'

I took care to ensure I was the first to leave The Hurdles that evening. I had no wish to confront Sarah with my failure to dent Rowena's delusions. Not least because I wasn't sure they *were* delusions. And that, I knew, was the last thing Sarah wanted to hear. Just as it was the last thing I wanted to admit. 'Perhaps it was too soon,' Sir Keith said by way of consolation as he saw me off in the darkness of the driveway. 'Perhaps we can try again when she's more receptive.' I muttered some vague words of concurrence and shook his hand in farewell, not daring to tell him what I'd realized at Frensham. Rowena's problem wasn't an inability to face the truth. It was a refusal not to.

A few days later, Sarah phoned me at work to propose a meeting before term ended at the College of Law. I detected in her voice an eagerness to remove any awkwardness between us before it grew into something more serious. It was an eagerness I shared. Probably on account of it, she agreed to let me take her to an expensive French restaurant in Haslemere. And probably for the same reason, she dressed for once as elegantly as her looks and figure deserved.

Rowena's name cropped up before the canapés, Sarah having no truck with prevarication. 'Daddy thinks it was a mistake to spring you on her. After she's thought about what you said, maybe she'll see things differently.'

'I wouldn't bank on it.'

'We have to. If she says any of those bizarre things in court, God knows what the consequences may be.'

'Does she have to be called?'

'It's not our decision. But, without her, the prosecution can't be as specific as they'd like to be about Mummy's movements and intentions. I'd be reluctant to dispense with her testimony if I were them. Apart from anything else, it would look so odd.'

'Your father mentioned a note your mother left for him in Biarritz. Wouldn't that be sufficient to—'

'Unfortunately, he threw it away before he'd heard about Mummy.'

'Then . . . what about the friend she was supposed to be staying with that night?'

'Sophie Marsden? No good either, I'm afraid. Mummy never contacted her. She must have been planning to surprise her with the picture.'

'I see.' Actually, I saw more than I liked. There was a disturbing vagueness about Louise Paxton's actions on 17 July. In the hands of a competent barrister, it could be made to amount to legitimate doubt. 'So . . . only Rowena . . .'

'Can testify to Mummy's exact plans on the day in question. Precisely.' Sarah didn't trouble to hide the concern in her voice.

'And it's vital Rowena *should* testify – if Naylor's line of defence is to be nipped in the bud.'

'But I can go some way to doing that myself.'

'I know. And I'm grateful. But we don't want to have to rely on the evidence of a stranger, do we?' She caught my eye and blushed. 'I'm sorry. I didn't mean— Well, you were a stranger to Mummy, weren't you?'

'Yes,' I said thoughtfully, my mind casting back to the glaring brightness – the dazzling unknowingness – of that day on Hergest Ridge. And to some lines of Thomas I'd read only recently. Which Sarah, if I'd spoken them aloud or even referred to the poem they occurred in, would have understood completely. As I couldn't allow her to – under any circumstances.

> The shadow I was growing to love almost,
> The phantom, not the creature with bright eye
> That I had thought never to see, once lost.

At the end of the meal, over coffee and petits fours, Sarah announced that Sir Keith was taking her and Rowena abroad for Christmas and New Year. It made good sense, with too many reminders of family Christmases past waiting for them in Gloucestershire. Biarritz was ruled out on the same grounds. So it was to be Barbados, where none of them had ever been before. Perhaps the novelty of the location would restore Rowena's sense of proportion. I endorsed the hope, though with little confidence. We parted on the pavement outside, in the icy splendour of a starlit winter's night. With a fleeting kiss and an awareness on my part that no recital of seasonal good wishes could strengthen the chances of a happy new year for Sarah or her sister.

> Which made me sigh, remembering she was no more,
> Gone like a never perfectly recalled air.

CHAPTER

SIX

The Timariot family celebrated Christmas 1990 much as we'd celebrated every Christmas since my parents' move to Steep. A festive gathering at the home of Adrian and his wife Wendy had become customary, if not obligatory. They lived in a large detached house on Sussex Road, overlooking Heath Pond. Large it needed to be, since they shared it with four children – two sons and twin girls – plus an overweight labrador. The rest of us were expected to revel in the resulting chaos. My mother certainly appeared to. As did Uncle Larry. But Jennifer's impersonation of a doting aunt was never convincing. And Simon, depressed at not spending the day with his daughter, tended to decline into drunken self-pity. Which left me to pretend I enjoyed listening to the wartime reminiscences of Wendy's father, interrupted as they frequently were by his grandsons' temper tantrums.

I'd always admired the way Hugh and Bella handled the ordeal. Hugh would inveigle Adrian into an intense shop-talking session, while Bella spent half her time in the garden, wrapped in a fur coat and puffing at a cigarette. Wendy had banned the practice indoors on account of the danger to the children from passive smoking. Which I thought mighty ironic, since I'd never known the horrors do anything *passive* in their lives.

This year, of course, Hugh was missing. So was Bella, whose links with us continued to grow more tenuous by the day. Superficially at least, it didn't seem to make much difference. Nor, I recalled, had my father's absence the first Christmas after his death. A family is more resilient than any of its members. It persists, amoeba-like, in the face of loss and division. It is infinitely adaptable. And therefore prone to change. At its own pace, of course. Which is sometimes too gradual for those it most affects to notice.

A straw in the wind came that afternoon in the form of a conversation I overheard between Wendy and her mother. The Gulf War was imminent and flying was suddenly considered a dangerous way to travel because of the supposed threat of Iraqi terrorism. But Adrian, it appeared, was planning to visit Australia. And Mrs Johnson was worried about her son-in-law's safety. If she was worried, I was puzzled. Adrian had said nothing to me about such a trip. Nor would he now, when I tackled him. 'Just an idea at the moment, Rob. Rather not elaborate till I'm clearer in my own mind. Sure you understand.' I didn't, of course. Nor did he intend me to.

By the time the first board meeting of the New Year took place, however, clarity of mind had evidently descended. Adrian wanted to take a close look at Timariot & Small's marketing arrangements in Australia. He reckoned there was scope for expansion. Maybe we needed to ginger up our agent there. Or find a new one. Either way, he and Simon ought to go out and see for themselves. Simon was all for it, naturally. And even if I suspected it was just an excuse for a holiday, I wasn't about to object. It was agreed they'd be away for most of February.

In the event, they had to come home early, for the saddest and most unexpected of reasons. It was the coldest winter Petersfield had experienced for several years. But my mother made no concessions to the weather. She took Brillo for a walk every afternoon whatever the conditions. On 7 February it snowed heavily. And out she went, despite a touch of flu which I'd advised her to spend the day nursing by the fire. She took a fall in one of the holloways and limped back to Greenhayes wet and chilled to the marrow. By the following evening, I had to call the doctor out, who diagnosed pneumonia and sent her off to hospital. Some old bronchial trouble and a latent heart condition caught up with her over the next few days. On 12 February, after a gallant struggle, she died.

I could have predicted my reaction exactly. Guilt at all the unkind words I'd ever uttered. Shame at my neglect of her. And a consoling grain of relief that, as exits go, it was swift and merciful. 'How she'd have wanted it to be,' as Uncle Larry said at the funeral. Which enabled Mother to infuriate me even from the grave. Charming as some people thought him, Brillo had never seemed worth sacrificing a life for to me. Had he tangled his lead in his mistress's legs – as so often before – and tripped her up in the snow? Mother had denied this when I'd suggested it and, for her sake, I tried not to believe it. But I wasn't sorry when Wendy volunteered to add him to her crowded household.

This left me alone at Greenhayes. It was now jointly owned by Jennifer, Simon, Adrian and me. But to sell straightaway, with the property market in such a parlous state, would have been perverse. From their point of view, I made an ideal tenant. Somebody they could rely on to keep the place looking presentable until the time came to cash in. The arrangement suited me too, so I went along with it, forgetting that it would work only so long as all our interests coincided.

I suppose the truth is that I chose to forget. My earlier dislike of the house had diminished as my enthusiasm for Edward Thomas's poetry had grown. I'd come to relish its proximity to his favourite walks and to follow them myself. After the blandness of the Belgian countryside, I'd returned to the sights and scents of rural England like a reluctant teetotaller to strong drink. All in all, it suited me far better to stay at Greenhayes than I cared to admit.

On the Sunday after the funeral, I was surprised by a visit from Sarah. She'd heard about my mother's death from Bella and wished to offer her condolences. There was no comparison between the circumstances of our bereavements, of course, but still they drew us briefly together. It was a cool dry cloudy day, with the snow long since washed away. We took a circular stroll up onto Wheatham Hill, passing one of Thomas's former houses in Cockshott Lane and another in Ashford Chace on the way back. We talked about the poems I'd come to know nearly as well as her. We discussed the bewildering consequences of death – the clothes parcels for Oxfam, the redundant possessions, the remorseless memories. And then, inevitably, we spoke of Rowena and the coming trial.

'Informally, we've been told it'll take place straight after Easter.'

'That's only another six weeks or so.'

'I know. But it can't come soon enough for me. Or Daddy. Once it's over, maybe we'll be able to start living again. I don't mean I want to forget Mummy. Or what happened to her. But we're all worn down by waiting. Especially Rowena.'

'How is she?'

'Better than when you met her. More controlled. More certain about what she has to do. I think she's going to be all right. In court, I mean.'

'And after?'

'She'll put it behind her. She has to. And she's stronger than you might think. Really.'

'Do you want me to see her again – before the trial?'

'Better not, I reckon. She hasn't said any of those . . . weird things about Mummy since . . .' She shook her head. 'Well, for a long time.' How long? I wondered. Had Sarah just stopped short of suggesting I was the cause rather than the cure?

'I'm sorry', I began, 'if I mishandled things . . . when Rowena and I . . .'

'Forget it,' she said, significantly failing to contradict me. 'It doesn't matter. It won't, anyway. Not once the trial's out of the way.' Assuming, she didn't add, that the trial went as smoothly as she hoped. And ended with the verdict she wanted to hear.

Sarah's information proved to be accurate. The trial of Shaun Andrew Naylor for rape and double murder opened at Birmingham Crown Court on Monday the eighth of April, 1991. I was notified that I'd be required as a witness, probably during the second week. Until then, I was left to follow events through newspaper and television reports like any other curious member of the public. I learned, just as they did, that Sir Keith Paxton was in court each day to hear the often harrowing medical evidence of how his wife had died. And I could only wonder, like them, how Naylor hoped to be acquitted when DNA analysis appeared to identify him as the rapist. Pleading not guilty was either a gesture of defiance on his part or there was something we were all missing.

I cut a pretty distracted figure at work during this period, my thoughts dwelling on events in Birmingham when I was supposed to be concentrating on matching cricket bat production to early season demand. As a result, I was a virtual spectator at the board meeting on 11 April, when Adrian unveiled his plans for penetration of the Australian market. An agency wasn't enough, according to him. Corporate presence was necessary. And Viburna, an ailing Melbourne sportswear manufacturer, was the key. He proposed a takeover, which would give Timariot & Small direct access to Viburna's customers, creating a perfect springboard for promoting combined cricket bat and accessories sales throughout the continent. Viburna could be ours for little more than a million. So, what were we waiting for? Nothing, apparently. Simon was keen. Jennifer said she'd look at the figures, but agreed we had to expand if we weren't to contract. And I made the mistake of thinking we could consider it in more detail later. Adrian and Jennifer were to report back after a fact-finding visit to Melbourne in May. Until then, no decision was to be taken. But already the idea had acquired a crucial momentum. It was Adrian's first big independent project as managing director. With the shares he'd inherited from Mother, he now held the largest single stake in the company. What he wanted, sooner or later, he would have. And so would the rest of us.

I travelled up to Birmingham the following Sunday and booked into the Midland Hotel. Sarah had told me she and her father would be staying there that night with Rowena, who was due to testify immediately before me on Monday morning. We'd agreed to dine together. It was the first time we'd all met since the lunch in Hindhead and I wasn't sure what to expect. But Sir Keith soon put me at my ease. He looked tired but determined, shielding his daughters as best he could behind a show of imperturbability.

As for Rowena, she'd changed, as Sarah had said. The intensity was still there, but the threat of imminent disintegration had vanished. She was in command of herself, though how certainly I couldn't tell. Her manner had become distant. I don't mean she was hostile towards me, or even cool. But she'd retreated behind a mask. And though the performance she gave was convincing, it was also expressionless. As if she'd willed herself to forget whatever was inconvenient or ambiguous in her recollections of 17 July 1990. At the cost of the most appealing part of her personality. She was still fragile. But somehow no longer vulnerable.

'I can't tell you', said Sir Keith when the girls had gone off to bed, 'what a help your sister-in-law's been to us these past few months.'

'Bella?' I responded, unable to disguise my surprise.

'She's a wonderful woman, as I'm sure you'd agree. She's put Rowena back on her feet in a way I don't think I'd have been able to.'

'Really?' This was news to me. And news I didn't much care for.

'I've found her company a genuine tonic. We have bereavement in common, I suppose. Her husband. My wife. Only those who've suffered in the same way can really understand, you know.'

'I'm sure that's true.' But I wasn't at all sure it applied to Bella. She must have given Sir Keith a vastly different impression of her reaction to Hugh's death from the one I'd received.

'I only wish she could have been in court last week. I'd have been glad of a friendly face. But the prosecuting counsel . . . Well, my solicitor actually . . . Some nonsense about how it would look if . . .' He puffed his cheeks irritably and sipped some brandy. 'Still, when this ghastly business is all over . . .' Then he grinned. 'Just wanted to put you in the picture, Robin. So it doesn't come as a shock. Some people can be damned prudish about this sort of thing. But not you, I dare say.'

'No. Of course not.' I smiled cautiously, trying not to show my incredulity. And something worse than incredulity. Disgust? Disapproval? Not quite. What I really felt was a form of jealousy. How dare Bella try to replace Louise Paxton? How dare Sir Keith even think of allowing her to? He should have loved Louise too much for such a thing to be possible. He should have loved her as I would have done in his place. Instead of which—

'I've you to thank for meeting Bella, of course. If you hadn't recommended Sarah to her as a lodger . . . Well, I'm grateful, believe me.'

Oh, I believed him. I'd be earning his gratitude twice over – though he wouldn't realize it – by what I said in court about his no longer irreplaceable wife. That's what made it so hard to bear. Sometimes, it's better to be cursed than to be thanked. And sometimes it's the same thing.

We went to the courts together next morning. They were housed in a modern city centre building externally similar to the offices of a prosperous insurance company. Inside, three galleried floors were crowded with lawyers, clients, policemen, journalists, witnesses and assorted hangers-on. Anxious consultations were underway in stairwells and corridors. And many of the faces were deadly serious. Some of its chain-smoking victims might think the law a joke. But none of them regarded it as a laughing matter.

Sir Keith and his daughters knew what to expect. They'd been there before. A few press cameras snapped as we entered, capturing Sir Keith impassive in three piece pin-stripe and old school tie, Sarah sombre and black-suited, Rowena pale but composed in a lilac dress. We climbed to the top floor and Sir

Keith went into Court Twelve while Rowena and I waited outside with Sarah. Within ten minutes of the start, Rowena was called. I wished her luck, which she barely acknowledged. Then she was shown in by an usher and Sarah followed, leaving me to kick my heels as the morning slowly elapsed.

I'd anticipated a lonely vigil and had brought Adrian's preliminary report on Viburna Sportswear to study while I waited. I couldn't concentrate on it, of course, but it gave me something to look at instead of the other hang-dog occupants of the landing. Which explains why the first I knew of Bella's arrival on the scene was when she sat down beside me.

'Hello, Robin,' she whispered. 'What's happening inside?'

'Bella! I didn't know you were coming.'

'Neither did I. Until I decided I wanted to. I shan't go in. Keith's forbidden me to. But I thought at least I could have lunch with you all. Perhaps dinner afterwards.'

'I'm sure Keith will be delighted to see you.'

'But you're not?'

'I didn't say that.'

'No. And you don't say half the things you mean. But I was married to your brother for nearly twenty years. I know the signs.'

'I'm sure you do. And I'm glad you haven't forgotten Hugh altogether.'

'So hard.' She looked at me more in disappointment than anger. 'The living are more important than the dead, Robin. Remember that.'

'I'll try to.'

'I'll put your tetchiness down to nerves. This waiting can't be easy for you.'

'I'm *not* nervous.'

'Good. That'll make your evidence all the more convincing.' She lit a cigarette and offered me one, knowing I'd given up years ago but enjoying the momentary hesitation before I refused. 'But then,' she added, blowing out a lungful of smoke, 'what can be more convincing than the truth?'

What I'd have said in reply I'll never know, because at that moment the door leading from the court opened and Rowena came out to join us. She was blinking rapidly and fingering her hair, much but not all of her composure gone. In its place I'd have expected to see relief, some visible sign of the liberation she should have felt. But instead there was more anxiety than when she'd gone in. As if testifying had added to her problems, not resolved them. As if she hadn't said – or been allowed to say – what she really wanted to. And there was a furtiveness as well. She looked as if she wanted to run away and hide. From all of us.

She saw Bella first and shaped an uncertain smile. Then Sarah appeared at her elbow and led her towards us. I tried to think of something both meaningless and comforting to say. But, before I could, the usher beckoned to me. My turn had come. And there was time to exchange no more than a glance with Rowena as I went in. But a glance was enough. The mask had fallen now. Beneath it, there was despair.

The court had none of the Dickensian appurtenances I'd somehow imagined. Glass-topped partitions, pale wood panelling and discreet grey carpeting drained away the archaism of gown and wig. It was a place where divorce settlements and tax evasion could be discussed in a seemly atmosphere. Rape and murder surely weren't topics that belonged in its antiseptic environment. Yet there was the judge, gorgeously robed. There was the coat of arms above his head. There, beneath him, were the lawyers and clerks in their orderly chaos of books and papers. And there, in the large glazed dock at the rear of the room, flanked by two prison officers, was the accused: Shaun Andrew Naylor.

I'd not seen him before, of course. And I hardly had the chance to study him now. A lean sallow-faced man with thick black hair leaning forward in his chair, as if straining to catch every word that was said. He looked up as I stepped into the witness-box and caught my eye for less than a second. I had the fleeting impression of someone bent on memorizing my features in every detail. Then I put the thought aside and took the oath.

The prosecuting counsel gave me an easy ride, as he was bound to. He let me present my well-rehearsed portrait of the relaxed and attractive woman I'd spoken to, briefly and inconsequentially, on Hergest Ridge. He encouraged me to specify the time at which we'd parted and to say how I could be so sure. And wisely he left it there.

The defence counsel didn't, of course. He wanted to know about the offer of a lift. Could it have been construed as the offer of something else? All this I parried easily enough, as he must have anticipated. But I couldn't deny the fact that she'd offered me a lift. Nor the theoretical possibility that she had more than a car journey in mind. These were purely negative points, of course. But he must have hoped they'd stick in the jurors' minds. I hoped he was wrong. Glancing across at them, I reckoned he probably was. They'd heard the evidence to date. They were already convinced – like the rest of us – that the defendant was guilty as charged. It was going to take more than logic-chopping to shift them.

As if to ensure this was so, the judge asked me to clarify my statement that there was nothing in Lady Paxton's manner or in anything she'd said to me that implied an ulterior motive. I was happy to do so. And while I was about it, he glared at the defending counsel as if to suggest he didn't like the line his cross-examination had taken. With that I was discharged. Sir Keith nodded appreciatively to me as I passed him on the way out. And I risked a single parting glance in Naylor's direction. But he was stooping close to the gap between glass barrier and wooden partition for a whispered word with his solicitor. He wasn't interested in me any more. My encounter with the man I believed to have raped and murdered Louise Paxton had been more fleeting than my encounter with Louise herself. I didn't expect ever to see him again. I didn't expect I'd ever need to.

Lunch was a rushed and frugal affair in the bar of the Grand Hotel, a short walk from the courts. Rowena said little. None of us, in fact, seemed to have much of an appetite and the satisfaction we expressed at the events of the morning had a faintly hollow ring. I hadn't heard Rowena's testimony, of course, and she hadn't heard mine. But, according to Sir Keith, who'd heard both, they'd been equally effective. As far as he was concerned, a convincing and coherent account of his wife's behaviour during the last day of her life had been placed on the record and was now unchallengeable. As to that, I assumed the defence counsel might still have something to say. But he couldn't know just how indefinable the doubts were that afflicted those who'd met Louise Paxton on 17 July 1990. We didn't put them into words, Rowena and I. But I was coming more and more to realize that we were both aware of them. And they were the same. The impression Louise had left on her daughter was the impression she'd left on me. She'd been changing before our eyes. Altering in mood and intention. Slipping out of sight and understanding. Retreating into camouflage we could never hope to penetrate. Or else discarding some long-worn disguise. Her past. Her life. Her death. Her future. They were all one now. But that day had seen them trembling on a razor's edge. And we'd watched, unwittingly, as they'd fallen.

Perhaps I should have tried to express some of this to Rowena.

Not for the purpose of striking up a sympathetic rapport. Just so she'd know she wasn't alone. But my thoughts were too confused. And nobody would have wanted me to, anyway, except perhaps Rowena herself. Her father and sister desired nothing more than a clean and simple end to the trial. Naylor convicted and locked up. The key thrown away. And the wife and mother they'd lost preserved for ever in the amber of their idealized memories.

Who could begrudge them? Not me. Nor Rowena, as I could tell by her strained but determined expression. She meant to see this through for their sakes. Perhaps Bella had reminded her, as she'd reminded me, that the living matter more than the dead. So we like to believe, anyway. So Rowena and I certainly believed. Then.

I didn't go back to court with them after lunch. I'd said my piece and suddenly wanted to be away, right away, from that room full of strangers where Louise Paxton's death was being slowly anatomized and her life progressively forgotten. But fleeing the scene achieved nothing. I couldn't escape the process. It stayed with me, keeping perfect pace, as the train sped south towards home. Naylor's face, half recalled, half imagined, in the flickering reflections of the carriage window. His eyes, resting on me as they'd rested on Louise. His mouth, curving towards a smile. Only he knew for certain why the mirror had been smashed that day. Only he knew the whole truth. Which he might never tell.

But what *would* he say? What version of the truth would he offer when he came to testify? He certainly couldn't avoid doing so. That became obvious as the prosecution case wound towards its close. DNA analysis suggested he'd had sex with Louise Paxton shortly before her death. There were sufficient signs of violence to suggest rape even if the circumstances hadn't been as conclusive as they were. His fingerprints had been found in several places around the house, including the bedroom *and* the studio. So had fibres which had been shown to match samples taken from a sweatshirt and a pair of jeans belonging to him. The jeans were also stained with three different types of oil paint shown to match paint types found on palettes, canvases and worktops in Bantock's studio. An unlicensed gun and a switch-blade knife had been discovered concealed beneath floorboards in Naylor's flat. Naylor himself had initially denied ever being at Whistler's Cot, only volunteering – or inventing – his story of being picked up by Lady Paxton when confronted with the forensic evidence against him. Finally, there were the witnesses who'd heard him boast of 'screwing the bitch and wringing her neck for her trouble'. A barman at a pub he used in Bermondsey called Vincent Cassidy, who'd phoned the police because what Naylor had done was 'out of order', 'too much for me to stomach', 'just not on'. And a prisoner he'd shared a cell with on remand called Jason Bledlow. 'He was proud of it. He wanted me to know. He just couldn't keep his mouth shut. Said he hadn't realized she was nobility, like. But he reckoned that made it better. I reported what he'd said straightaway because I was disgusted, really sickened, you know?' And it was impossible to believe the jury didn't know. It was inconceivable he could say anything to dislodge his guilt from their minds. He was going down.

But not without a struggle. *The trial will resume on Monday,* reported Saturday's newspaper, *when the defence will present its case.* But what case? I knew then I'd have to hear it myself, in his own words. Every lie. Every evasion. Every badly constructed piece of the fiction he'd be forced to present. I needed to be certain. I'd never met the witnesses. I'd never studied forensics. I had to look him in the face as he protested his innocence to be sure of his guilt. Because that's what I needed to be. Sure. Beyond even unreasonable doubt.

Telling Adrian I needed to take a few days' leave so soon after the day I'd already spent in Birmingham was the easy part. Explaining myself to the Paxtons was next to impossible. In the end, I didn't even try, travelling up by an early train on Monday morning and squeezing into the court just before proceedings began. Sir Keith spotted me at once, of course, and was clearly puzzled. But he was on his own, which was a relief as well as a surprise.

There was time for us to have a quick word before the judge entered. To my astonishment, Sir Keith seemed to think I'd come for his benefit. 'Sarah's had to go back to college for the start of the summer term and Rowena's staying with her in Hindhead. Bella can keep an eye on her there. Besides, I didn't see why she should have to listen to Naylor's lies. It's bad enough any of us should have to. I don't mind admitting I'm glad I shan't be sitting through it alone, though. This is much appreciated, Robin, believe me.'

The court was fuller than it had been on the day I'd given evidence. There was a buzz of expectancy, an unspoken but unanimous understanding that we'd come to the crunch. Naylor was already in the dock, staring into space and chewing at his fingernails, right leg vibrating where it was angled under his chair. His nervousness was hardly surprising in view of the sledgehammer blows the prosecution had been able to deliver. He looked what we all thought he was: a hardened over-sexed young criminal with a streak of malicious violence he couldn't control. But he was trapped now. And the only way out was to persuade the jury he'd been wrongly accused. Which he didn't look capable of doing. Not remotely.

The jury filed in. Then the judge made his entrance. And Naylor's barrister rose to address the court. His opening speech was short and to the point. 'Mr Naylor has nothing to hide, members of the jury,' he concluded. 'Which is why I propose to call him to give evidence in his own defence.'

And so it began. Naylor was taken from the dock to the witness-box and sworn in. He spoke firmly and confidently, almost arrogantly. His answers were casually phrased but cleverly constructed. Too cleverly, I suppose. Some mumbling show of awe might have won him a few friends. Instead, he came across as somebody so contemptuous of the world that he couldn't believe it had turned against him now. And he seemed positively proud to admit how he made a living.

'I'm a thief. That's what I am. I clock targets while I'm doing the day job. Call back later to collect. Thieving's what I do. But I don't murder people. I might lay somebody out if they tried to stop me getting away, though I've never had to. But I wouldn't kill them.' And rape? What about that? 'I'm no rapist. I reckon they're the lowest form of life there is. Them and child molesters. I'm a married man with children. But like my wife'll tell you, I'm no saint. I've never been able to say no to women. They like me. I've never had to force them into it. I've never wanted to. I never would.'

That much *seemed* credible. He had the cocksure manner and smouldering looks some women find attractive. But he also had such confidence in his own irresistibility that it was easy to imagine him reacting violently to rejection. As for murder, well, he'd more or less said it himself. If Bantock had tried to stop him, worse still to apprehend him, he'd have done whatever was necessary to escape. Candour was his only hope. But candour revealed him as a man quite capable of committing the crimes he'd been charged with.

So, what *was* his version of events? It took him the rest of the day to spell it out. But what it amounted to was this. He'd gone to stay with a friend in Cardiff while the dust settled on a row with his wife. The usual cause – his chronic infidelity – had been aggravated by the latest piece of skirt being her sister. He reckoned a trip to Disneyworld for her and the kids might patch things up. So, he set about raising some cash to pay for the holiday by breaking into likely looking rural properties, all of them far enough from Cardiff to avoid embarrassing his friend. A house near Ross-on-Wye on the night of 14/15 July. Another near Malvern on 15/16 July. And a third near Bridgnorth on 16/17 July. He stayed in the area next day and looked around the Ludlow-Leominster-Bromyard triangle, spotting a couple of possibilities. Then he drove towards Kington and stopped at the Harp Inn, Old Radnor, to while away the evening before deciding which one to try. And that's when his plans changed.

'I was sitting outside in the sun. What was left of it. The place was pretty busy. Lady Paxton – I didn't know her name then, of course – walked up and asked if she could share my table. I said yes and offered to buy her a drink. She didn't go into the pub herself. And she'd left her car a little way down the lane, near the church. We talked. Like you do. It was obvious . . . Well, I got the pretty clear impression she was . . . interested. We had another drink. She got friendly. Started to flirt with me. Eyefuls of smile. Hand brushing my thigh. You know. I got the message. And I thought: why not? Beautiful woman. Lonely and a long way from home. Who wouldn't? She didn't say much about herself. Or ask me much about myself. We left about eight forty-five, I suppose. It was getting dark by then. She suggested we go back to a friend's house nearby. Said the friend wouldn't be there and . . . she could use it. She led the way in her car. I followed in mine. It wasn't far. A cottage up a narrow lane near Kington. The friend was a painter. A woman, she said. She showed me her studio. I didn't spend long looking around. We both knew what we were there for. It started in the studio. But there were too many things to bump into. So she took me upstairs to the bedroom. I didn't rape her. I didn't need to. She was . . . a willing partner. And she . . . well . . . liked it a bit rough. But that's not rape. Not anything like. I didn't stay long afterwards. She said her friend was due back around eleven and she wanted time to clear up. So, I made myself scarce. It can't have been much later than half past ten when I left. She was still in bed then, alive and well. I stopped for a drink at a pub in Leominster just before closing time. The Black Horse. Then I went on and did the place near Bromyard. Big house at Berrow Green. I got a good haul there. Felt pretty pleased with myself. I got to Cardiff around dawn. Next day, I set off back to London. Reckoned I'd got enough to pay for the Florida trip. And it was about time I made it up with the wife.

'I heard about the murders on the telly. At first, I couldn't believe it was the same woman. But when I saw her picture in the papers . . . . I knew. And I knew the best thing I could say was nothing. I mean, I had to be in the frame, didn't I? They said she'd been raped. And I knew they could tie me to that. Probably to the cottage as well. So I laid low. Didn't go down the Greyhound. Let alone say anything to Vince Cassidy. What he says I said . . . It isn't true. Any of it. She was alive when I left the cottage. And the painter wasn't there. I don't know who murdered them. Or why. But it wasn't me.'

'At times he was almost plausible,' said Sir Keith over a drink in the bar of the Midland Hotel at the end of the afternoon session. 'I mean, if you didn't know Louise, that is.'

'He didn't seem plausible to me. A slick liar, yes. But nobody was taken in.'

'I hope you're right. I don't want Louise's memory sullied by any of the things he said about her.'

'It won't be. He can't achieve anything this way – except a longer sentence.'

'I'd give him a short sentence if I could. The shortest one of all.'

'Yes,' I said, lowering my voice. 'I rather think I would too.'

'The evil-minded bastard,' Sir Keith muttered, massaging his brow. 'God, I'm glad the girls didn't hear any of that.'

'They'll read it though, won't they?'

'Yes. They're bound to. But at least they won't have to watch his weaselly eyes while they're about it. Or listen to his Jack-the-lad voice reeling off lies like grubby fivers from a wad in his back pocket. I expected to hate him, of course. To despise him. To want him dead. But I didn't know he was going to make my flesh creep. Well, tomorrow he'll be cross-examined. I hope the prosecuting counsel puts him through hell. Because that's what he deserves.' He broke off and shook his head, bemused, it seemed, by the force of his response. 'Sorry. I didn't mean to get carried away.'

'Don't apologize. I agree with you. One hundred per cent.'

Sir Keith and I drank too much and stayed too long in the hotel bar that night. Sickened by the way Naylor had sought to portray his wife as some kind of ageing nymphomaniac, his anger gave way in the end to grief. I sat and listened to his increasingly tearful reminiscences of their life together. How they'd met when Louise had been working as a hospital receptionist during a university vacation. How he'd fought off the younger rivals for her affections. How they'd married despite her parents' opposition.

'Both dead now, thank God. I wouldn't have wanted them to go through this. Even though they never liked me. Well, I was fifteen years older than Louise with a divorce behind me. I wasn't what they had in mind for their daughter at all. She was an only child and naturally they wanted the best for her. And they thought she could do a great deal better than me. Maybe they were right. I didn't have the knighthood then, of course. I didn't have the lifestyle I have now. But that didn't deter Louise. She was never a gold-digger. She accepted me for what I was. And for what I might become.'

In the event, Sir Keith had given his wife wealth and status as well as love. They'd been married for twenty-three years and he'd never once regretted it. A beautiful wife and two lovely daughters to adorn his middle age. He'd known he was lucky, blessed with more than his fair share of good fortune. But he'd never supposed there'd come such a savage reckoning. He'd never imagined he might have to pay so dearly for the joy and fulfilment Louise had brought into his life.

'And now it's so empty, Robin. Like a husk. I've felt so old since Louise died. So tired. So decrepit. And I'm not very good at being alone. I suppose that's why . . . well, why Bella . . . She's been good for me. Good for all of us. She can never replace Louise. Nobody can. But . . . it helps . . . to have somebody . . . It helps her as well, I think. She loved Hugh very much, didn't she?'

I probably said yes. I certainly didn't disabuse him of the notion. What would have been the point? I felt sorry for him. I even felt I understood. That night, indeed, I began to imagine I understood more about Louise Paxton than Sir Keith ever had. The lonely childhood and the disapproving parents were two more pieces of the jigsaw. Somewhere still, out there, she was waiting to surprise me. I dreamt of her sitting beside me outside the Harp Inn, as Naylor had claimed she'd sat beside him. The setting sun was behind her. I couldn't see her face clearly. Her hand brushed my knee. And she laughed. *'Follow me,'* she said. *'You can't imagine what I have in mind.'*

* * *

The prosecuting counsel spared no effort in his cross-examination of Naylor. Yet for all his remorseless probing, Naylor's story remained intact. He didn't make the mistake of taking up counsel's invitation to explain the improbabilities and inconsistencies in his account. Why should a respectable married woman like Lady Paxton seek sex with a man like him? He didn't know. Why should she take him to the house of somebody she knew only slightly? Again, he didn't know. Why should anybody but him want to murder her? Yet again, he didn't know. Didn't he have any remorse for inflicting such a distasteful lie on Lady Paxton's family? No, because it wasn't a lie. Why, then, had he initially denied all connection with the case? Because he'd panicked. Simple as that. It had been an act of stupidity, not guilt. Did he seriously expect anyone to accept that? Yes. Because it was the truth. 'And truth's stranger than fiction, don't they say?' He was still confident, still giving as good as he got. 'I'm putting my hand up to four burglaries. I'm admitting the kind of man I am. I'm not trying to pretend anything. I'm just saying this. I've never murdered anyone. I've never raped anyone. I'm not guilty.' Sometimes, just sometimes, you could think he believed it. But, glancing round the court, you could sense what he must have sensed as well. If he really did believe it, he was the only one.

I went back to Petersfield that night. Sir Keith, who meant to see the trial through to its end, saw me off at New Street station. 'It'll be over by early next week, I reckon,' he said as I leant out of the train window for a parting word. 'And I want to be here to see how he takes the verdict – and the sentence. Will you be coming up again?'

'I don't think I'll be able to. Pressure of work, you know.'

'Of course, of course. I won't forget the support you've given us, Robin. Helping Rowena. Sarah too. And listening to me ramble on last night. Other people's lives. Other people's problems. They can be hard to take, I know. And it's not as if you even knew Louise, is it? Not really.'

'No. I never did.'

Not *his* Louise, anyway. Another one maybe. A version of her as far removed from the person he'd lived with for twenty-three years as Naylor's version of events was from the truth as I thought I knew it. The light faded as the train rushed south towards London. And the darkness grew. Who could be sure, absolutely sure, of anything? Where she'd gone that night after leaving Hergest Ridge. What she'd done and why. What she *would* have done if I'd gone with her. And where we'd all be now if I had.

The defence called four more witnesses after Naylor himself. The friend he'd stayed with in Cardiff, Gary Newsom, who spoke up for him as a bit of a rogue but no murderer, who'd returned to Newsom's home in Cardiff on 18 July 1990 'relaxed and a bit pleased with himself, but looking forward to going back to London'. A customer at the Harp Inn the night before who recognized Naylor as 'a man I saw sitting outside with a good-looking woman; it was definitely him and the woman could have been Lady Paxton, but I can't be certain'. A barmaid at the Black Horse, Leominster, who remembered serving Naylor just before closing time that night. 'He bought me a drink and chatted me up a bit. He seemed nice enough. I quite took to him, as a matter of fact.' And lastly Naylor's wife, Carol. 'It's true about the row. A real up-and-downer. And about the holiday. He was full of it when he came back. I knew how he'd got the cash. The stuff he stole was in his van. Like he says, thieving's in his blood. Always has been. But murder ain't. Nor's rape. My Shaun would never go in for that sort of thing.'

It didn't sound to me as if any of this amounted to very much. As the prosecuting counsel pointed out in his closing speech, Naylor might well have been at the Harp that evening. But the witness hadn't been able to put a definite time on the sighting or identify Lady Paxton as Naylor's companion. She could have been anyone, given Naylor's roving eye. As for his late visit to the pub in Leominster, that could have been a futile attempt to set up an alibi. Futile because there was still plenty of time for him to have gone to Whistler's Cot, murdered Bantock, raped and murdered Lady Paxton, then driven the fifteen miles to Leominster before eleven o'clock. By Naylor's own admission, he'd had sexual intercourse with Lady Paxton. Did anybody seriously believe this was with Lady Paxton's consent? If it was, why should she choose Whistler's Cot as a venue? And why take Naylor into Bantock's studio first? Because, of course, Naylor had to say she did so in order to account for the forensic evidence of his presence in the studio: the paint and the fibres. Whereas the real explanation was that he'd torn his clothing and stained his jeans during the fatal struggle with Oscar Bantock. When Lady Paxton had surprised him at the scene of the crime, he'd forced her to go upstairs and undress, probably threatening her with the knife or the gun. He'd raped her, as was shown by the amount of vaginal bruising, which he'd attempted, with breathtaking impudence, to attribute to masochistic tendencies on Lady Paxton's part. Finally, he'd strangled her as he had Oscar Bantock, using a ligature of picture-hanging wire taken from the studio. Then he'd fled, the original purpose of his visit to the house forgotten. These were crimes of horrifying brutality, motivated by material and sexual greed and made possible by a complete indifference to the pain and suffering of others which Naylor had continued to exhibit in his outrageous mockery of a defence. Guilty verdicts on all three charges were the only appropriate way to respond.

Strong stuff. But Naylor's barrister responded by pointing out that his client's explanation of the events of 17 July 1990 *was* consistent with the evidence. He'd met Lady Paxton at the Harp, where they'd been seen together. They'd gone to Whistler's Cot and had vigorous sexual intercourse, Lady Paxton having some good reason to believe the owner of the house wouldn't return until later. Naylor had then left. Subsequently, a person or persons unknown had entered the house and murdered Lady Paxton and Bantock, who was either on the premises by then or arrived while the murderer was escaping. The estimated time of death, 9 to 10 p.m., was only that: an estimate. It certainly didn't rule out such a sequence of events. As for the identity or motive of the murderer, who knew? The police had stopped looking once they'd found Naylor. He specifically denied making the confessions attributed to him by two witnesses, one of whom had a criminal record. Those witnesses were either mistaken or were lying for reasons of their own. Finally, it should be remembered that Naylor had been completely honest about his criminal lifestyle. He'd admitted four burglaries in the Kington area, all confirmed by the police. One of them had taken place only a few hours after he was supposed to have committed rape and double murder at Whistler's Cot. Was this really what he'd have done after carrying out such horrendous acts? Surely not, his barrister urged the jury to agree. They should give his client the benefit of the doubt.

Yet very little doubt seemed to exist in the judge's mind when he summed up. To accept Naylor's version of events, he stressed, it was necessary to suppose that Lady Paxton had gone to Kington not simply to buy a painting but to satisfy a craving for casual sex with a stranger. If the jury found that improbable, they might well conclude that the defendant was guilty as charged.

Naturally, they should give due weight to the possibility that he was telling the truth, but they should also remember that he had, by his own admission, lied in his initial statement to the police. The coincidence of an unknown murderer arriving at Whistler's Cot shortly after his departure was, moreover, bound to strain credulity. The judge's implication was clear.

And it wasn't lost on the jury. Sent out rather later than Sir Keith had predicted, they returned within four hours and found Naylor guilty on all three counts. The judge condemned him for adding to the grief of the Paxton family with his mischievous and implausible defence and described him as a depraved and dangerous individual whom the public had every right to expect would be kept behind bars for a very long time. He sentenced Naylor to life imprisonment for each of the murders and ten years for the rape, all to run concurrently. As a final touch – much applauded by the press – he recommended a minimum term in custody of twenty years. Still protesting his innocence but no longer being listened to by anyone, Shaun Naylor was taken away to begin his sentence.

CHAPTER SEVEN

It was over. Louise Paxton was dead and buried. And now, with her murderer's conviction and imprisonment, she could rest in peace. While I began the reluctant but inevitable process of forgetting her. Which is what I thought I would do. But, as the gap stretched between me and the one brief intersection of our lives, the recollection of our meeting grew somehow clearer, not fainter. I assumed this would eventually cease. The rational part of my mind dismissed it as a caprice of the imagination and waited patiently for it to fade. But it didn't fade. It seemed to draw a curious energy from the passage of time, to become slowly more elusive yet more potent by the day. Whenever I was tired or alone or thinking of nothing in particular, the components of that evening on Hergest Ridge would reassemble themselves in my mind. The quality of the light. The pitch of the slope. The colour of the grass. The shade of her hair. The look in her eye. And her words. Every phrase. Every nuance. Yet always the question was the same. *'Can we really change anything?'* And whatever answer I chose made no difference. Because she was out of earshot now. For ever.

Louise Paxton's memory may not have withered, but my association with her family showed every sign of doing so. Sarah invited me to a party at The Hurdles on the last Saturday in June. A crowd of her fellow students from the College of Law were there to celebrate the end of the course, with Bella presiding good-humouredly over their exuberances. I felt old and out of place and wished I hadn't gone. Sarah was busy playing the part of hostess and couldn't spare me much attention. It was Bella, in fact, who brought me up to date with her plans.

'Rowena's going to take up a deferred place at Bristol University in the autumn. Keith thinks she'll be able to cope with student life by then. And he hopes Sarah will be able to help her. She's trying to arrange to do her articles in Bristol. Then they could live together. That would give Rowena some of the security she needs. I shall be sorry to be left alone here again, but . . . well . . . maybe I won't be for long.'

'Another lodger?'

'Not exactly. Not yet, anyway. I'm planning to go abroad next month.'

'Where to?'

'Biarritz, as a matter of fact. Keith's asked me.'

'Really? Well, I . . . I hope . . .'

'We enjoy ourselves? Thank you, Robin. I'll try to make sure we do.'

So Sir Keith was in Biarritz with Bella, and his daughters – I later learned – were on a Greek island together when the anniversary of the Kington killings came round. I hardly remember where I was. But I know where my thoughts were dwelling.

The summer of 1991 was a good one for Timariot & Small. The cricket bat business was relatively unaffected by the general economic recession. I suppose that's why we had so few qualms about the takeover of Viburna Sportswear following Jennifer's favourable report on its finances. She and Adrian went out there again in August to finalize the terms and Simon was looking forward to spending much of the Antipodean spring in Melbourne, setting up various cross-promotional schemes. As works director I had no need to go myself, since Viburna's former chairman and chief executive, Greg Dyson, was staying on to manage production at the Australian end. Viburna Sportswear formally became a subsidiary of Timariot & Small on 1 October 1991. The way was clear for Adrian's international ambitions to take flight.

My own ambitions were less easy to define. I was on top of my job and deriving satisfaction from seeing some of my innovations work well there. In less than a year, I'd settled into the company as if it were an old and comfortable jacket. I liked the staff and relished accommodating my ideas to their idiosyncracies. I enjoyed the blend of tradition and efficiency, of ancient craft and modern commerce. But outside the hours I spent at the factory there was an emptiness in my life I should have wanted to fill, a solitude I should have regarded as loneliness. Instead my efforts to meet people and make friends were half-hearted, almost insincere. There were a few contemporaries from Churcher's I'd see from time to time, most of them married with children. There were the regulars at the Cricketers to while away an idle evening with. Or Simon to get roaring drunk with if I felt in the mood, as occasionally I did. But that was all.

At least until Jennifer tried to pair me off with a friend of hers who ran an interior design business in Petersfield and was recovering from an acrimonious divorce. Ann Taylor was an attractive and sensitive woman of my own age. I liked her from the first. Her vivacity. Her humour. Her subtlety. And she liked me. There was no mistaking that. It could have worked between us. It could have led to something. Instead, I let it slip through my fingers. A horribly misjudged weekend in Devon forced us both onto the defensive. After that, there was no dramatic breach, no final parting of the ways. Just a drift into brittle indifference.

'What's wrong with you?' demanded Jennifer in her exasperation. 'You were made for each other.' And maybe she was right. Or would have been. But for a memory I couldn't discard.

'Who's Louise?' Ann had asked me in our hotel room in Devon the morning after the fumbled night before. 'You seemed to be speaking to her in your sleep. Something about a mirror.'

'You're mistaken.'

'I don't think so. The name was quite clear. I don't mind . . . if it's somebody you once . . . knew well.'

'No. It's nobody I ever knew.'

> The simple lack
> Of her is more to me
> Than others' presence,
> Whether life splendid be
> Or utter black.
>
> I have not seen,
> I have no news of her;
> I can tell only
> She is not here, but there
> She might have been.

*   *   *

One Sunday morning in the middle of October, I was surprised by a telephone call from Bella, inviting me to join Sir Keith and her for lunch at Tylney Hall, a country house hotel near Basingstoke. I accepted at once, even though I knew I wasn't being asked for the pleasure of my company. The drive up was idyllic, autumnal sunshine bathing the trees and hedges in golden light. Some of the same fleeting lustre seemed to cling to my hosts, who were waiting for me on the terrace when I arrived. Sir Keith wasn't just smiling. He was clearly extremely happy. A healthy glow warmed his features, a button-hole and jazzy tie signalling relaxation and indulgence. While Bella looked more than usually glamorous in a tight-waisted pink suit and shot-silk blouse. The glitter of diamonds drew my eyes to her wedding finger. And there, beneath an engagement ring I'd never seen before, was a plain band of gold.

'I wanted you to be one of the first to know, Robin,' said Bella as she kissed me. 'We were married on Thursday.'

'I hope you'll excuse the secrecy,' put in Sir Keith. 'But we thought a low-key ceremony was best. You know how some people can be.'

'But not you, Robin,' said Bella, smiling sweetly. 'We trust.'

'No,' I hurriedly replied. 'Of course not. My . . . heartiest congratulations.'

So it was done. Bella had become the second Lady Paxton. No doubt she'd have preferred a grandiose celebration of this apogee of her social achievement, but Sir Keith had insisted on discretion and it was easy to understand why. Fifteen months wasn't long, some would have said, to mourn a wife of twenty-three years. I'd have said so myself, come to that. Fifteen *years* wouldn't have seemed sufficient to me. Not when Louise was the wife he'd lost. And the sort of wife he'd never find again.

Naturally, however, I gave them no hint of my true opinion. I supplied instead a fair impersonation of just what Bella wanted me to be: the token relative, expressing his well-bred pleasure at their news. We lunched lavishly and lengthily in the oak-panelled restaurant and I listened politely while they poured out their hopes and expectations of a new life together.

'I'm winding up the London practice and giving up my consultancies,' Sir Keith announced. 'I'm sixty-one, so perhaps it's about time. I suppose I'd have carried on for another five or six years if it hadn't been for . . . Well, retirement is a fresh start. For both of us. We'll be able to spend more time in Biarritz. And anywhere else Bella wants to go.'

'The girls have been quite splendid about it,' said Bella. 'No resentment. No resistance. They just want their father to be happy. And I mean to see he is.'

'I suppose it's easier because they've both flown the nest,' Sir Keith continued. 'Sarah's with an excellent firm of solicitors in Bristol. And Rowena's started her course at the university there. She's settled in well. Put last year's . . . difficulties . . . firmly behind her. They're sharing a flat in Clifton. Cosy little place. You ought to go up and see them. They'd like that.'

'Meanwhile,' said Bella, 'Keith's going to take me round the world in style on a luxury cruise ship. She sails from Southampton the day after tomorrow. Quite a honeymoon, don't you think?'

But what I really thought I wasn't about to let slip. As Bella must have realized. For when Sir Keith left us for a few minutes, her effervescent tone went suddenly flat.

'You reckon I've married him for his money and nothing else, don't you, Robin?'

'No. There's the title as well.'

'Very clever. But not true. I happen to like him a lot.'

'Like – but not love?'

'It might come to that. To start with, we can just have fun together.'

'I'm sure *you'll* have fun, Bella. You always do.'

'Try it yourself. It's not a bad way to live. Instead of vegetating in Petersfield.'

'Is that what you think I'm doing?'

'Isn't it?'

'No. Of course not.'

'Then what *are* you doing? When I first met you, I thought you were the one member of your stick-in-the mud family who might actually do something with his life. Instead of which, here you are, working at that bloody factory like the rest of them. You've disappointed me, Robin. You really have.'

'Sorry about that,' I responded, smiling sarcastically. Then I saw her glance past me. Her husband was about to rejoin us. But before he did, there was time for me to add: 'Let's hope *you* don't disappoint Sir Keith, Bella. And vice versa, of course.'

A month passed, halfway through which I received a triumphantly self-satisfied postcard from Bella, despatched during a stop-over in Egypt. *'Pyramids are so much more interesting than cricket bats.'* Then, one uneventful Friday afternoon at work, Sarah telephoned me from Bristol. 'I'm in the office, so I can't talk long.' She sounded more stilted than the length of time we'd been out of touch could account for. 'Do you think . . . Look, would it be possible . . . for you to come up here . . . at short notice? Like . . . tomorrow?'

'Tomorrow? That . . . er . . . could be tricky.' This was a lie prompted by some play-hard-to-get instinct. 'I mean, I'd love to see you. And Rowena. But . . . why the rush?'

'Rowena's why. I can't explain over the phone. But it *is* urgent. She's . . . not well. And I thought . . . But if you can't make it . . .'

'No, no. It's all right. I can rearrange things. What's wrong with her?'

'I can't go into it. Not now. But tomorrow . . .'

'OK. I suppose I could get up there around midday. I'll need your address.'

'It's a long way. Wouldn't it be quicker if you drove to Reading and caught a train from there? Then I could pick you up at the station.'

'Oh there's really no—'

'I've got a timetable for that line. We could fix it up now. It'd be easier this way, Robin. Believe me.' And something almost pleading in her tone stopped me offering any further resistance.

She was waiting for me at Temple Meads as promised, anxiety lending a briskness to her self-controlled manner. There was some other more lasting change at work as well. Her style of dress had altered – black sweater and leggings under a short snappy overcoat – but no more so than the transition from student to professional lawyer could have explained. Her appearance was designed, if anything, to conceal her personality. And perhaps that's what I noticed. An invisible barrier between us. A layer of caution her mother's death had temporarily peeled away. Now, it was back in place.

An exchange of platitudes about our careers carried us as far as her car. I didn't ask – though I wondered – if collecting me from the station was a ploy to give her time to prepare me for what was awaiting us in Clifton. Rowena, presumably. Who wasn't well. Whatever that meant.

What it meant Sarah swiftly explained as we headed west along the riverside. The day was cold and grey, overnight fog still lingering. Autumn's consolations were nowhere to be seen – or sensed. 'Rowena tried to commit suicide last Monday, Robin. She's all right now. But it was a serious attempt, according to the doctors. Aspirin, tranquillizers and gin in sufficient quantity to have killed her if I hadn't popped back to the flat at lunchtime – which I don't normally do.'

'Good God.'

'Yes. Quite a shock.'

'But surely . . . I thought your father said . . . how well she was doing.'

'That's what he chose to believe. With Bella's encouragement. Actually, Rowena did put up a pretty convincing show for them. Fooled me too. But that's all it can have been. A show.'

'Is your father . . . Well, are they . . .'

'Coming back? No. Because they don't know. I honestly don't think Daddy – far less Bella – would be any help to Rowena at the moment. He's besotted with Bella, you know. Well, of course you know. She's your sister-in-law. Sorry. That sounded like an accusation. Bella is what Bella is. Far more than Daddy can resist. I'd think it was laughable if he weren't my father. As it is, it's positively embarrassing.'

'But . . . I understood . . . They told me you'd given them your support. Quite willingly.'

'There was no point doing anything else, was there? No point letting that scheming bitch – sorry, letting my stepmother – see what I really thought.'

'Is this why Rowena took an overdose?'

'I'm tempted to say yes. It'd suit me quite well to blame Bella for what's happened to Rowena. But let's not kid ourselves. She's not the reason.'

'Then what is?'

She glanced round at me, but didn't reply directly. I suppose I already knew the answer. Sir Keith hadn't been told. But I had. Because I might understand. We were crossing the river now. Ahead, I could just make out the blurred lines of the suspension bridge spanning the murk-filled Avon Gorge. We were nearly there. In more ways than one. 'That afternoon at Frensham Pond,' said Sarah. 'Remember? Nearly a year ago. I thought it was only a question then of putting the trial behind us. I thought Rowena was just in mourning. Like I was. But she wasn't, was she? It was always more than that. I realized you knew what it was. I told myself it was nothing. I went on pretending it was nothing. But pretending hasn't got us very far, has it?'

'You're wrong, Sarah. I didn't know and I still don't.'

'But you've a faint idea. Haven't you?'

'Maybe. An inkling, perhaps.'

'About Mummy?'

'Something about her, yes. About how she was . . . that last day.'

'Which you and Rowena share?'

'In a sense. But . . . Well, I think so. Yes.'

'Then help her put it to rest, Robin. Please. For all our sakes.'

They lived in a second-floor flat in a graceful Regency terrace on the edge of Clifton Village, decorated in a strange blend of exoticism and formality. Rowena behaved more normally during our awkward lunch party than I'd expected, referring obliquely to her 'illness' and talking about resuming her mathematics course as soon as possible. Afterwards, Sarah said she had to go out but would be back for tea. I was left in the lounge while the sisters conducted a strained and whispered conversation at the door. 'Just talk to him, Ro,' I heard Sarah say. 'It's all I ask.' Then the door closed. Rowena went from there to the kitchen and showed no sign of joining me. Eventually, *I* felt forced to join *her*.

'Is that coffee you're making?' I asked, seeing the kettle in her hand. She started violently, sending a spout of boiling water sizzling across the hob. 'I'm sorry. I didn't mean to—'

'It's all right,' she said, leaning against a worktop and closing her eyes for a second. 'My nerves. They're a bit . . . frayed.'

'Of course. I quite understand.'

'That's what Sarah thinks, doesn't she? That you understand, I mean.' Her eyes were open now and trained squarely on me. I'd forgotten how disconcertingly huge they were, as wise it seemed as they were innocent. Then she looked away. 'I'm not allowed coffee. But if you—'

'Whatever you're making.'

'Herbal tea.' She smiled. 'Supposed to be calming.'

'Tea it is, then.'

She spooned some of the dustily unappetizing leaves into a mug for me, added water to her own and mine, then led the way back to the lounge. She sat by the window, her mug cradled in her hands, inhaling as she drank. Perhaps the herbs were working. She seemed calm enough. Almost contemplative. As if she'd seen reason. Or given up hope of seeing it.

'I was sorry,' I hesitantly began, 'to hear about . . . your trouble.'

'Were you?'

'Of course.'

'Why? We hardly know each other.'

'No, but—'

'I didn't plan it, Robin. I didn't spend weeks building up to it. I'd even forgotten it was Mummy's birthday. November the eleventh. I just saw it on the calendar in the kitchen. Sarah had already gone to work. And it was so grey. Like today. Mummy's birthday. And Daddy away on a cruise with a . . . new wife. Do you think he remembered?'

'I'm sure he did.'

'It's funny . . . to have so little control. To see yourself . . . as if you're disembodied . . . weeping and wailing. As if your emotions are just . . . too powerful to contain.'

'Rowena—'

'They want me to forget her. Daddy. Sarah. And Bella of course. They all want me to forget her. "Put it behind you," they say. "Accept. Adjust. Go on." They seem to think it's so simple. Like the doctors. And the counsellors. And that psychiatrist Daddy found for me last year. They all think the same. That this is just grief. A refusal to come to terms with reality.'

'Your mother *is* dead, Rowena. Nothing can bring her back.'

'But *why* is she dead?'

'Because Shaun Naylor murdered her.'

She shook her head slowly, more in sorrow it seemed than disagreement. 'I've gone over it all so many times. What she said. How she said it. Like I had it on videotape and could replay it over and over again. In slow motion. Frame by frame. Looking for the clue.'

'What clue?'

Her gaze circled slowly round the room, from the window to where I was sitting. 'You know, don't you?'

'No. Tell me.'

'When Mummy left that afternoon, she said to me . . . We were standing by the car. She was ready to go. Hesitating a bit. She wouldn't have normally. We'd said goodbye. And, anyway, it wasn't supposed to be a lengthy parting. She said . . . I remember the words exactly. There's no mistake. Sarah thinks I misheard. But I didn't. I misunderstood. That's what I did. She said: "I may not be back for quite a while, darling." I thought she meant she was going to stay with Sophie Marsden. To show the picture off to her. Well, she'd mentioned she might. So all I said was: "You'll be with Sophie?" And she thought for a moment. And then she replied: "Of course, darling. That's where I'll be." Then she kissed me and drove away.'

'I don't see—'

'I testified in court that Mummy was quite specific about her plans. But she wasn't. Not really. Otherwise she'd have phoned Sophie before setting off. She told me she was going to Kington to buy one of Oscar Bantock's paintings. But at the end . . . as she was leaving . . . I think she meant to say something else. It was like . . . she knew she might never see me again.'

'Surely not.'

'If I hadn't jumped to conclusions, she might have . . . And then there was the ring. I noticed her checking the finger she'd worn it on with her thumb. As if . . . she hadn't lost it . . . but was checking . . . reassuring herself . . . that it wasn't there.'

'A reflex. Nothing more.'

'What she never put into words . . . What I can't exactly describe . . . You felt it too, didn't you?'

'I'm not sure what you mean.'

'She was on the brink. She was about to step off. Into the void. She knew it. And still she stepped. Why?'

'I don't know.' I rose and walked across to the window. She sat beneath me, looking where I was looking. Out into the blanketing greyness of the sky beyond the neighbouring rooftops. 'Truly, Rowena, I don't.' On an impulse, I crouched beside her chair and took her hand in mine. She let me do so, studying me gravely through those immense far-questing eyes. 'I often think – like you, apparently – that there was something amiss, something adrift, that evening. She was . . . like a beautiful yacht in full sail with nobody at the helm . . . waiting for the breeze to pick up, the current to move her. I've never understood it. Never been sure I'm not investing what happened with too much significance because of what followed. I don't think I am. I don't think you are. But . . .'

She smiled with relief. 'It means a great deal to me that I'm not completely alone, Robin. It means I'm not the victim of my own delusions after all. Unless we both are.'

'She wouldn't have wanted you to brood like this. To suffer on her account.'

'I know.'

'She'd have wanted you to be happy. Wouldn't she?'

'Oh yes.'

'Then can't you be? For her?'

'But I am. Sometimes. Don't you see? What I've lost isn't happiness. It's balance. Equilibrium.' Suddenly, her expression crumpled into tearfulness. She tensed, as if to suppress a sob, released my hand, set the mug down and sighed. 'They never tell you that about suicide. The thought of it . . . can be so exhilarating. So tempting.' She shook her head. 'But I'm over it now. There's nothing in the least bit tempting about a stomach pump. Take my word for it.' At that she smiled. And so did I. 'Let's go for a walk, Robin. I haven't been out since they released me from hospital. We can leave a note for Sarah.'

We walked out onto Observatory Hill, then circled back to the suspension bridge. She meant to cross it, I knew. To tease me with the classic suicide's view of the gorge. To test whether I'd try to stop her. But if I did, some slender thread of trust would snap between us. So I let her walk ahead, running her fingers along the railing as she went, squinting up at the high curving cables, or down at the grey winding snake of the river. She stopped in the centre and I caught her up. To find her eyes wide with joy.

'It's good to be alive,' she said, turning towards me. 'Isn't it?'

I nodded. 'Yes. It is.'

'I thought so even on Monday. It's just . . . for a moment . . . for an hour at most . . . death . . . or oblivion . . . seemed even more attractive.'

'But not any more?'

'No. The world's too wonderful to give up. I haven't had my fill of it yet.'

'You never will.'

'I hope not. Except . . . do you think Mummy might simply have . . . had enough of the world?'

'I'd say the exact reverse.'

'I'm sure you're right. It's funny, though. When I saw her . . . in that place . . . the mortuary . . . she looked so . . . very very beautiful.'

'She was beautiful when she was alive.'

'But even more so when she was dead. Her skin was so pale. Like . . . flawless alabaster. And so cold. When I touched her, she opened her eyes, you know.'

'What?'

'Oh, it was an hallucination, of course. A figment of my overstressed imagination. But it seemed so real. And the oddest thing was . . . how happy she looked.' Rowena took a deep breath, then started back towards the Clifton side of the bridge. As I fell in beside her, she said: 'One of the things I used to like about mathematics was the certainty. An answer was either right or wrong. And if it was right, it was *absolutely* right and always would be. First principles governed everything. Two plus two equalled four and could never equal anything else.'

'Surely that's still the case.'

'In mathematics, perhaps. But not in life. The variables are too great. It would be possible to rerun the events of the seventeenth of July last year a hundred times within the same parameters and produce a hundred different results. Many of them would be similar, of course. But none would be identical. Not exactly. Some would be dramatically different. Almost unrecognizable. A lot of times – maybe a majority of times – Mummy wouldn't die. Wouldn't even be in danger. Just because of some tiny scarcely noticeable variation. Like what she said to me. Or to you. And what we said in reply.'

'But we can't rerun those events. Any more than we can – or should – take responsibility for the fatal variation.'

'I know.' She looked round at me and smiled. 'That's why I'm going to stop trying to.'

Rowena stayed behind when Sarah drove me to the station early that evening. Sarah, indeed, encouraged her to on the grounds that she should take her convalescence seriously. She was so emphatic on the point, however, that I suspected another reason was at work: an eagerness to compare notes with me on her sister's state of mind. And so it turned out. No sooner had we left Clifton than she proposed we stop on the way for a drink. There were plenty of later trains than the one I'd been aiming for, so I was happy to agree.

A hotel bar supplied the privacy Sarah was seeking. She insisted on buying the drinks, as if I merited some reward for coming so far. Perhaps my willing response to her call had struck her as unusually – even oddly – generous. She wasn't to know how helpless I was to resist any summons emanating from her family. I couldn't have begun to explain why I should be. But I was. What she might regard as altruism was in reality a compulsion.

'I think seeing you's done Rowena some good. She seemed much more relaxed this afternoon.'

'I didn't do very much. Apart from listen.'

'Perhaps not. But she thinks you're the only one who can understand what she experienced the day Mummy died.'

'I can try to. Though I don't share her belief that your mother somehow foresaw her death.'

'No. Well, obviously she didn't.'

'Nevertheless, her parting words to Rowena were . . . a little strange, weren't they?'

'Ah. She told you them, did she?' Sarah toyed with her glass, rattling the ice cubes against each other and frowning, as if considering a complex legal question. 'I do wish she'd forget what Mummy said and what it might have meant.'

'Why?'

'Because I'm running out of ways to avoid explaining to her that there's a much more plausible interpretation than her fanciful ideas of precognition.'

Now it was my turn to frown. 'Meaning?'

'Oh, come on. Mummy had lost her wedding ring. She'd brought a suitcase full of clothes back from Biarritz, but she didn't leave it at home. It went with her in the car, on the grounds that she had no time to unpack.'

'I still don't—'

'She was leaving Daddy. That's what I think, anyway. It's probably what she told him in the note he threw away. And it's probably what she meant to tell Rowena. Until she thought better of it. Thank God.'

I wanted to contradict her. I wanted to deny that the mystery and ambiguity surrounding her mother's death could be reduced to a simple act of marital desertion. But I was aware before I spoke that my protests would seem inexplicable. Why should I care whether it was true or not? Why should it be any of my business? In the end, I said nothing.

'I can't be certain, of course. It's not something I was expecting. Or had any reason to expect. But Mummy would have been quite capable of putting up a convincing front. Even Daddy might not have known she was planning to leave him. I can't exactly ask him, can I? I'd have to accuse him of lying about the note – and of destroying material evidence.'

She'd thought this all along. Since before we'd met in Brussels. It was safe to tell me now, of course. The trial was out of the way. My testimony could no longer be tarnished by doubts about her mother's image of impeccable virtue. Disgust at her father's marriage to my sister-in-law must also have played its part. She probably took some small pleasure in enlightening me. Saw it as a vicarious slap in the face for Bella.

'Hadn't it occurred to you, Robin? I mean, just as a theoretical possibility?'

'No. It hadn't.'

'I was so worried it must have. And that you'd say so to Rowena. She mustn't be allowed to think of it. It would be disastrous. She sees Mummy as perfect in every way.'

'But you don't?'

'She was human. Like the rest of us. And she kept a great deal to herself. If she'd had enough of her marriage, it would be just like her to conceal the fact from Rowena and me. And to endure it until we were no longer dependent on her. Well, I was already off her hands. And Rowena was about to follow. Maybe last year seemed the obvious time to make the break.'

'Where would she have gone?'

'I don't know. Perhaps she didn't either. Perhaps it was sufficient just to strike out on her own. A few days with Sophie, then . . . If she really meant to go to Sophie's, that is.'

'You're not suggesting she and Oscar Bantock—'

'No, no. I'm sure not. But . . . perhaps some other man I never met was waiting patiently. Somebody she'd known years before, still carrying a torch.'

I remembered the man who'd nearly driven me down in Butterbur Lane and was tempted to describe him to Sarah in case she knew him. Then resentment of her honesty overcame me. Why say anything to support her theory when she'd kept it from me so long? Why reinforce a suspicion I wanted no part of? 'You could be wrong about this, couldn't you?' I asked, silently willing her to agree. 'As a lawyer, wouldn't you say the evidence was purely circumstantial?'

'Oh yes. I could be wrong. Easily. I hope I *am* wrong. I love my father. I don't like to think of what he must have gone through if I'm right. To learn Mummy had deserted him only a few hours before he learned she was dead. And then not to be able to tell anyone. To love her and to lose her. Twice over. That's real suffering, don't you think?'

'I think you've all suffered. In your different ways.'

'And Rowena responds by trying to commit suicide. While Daddy makes a fool of himself with a glamorous widow.' She smiled, mocking me as well as herself. 'Where does that leave me, Robin?'

'It leaves you taking it in your stride. Apparently.'

'Don't you think I am?'

'You tell me. Being the strong dependable sister can't be easy. If you'll forgive me for saying so . . .'

'Yes?'

'You look . . . just a little stretched.'

'Rubbish.' She reddened and took a sip of her drink. 'Absolute rubbish.'

'Is it?'

'I believe in facing facts.' She tossed her head, the haughty public schoolgirl peeking from behind the composed professional. 'If necessary, facing them down.'

'But these aren't facts, are they? Only suppositions.'

'Exactly.' She stared at me impatiently, as if I were being irritatingly obtuse. 'That's why I want to protect Rowena from them. Because what can't be proved can't be disproved.'

'Then stop worrying. She'll learn none of this from me.'

'No. I don't suppose she will.' She sat back and studied me intently through narrowed lids. 'You're a puzzle, Robin. You really are.'

'In what way?'

'Why do you care about us so much? We don't give you much encouragement. We're not even as grateful as we should be. When you met Mummy on Hergest Ridge— By the way, that *was* the first time you'd met her, wasn't it?'

'Of course.'

'It's just . . . well . . . we only have your word for it, don't we? That it was a chance meeting, I mean.' Yes. They did. So did I. Only my word. Only my fallible recollection. And now, worming its way into Sarah's mind, was the half-formed thought that had already strayed into mine. I'd met Louise Paxton by chance. The purest of chances. It couldn't have been anything else. Could it? 'Go on then, Robin. Say that's what it was. Why don't you? What's stopping you?'

'Nothing.'

'But still you don't say it.'

'Because I can't prove it. To you. Or to anyone else.' Her eyes were open wide now, staring at me in amazement. This was the last reply she'd expected. And the last one she'd have wanted to hear. 'I can't prove it, Sarah. Even to myself.'

Waiting for the train at Temple Meads, sobered by cold air and the rowdy dregs of a football crowd further down the platform, Sarah and I looked sheepishly at each other. We both regretted the turn our conversation had taken. We were ashamed of the accusations we'd almost levelled, the inner truths we'd almost revealed. They were intimacies we weren't ready for. Arenas we weren't prepared to enter.

'I'm sorry,' she said haltingly, 'for some of the things I . . . Forget it. Please. All of it.'

'Consider it forgotten.'

'But it isn't, of course, is it?'

'No.' I risked a smile and she bowed her head in understanding. 'Shall we agree . . . simply not to mention it again?'

'Let's.'

'If there's anything more I can do to help Rowena . . . or you . . . you'll let me know, won't you?'

'If you're sure you want me to. Wouldn't it be safer . . . to walk away from us altogether? Safer for you, I mean.'

'I don't know. Maybe. But I can't. So . . .'

'I'll remember the offer.' She looked round. 'Here's your train.' Then she leant up and kissed me. 'Safe journey, Robin.'

Sarah was wrong. I told myself so over and over again as the train sped towards Reading. She was wrong, even though her explanation fitted the facts with greater exactitude than any other. She was wrong, even though, in my weaker moments, I feared she might be right.

CHAPTER

EIGHT

My mother's death deprived the Timariot family of a centripetal force I'd never realized she embodied. This first became apparent over Christmas 1991, when the traditional mass gathering at Adrian and Wendy's went by the board. I spent the day alone, tramping the lanes around Steep and wondering whether I oughtn't to feel deprived or deserted – rather than strangely content.

On Boxing Day, I drove down to Hayling Island to see Uncle Larry. He lived in a chalet bungalow overlooking Chichester Harbour, with a telescope permanently erected in the bedroom window to study the comings and goings of sea birds on the mud-flats. His other passion – cricket – was evident in the daffodil ranks of *Wisden*s on his bookshelves and the desk-load of notes and documents he'd been trying for ten years or more to distil into a definitive history of Timariot & Small. But the company's future, not its past, was what he wanted to discuss with me.

'I had lunch with Les Buckingham the other day,' he announced. (Les Buckingham had been his opposite number at one of our biggest rivals in the bat-making business.) 'He said something about Viburna Sportswear that worried me. I didn't know what to make of it. He's probably got the wrong end of the stick, but, according to Les, Viburna are very much in Bushranger's pocket. Bushranger Sports, that is.' The clarification was unnecessary. Bushranger Sports of Sydney and Auckland had been making cricket bats for less than twenty years, but had already carved out a large chunk of the Australian market for themselves. 'He doesn't see how they'd let Viburna get away with selling our bats under their very noses.'

'They can hardly stop them now we effectively *are* Viburna.'

'That's what I said. But Les . . . Well, he was unconvinced. Reckoned Bushranger had . . . ways and means. Couldn't say *what* ways and means, of course. That's why I thought he was just flying a kite. But I wanted to check you'd heard nothing similar. We've invested a lot in this takeover. And borrowed to do it, Jenny tells me. With interest rates where they are at the moment, we can't afford to have it turn sour.'

'I agree. But it's not going to turn sour.'

'You're sure?'

'Well, Adrian, Jenny and Simon are sure. So I am too. As for Les Buckingham, now he's retired, isn't he bound to be just a bit . . . out of touch?'

'Like me, you mean?'

'No, of course not.'

'Well, you may be right. You've all got your heads screwed on. I suppose I ought to just let you get on with it.'

'Probably.'

'And stop worrying?'

'Yes. Believe me, Uncle, there really is nothing to worry *about*.' But there was, of course. Plenty.

The truth emerged in progressively more disturbing morsels during the first few months of 1992. Rumours no more substantial than Les Buckingham's began to coagulate into doubts nobody quite seemed able to pin down or dismiss. Unexplained problems delayed – then prevented – placements of Timariot & Small bats in Viburna's retail outlets. Technical hitches, according to Greg Dyson. Rather more than that, I began to suspect.

Then, in March, came two simultaneous bombshells. Danziger's, the nationwide Australian sports goods retailer, confirmed in writing that a legally enforceable agreement with Bushranger Sports prohibited them from handling cricket bats originating from Bushranger's domestic rivals. Our ownership of Viburna meant we now fell within that classification. The whole point of taking them over in the first place – readier access to the Australasian market – was vitiated if Danziger's doors were closed to us. And the lawyers agreed they *were* closed – *if* the agreement was valid. Well, Bushranger were bellicose enough in their assertions to suggest they had no doubts about its validity.

And Danziger's insisted Greg Dyson had long known of its existence. Naturally, we wanted to hear Dyson's response to that. But he chose this moment to send us a perfunctory letter of resignation and quit Melbourne without leaving a forwarding address behind him.

There was worse to follow when Adrian and Jennifer hurried out to Melbourne to investigate. Previously undisclosed creditors of Viburna came to light. Along with details of substantial foreign exchange transactions in the last few weeks of Dyson's tenure of office which he'd apparently used to camouflage the diversion of Viburna funds to overseas bank accounts held in names which sounded horribly like aliases. Viburna funds were of course Timariot & Small funds. More ominously, they represented moneys lent to us on the assumption that we could repay them from the profits our takeover of Viburna would bring in. But now there weren't going to be any profits. Just escalating losses made worse by legal fees, hidden debts and outright theft. I don't know whether Dyson had ever tried his hand at sheep-shearing. But he'd certainly done a thorough job of fleecing us.

The recriminations began straightaway. Simon and I felt Adrian, who'd had more dealings with Dyson than the rest of us, should have realized he was a crook. We also reckoned Jennifer should have spotted the holes in Viburna's books. There were acrimonious meetings and blazing rows; simmering resentments and incipient feuds. Adrian brazened it out, insisting we'd been taken in by a master fraudster: no blame could attach to him. Jennifer took a different line, admitting she should have smelt a rat sooner and offering to resign her directorship. She was genuinely appalled that we'd been so easily deceived. Well, so were all of us. In the end, there was nothing to be gained by making Jennifer a scapegoat. Her offer was never taken up. And Adrian remained in charge. But his authority – along with our faith in him and in each other – was damaged beyond repair. The anxious debates and stifled accusations left us divided and dispirited. Timariot & Small could never be the same again.

Worse still, it couldn't be prosperous either. The Petersfield operation remained as viable as ever. We were actually doing very well. But the Viburna connection was an open wound we couldn't staunch. To cover the debts Dyson had accumulated on our behalf and wind up Viburna Sportswear committed us to several years of corporate loss. Nothing could change that, even if the Australian authorities caught up with Dyson – which they showed no sign of doing. Uncle Larry never once said 'I told you so'. But the affair saddened him more than any of us. He'd been researching Timariot & Small's financial record for his company history and knew a profit, however small, had been turned in every year of its existence. Every one of a hundred and fifty-six years, to be precise. But the hundred and fifty-seventh was going to be different. And so were quite a few more after that. The future had lost its certainty. It was no longer a safe place to go.

Caustic though she was in her criticism, Bella refused to become embroiled in the consequences of the Viburna disaster. As Lady Paxton, I suppose she thought she should remain aloof. And Sir Keith's money meant she could afford to. They'd sold the London house and taken to using The Hurdles as their base in England. More and more of their time, however, was spent in Biarritz, which Bella found convenient both for Pyrenean skiing and Côte d'Argent sunbathing. I saw little of them and remained unsure whether Sir Keith had been told about Rowena's suicide attempt. If not, I didn't propose to break the news. Especially since she seemed to have recovered from it so well.

My evidence for that assessment was admittedly limited. But it was persuasive. Early in April, I was driving back through Bristol from a visit to an engineering firm in Pontypool who claimed they could solve our sawdust extraction problems at a stroke. I diverted on a whim to Clifton and called at the flat in Caledonia Place on no more than an off-chance that anybody would be at home. It was, after all, the early afternoon of a working day. But Rowena's Easter vacation had just begun and she welcomed me warmly, plying me with non-herbal tea and repeated assurances that she'd put the neuroses of the autumn well behind her. I found it easy to believe. She looked, sounded and behaved like a relaxed and self-confident twenty-year-old. The baggy black outfit she wore was unflattering, the taped music she turned down for my benefit excruciating, but both were fashionable. She hadn't cut her hair though and I hoped she never would, but it *was* tied back under some sort of bandana. Her strangeness – her ethereality – was fading. And part of me regretted its going. But I knew she'd be happier without it.

One other encouraging sign came in a telephone call which occupied Rowena for a whispered ten minutes in the hall. A boyfriend called Paul, she later admitted. 'It's nothing serious,' she added. But I couldn't help suspecting her blushes told me more than her words.

I'd studied a framed photograph that stood on the mantelpiece while she was out of the room. It was of her and Sarah with their mother and couldn't have been more than two or three years old. An unremarkable snapshot, casually posed. But even there, in Louise Paxton's distant half-quizzical smile, you could read the tentative beginnings of her enigmatic end. From the shadow of which Rowena was at last emerging.

> What shall I give my daughter the younger
> More than will keep her from cold and hunger?
> I shall not give her anything.

By June, I'd had a bellyful of Timariot & Small's intractable problems and was in need of a break. To my surprise, Bella offered me one, in the form of an invitation to visit her and Sir Keith in Biarritz. I'd been too preoccupied to book any kind of a holiday for myself, so I accepted with well-disguised alacrity.

I went out as soon as I could arrange a fortnight's leave and found the resort still hanging back from the tumult of high summer. Its white façades and terracotta roofs lined three miles of surf, sand and crumbling rock with dilapidated but undeniable dignity. Torquay with a Gallic swagger, if you like. And like it I did. Its empty dawn beaches. Its stinging salt winds. Its dazzling afternoons and langorous evenings. Its never obsequious air of being every man's haven. And every woman's too.

L'Hivernance was at the northern end of the town, where the Pointe St-Martin and its lighthouse stood guard over the Plage Miramar. The villa had been built in the twenties for an exiled Chilean politician. Its site was sheltered but panoramic, its design plain yet boldly curvaceous, all peach-washed bays and balconies, with wide arched windows like the heavy-lidded eyes of some bosomy dowager. It was easy to imagine its first owner glaring out at the Atlantic as he'd once glared out at the Pacific, ruminating on the rights and wrongs of the latest *coup* in Santiago. Perhaps because he'd been afraid of political enemies sending agents in search of him, there was no entrance visible from the street. Just a doorless frontage commanding a prospect of the ocean, flanked by the sub-tropical foliage of the garden. A driveway, leading in by one gate and out by another, curved round to the rear, where access could be discreetly obtained. Or not, as the case might be.

The interior was altogether less discreet. High ceilings and broad staircases suggested a larger and grander residence than it actually was. Dudley Paxton had loaded its conventional comforts with assorted ethnographia collected during his African postings. His son assured me most of it was now mouldering in a museum basement in Bayonne, but plenty of ivory, beaten copper and bolt-eyed statuary remained, along with leopard-skin antimacassars and elephant-foot wastepaper bins.

What Louise had made of this gruesome clutter I couldn't begin to conjecture. She'd evidently thought better of trying to impose her personality on the villa, however, contenting herself with converting just a couple of rooms to her vision of what it should have been. An airy pale-curtained boudoir with its own south-facing balcony. And a gallery at the back of the house devoted to a dozen or so Expressionist paintings. Not the best, of course. They'd always stayed in England. Latterly in a bank vault, Sir Keith told me. There were a couple of Ensors in the vault. And a Rouault, Louise had always believed, though it still awaited accreditation. The pictures left at L'Hivernance were strictly second division. Which was where the critical establishment had placed Oscar Bantock. So it was no surprise to find him represented by a pair of vividly tempestuous works. *The Drowning Clown* and *Face at the Window*. With an empty patch of wall between them where *Black Widow* may have been destined to hang. But about that Sir Keith was saying nothing.

Staying at the villa focused my mind on Sarah's all too plausible theory of what had happened there in July 1990. I couldn't ask whether it was true, of course. Bella and I had struck an unspoken bargain when I accepted her invitation. Her side of it was to avoid cross-questioning me about the Viburna fiasco. Mine was to play the part of a cultured but reticent relative whose presence reassured her new friends that her background in England wasn't a discreditable blank. Hence, I assumed, the hectic round of dinner parties she arranged while I was with them. And hence the embargo on any expressions of curiosity by me about the first Lady Paxton – and the circumstances of her last departure from L'Hivernance.

But that didn't stop me thinking. Or imagining. Slammed doors and raised voices echoing through the sea-lit rooms. Louise standing on the beach at sunrise, slipping a ring from her finger and hurling it towards the cream-topped breakers. Or sitting on the boudoir balcony, writing a farewell note to her absent husband. *By the time you read this, Keith . . .* I looked at him often when he didn't realize he was being observed and wondered just what her message had been. If Sarah was right, you couldn't blame him for destroying it. It made no difference, after all. Nothing could bring Louise back to life. Certainly not the missing jigsaw-pieces of the truth about how she'd died. Even if I found them, I could never find her. She was gone for ever. Though sometimes – when a curtain moved or a silence fell – you could believe she wasn't quite out of reach.

My fortnight in Biarritz was half done when Rowena telephoned her father with news that clearly took him aback. She'd got engaged and wanted to come out straightaway to introduce him and Bella to her fiancé. His name was Paul, as I could have predicted. Not a student, apparently, but a risk analyst for Metropolitan Mutual, an insurance company with headquarters in Bristol. In a separate call, Sarah explained that Rowena had met him through her. She and Paul Bryant had been a year apart at King's College, Cambridge. He'd looked her up on realizing they were both living in Bristol and had instantly fallen for Rowena. As she had for him. Sarah reckoned Sir Keith couldn't fail to like him.

She was spot on. Rowena and Paul arrived a few days later and were hardly through the door before their compatibility and affection for each other – as well as Paul's suitability as a son-in-law – became abundantly obvious. He was a young man of charm, humour and evident sincerity. Dark-haired and handsome in a fashion-poster style that clearly appealed to Bella every bit as much as Rowena, he also possessed a keen and probing intellect. Along with a disarming facility for drawing people out about their achievements and ambitions while saying remarkably little about his own. I couldn't decide whether this was a deliberate technique or a personality trait. Nor whether it was as apparent to others as it was to me. But, strangely, it didn't make him any less likeable. Quite the reverse. Especially where women were concerned. He was according to Bella, '*the least vain good-looking man I've ever met*'. Which, coming from her, was quite a compliment. Though where it left me I didn't like to speculate.

Something else about Paul Bryant puzzled me from the first. His amiability – his lack of the slightest hint of sarcasm – was as intriguing as it was endearing. There was either more or less to him than met the eye. But which? His manner deflected any attempt to decide. He could be naïve as well as profound, gauche as well as sensitive. He could be, it sometimes seemed, anything he judged you wanted him to be.

But his love for Rowena was genuine beyond doubt. To watch him watching her was to glimpse true devotion. And it was devotion that never threatened to smother. He knew how much support to give her and how much independence. He protected her without dominating her. He encouraged her to bloom and stepped back to study the result. He was the best friend she could hope to have. And would make the perfect husband. As she well knew. 'Meeting Paul was like recovering from colour blindness,' she told me. 'He's banished the drabness from my life. Not the sadness. Not all of it, anyway. Not yet. But soon he will. With Paul I can lead a happier life than I ever expected to.'

There was never any likelihood that Sir Keith would object to the match. Since Paul worked in Bristol and already owned a home there, marriage needn't disrupt Rowena's studies in any way. When she revealed they'd been thinking of a September wedding, her father was almost more enthusiastic than she was. 'Yes, make it September,' he urged. 'It'll be more than a wedding. It'll be the day this family puts the past behind it and goes forward together.' Fine words. Fine sentiments. With every prospect of fulfilment.

While I was in Biarritz, there was only one occasion when I talked to Paul on his own. It was the day before I was due to leave. Sir Keith was at the golf course, while Bella had taken Rowena to experience the delights of thalassotherapy, the latest beauty treatment with which she hoped to stave off middle age. We'd agreed to meet them afterwards for tea. Leaving the villa with plenty of time to spare, we strolled down the beaches – emptied by grey skies and a keen wind – to the old fishing port, then climbed by zig-zag paths up through the tamarisk trees to the Pointe Atalaye. At its summit, we leant against some railings and looked back along the sweep of the bay to the lighthouse and the nestling roof of L'Hivernance. And Paul suddenly answered a question I'd not had the courage to ask.

'I know about the suicide attempt, Robin. You don't have to avoid the subject for my benefit.'

'Good. I'm glad. That you know, I mean.'

'She told me right at the start. She's still not ready to tell her father, but . . . we'll get there in the end.'

'I'm sure you will. You seem to be just what she needs.'

'Glad you think so. It makes it easier for me to mention something that's been on my mind.'

'Oh yes?'

'Well, Sarah and Rowena have both told me how kind you've been to them since their mother's death. How generous with your time and attention.' It was a curious choice of phrase. He kept his eyes trained on the distant lighthouse as he continued. 'Sarah and I saw quite a lot of one another at Cambridge. I feel I know her almost as well as Rowena. I even met their mother once. And the infamous Oscar Bantock.'

'Really?'

'Sarah took me to an exhibition of his work in Cambridge. Pretty crappy stuff.' He chuckled. 'I think I may have let Bantock realize what my opinion was. I expect I was a bit drunk. Tongue ran away with me. I've learned to control it better since. Anyway, Louise Paxton was there. I exchanged a few words with her. Nothing more. Like you, I suppose.' Now he did look at me. 'Just a fleeting encounter. But enough to be able to imagine what losing her must have meant to her daughters.'

'They've suffered, no question.'

'But Sarah's ridden it out. And, with my help, Rowena will too.'

'Good.' I smiled to cover my puzzlement. He was making some kind of point. But I couldn't grasp what it was. 'I hope you're right.'

'Oh, I am. I'm sure of it. Surer than I've ever been of anything. Rowena and I are made for each other. Which means . . .' He smiled. 'What I'm saying, Robin, is that you can stop worrying about her. She's got me to look after her now.' *And she doesn't need you any more,* his dazzling smile declared. 'You've been a real help to her. And to Sarah. But from here on . . . Well, you can let me handle things.' I was being warned off. Politely but firmly told to keep my distance. He obviously didn't see me as a rival for Rowena's affections. Then what did he see me as? Somebody who knew a little too much for comfort? Somebody who might possibly know more than he did? Was that what he feared? Or did he just want rid of me for Rowena's sake? There was nothing in his expression or tone of voice even to hint at the answer. Candour and concealment were in him almost the same thing.

I smiled back and made a calculated attempt to catch him off guard. 'Tell me, Paul – Does Rowena still believe her mother went back to England that last time purely in order to buy one of Bantock's paintings?'

The question was as much a test of Sarah as of Paul. I needed to know whether she trusted him as completely as he'd implied. His response was swift. But it didn't quite dispel the doubt. 'She believes it. And I think it's best she should. Don't you?'

He had me where he wanted me. The only slight advantage I

could deny him was the pleasure of hearing my explicit agreement. I glanced at my watch and nodded down towards the Hôtel du Palais, a mansarded monument to Second Empire opulence that dominated the shoreline – and was the chosen venue for our tea party. 'I think we ought to start back,' I said, grinning at him. 'Don't you?'

Tea amid the chandeliered splendour of the Hôtel du Palais – the Ritz-sur-mer, as Bella called it – was superficially a delightful experience. For Bella it was an opportunity to show off her possessions before an appreciative audience of *après-midi* society. Her jewellery. Her suntan. Her shapely thighs. Her pretty stepdaughter. And her stepdaughter's handsome fiancé. Paul and Rowena played their parts so well that my own mood made no impact. When Bella did notice my lack of contribution to the sparkling banter, she attributed it to depression at the thought of returning to England. And I let her think she was right.

In a sense, I suppose she was. But it wasn't the prospect of leaving behind the charms of Biarritz that weighed me down. It was the knowledge that Paul's marriage to Rowena really would raise the drawbridge between us. Between me and the only other person who'd met Louise Paxton on the day of her death – and glimpsed the indecipherable truth. It shouldn't have mattered as much as it did. It shouldn't have mattered at all. But still, two years on, I couldn't forget. I didn't want Rowena to either. I didn't want Paul Bryant to make her happy at the expense of her mother's memory. But I knew he meant to. And I was very much afraid he would succeed.

Rowena Paxton and Paul Bryant were married at St Kenelm's Church, Sapperton, on Saturday the twelfth of September, 1992 – a gorgeous late summer's day of mellow sunlight and motionless air.

As I drove up across the Berkshire Downs and the Vale of the White Horse that morning, I could already picture the scene awaiting me: the Cotswold stone; the stained glass; the lace ruffs of the choristers; the silk dresses of the ladies; the grey top hats of the gentlemen; and the deep black shadows cast by ancient yews across the gravestones. The blessings of nature and the contrivances of man would weave their familiar spell and for a single afternoon we'd believe we really were witnessing the perfect union of two lives.

The reality was almost exactly that. Sapperton lay deep in *Ideal*

Home country: a neat little village of restored cottages and secluded residences perched on the eastern slopes of the Golden Valley. The cars were parked two- or three-deep along the lane leading to the church. Inside, family and friends were massed in their finery. I caught a glimpse of Bella at the front before being relegated to a distant pew. From there I was happy to spectate anonymously as the bride made her entrance on her father's arm. Rowena's delicate features were transformed into fairy-tale beauty by a narrow-bodiced wedding dress. While Paul, slim and elegant in his morning coat, resembled her saviour prince as closely as anyone could demand. Sir Keith swelled with paternal pride as he led his daughter up the aisle, Sarah and two other bridesmaids following with the page-boys. The priest welcomed us with a nicely judged reference to the bride's mother. Paul and Rowena recited their lines without a stumble. The marriage was pronounced. Prayers were said. Hymns were sung. Eyes were dabbed and throats cleared. And I saw such unalloyed happiness in Rowena's expression that I rebuked myself for doubting this would turn out to be the best thing she'd ever done. Clearly, she was confident it would. So who was I to quibble?

The Old Parsonage stood so close to the church that the bride and groom's conveyance there by pony and trap was the shortest of superfluous trots. It was a handsomely gabled house made to seem larger than it was by its lofty setting above the valley. The terraced garden led the eye towards the winding course of the river below and the wooded slopes on its other side: a ruckled blanket of green up which a tide of shadow slowly climbed as the afternoon advanced.

A marquee had been set up at the top of the garden, adjoining the house. Here, as a string quartet played and waitresses dispensed champagne with limitless generosity, I did my best to amuse the guests I shared a table with: the couple who lived next door and their daughter; an old medical colleague of Sir Keith's; and a cousin of Paul's who seemed to know him about as well as I did. 'Smart and close, our Paul,' he remarked with a frown. 'Always has been.'

I exchanged a few words and a kiss with Rowena, a handshake and garbled best wishes with Paul. I suppose I didn't expect more. My invitation was something of a farewell gesture. I knew that and so did they. My connection with Bella meant there'd probably be the odd fleeting encounter over the years. But nothing more. Paul had become the master of Rowena's destiny. And I didn't feature in his plans at all.

This awareness stayed with me throughout the day. It was there when I followed the usher across the church. When I applauded the speeches and toasted the happy couple's future. When I stood in the crowded lane and cheered them off. And it would still be there, I knew, when I made my solitary journey home. For them, this was a glorious beginning. For me, a solemn end.

'It went well,' Bella said to me as they drove away, letting me see some of the relief she would have hidden from others. She'd done the bulk of the planning and, in a sense, this was as much a celebration of her marriage as Rowena's. The first full-scale public occasion she'd presided over as Lady Paxton. Its success was a measure of her acceptance. And it had been a success. If anybody had compared her unfavourably with the first Lady Paxton, they'd done so in the privacy of their own thoughts. Bella was safely installed.

I'd always known she would be, of course. Her dress sense might occasionally betray her. Some, for instance, would have said she shouldn't have been showing so much cleavage at her stepdaughter's wedding. But that wouldn't have included any of the male guests. Her *joie de vivre* was irrepressible. And so was her social ambition. The council-house girl had become what my mother had always said she wasn't: a lady.

Sir Keith paid her a special tribute in his speech, describing her as 'the woman who's helped me and my daughters recover better than we ever thought we could from the loss we suffered two years ago'. He was equally fulsome in his praise of his new son-in-law. 'Paul is a remarkable young man. As strong as he is sensitive. As honest as he is perceptive. Rowena has found herself a fine husband.' He meant it too. The conviction in his voice was unmistakable. Sir Keith Paxton was a man well pleased with the compensations life – and death – had handed him.

And who could blame him? He'd not been married to Bella long enough to see her crueller side. While Paul was the sort of son-in-law fathers dream of. I watched him charming the aunts and chucking the page-boys. I listened to his witty well-ordered speech. I studied him long and hard as he posed with his parents and sisters for yet another photograph. Mr and Mrs Bryant were a gauche good-hearted couple, overawed in the company of medical grandees and Cotswold weekenders. But their son wasn't. Paul Bryant went in awe of nobody. Metropolitan Mutual employed him as a risk analyst and it was easy to see why. Because for him risk spelt no danger. He was in smooth and complete control of his life. And now of Rowena's too.

* * *

The party slowly broke up after the bride and groom's departure. Some guests left promptly. Others lingered, chatting over tea and coffee in the marquee or strolling in the garden. Bella circulated among them, making new acquaintances and sealing old ones, her energy apparently inexhaustible. Sir Keith too kept up the round, paying me little heed when I said goodbye. 'Delighted you could come, Robin. Delighted. It's been a splendid day, hasn't it?' He didn't stay to hear my answer. But he wouldn't have been disappointed if he had.

I'd not spoken to Sarah all afternoon, so I went in search of her before leaving. A friend of hers I vaguely recognized said she was in the house. I traced her to a small room at the front fitted out as a study, about as far from the party as she could be. There was a woman with her. Tall, fair-haired and elegant, aged somewhere in her forties. I hadn't noticed her at the top table or close to the centre of the celebrations. But she obviously knew Sarah well. They were talking softly as I entered, almost whispering. And, whatever they were saying, they stopped as soon as they saw me.

'Robin!' said Sarah, jumping up. 'How lovely. I was hoping to see you before you left. I'm sorry to have neglected you. But it's been *so* hectic.'

'Of course,' I said, smiling. 'I quite understand.'

'You've been well looked after?'

'Absolutely. Couldn't have been better.'

'Just what I was saying,' her companion remarked. 'I'm Sophie Marsden, by the way.' She rose and stepped towards me, extending a kid-gloved hand.

'Robin Timariot.' I looked at her as we shook, my attention raised now I knew who she was. Louise Paxton's friend. The one who'd shared her enthusiasm for Expressionist art. And who'd shared a few secrets along the way, perhaps? There *was* a similarity to Louise. Not in looks so much as manner. A hint of distance. An involuntary implication that much of her mind dwelt on subjects no-one else could understand. It was there in Sophie, albeit more faintly – more impermanently – than it had been in the woman I'd met on Hergest Ridge. But it *was* there. Like a palm-print. An impression. A dried flower preserved between the pages of a book. No scent. No sap. No life. But stronger than a memory. More than chance likeness or fading recollection. More than could ever be forgotten.

'Sarah's told me about you, Mr Timariot. What a help you've

been to her and Rowena. And to Keith, of course. In introducing him to Bella.'

'Well, I . . .'

'Louise was a great believer in life, you know. In making the most of it. In casting off past sadnesses. She really would have been pleased at how things have turned out.'

'I . . . I'm . . .' I groped for an adequate response. Part of me wanted to echo her sentiment. To draw a neat straight line with Louise Paxton on one side and me incontrovertibly on the other. But another part of me wanted to protest. To rage against a travesty I couldn't define. To cross the neat straight line. 'I'm so glad . . . to hear a friend of hers say so, Mrs Marsden.'

'Actually, Robin,' said Sarah, 'I was about to take Sophie to see Mummy's grave. She's not visited it since the funeral. Rowena's asked me to put her bouquet on it along with mine. Would you like to come with us?'

'I'd be delighted,' I said. With sudden and utter sincerity.

The graveyard of St Kenelm's Church had been full for fifty years or more. Since then, burials had taken place in a small cemetery just outside the village. I drove Sarah and Sophie there at the start of my journey home. Though it was less than a mile from The Old Parsonage, we seemed to have been transported a vast distance from the gabbling gaiety of the wedding party. The cemetery was still and silent, its graves clustered around an avenue of yew trees at one end while the other end stood empty and overgrown, awaiting future use. I didn't ask why Sir Keith hadn't come. Why Rowena had felt unable to do this herself. Why Sarah had asked Sophie and me to go with her. Did she, I wondered, regard us as more likely to understand her feelings than her father? Were we the only two she could trust with a share of this experience?

We walked slowly and self-consciously along the gravel path, Sarah a few steps ahead, cradling the bouquets in her arms. She went straight to the grave and placed the flowers beneath the headstone. Sophie and I stood behind her and watched as she knelt beside it. Dew still clung to the grass in the shadow cast by the nearest yew. Its moisture was darkening the hem of her full-skirted dress, turning rose pink to blood red. There was meaning everywhere, if you cared to look. As I looked now, at the inscription on the headstone.

LOUISE JANE PAXTON
11 NOVEMBER 1945 – 17 JULY 1990
FIRST KNOWN WHEN LOST

The phrase was from a poem by Thomas. Only Sarah could have chosen it. Only she could have known what the choice meant. Though in that moment I seemed to as well.

We stayed a few minutes, no more. Then Sophie and I started diplomatically back towards the gate, while Sarah lingered by the grave. They meant to walk back to the house, so I'd soon be on my solitary way. There was much I wanted to ask Sophie, but there was too little time and no obvious pretext for extending it. Besides, my curiosity about her dead friend would have seemed odd, suspiciously inappropriate. A few mumbled trifles were all that should have been expected of me.

'A peaceful spot,' I ventured, as we reached the gate and looked back at Sarah.

'Yes. I'm glad to have come back. You've not been here before?'

'No.'

'You didn't come to the funeral, of course. But I thought perhaps afterwards . . .' She glanced round at me, her eyes narrowing beneath the brim of her hat. I sensed suspicion on some score I couldn't fathom. I sensed there was a question she longed to ask me. But something held her back. 'Sarah told me you manage a cricket-bat factory in Petersfield. Is that right?'

'Yes.' The point seemed deliberately banal, provoking me to respond in kind. 'What about your husband, Mrs Marsden? What line is he—'

'Agricultural machinery. But you don't want to hear about that. *Very* boring.'

'No more so than the cricket-bat business, I'm sure.'

'Believe me, it is.' Abruptly, she changed the subject. 'Have you heard from Henley Bantock, by the way?'

'I'm sorry?'

'Oscar Bantock's nephew. He's writing his uncle's biography. *Has* written it, I suppose. It's due out next spring. He came to see me a few months ago. I have two Bantocks on my drawing-room wall and he wanted to photograph them for the book. Wished I hadn't agreed in the end. Appalling little creep.'

I smiled. 'He is rather, isn't he?'

'Oh, so you *have* met him?'

'Once, yes. But not about the book. There's nothing I could have told him anyway.'

'No?'

'Of course not.' Her questions were becoming more and more baffling. I could have believed she was trying to provoke me into disclosing something, but for the fact that there was nothing to disclose. 'I never knew Oscar Bantock.'

'No. But you knew his foremost patroness, didn't you?'

I frowned. My bemusement must by now have been apparent to her. Along with my growing irritation. 'You mean Louise Paxton?'

'Who else?'

'You've lost me. I met Lady Paxton for a few minutes on the day she died. That's all. We didn't discuss Oscar Bantock's painting career.'

'Then what made you contact the revolting Henley? It's *you* who've lost *me*.'

We stared at each other, incomprehension battling with incredulity. I sensed it would be foolish – perhaps dangerous – to try to explain how I'd met Henley. But why I couldn't have said. Sophie Marsden seemed not just to know something I didn't, but to know it *about me.* I couldn't decide which might be worse. To find out what it was. Or never to.

'Are you two all right?' asked Sarah, surprising both of us, even though her approach along the gravel path can hardly have been stealthy.

'Fine,' replied Sophie. 'Just chatting.'

'Yes,' I said. 'But as a matter of fact—' I glanced ostentatiously at my watch. 'I think I ought to be starting back now. I've . . . er . . . a long drive ahead of me.'

'Of course,' said Sarah, smiling warmly. 'It's wonderful you were able to share the day with us, Robin. Rowena really appreciated it, I know.'

'Wouldn't have missed it for the world,' I responded, leading them out through the gate and moving round to the driver's door of my car. 'Well, I . . .'

'Goodbye,' said Sarah, stepping forward to kiss me. 'Lovely to see you.'

'You too,' I murmured. Then I turned to shake Sophie's hand. 'Goodbye, Mrs Marsden,' I said, hoping my grin wouldn't look too stiff.

'Please call me Sophie,' she replied, fixing my eyes with hers as she added: 'After all, I'm sure we'll meet again.'

CHAPTER

NINE

Timariot & Small's financial circumstances didn't improve as 1992 faded towards 1993. There were, to be honest, no grounds for expecting them to. Jennifer spent nearly as much time in Melbourne as Petersfield, but the more she learned about Dyson's management of Viburna Sportswear, the worse the outlook seemed to grow. While Adrian's attempts to negotiate an exemption for us from Bushranger's agreement with Danziger's came predictably to nothing. The road back to profit and self-respect was going to be long and hard.

But we had no obvious choice other than to tread it. For my part, I took some comfort from being the least blameworthy member of the board and concentrated on running the Frenchman's Road operation as efficiently as possible. The workforce knew about the Viburna disaster, of course. How couldn't they? It led to some cynicism about the calibre of the directors, but no more than I'd have expected. Less, in some ways, than was justified. Don Banks had been making cricket bats of consistently high quality for as long as I could remember. It had taken him fifteen years just to learn how. His standards were as demanding as ever. And he was no moaner. A stern reticent deferential man was Don. But I saw the look on his face as Adrian and I stood talking in the workshop one day. And I knew what the look meant. We'd let him and his fellow craftsmen down. We'd failed to live up to *their* standards.

I think it was people like Don who made me determined to see it through. I could have scuttled back to Brussels and index-linked security any time I liked. I often thought of doing so, I can't deny. The Maastricht Treaty was bulldozing its way through the parliaments of Europe and lots of juicy new posts were sure to follow in its wake. One of them might have my name on it. Nobody could blame me for grabbing a ripe plum from the laden bough. Except Don Banks and the rest, of course. Except all their predecessors and successors for whom Timariot & Small had meant and might yet mean something more satisfying than an adequate living. Except, in the final analysis, me.

So I stuck to the task, over-compensating for the board's strategic deficiencies by working excessive hours and paring back my life until it comprised little more than the short-term worries and long-term problems of the family firm. Hugh's example should have deterred me from becoming a workaholic. But during an evening of home truths and brotherly bonding in the Old Drum, Simon assured me that was just what I was turning into. And he was right, however reluctant I might be to admit it. I had few friends and no leisure pursuits besides country walking. Since the break with Ann, I'd deliberately avoided intimacy with another human being. Not just sexual intimacy, but any kind of lowering of the psychological defences. I found the limitations of my existence strangely comforting in an ascetic sort of way. More and more, I was coming to see how safe – how undemanding – the solitary life really was. And I was beginning to think I'd probably settle for it.

Thanks largely to Bella, I stayed in distant touch with the Paxtons. She invited me to a Boxing Day lunch at The Hurdles, which Paul and Rowena also attended, along with Sarah and a humourless young lawyer called Rodney who was clearly more taken with her than she was with him. That and a few similar occasions apart, however, our worlds no longer overlapped. Sir Keith had given his daughters the use of The Old Parsonage as a weekend retreat within easy reach of Bristol, while he and Bella divided their time between Biarritz and Hindhead. The lives of Louise Paxton's husband and children were back on an even keel. Sir Keith was settling into marriage and retirement. Sarah was looking ahead to her career as a solicitor. And Rowena was probably only waiting to finish her degree course before starting a family. Equilibrium had been restored. As for Louise and her stubborn but elusive memory, those who couldn't forget her didn't speak of her. Those, like me, who couldn't stop wondering, knew better than to wonder aloud.

In March 1993, however, the Kington killings' slide into a discarded past came abruptly to a halt. That month saw the publication of *Fakes and Ale: the Double Life of Oscar Bantock*, by Henley Bantock and Barnaby Maitland. I remember clearly the moment when I came across a review of the book and learned of its existence for the first time. It was an unremarkable Thursday afternoon. I was eating a snack lunch at my desk, waiting for our timber agent to return a call and leafing idly through the newspaper. Then the headline caught my eye. NEGLECTED EXPRESSIONIST'S LAST LAUGH AT ART WORLD. What had apparently already been made much of in the specialist art press was summarized in the column below.

This entertaining if sometimes uneven biography of Oscar Bantock, the eccentric English Expressionist who was murdered three years ago, is a collaborative venture between Bantock's nephew Henley and the unorthodox art historian Barnaby Maitland. It reveals that Bantock, written off in his lifetime as a prickly drink-sodden recluse determined to plough a lonely and deeply uncommercial Expressionist furrow, was actually a womanizer of considerable charm, a popular and sociable pub-goer and a gifted forger of several different artists and styles. His scorn of naturalistic and sentimental work emerged in subtle pastiches of its most popular examples from which he made far more money than he ever did painting in his own name. Maitland's researches are based on journals inherited from Bantock by his nephew and meticulous cross-checking with the records of dealers named in them, often to those dealers' vigorous displeasure. They reveal the curmudgeonly idealist's double life as the most mercenary of forgers. He seems to have stuck at first to middle-rank recently dead artists, notably a clutch of Edwardian specialists in drawing-room or garden scenes of children and pets, greetings card material in reasonable demand but not famous or pricey enough to attract expert attention. In the last few years of his life, however, he became more ambitious, mining his own Expressionist vein to produce several brilliant fake Rouaults and Soutines. Henley Bantock's insight into his uncle's drift towards cynicism supports Maitland's contention that this change was triggered by the artist's acceptance that he could not hope for recognition in his own right and that material reward represented his only prospect of satisfaction. If they are correct, which many irate dealers, auctioneers and owners will say they are not, Bantock and one of the few tireless fans of his own work, the late Lady Paxton, paid a heavy price for his revenge against the artistic establishment. The authors' most startling conclusion is that the murders of Bantock and Lady Paxton in July 1990 may have had more to do with his output of fake art than any of the motives imputed to the man convicted of the crimes. If this sad and fascinating tale of frustration and forgery turns, as it well might, into a cause célèbre of miscarried justice, then the authors will have exposed a legal as well as an artistic scandal. But that, as they say, is another story.

I was dumbstruck. What had Henley been thinking of? His uncle a forger. Well, that was between him, his conscience and his customers. I didn't care one way or the other. But I did care about Louise Paxton. And it was being suggested according to the reviewer – on what evidence he didn't bother to mention – that there was more to her murder than met the eye. More, by implication, than could be laid at Shaun Naylor's door.

I telephoned Sarah that evening. Before I could explain why I'd called, she guessed.

'You've read *Fakes and Ale*?'

'No. Just a review.'

'Then you might be making more of it than you should. Henley Bantock sent me an advance copy. Crowed about his theory in a covering letter. Said I'd be bound to find it persuasive. Well, I don't. He hasn't produced a shred of evidence to support it.'

'But what *is* his theory?'

'That Oscar was murdered because several dealers he'd sold fakes to were afraid he meant to go public with the story of how he'd duped them. And that Mummy had the bad luck to be there when it happened. But he can't back it up. The forgery business seems to be true. But obviously that wasn't sensational enough for the publisher. So, Henley's gilded the lily with this wild idea that just happens to tally with Naylor's defence.'

'But surely, if there's no evidence—'

'It'll come to nothing. Exactly. That's why I didn't bother to tell you about it. But look, I have to go out and . . .' She seemed to be whispering to somebody in the background. 'Why don't I send you the book, Robin? It'll be quicker than you ordering a copy. Then you'll see what I mean.'

It arrived two days later. The cover illustration was one of Oscar Bantock's own paintings, a blurred but eye-catching self-portrait depicting the artist standing in a luridly decorated bar drinking from a tankard shaped in the likeness of a death's head. There was a queasily prophetic quality to it that made me think Sarah might have been glad to get it off her hands.

According to the blurb on the dust jacket, Henley Bantock was a *former* local government officer. Presumably, he and Muriel had already earnt enough from Uncle Oscar's art to quit the bureaucratic life. Now they were aiming to cash in on his scandalous secrets while enjoying the luxury of condemning them. With Barnaby Maitland to lend the whole thing some scholarly gloss. Maitland had books on two other twentieth-century forgers – the notorious 'Sexton Blaker' Tom Keating and the Vermeer specialist, Hans van Meegeren – to his credit. He must have seemed an obvious choice as co-author. Just as the journals Henley had discovered at Whistler's Cot must have been too succulent an opportunity for Maitland to resist.

I read the book in one long sitting, enduring Henley's self-serving hatchet job on his uncle's character for the sake of Maitland's convincingly detailed account of how and why he'd taken to forgery. And even that was only a necessary preamble to what really concerned me. We came to it slowly, via Maitland's meticulous verification of the output of forgeries recorded in the journals. Oscar had wanted the truth to come out after his death, of course. That was the point of them. To show what fools the experts were to denigrate his work. To prove they couldn't tell good from bad, true from false, real from fake. And he'd proved his point. Perhaps too well. The Rouaults and Soutines were his fatal mistake, in Maitland's opinion. They fetched high prices despite doubts about their authenticity. Such high prices that the truth about them threatened the reputations and livelihoods of influential dealers and powerful middle-men. The authors reckoned Oscar let it be known he meant to publish the facts. It would have been his glorious V-sign to the self-appointed arbiters of taste who'd done him down. It would have fulfilled his true motive for turning out fakes, which was never really money in their opinion so much as distorted pride.

Sarah was right. They hadn't uncovered any evidence to support their theory. It was a shallow invention designed to boost sales. But to the ill-informed it might sound plausible. A contract killing that claimed Louise Paxton as an extra victim because she was in the wrong place at the wrong time. Where did that leave Naylor? The authors didn't know. But Maitland doubted he was the sort to be employed as a hit-man. So, in the end, their implication was clear. But unstated. That was the worst of it. They never came out and said what many readers would infer. That Naylor was innocent.

I felt so angry after finishing the book that I wrote to Henley Bantock care of his publisher, accusing him of a gratuitous attack on a fine woman's memory. It was a stupid thing to do, since it merely elicited a sarcastic reply that deliberately missed the point I'd made. *'You were not above deceiving me about your connection with Lady Paxton,'* Bantock wrote, *'so your high moral tone is scarcely justified. Our conclusions about the Kington killings represent a reasonable extrapolation of the known facts. I am sorry if they offend you, but I wonder if that is not really because you resent us seeing matters in a clearer light than you.'* I didn't pursue the correspondence. Nor did I comply with his closing request. *'Please pass on my best wishes to your sister.'*

According to Sarah, the only sensible course of action was to ignore the book. 'Treat it with the contempt it deserves, Robin,' she said in a telephone conversation shortly after I'd finished it. 'Chuck it on the fire if you like. *I* don't want it back.'

I didn't destroy it, of course. I slid it into a bookcase out of sight, spine turned to the wall, and did my best to forget all about it. Oscar Bantock's career as a forger would no doubt run and run as a story in the art world. But I didn't move in the art world. As for its supposed relevance to Naylor's conviction as a rapist and double murderer, that was surely a kite that wouldn't fly. With or without *Fakes and Ale,* Shaun Naylor was staying where he belonged: in prison. And the truth was staying where *it* belonged. The Kington killings weren't going to come back to haunt us. Not so long after the event. Not in the face of so much certainty. They couldn't. Could they?

I had lunch with Bella and Sir Keith over Easter. They took the same line as Sarah. Dignified silence was the only way to respond to Henley Bantock's money-grubbing. 'I'm glad Louise never knew old Oscar was into forgery,' said Sir Keith. 'She thought he was a neglected genius – and an idealist to boot. The real irony is that this will actually increase the value of genuine Bantocks. Like the ones Louise bought for next to nothing. *And* Sophie Marsden. She should be pleased. But Henley's the big winner, isn't he? Royalties from his nasty little book. And God knows what per cent whacked onto his stockpile of Bantock originals. With all that to look forward to, you'd think he could have had the decency to leave the murders out of it. But people never are *moderately* greedy, are they? They always want more.'

I enquired tentatively about Rowena's reaction to the book. But as far as Sir Keith knew, she was unaware of its existence.

'Too busy trying to combine being a student and a housewife to comb through reviews. Paul hasn't drawn it to her attention and, frankly, I think he's wise not to. We don't want any repetition of those problems she had before the trial, do we? In fact, I'd be grateful if you took care not to mention it next time you meet her. With any luck, it'll pass her by completely. Leave her free to concentrate on making me a grandfather as soon as possible.'

I promised to say nothing, even though I wasn't sure keeping Rowena in the dark was either feasible or sensible. Too many secrets were piling up for my liking. Presumably, Sir Keith still didn't know about her suicide attempt. Now she wasn't to know about Henley Bantock's alternative explanation for her mother's death. If and when she found out, the efforts to shield her from it might give the theory some of the credibility it didn't deserve. 'It'll end in tears,' my mother would have said. And I'd have been bound to agree with her. Tears. Or something much worse.

Vindication of my scepticism came within a matter of weeks. It was heralded by a telephone call at work from a researcher for the television series *Benefit of the Doubt*. I'd heard of it, of course, and seen it a couple of times. Nick Seymour, the presenter, set about drawing public attention to a possible miscarriage of justice during a thirty-minute assessment of the evidence that had sent one or more people to prison. He'd helped bring about acquittal and release in several cases and become a minor celebrity in the process. Now he planned to devote a future edition to the Kington killings – and the conviction of Shaun Naylor. As a witness at Naylor's trial, would I be prepared to record an interview for the programme? I said no. But Seymour wasn't the man to leave it there. A couple of days later, he rang me personally at home.

'I'm trying to get as full and fair a picture as possible, Mr Timariot. All I'd want you to do is repeat what you said in court. Set the scene for the viewer. Give your first-hand impression of Lady Paxton's state of mind on the day of the murders.' His voice was rounded and reasonable. But there was an edge of impatience in it as well. He didn't like being turned down.

'The problem is, Mr Seymour, that I have to assume you'll be trying to suggest Naylor's innocent. And I simply don't believe he is.'

'Have you read this new biography of Oscar Bantock?'

'*Fakes and Ale*? Yes. And if Henley Bantock's unsubstantiated theories are what—'

'They're part of it, of course. But if you're so sure they're unsubstantiated, why not say so on TV? I'm offering you that chance.'

'But the programme will be geared to backing Henley's interpretation, won't it? Otherwise you wouldn't be doing it.'

'True. But look at it this way. Naylor claims Lady Paxton picked him up that night. If you think he's lying, why not tell it on air the way you saw it? After all, you're the only other person who met her that day. Apart from her daughter. And I don't really want to bother her. Unless I have to, of course. Unless you leave me no choice in the matter.' The pressure was subtle but definite. I wasn't warming to Mr Seymour. But I was beginning to think I'd better cooperate with him. If only for Rowena's sake.

'How do I know you'd transmit what I said? I can tell you now none of it would help you paint Naylor in a sympathetic light.'

'Then I might not use it. But at least I couldn't say you'd refused to talk to me, could I?'

'All right, Mr Seymour. You can have your interview. For all the good it'll do you.'

The interview was fixed for Thursday the twentieth of May. Seymour and a cameraman would come to Greenhayes at six o'clock that evening and be gone again within the hour. They'd be punctual and I'd be put to minimum inconvenience. So Seymour assured me, anyway. And I believed him. I also believed he wouldn't want to linger after he'd heard what I had to say.

At the time I scribbled the appointment in my diary, Thursday the twentieth of May seemed just one handy blank in an otherwise busy week. But it didn't turn out to be. Adrian was supposed to return to the office on Monday the seventeenth after a fortnight in Australia. The trip was a last ditch attempt to strike some kind of deal with Bushranger Sports. Adrian believed – unlike the rest of us – that he might still be able to sweet-talk Bushranger's notoriously hard-nosed chairman, Harvey McGraw. And McGraw had agreed, apparently, to let him try. I arrived at Frenchman's Road on the seventeenth expecting to hear Adrian's account of his failure. Instead, his secretary announced his return had been delayed by forty-eight hours. Whether that was a good sign or not he'd declined to tell her. We'd just have to wait and see.

Adrian was home by Wednesday. But nothing was seen of him at the factory. He phoned in to say jet-lag had claimed him, but he'd be fit to chair an informal board meeting on Thursday morning to which he'd report the outcome of his trip. By now, I was beginning to smell a rat – or the marsupial equivalent. Simon and Jennifer were as puzzled as me. And so was Uncle Larry, who called me that night. 'Why does Adrian want me to attend this blasted meeting, Robin? What's he up to?' I couldn't tell him. But we didn't have to wait long to learn the answer.

It rained that morning. All that day, as it turned out. The rain ticked at the boardroom windows and ran in reflected rivulets down the glazed face of Joseph Timariot. He seemed to be listening to us as we conferred. Measuring our achievements against his. And taking silent note of the disparity.

We were expectant and uneasy. All of us were uncomfortable, though some more obviously so than others. Even Adrian looked strangely abashed. As if what he had to report was something worse than simple failure to strike a deal with Bushranger Sports. And so it was. Far worse. It was what he called success. But success often has a higher price than failure. And he was about to invite us to pay it.

'I spent quite a long time with Harvey McGraw. I got to know the man pretty well. He *is* hard. But fair. He made me an offer which, after I'd thought about it, I realized was both of those things. Hard to accept. But fair. And in the circumstances, the best we can hope for. As I'm sure you'll agree when you've reflected on it. I don't want instant reactions. That's why I've kept this meeting informal. I want your mature thoughts when you've mulled it over.'

'Mulled what over?' asked Simon impatiently. But by now, I suppose, we all had an inkling of what was coming.

'McGraw's offering to buy us out.'

'Of Viburna? The guy must be—'

'Not Viburna. Not just Viburna, anyway. McGraw wants the whole operation.'

'You mean Timariot & Small?' put in Uncle Larry.

'Yes.'

'Good God.'

'But you told him we're not for sale, didn't you?' I asked disingenuously.

'Not exactly. He knows we're in the mire. He knows we have to listen.'

'Why?'

'Because it's a good offer. He'll cover Viburna's debts. And pay us two and a half million on top.' Adrian risked a smile. 'Pounds, that is.'

There was momentary silence. Then Uncle Larry said: 'Am I to take it that you're recommending acceptance?'

'I am.'

Uncle Larry stared at him in stupefaction. 'You're advocating the sale of this business? After more than a hundred and fifty years of independent trading? To an Australian? Good God almighty, Harvey McGraw's great-grandfather was probably in chains on a convict ship bound for Botany Bay when my great-grandfather—'

'Reciting the firm's history isn't going to help,' snapped Adrian. 'We're staring crippling losses in the face.'

'But we wouldn't be, would we?' I couldn't help asking. 'Not if we hadn't bought Viburna in the first place.'

Adrian glared at me, but didn't speak. Instead, Jennifer tapped her pen on her note-pad and said: 'It's a good offer. From a strictly financial viewpoint. It's more than we're really worth. At the moment. And for the foreseeable future.' She turned to Adrian. 'Any strings?'

'None.'

'There don't have to be, do there?' said Simon. 'Bushranger can make a go of Viburna thanks to their deal with Danziger's. And they can use us to expand over here just like we planned to use Viburna to expand over there. When we dipped our toe in Australian waters, I thought we might get it bitten off. I never expected we'd be swallowed alive, though.'

'I had reservations about the Viburna takeover,' I said, looking accusingly at Adrian. 'But you trotted out some cliché about having to get bigger if we weren't to get smaller. Now it seems what you mean by getting bigger is going out of business.'

'Recriminations won't help,' said Jennifer, ever the conciliator.

'Nor will acquiescence. We're being asked to sell the workforce down the drain to pay for our mistakes. The mistakes of some of us, anyway.'

Adrian was angry. That last shaft had hit home. I could tell by the tic working in his cheek. But not by the tone of his voice. It stayed calm and reasonable. 'Bushranger want to take us over, not close us down. The workforce will be fully protected. Timariot and Small will become a subsidiary of Bushranger Sports, that's all. In some ways it'll be a bigger and more challenging operation. We'll be marketing Bushranger's products along with—'

'Who's *we*? Who's going to head this subsidiary? Our current chairman?'

Adrian flushed. 'Perhaps. But—'

'No doubt a seat on the Bushranger board will go with the job. I can see you'll have done very well out of taking this company from profit into self-inflicted loss.' I was angry too. Angrier than I could ever have foreseen at the terminal consequences of my smooth-talking wide-horizoned brother's leadership. And at my own naïvety. I should have nipped his ill-considered ambitions in the bud long ago. I should have known better than to trust him with stewardship of the values and traditions bound up in Timariot & Small. I should have realized he saw them merely as a stepping-stone to something bigger and grander. Bigger and grander, that is, for him.

'Your share of two and a half million won't be a bad return for three years' exile from the fleshpots of Brussels,' said Adrian, his face darkening.

'Won't? Don't you mean wouldn't? *If* we compounded your errors of judgement by accepting this offer?'

He sat back and composed himself, refusing to let me draw him into open confrontation. 'I'm confident this board *will* accept the offer, when it's had time to consider its merits. For the moment, that's all I'm asking it to do. Though I should tell you I stopped off in France on my way back from Australia. I visited Bella in Biarritz and put her in the picture. She, like me, favours acceptance.'

So there it was. The virtual declaration of his victory. Between them, he and Bella controlled more than 40 per cent of the company's shares. If Jennifer voted with them – as her guarded remarks had suggested she would – Adrian would be home and dry. Simon was bitter enough when I cornered him in his office later. But he was already becoming philosophical. 'This could net me more than three hundred thou', Rob. Enough to keep Joan at bay and then some. I've got to go for it. You do see that, don't you?' Oh, I saw. I saw all too clearly. 'Anybody who votes no will get the chop if it goes through. That's obvious. And it will go through. You know it will. So why fight it?'

Why indeed? It was hard to explain to somebody who didn't understand. Uncle Larry understood, of course. I went out with him for a long lugubrious lunch at the Bat & Ball on Broadhalfpenny Down, the cradle of organized cricket. Afterwards, we stood outside in the rain, gazing over the fence at the famous ground, its old thatched pavilion and memorial stone bearing witness to the legendary exploits of the Hambledon club more than two hundred years ago.

'John Small played here many times,' said Uncle Larry. 'Old John, I mean. He was a bat maker for more than seventy years, you know.' I knew very well. He was also grandfather of the John Small who'd gone into business with Joseph Timariot in 1836. 'I suppose you could say he was our founder in a sense.'

'I shall vote against,' I solemnly declared.

'So shall I. But we'll lose, won't we? Adrian has his children to consider. Simon needs the money. Jenny can't stop thinking like an accountant. And to Bella it's all antediluvian nonsense. Our goose is cooked.'

'But not served or eaten. Not yet.'

I drove straight home from Broadhalfpenny Down and telephoned Bella. But she wasn't in. Instead, Sir Keith came on the line.

'Anything I can do for you, Robin?'

'I don't think so. I wanted to talk to Bella about the Bushranger bid.'

'Ah yes. Your brother told us all about it. Seems a neat way out of the hole you've dug yourselves into. Bella certainly seems to think so.'

'Does she?'

'I suppose you're mightily relieved.'

'Not exactly.'

'You should be. Salvation of this order doesn't often present itself. I'm glad you called, by the way. My solicitor tells me that TV programme *Benefit of the Doubt* is going to take a sceptical look at Naylor's conviction. Have you heard anything from the producers?'

'No,' I heard myself lie. 'Not a thing.'

'Well, if you do—'

'I'll know what to tell them.'

Looking back, I can see why it happened. My anger at the probable demise of Timariot & Small and my frustration at being unable to do anything to prevent it had to find an outlet. I didn't think it through on a conscious level. I didn't plan to lash out at Bella by upsetting her husband's cosy assumptions. But that's what I did. I'd spent a couple of hours at Greenhayes, drinking scotch and watching the rain sheet across the garden, when Seymour and his cameraman arrived, dead on time, at six o'clock. I'd worked up a fine head of resentment by then. Resentment of the greed that had dragged down Timariot & Small; of the ease with which Adrian and the rest seemed able to turn their backs on the labour of four generations; of the readiness I and others had displayed to mould the memory of Louise Paxton to fit our requirements. The ends seemed to have justified the means once too often. I wanted to give honour and tradition a solitary triumph over commercial expediency; honesty and sincerity a single victory to savour. I wanted to speak my mind without tailoring my words to their audience and my thoughts to their results. I wanted my own blinkered form of justice. And Nick Seymour gave me the chance to have it.

I'd expected to dislike him. In the event, his self-deprecating humour and affable manner won me over. He had wit and patience. The wit to see I was in the mood to talk. And the patience to let me. He had a long list of questions to ask. I saw them typed out on a sheet of paper in his hand. But he didn't need to reel them off. I answered them without prompting. I tried – for the very first time – to describe my meeting with Louise Paxton fully and accurately. I had enough sense not to contradict or withdraw anything I'd said in court. But I also had enough courage – or stupidity or recklessness or all three rolled together – to try to define what it was that had lodged in my mind after our fleeting encounter on Hergest Ridge.

After Seymour had gone, evidently pleased with the material he'd got on tape, I couldn't remember exactly what I'd said to him. Not every word and inflection. I certainly couldn't imagine how it would look and sound on television several weeks down the road. And I didn't much care. Not at the time. It was sufficient to have unburdened myself. To have told it as it really was. Or as it had seemed to be that day. Recalled at last. Without distortion or evasion. Without fear of whatever the consequences might be.

I poured myself another drink and toasted the fragile truth that was all I could throw back at Bella and Sir Keith and my hard-hearted siblings. I'd paid my dues to Louise Paxton. Late but in full. I'd cleared my debts. Now I was free to remind others of theirs.

CHAPTER TEN

Sentimental appeals proved even less effective than recriminatory arguments. I tried both over the next couple of weeks without making the slightest impact on Adrian's determination to push through acceptance of the Bushranger bid. From his point of view, it solved our problems at a stroke, never mind that the problems were of his creation and the solution an humiliating end to a proud piece of history. Simon and Jennifer went along with him, Simon because his share of the sale price would get Joan off his back and Jennifer because she could see no other way out of deficit. As for Bella, when I eventually succeeded in speaking to her, it became apparent that she regarded the dissolution of Timariot & Small as tantamount to a mercy killing. 'Hugh should have negotiated something like this years ago. Then he might not have worked himself into an early grave.' My hope that Sir Keith might consider injecting capital into the company to make it independently viable was abandoned before I'd even expressed it.

That left Uncle Larry and me in a decisive minority. Adrian dismissed us as unrealistic romantics and I suppose he had a point. Uncle Larry's reluctance to see the family firm taken over could be seen as no more than an old man's refusal to live in the present. While the irony of my position was that I'd become more committed to Timariot & Small – past *and* future – than my brothers or sister, despite remaining aloof from it far longer than any of them. Perhaps that was the point. Perhaps I understood what we'd lose by selling out just because I'd spent twelve years away from it. And perhaps they failed to because they hadn't. Familiarity had bred contempt. Later, I knew, they'd regret it. But their regrets would be futile. We could only destroy what our forefathers had created once. It was an irreversible act. But it was an act they were clearly set on carrying out.

Busy chasing false hopes and faint chances of staving off the Bushranger takeover, I gave little thought to my *Benefit of the Doubt* interview besides savouring the prospect of any small embarrassment it might cause Bella. Seymour had told me the programme would go out some time in mid-June and had promised to send me a video of it in case I didn't catch the broadcast. I'd intended to check *Radio Times* to see when it was coming up, but somehow never got round to doing so. If I had done, I'd have known a week in advance that it was scheduled for transmission at eight thirty on Wednesday the sixteenth of June. In the event, my first inkling of that was when I returned home from work two nights before to find a parcel small enough to fit through the letter-box lying in wait for me on the doormat. It was the promised video. I played it straightaway. And long before the end I realized just how big a fool I'd been.

Seymour wasn't just a handsome front man. He was clever as well. If I hadn't known that before, I found it out now. The doubt he sowed in the viewer's mind about Naylor's guilt wasn't based on clinching facts or convincing arguments. It relied instead on impressions and implications. The programme started out as a straightforward summary of the case from the discovery of the murders to Naylor's conviction. Then Seymour turned his attention to Naylor's defence. 'Let's see if this stands up,' he coolly said. 'Let's suspend disbelief for the time it takes to subject Shaun Naylor's version of events to some obvious tests. We'll begin where he says it began, at the Harp Inn, Old Radnor.' The camera panned across the pub's façade, then moved to the man who'd testified at the trial that he'd seen Naylor there with a good-looking woman on the evening of 17 July 1990. He seemed more confident now than before that it was Louise Paxton. 'I reckon it was, yes. They were getting on well together. Laughing and joking.' If he was right, Seymour pointed out, they could only just have met. At the very least, this indicated a willingness for flirtation on Lady Paxton's part. Was that credible? Did that fit her character?

Suddenly, Sophie Marsden was on screen, relaxing in the

horse-brassed black-beamed interior of her Shropshire home. She looked as much at ease as Seymour had made me feel, perhaps more so. And she was talking freely about the friend she'd known. 'Louise wasn't really the saintly wife and mother she's been portrayed as. She was a lot of fun. She lived life to the full. Sometimes she flirted with strangers. And sometimes it may have gone beyond flirting. I know of at least one occasion when it certainly did. She told me about it. She wasn't boasting. It was . . . the kind of secret we shared.'

Before I could absorb the full ramifications of what Sophie had said, Seymour was in picture, striding up the track from Kington to Hergest Ridge. 'So, according to Lady Paxton's best friend, Shaun Naylor's account of how they met *is* feasible. What's more, we know she met at least one other man that evening under similar circumstances. Up here, on Offa's Dyke, where solitary male walkers are often to be found.'

Then my face was staring out of the screen at me, the sitting-room at Greenhayes visible in the background, including part of the very television set I was watching. And I was saying what Seymour wanted to hear. 'Lady Paxton was friendly and approachable. She seemed to want to talk. Not just about the weather. About something else. But she was reluctant to talk at the same time. As if . . . Well, I've never really been able to describe her state of mind, even to myself. It was so difficult to assess. When she offered me a lift, I thought it was just a kindly gesture. Now I'm not so sure. I think she must have wanted me – wanted somebody – to stay with her.' Then we were back with Seymour on Hergest Ridge. Leaving me to shout at his video-recorded face: 'Hold on. What about the rest? That's not all I said, you devious bastard.' Just how devious he'd been sunk in only when I replayed the interview several times. Then, at last, I was able to recollect exactly what I'd gone on to say. *'I think she must have wanted me – wanted somebody – to stay with her. To give her some disinterested advice about a problem she was trying to solve. To listen while she talked whatever it was out of her system.'* What I'd recounted couldn't possibly be regarded as a sexual proposition. But Seymour's edited version of it could be. *'I think she must have wanted me – wanted somebody – to stay with her.'* The phrase echoed in my mind as Seymour quoted it to camera. 'Failing to find that somebody in Mr Timariot, did Lady Paxton strike luckier half an hour later at the Harp Inn? The evidence available to us suggests she may have done.'

The film cut to the frontage of Whistler's Cot. Seymour strode into picture. 'The prosecution argued at the trial that Lady Paxton would hardly have risked using somebody else's house for illicit sex. But her relationship with the owner was never explored. We know she was in effect his patron. He owed her a good deal. Might he have been willing to repay that debt by making his cottage available for her use? Or might she have known he wasn't going to be there until later that night? With both of them now dead, we cannot hope to find out. But Lady Paxton's friend, Mrs Marsden, did say this.'

Sophie returned to the screen. 'Louise and Oscar got on well together. There was a spark between them. An understanding. That's why she appreciated his paintings better than most. You'd think they had nothing in common to look at them. In fact, there was an intuitive bond between them. Platonic, but genuine.'

Then we were back with Seymour. 'If the jury had heard that, they might not have been so sure Shaun Naylor was lying about being brought here by Lady Paxton. But they'd still have come up against a substantial objection to his version of events. If he didn't murder Oscar Bantock and Lady Paxton, who did? And why? Until three months ago, there seemed no other conceivable suspect or motive. Then this book' – he brandished a copy of *Fakes and Ale* – 'was published. And suddenly the situation became rather more complicated.'

Henley Bantock I recognized at once. A caption identified his pudgy bow-tied companion as Barnaby Maitland. They seized the chance of a free peak-time advertisement for their book with ill-disguised glee. But they also set out their alternative explanation for the Kington killings with undeniable facility. 'Fine art and the criminal underworld have many points of overlap,' expounded Maitland. 'Forgery is perhaps the most remunerative – and hence the most dangerous.' 'My uncle often told me he could humiliate the art establishment if he chose to,' contributed Henley. 'Only when I found his journals did I realize it was true.' 'It has to be said,' Maitland resumed, 'that there were many reasons why poor old Oscar was worth more dead than alive in the summer of nineteen ninety.'

'Many reasons,' echoed Seymour. 'None of which were considered at the trial. If they had been, would they have made any difference to the outcome? Shaun Naylor's solicitor, Vijay Sarwate, thinks they might have done.'

We switched to the cramped and crowded interior of Sarwate's office. He was a lean weary-sounding man who looked as if he wasn't sure whether to be grateful or bitter about the legal-aid lottery that had handed him such a case. But about one thing he *was* sure. 'Evidence concerning Oscar Bantock's activities as a forger would have been very valuable to my client. It would have supplied the missing link in his defence: a credible explanation for the events that took place that night *after* he left Whistler's Cot. Circumstantial evidence is often the most difficult kind to refute because, at the back of the jury's minds, the unspoken question is always there: *If he did not do it, who did?* That question went unanswered at the trial, to my client's undoubted detriment. Obviously, in the light of these revelations, it would not go unanswered again. Indeed, I am already exploring with counsel the possibility of seeking leave to appeal against the convictions on precisely those grounds.'

'While his solicitor takes advice,' Seymour went on, 'Shaun Naylor's wife and children wait and wait for the hsuband and father the law decided should be kept away from them for at least twenty years. By then, Mrs Naylor will be nearly fifty years old.'

The Naylor flat in Bermondsey. Garishly decorated and littered with discarded toys, but clean and homely in its way. Carol Naylor, a thin haggard and obviously hard-pressed young woman, perched on the edge of a black leather-look sofa, drew nervously on a cigarette and glanced at a framed photograph of Shaun dandling their youngest on his knee four Christmases ago. 'What makes you so certain of his innocence?' asked Seymour. 'I've known him all my life,' she replied. 'We grew up six doors apart. I've been married to him eight years. I know him better than he does himself. He can be short-tempered and arrogant. But he's not a rapist. Not a cold-blooded murderer. It's just not in his nature.' She fought back tears. 'He didn't do what they said he did. He couldn't have done. I've known that from day one.'

'And from day one,' said Seymour, taking up the story outside a prison wall, 'Shaun Naylor has consistently denied committing rape and double murder that night in July nineteen ninety. He's been held here, at Albany Prison on the Isle of Wight, since his conviction. Home Office regulations prevent us visiting him, but we have exchanged letters with him. In his most recent communication, he says this.' Seymour held up the letter and read from it. '"I'm hoping this forgery business will make the authorities reopen my case. It's the first chink of light there's been since I was sent down. In the end, they'll realize I really am innocent. I have to believe that. Otherwise, I'll go mad thinking about the injustice of what's happened to me."' Seymour paused for effect, then said: 'Shaun Naylor still maintains he is the victim of a miscarriage of justice. Faced with what we now know and can legitimately conjecture about the events of July seventeenth, nineteen ninety, there may be many who agree with him and who feel he has been denied that most crucial component of justice: the benefit of the doubt.'

As the credits rolled, I switched the set off and stared blankly at my reflection in its screen. My few minutes of air-time solidified in my mind as a single hideous recollection, irredeemable and unalterable. In forty-eight hours, I'd be seen and heard in thousands of homes. Those of my colleagues and subordinates. Those of Naylor's friends and relations. And those of Louise Paxton's. To them I wouldn't be fanning a flame of hope. I'd be betraying a fine woman's memory. And my own solemn pledge. Sophie Marsden's candour would probably do more damage than mine. But mine was the less forgivable. And complaints of selective editing would probably only make it worse.

I thought of phoning the television station and demanding to speak to Seymour. But I knew it would do no good. Even if I succeeded in contacting him, he'd only deny the charge. Editing of taped interviews was commonplace. Whether it amounted to deliberate distortion depended entirely on your point of view. Besides, I had no record of our conversation to set against his. I had no proof he'd set out to misrepresent what I'd said. Not a shred.

Which left me to consider the fall-out from my contribution to his rotten programme. One thing was certain. If I let Sarah or Rowena or Sir Keith simply come across my interview without warning, they'd be justified in thinking the worst of me. I had to prepare them. I had to explain what I'd been duped into doing. And I had to explain it very quickly.

I phoned Sarah, reckoning she'd at least try to understand. But there was no answer. I left a message, emphasizing its urgency. Two anxious hours passed, during which I replayed the video several times. Then, just as I was about to call Sarah again, she rang back.

'I need to see you, Sarah. Tomorrow. There's something I have to tell you.'

'What?'

'It's too complicated to go into over the phone. Can we meet?'

'Well . . . I suppose so. But tomorrow's difficult.'

'It can't be delayed. Honestly.'

'It may have to be. I'm tied up all—'

'Rowena's involved,' I interrupted, calculating that her name would persuade Sarah where any amount of pleas in my own right might fail.

'What's this about, Robin?'

'Meet me tomorrow, Sarah. Please.'

'It really is urgent?'

'Yes. I'll come to Bristol. Wherever suits you.'

'All right. College Green, twelve thirty sharp. Wait on one of the benches there. I work nearby. But a long lunch is the last thing my schedule needs at the moment, so please don't be late.'

'I won't be, I promise.'

I drove up to Bristol early enough the following morning to be absolutely certain of being on time. It was a warm sunny day. When I arrived, the benches on College Green were already occupied by groups of idle youths and weary shoppers in search of a tan. A heat haze blurred the perspective of Park Street and the soaring elegance of the University Tower, while traffic roared by and exhaust fumes swirled in the motionless air. I stood in the centre of College Green's triangle of grass, studying the ceaseless bustle of the world and reflecting how powerless I was to halt or alter its course in any way. What would be would always be.

She appeared promptly at half past twelve from the mouth of a narrow street between the cathedral and the Royal Hotel. A slight hurrying figure in a grey suit and white blouse. It struck me, watching her approach, that at twenty-five she'd begun to lose some of the youthful traits I'd noticed at our first meeting. Which wasn't just a measure of her professional cares, but an indicator of how long I'd known her. Her mother had been dead nearly three years. Yet still, in so many ways, she lived.

'I don't have long, Robin,' Sarah announced, greeting me with a fleeting kiss. 'Shall we to go a pub? There's a decent one just round the corner.' Then she noticed the plastic bag in my hand. 'Been shopping?'

'Not exactly.' Her innocent question spared me the task of constructing a painful preamble. I launched straight in. 'Did you know there's to be a programme about your mother's murder on television tomorrow night?'

'*Benefit of the Doubt*? Yes. Daddy's solicitor got wind of it.'

'This is a recording.' I held up the bag. 'It's why I'm here.'

'What are you doing with a recording of a programme that's not yet gone out?'

'It's a complimentary copy. A gesture of thanks from the presenter. I'm in it, you see. In more ways than one.'

* * *

We sat in a cool and shadowy alcove of the Hatchet Inn, privacy guaranteed by the hubbub of fruit machines and bar-rail conversations. Sarah listened patiently to what I had to say, pressure of commitments forgotten now I'd drawn her out of her daily preoccupations to consider once more the doubts and difficulties her mother's death had bequeathed to her – and which she must have heartily wished could be put behind her for good and all.

'I was a fool to agree to the interview. And a bigger fool to let him set me up the way he did. The Bushranger bid was what did it. But for all that spinning around in my head, I'd never have let my tongue run away with me. I was a bit drunk, a bit resentful, a bit . . . Well, there it is. It's done. And it can't be undone. Seymour's edited the tape to make it sound as if I think your mother tried to pick me up. I didn't say that. I didn't mean that. But it's how it comes out. I'm sorry. Sorry *and* ashamed. There's nothing I can do to stop it. Or change it. I just wanted you to know . . . beforehand . . . that it wasn't intentional. God knows what Sophie was thinking of, but I was . . . thinking of all the wrongs things. Not concentrating. Not considering the consequences. Not . . . seeing clearly.'

'I don't understand. No amount of editing could put words in your mouth.'

'It can seem to, believe me. Seymour twists what I say by leaving odd sentences out. It's subtly done. You might not notice if you didn't know it had happened.'

'And that's why you wanted us to meet? So I *would* know?'

'Partly. But I'm also worried about Rowena.'

'You and me both. This couldn't have come at a worse time. She's been . . . a bit down lately. Fretting about her exams, Paul reckons. But they're out of the way now and she hasn't perked up. They say depression is a recurring illness and I think it may have recurred in her case. Not because of Mummy, though, or this bloody book. I'm not even sure she knows it's been published.'

'Why, then?'

'Your guess is as good as mine. Paul's her confidant now, not me. Or he should be.'

'The marriage hasn't run into trouble, has it?'

'No. At least . . . Well, *lack* of trouble may be the problem. Paul loves Rowena. That's obvious whenever you see them together. But there's such a thing as too much love, isn't there? It can become stifling, even oppressive. Rowena's only twenty-two. No age really. She grew up late. Maybe she's only just started to grow up. Maybe she's regretting settling her future so soon. It's all mapped out for her now. Paul's wife. The mother of Paul's children. A fixture in Paul's life. A part of Paul. Where's Rowena?'

'If that's the way she's thinking . . .'

'A renewal of doubts about Mummy's death isn't going to help. Exactly. Fortunately, Rowena hardly watches television from one week's end to the next. With any luck, she'll know nothing about *Benefit of the Doubt.* I'm going out to dinner with her and Paul tomorrow night. Just to make sure.'

'Was that your idea?'

'Mine *and* Paul's.'

'It could look like a conspiracy to Rowena. If she ever finds out. Not mentioning the book to her. Not telling her about the TV programme. You and her husband censoring what she can be allowed to know. It's a dangerous—'

'You have a better idea, do you?' She was angry. It happened suddenly and only now, too late, did I realize why. I'd crossed the invisible boundary between legitimate concern and unwelcome interference. 'What do you suggest? Dig up all those uncertainties again? Start her chasing after that crazy idea about Mummy foreseeing her death?'

'No. Of course not. But—'

'Or is this interview your way of taking the decision out of our hands?'

'You know it isn't.'

'Do I?'

'Would I have warned you about it if it was?'

'Perhaps not. But . . .'

'Evasion and concealment breed problems, Sarah. Don't you see that? Oh what a tangled web we weave, etcetera. If you'd been honest with Rowena about the possibility that your mother meant to leave your father, precognition might never have entered her head as an—'

'That's it, isn't it?' She stared at me, appalled. 'That's why you've done this. I knew I should never have told you about Mummy leaving Daddy. You resented me keeping it from you till after the trial, didn't you?'

'Why should I have resented it?'

'Because what you said in court might have been different if you'd know about it then. And you think that's why I held it back. What's more, you're right. I only told you when I did because I thought Rowena's suicide attempt would have made you understand just how damaging complete honesty could be. But you didn't understand. And you still don't. As I expect this proves.' She pointed at the bag lying on the table between us. 'So now you want to have it both ways. The truth – or your version of it – out in the open. And my generous pardon. Justified by some crap about selective editing.'

'You've got it wrong, Sarah. I'm simply trying to—'

'Force your opinion of us down our throats. Well, I'm not going to let you.' She rose abruptly, her chair scraping back across the floor, and grabbed the bag. 'I'll watch the tape, Robin. And I'll be the judge of what I see. Thanks very much.' She turned on her heel and slipped through the crowd towards the door.

'Sarah, wait! I—' But she was gone. And pursuit now would only make matters worse. A blazing argument in the street to add to our misunderstandings. I sank back in my chair and contemplated the ruins of my strategy. There was a grain of truth in what she'd said. I wanted her approval, even her esteem. Perhaps, buried too deep for confession or recognition, I wanted some part of her that would remind me of her mother. But a greater desire always prevailed in the end. A desire to possess the secret Louise Paxton had taken to her grave. *'Can we really change anything, do you think?'* No. We couldn't change a single thing. Unless we discovered it first. And then . . . Maybe. Just maybe.

I stayed longer in the pub than I should have, then wandered out, slightly drunk, into the hot afternoon. The visit to Bristol had been a mistake. I knew that only too well. Sarah couldn't have thought worse of me if I'd kept clear and let her see the programme unprepared. I'd tried to forewarn her of Seymour's duplicity. But I'd only succeeded in alerting her to mine.

I made my way back to College Green and headed vaguely towards Queen Square, where I'd parked the car. But it was obvious some strong coffee would be needed before I drove anywhere. The warehouses running down the western side of a narrow reach of the harbour just below the Royal Hotel had been converted into a complex of shops, restaurants and art galleries. A couple of *espressos* in a café there cleared my head. I emerged ready to face the journey back to Petersfield.

Only to stop in my tracks when I glanced across the reach to see Rowena walking slowly along the other side. She was wearing a long loose flower-patterned dress. Her hair hung unbraided to her waist, a splash of palest gold in the sunlight, waving slightly with each step she took, as a field of wheat might when stirred by a breeze. She was heading south, bound presumably for home. I knew from Sarah that she and Paul lived in one of the smart dockside town houses that had sprung up in the area since its commercial decay. Convenient for Metropolitan Mutual *and* the university. But she didn't seem to be in a hurry to get back there. She was dragging her feet, fiddling with the strap of her shoulder-bag as she walked, alternately gazing up at the sky and staring down at the cobbles. She looked neither to right nor left, but, even if she'd glanced in my direction, she'd probably not have seen me in the shadows of the colonnade that ran the length of the warehouse block. The reach was narrow, of course. If I'd stepped forward and shouted to her, she would have heard. But something deterred me. Something in her bearing and my shame. Something that told me chance meetings were best avoided.

Nevertheless, I found myself walking in the same direction as her. And at the same pace. Keeping track for as long as our routes ran parallel. Hers down past the Unicorn Hotel to the Arnolfini building at the corner of the quay. Mine to where the colonnade ended and a permanently moored ship got up as a floating pub blocked my view of her. Hurriedly, I went aboard, ordered a drink I didn't want and took it to the starboard window. But Rowena had stopped at the quayside opposite me, almost as if she'd known I'd need a few moments to catch up. She couldn't see me, I was certain. Not with the sun in her eyes as it was. She seemed to be looking for something, squinting out across the water. She took a step closer to the edge and for a second I was alarmed. But there was no need. She tossed her head, setting her hair bouncing across her back, then turned and walked away towards the swing-bridge across the harbour.

She'd soon be out of sight. Distance would claim her as one of its own. I watched her cross the bridge, then turn to the left, heading further away from me than ever along the wharves on the far side of the harbour. A pale speck amidst the visual chaos of masts and rooftops, speeding cars and sprawling crowds, glaring sky and sparkling water. A few seconds, as my eyes strained to follow her. A farewell flash of sunlight on her hair. Then she was gone. I waited to be certain. But there was no longer any trace of her. Not so much as a blur.

I left my drink and walked off the ship. There, opposite me, on the quay, she'd stood only a few minutes before. I could have hailed her. I could have urged her to wait while I hurried round to join her. And if she'd still been standing there, I believe I would have done. But belief can so often be self-deception. I'd had the chance. And I'd turned it down. Now there was nothing to do but to walk away.

I heard nothing from Sarah between my return to Petersfield and the *Benefit of the Doubt* broadcast. She'd had ample time by then to play and replay the video until every word of mine Seymour had used was imprinted on her memory. But her only response was silence. Perhaps, I thought, that was to be my punishment. My exclusion, so far as she could engineer it, from Rowena's life as well as hers. My forfeit of the confidence they'd once invested in me.

I recorded the transmission myself, but I didn't watch it. I'd seen it too many times already. The awareness that I couldn't force Seymour to admit he'd deliberately distorted what I'd said any more than I could force Sarah to acknowledge he'd done so dragged my exasperation down into exhaustion. Until a show of indifference was the only riposte I felt capable of.

Adrian had got hold of a couple of tickets for the opening day of the Lord's Test and had offered them to Simon and me, claiming he was too busy to go himself. Simon and I both realized it was more in the nature of a bribe, with the company's response to Bushranger's bid still formally unsettled. But that didn't stop us accepting. In my case, it was just what I needed: a day's refuge from any possibility of an irate call from Bella or Paul or Sir Keith about my interview on *Benefit of the Doubt* the night before. Simon gave me his opinion of it, of course. 'I said you should never have got mixed up with that in the first place, Rob. You should have listened to your big brother.' All of which was thoroughly predictable. As well as being uncomfortably close to the truth. But as soon as the champagne started to flow, he gave up lecturing me and a moratorium on the subject of Bushranger meant we had an enjoyably light-hearted day. Even if Australia's dominance of England did seem to point a dismal moral for Timariot & Small.

I got back to Greenhayes late that night, overslept and reached the office nearer ten o'clock than nine the following morning, my hangover made no more bearable by the knowledge that Simon's was probably worse. A pile of messages had accumulated in my absence and I was sifting aimlessly through them with one hand while trying to prise a disprin out of its foil wrapper with the other when my secretary put her head round the door to announce she had Nick Seymour on the telephone.

'That's *the* Nick Seymour,' she said, apparently impressed.

'What does he want?' I barked ill-temperedly.

'He wouldn't say. It couldn't be anything to do with what's in the paper, could it?'

'I don't know. I haven't seen a paper.'

'Oh. You don't know, then.'

'Didn't I just say that?'

'Sorry,' she said, bridling. 'It's just—'

'Put *the* Nick Seymour through, Liz. Without wasting any more time, eh?' I waved to her dismissively and she took the hint. A few seconds later, the telephone rang.

'Mr Timariot?' It was Seymour all right, a grain of apprehensiveness scarcely denting his self-assurance.

'Rung to apologize, have you?'

'What do you mean?'

'You know very well.'

'Listen, I haven't got time to play games. I'm simply trying to make sure we take a consistent line on this. In both our interests.'

'I don't know what you're talking about.'

'Come on. The Paxton girl. Or Bryant. Whatever the right name is. The tabloids are trying to blame me for what's happened.'

'What *has* happened?'

'Don't you know?'

'I wouldn't ask if I did, would I?'

'I thought you must do.'

'Just tell me.'

The tone of my voice silenced him for a moment. Then he said: 'Lady Paxton's younger daughter committed suicide yesterday afternoon.'

'What?'

'Threw herself off Clifton Suspension Bridge, apparently.'

'Rowena's dead?'

'Yes. And the newspapers are trying to say she only did it because she'd seen my programme on Wednesday.'

'Oh my God.'

'So you see it's vital we stick together. The papers may not contact you. But, if they do, you'd be well advised to—'

I cut him off before he could say any more and slowly replaced the handset. Beneath me, amidst the confetti of Liz's neatly typed messages from the day before, was one that was shorter than most. *Mrs Bryant rang on a matter of urgency. She will call back.* And there, in my mind's eye, was the sunlight flashing on her hair as she turned from the quayside.

I jumped from my chair and ran into the outer office, clutching the scrap of paper in my hand. Liz looked up in surprise. 'What's wrong?'

'This message.' I slapped it down in front of her. 'When did you take it?'

'Mrs Bryant,' she mused. 'Oh, I remember. Said she was in a call-box. Sounded anxious.'

'When?'

'Er . . . during the lunch hour. Yes. Just before two. Or just after.'

'Let me see your paper.' Her *Daily Mail* was poking out of the desk drawer beside her.

'You don't mean . . . Rowena was the Mrs Bryant who phoned you yesterday?' Horror began to dawn on her. 'I never—'

'Give me the paper!' She handed it over and there was the headline, staring at me from the front page. DAUGHTER TAKES LIFE THREE YEARS AFTER MOTHER'S MURDER. *The daughter of one of the victims of a double murder three years ago yesterday took her own life in a fatal dive from Clifton Suspension Bridge, the notorious Bristol suicide spot.* My eyes scanned the paragraphs in search of the information I both wanted and dreaded. *Rowena Bryant, a twenty-two-year-old married student at Bristol University, is said to have become depressed over recent weeks. It is thought her suicide was prompted by seeing a video recording of Wednesday night's* Benefit of the Doubt *programme, in which controversial presenter Nick Seymour aired doubts about the guilt of the man convicted of the rape and murder of her mother, Lady Paxton, in July 1990. Shaun Naylor, 31, is serving a—* But where was the time – the precise time? When did it happen? *Onlookers were amazed to see Mrs Bryant walk calmly to the middle of the bridge shortly after two o'clock yesterday afternoon, climb onto the railings and—* Shortly after two o'clock. So it was even worse than I'd feared.

'Are you OK, Robin?' asked Liz.

She got no answer. I closed the newspaper, dropped it onto her desk and picked up the message she'd taken just before two o'clock the previous afternoon. Or maybe just after. *Mrs Bryant rang on a matter of urgency. She will call back.* 'Is this really all she said?' I demanded.

'Yes. She was only on for a minute or two. Said it was urgent and personal. When I explained you were out, she sounded disappointed. I suggested she call back. She said she would. Then . . .'

'Then what?'

'She rang off.'

She rang off. And walked the short distance from the call-box to the bridge. She must have used the kiosk on the Clifton side. I could remember passing it with her that day in November 1991 when I'd gone up to Bristol at Sarah's urging to help Rowena forget the mystery of their mother's death. We'd talked of her suicide attempt a few days before; of how good it was to be alive; and of the strange appeal death could still seem to hold. For a moment, for an hour at most, she'd said, death had seemed more attractive than life. And now it had again. But an overdose was neither certain nor instant. Whereas a leap from the bridge—

'It doesn't make any sense,' murmured Liz. 'She said she'd call back. I'm sure of it.'

'Don't worry. It wasn't your fault. You weren't to know.'

She looked up at me gratefully. 'I don't suppose anybody was, were they?'

I wanted to agree, to affirm wholeheartedly that this was a bolt from the blue nobody could have predicted or prevented. But something stopped me. Rowena's own words – her irrational sense of guilt for the fate that had overtaken her mother – stood between me and the denial of responsibility I'd otherwise have been glad to utter. *'It would be possible to rerun the events of the seventeenth of July a hundred times and produce a hundred different results. A lot of times – maybe a majority of times – Mummy wouldn't die. Wouldn't even be in danger. Just because of some tiny scarcely noticeable variation. Like what she said to me. Or to you. And what we said in reply.'* I'd persuaded her then to agree that, even if this was so, nobody could foresee or be blamed for the fatal variation. But perhaps I hadn't really believed that any more than her. Perhaps we'd both known better, but hadn't dared to say so. For fear of what it meant.

'Can we really change anything, do you think?' Yes, Louise. I could have saved you. And I could have saved your daughter. If I'd refused Seymour his interview. If I'd been more careful about what I said. If I'd given him no scope to finesse the result. If I'd gone to Rowena straightaway. If I'd called to her across the harbour. If I'd been in the office to take her call. If I'd told her the truth all along. If I'd simply trusted her as she wanted me to.

If I'd only made one right choice instead of a dozen wrong ones. Then – and only then – it might have been so very different. But it wasn't going to be. Any more than Rowena was going to call back. Not now. Not ever.

CHAPTER ELEVEN

I'm not sure now how I got through the rest of that day. For most of it, I was shut away in my office, struggling to articulate a response to Rowena's death. I knew contact with Sarah at this stage would be counter-productive. She'd be bound to blame me for what had happened. Although I longed to ask her how Rowena had come to see the video, to do so was to all intents and purposes impossible. Paul was a virtual stranger to me. To approach him in the midst of his grief was inconceivable. Bella was a possible go-between and I did risk a call to her in Biarritz, only to be told she and Sir Keith had already left for England. So I was left in limbo, unable to act because every action I considered led me nowhere.

One decision I did take was to play along with Seymour, though for my own reasons. I instructed Liz to tell any journalists who rang that I was out. She heard from several. But they weren't going to hear from me. An interview had started all this and I knew public recriminations would only prolong it. If Sarah wasn't prepared to believe the explanation I'd given her face to face, seeing a garbled version of it in the tabloid press wouldn't make any difference. I let Seymour imagine what he liked, though. I was out to him as well. And meant to go on being.

I went home as early as was consistent with a pretence of putting in a day's work, but didn't stay there longer than it took to change my clothes. I dreaded the telephone ringing with Sir Keith or some muck-raking newspaperman on the line, yet knew I'd have to answer in case it was Sarah offering me an olive-branch. To walk myself into a state of exhaustion round the lanes and hangers was preferable to an agony of suspense at Greenhayes, so out I went. I finished up at the White Horse, an old haunt of Thomas's on the Froxfield plateau, where I was mercifully unknown and could drink steadily away until the demons were dulled, though scarcely banished.

It was nearly midnight when I got back to Greenhayes. But the telephone rang before I'd so much as locked the door behind me. And I was too drunk to hesitate before picking it up.

'Robin?'

'Oh, Bella . . . It's you.'

'I've been trying to contact you all evening.'

'Sorry. I was . . . out.'

'I assume you've heard about Rowena.'

'Oh yes. I've heard.'

'Is that all you can say?'

'What else do you want me to say?'

'I should have thought we were owed an explanation from you at the very least.'

'I'd be happy to give one. If you thought it would be listened to.'

'I'll listen, Robin.'

'But will Keith? Will Paul? Will Sarah?'

'Probably not, no. Can you blame them? They think you and this Marsden bitch are partly responsible – if not chiefly responsible – for what Rowena did.'

'And no doubt you agree with them.'

'What I think isn't very important at the moment. Now listen to me. Keith's spending the weekend with Sarah and Paul. But I'm coming down to Hindhead tomorrow. I'd like to see you. Come to The Hurdles at . . . say . . . four o'clock?'

'All right. If you think it'll serve any—'

'Just be there, Robin.' And she hung up before I had a chance to prevaricate any further. Not that I would have done. I had as many questions for her as she had for me.

I reached The Hurdles halfway through a blazing hot summer's afternoon. The lawn was loud with grasshoppers. The plop-plop of a tennis game could be heard from beyond the neighbour's fence. And a distant growl from the deep blue sky as a light plane towed a glider up into the thermals. Death seemed as remote as winter. But death was what had brought me there.

Bella greeted me with a complaint about the heat. 'I'd forgotten how humid it can be in England,' she said. 'God, what a time for this to happen.'

'Could there be a good time?'

'You know what I mean. Do you want a drink?'

'Why not?'

'There's a beer in the fridge. About all there *is* in the fridge. Bring it onto the terrace.'

I fetched a can and a glass and followed her out to the rear of the house, where she'd arranged a couple of directors' chairs beneath the pergola. She already had a drink, something cool and lemon-coloured, with a straw in it. A sheaf of ripped-open letters beside her chair testified to the length of her absence. And she didn't look happy to be back. She was smoking, which wasn't a good sign. Nor were the sunglasses she hid her eyes behind. I might have betrayed her husband and stepdaughter. But I'd inconvenienced her. A heinous offence indeed.

'Sarah told me you'd claimed to be a victim of selective editing.'

'It's true. I was.'

'Bullshit. I've seen the tape, Robin. What *did* you think you were doing?'

'Trying to tell it how it really was.'

'And was that worth driving Rowena to suicide for?'

'No. Of course not. I had no idea—'

'You knew about the first attempt. How can you claim to have had no idea?'

'Ah. Sarah's mentioned that, has she?'

'Yes. And I wish she'd done so at the time. Then Keith and I might have been able to— Oh, never mind.' She rose and walked up and down, puffing at her cigarette. 'It's not *all* your fault. I'll say that much. Sarah was a fool to keep us in the dark. And she should have realized what might happen if Rowena found out about the programme.'

'How *did* she find out?'

'A stroke of bad luck. With her exams finished and term all but over, she wasn't going into the university last week, so Paul thought she probably wouldn't meet anybody who'd seen the programme. But another maths student she knew quite well *had* seen it. She called round for coffee on Thursday morning and asked Rowena about it. But Rowena didn't know it had even been made, let alone broadcast. She was shocked. Outraged, I suppose, that it had been kept from her. I knew that was a mistake all along. I should never have let Keith . . . Anyway, about half an hour after her visitor left, Rowena was spotted by another resident going into Sarah's flat in Caledonia Place. She still had a key from when they shared it. She must have guessed her sister had recorded the programme while she was out with her and Paul the night before. But Sarah hadn't needed to record it, had she? Because you'd given her a tape of it, neatly labelled, which Rowena found and watched on Sarah's TV. It was still in the video recorder when Sarah got back. Can you imagine the effect it must have had? Sophie Marsden implying her mother was some sort of nymphomaniac.'

'She didn't exactly—'

'And you backing her up. Reviving Rowena's delusions about second sight and missed opportunities. Making her feel guilty for aiding Naylor's conviction. Making her suspicious of her own family for keeping so much back. Making her afraid of what it all might mean. God knows how many times she watched that video over the next couple of hours. But it was too many times for her to bear. She drank about half a bottle of gin, you know. Then walked up to the bridge and threw herself off. They think she may have tried to phone somebody just before she did it. They found her diary in the call-box on the Clifton side.'

'It was me.'

Bella stared at me in astonishment. 'You?'

'Yes. But I was at Lord's all day. With Simon. She told my secretary she'd call back.'

'Oh, perfect! Our last chance of saving her blown. Because you go to bloody Lord's and get pissed with Simon. That really is wonderful.'

'For God's sake, I wasn't to know.' If blame was to be distributed, I didn't mean to take more than my share. 'Sarah swore me to silence about Rowena's overdose. And *your husband* pleaded with me to say nothing to her about *Benefit of the Doubt.* Maybe if you'd tried to understand her misgivings before the trial; maybe if you'd trusted her just a—'

'Keith didn't plead with you to give Seymour an interview. Or to pour out some psycho-babble to the wretched man about Louise's state of mind the day she died.'

'No, but—'

'And since you seem to be trying to shuffle off responsibility for what's happened, I may as well mention something I was intending to spare you. But it makes more sense now you've admitted it was you she rang, so you may as well know. When Sarah got back to her flat, the TV was still on. With the *Benefit of the Doubt* video freeze-framed on the interview with you. So now you know why she wanted to speak to you, don't you?'

'To ask which version was the truth,' I murmured in reply, as much to myself as to Bella. 'The one I told at the trial. Or the one I hinted at in the interview. The one she forced herself to believe. Or the one she could never quite forget.'

'And what would you have told her?'

'I don't know. I'm not sure of the answer any more. I suppose I never was.'

Bella sat down again, stabbed out her cigarette and glared across at me. 'Why couldn't you just leave it alone, Robin, eh? She was getting over it. They all were. Keith's been so happy recently. Really enjoying his retirement. And now . . .'

'I'm sorry, Bella. Sorry for everything. But even if I'd done and said nothing, Bantock would still have written his book. Seymour would still have made his programme. The questions – and the doubts – would still have been raised.'

'And maybe Rowena could have borne them. But for your intervention. Have you considered that?'

'Yes. I've considered it. Kind of you to point it out, though.'

Bella plucked off her sunglasses and stared at me. I think she may have felt she'd gone too far. But a softening of her tone was the only concession she offered. 'Keith, Sarah and Paul are going to need all my help to recover from this. It's like a blow to an unhealed wound. I have to think of them before anyone else.'

'I understand that.'

'I'm not sure exactly when the funeral's going to be, but I think it would be best if you left them alone until it's out of the way, don't you? Until it's *well* out of the way.'

I'd expected it, of course. This exile from their company as well as their affections. I'd brought it on myself. Yet it still hurt. 'You'll let me know when and where? I'd like to . . . send some flowers.'

'I'll let you know.'

'If there's anything—'

'There is, as a matter of fact.'

'What?'

'Speak to Sophie Marsden. Find out what the hell she meant by saying those things to Seymour. It's eating Keith up. The fear that there was some truth in it. I doubt there was, personally. Louise was no good-time girl. Not according to everybody I've spoken to about her. In which case, I'd like to know why Sophie Marsden chose to depict her as one. Keith looked on Sophie as a friend. Her behaviour's shocked him even more than yours.'

'What makes you think she'll open her heart to me?'

'You're on her side, aren't you?'

'Of course not. There are no—'

'Besides, I wouldn't trust myself in her presence. I need an intermediary. If you want to repair some of the damage you've done . . .'

'All right. I'll be your messenger boy.' My reluctance was mostly show. I wanted to prise Sophie's motives out of her as much as Bella did, if not more so. Our one brief meeting at Rowena's wedding had left me with the strange and disturbing impression that she knew something about me that I didn't even know myself. It was high time I found out what it was.

Bella had given me Sophie's phone number. I tried it as soon as I got home. But Sophie was out, according to her husband.

'You're not another of these bloody journalists, are you?'

'No. More like another victim of them.'

'I'll tell her you called, in that case.'

There was something faintly familiar in his mournful voice. I could almost have believed I'd spoken to him before. But when would I have crossed paths with somebody in the agricultural machinery business? Never seemed the likeliest answer.

No less than five hours later, rousing me from drink-deepened slumber, Sophie called back. She didn't sound in the least drowsy, even though the hall clock had struck one as I stumbled to the phone. Nor, to my fuddled surprise, did she seem at all reluctant to meet.

'I think we probably should, don't you? In the circumstances.'

'Well, obviously I do. But—'

'Would London suit you? We have a small flat in Bayswater. I'm thinking of going down there for a few days next week. The summer sales may cheer me up. I've felt quite awful since the news about Rowena.' The idea that a spendthrift spin round Harrods could reconcile her to the needless extinction of a young girl's life disgusted me more keenly than for the moment my tired brain could grasp. 'Why not come to tea on Tuesday?'

'All right. Where do you—'

'Six, Godolphin Terrace. I'll expect you about three thirty.'

'OK. I—'

'See you then. 'Bye.'

By the time I got back to bed, I was alert and fully awake. Had she delayed her call until her husband was asleep, I wondered? If so, why should she want to keep our appointment secret? Anyone would think it was an illicit *liaison.* And why – yes why – was she not just willing but eager for us to meet?

Such thoughts pushed sleep effortlessly aside and left me to toss and turn through the brief summer's night, tracing and retracing in my mind the sequence of events leading from Louise Paxton's murder to her daughter's suicide. Rowena's self-destruction was in some senses the more awful death. She was so fragile, so vulnerable, so patently in need of protection. There should have been some way to save her. There should have been and probably there had been. But it had been neglected, over-ridden in the pursuit of other claims, other fleeting impulses. By me among others. And what did the others really matter when I closed my eyes and saw, in images I couldn't suppress, that slender figure falling from the bridge, arms outstretched, with a diary left behind her on a call-box shelf and my face blurred and flickering on a television screen?

Dawn was only a few hours away. When it came, I was already washed and dressed. The idea of spending a solitary Sunday lying low at Greenhayes wasn't just intolerable. It was quite simply inconceivable. Bella had told me to leave them alone and so I would. The living, that is. But nobody could stop me going in search of the dead. I'd stood in the room where Louise had been murdered. Now I had to stand on the bridge from which Rowena had leapt. It wasn't a matter of choice. It was something I had to do.

Clifton was still and quiet as the grave so early on a Sunday morning. But the sun was already warm on my back as I walked up Sion Hill and risked a glance along Caledonia Place. A milk float was humming towards me from the far end. I watched as it chinked to a stop near Sarah's door and wondered, if I waited, whether I'd see her come out to collect a bottle. She'd be awake, I had no doubt. She wouldn't have slept any better than me. But at the thought of what might happen if she spotted me, I pressed on.

Now I was probably retracing Rowena's footsteps of three days before. Following the curve of Sion Hill, with the suspension bridge dominating the view to my left. The hangers looked no thicker than twine from this distance. And the depth of the gorge wasn't apparent. It could have been a footbridge across a shallow stream. Except I knew it wasn't.

A path led up across a broad grass bank to the bridge road. As I turned onto the pavement, all possible routes converged. For there, ahead of me, was the call-box Rowena had used. I paused beside it and pulled the door open. I don't know why, really. There was nothing to distinguish it from a thousand others. The phone. The printed instructions. The rank smell. The sundry graffiti. And an empty shelf.

I moved on. Past the control-box and the toll barriers. Round the giant left foot of the pylon. And out onto the bridge. The railings were about five feet high, fenced in with flimsy mesh and topped with blunt wooden spikes. No real obstacle for the desperate or the determined. And Rowena must have been both that day. They said she'd jumped from the centre. I glanced ahead and behind as I went to make sure I knew when I'd reached the point where she must have stopped. When I had, I stopped too. And looked down for the first time.

So far. So awesomely far. Sunlight twinkled benignly on the winding river and gilded the fat wrinkled mud-banks. The Bristol to Avonmouth main road hugged the eastern side of the river and the height I was above it sowed a fleeting illusion in my mind. That it and the few cars moving along it were toys I'd laid out on my bedroom floor as a child. Toys I could pick up or dismantle at will. Then the huge gap of empty air rushed into my consciousness and I stepped back, appalled. Good God almighty. What a thing to do. What an act to have not just the wish but the courage to carry out. To find a foothold and climb onto the railings. And then what? Leap from there? Or lower yourself down until your toes were resting on the narrow sill at the foot of the railings, then turn round and let yourself fall? The deliberation. The decision. And the deed. All reversible. All nullifiable. Until the fraction of a second after letting go, when wind and gravity plucked your freedom away. And your life had only that long plummeting moment to last.

Why had she done it? Standing there in the centre of the bridge, I felt a wave of nausea sweep over me. I stared up into the sky until it had passed. Then I looked down again. And knew. It wasn't the lies we'd told you, was it, Rowena? It wasn't the thought that we'd implicated you in a possible miscarriage of justice. Nor the fear that you'd never known your mother for what she truly was. It was none of those things. Not in the end. Not when you came to the point of no return. '*She was on the brink*,' you'd said of her. '*She was about to step off.*' I remembered now. '*Into the void.*' Your words. '*She knew it.*'

Your every word. *'And still she stepped.'* You had to know, didn't you? You had to find out. *'Why?'* I couldn't tell you. Nobody could. You knew that. And, watching the video, you must have realized it would never be any different. Unless you followed her. Unless you surrendered to the impulse you'd tried to bury. *'The thought of it can be so exhilarating.'* Yes. Of course. *'So tempting.'* And so very very final.

It was mid-morning before I left Bristol. I drove slowly, hardly knowing whether it was better to stay or to go. Somewhere near Warminster, I turned on the radio and found myself listening to the cricket commentary from Lord's. The Test Match was still going on. When it had started, I'd actually been quite interested in the outcome. But Rowena had been alive then. Now it seemed like a transmission from another planet. There were tears filling my eyes as I stabbed the 'off' switch. And there was comfort in the silence that followed.

Tuesday came. And with it my appointment in London. After putting in a desultory morning at work, I walked to the station and caught a lunchtime train to Waterloo. Then I took the long way round the Circle line to Bayswater and tracked down Godolphin Terrace.

It turned out to look less grand than it sounded. The houses had all the traditional touches: four stuccoed storeys plus attic and basement, complete with pillared porch and dolphin door-knocker. But some were beginning to look dilapidated. One or two would be ripe for squatters if the residents didn't watch out. Though Sophie Marsden, I felt sure, could be relied on to do that.

Number 6 was in good order, brasswork polished, paint gleaming. When I rang Sophie's bell, she answered promptly.

'Robin?'

'Yes.'

'Push when you hear the buzzer. I'm on the second floor.'

I was in. And when I reached the second landing, she was waiting at her door. Newly coiffured, I reckoned, though presumably not for my benefit. But her close-fitting dress made me think, as I followed her into a tastefully furnished lounge, that I might be wrong. Perhaps flirtation was to be her counter to whatever line she expected me to take. If so, I didn't propose to let it work.

'There's tea, of course. But I fancy a gin and tonic myself. You?'

'All right.'

I moved to the window while she poured them and gazed down into the street. Sooner than I'd anticipated, she was at my elbow, glass in hand, smiling enigmatically. 'Afraid someone might be following you, Robin?'

'No. Of course not.'

'Here's your drink. Let's sit down.'

A sofa and two armchairs were arranged around a low table in front of a huge marbled fireplace, an aspidistra in a copper pot filling the grate. A mass of gold-edged invitations crowded out the bric-à-brac on the mantelpiece, above which hung a gloomy oil painting of what looked like the Tower of Babel. Sophie took one end of the sofa and patted the cushion of the adjacent armchair. I sat down and sipped at my drink, resisting a powerful urge to take several large gulps. Then I noticed the Bantock hanging on the wall facing me. As I'd been intended to, of course. A Madonna and child. Or an old woman with a doll. It was hard to tell.

'What's your opinion of Expressionism, Robin?'

'I'm really not qualified to—'

'We're all qualified, surely. To judge whether something's good or bad. Right or wrong. I've never been entirely sold on Oscar's work myself.'

'Then why—'

'As an investment. Louise was the enthusiast. I trusted her taste. And it's paid off. Though ironically only because Oscar's dead. And Louise with him.'

'Sophie, I didn't come here to—'

'Discuss art? No. I suppose not.' She jiggled the ice in her glass and took rather more than a sip. 'Ah, I needed that.' She smiled. 'The first taste is always the best, isn't it? Of everything.'

'Why did you say what you did to Seymour?'

'You believe in coming to the point, don't you? Is that what— Well, we'll come back to that later, I expect.'

'Come back to what?' She was playing the same game with me she'd started in Sapperton. The same cat-and-mouse progression towards a meaning we never quite reached. And the resemblance to Louise was growing again. Or I was noticing it more. But perhaps resemblance wasn't the right word. It was more an imitation. An expert recreation of parts of her she knew I'd recognize. The soft voice. The toss of the head. The balancing on the brink.

'I was shocked to hear about Rowena. A young life snuffed

out. So tragic. I always envied Louise her children, never having had any myself. But I suppose they bring as much grief as joy. How is Keith bearing up?'

'I haven't seen him. Or Sarah. Or Paul.'

'Ah. Giving them a wide berth, are you? I quite understand. I thought I ought to do the same. In the circumstances.'

'I've spoken to Bella.'

'Of course. Your sister-in-law. Lady Paxton, I should say. Though the name doesn't quite fit, does it?'

'She tells me they're all extremely upset. As you'd expect. And they hold you and me to blame for what's happened. As you'd also expect.'

'So we're in the same boat, then.'

'In a sense.'

'Mmm.' She leant back and stared up thoughtfully at the ceiling. 'In that case, why don't *you* tell *me* why you cooperated with the charming Mr Seymour.'

'To stop him harassing Rowena.'

'You think he meant to?'

'I don't know. It was an effective lever of persuasion, though. And once he'd got me talking, he knew a little creative editing would do the rest.'

'That's your cover story, is it?'

'It happens to be—'

'Come on, Robin. Nobody's going to swallow it, least of all me. Neither of us thought Rowena would be so . . . drastic. So . . . extreme. It wasn't our fault.'

'Wasn't it?'

'No. So let's stop pretending we were set up by Seymour. Even the papers seem to have given up portraying him as the villain of the piece. We both knew exactly what we were doing. And why.'

'Maybe. But I doubt our reasons were the same.'

'Really? I'd have said they were identical. You've never believed the official account of Louise's death. And you were hoping Seymour might be able to cast enough doubt on it to make others share your disbelief. So you decided to give him a little help. That's all.'

'Are you saying . . . that's why you . . .'

'Of course. If I'd known you thought the same way—'

'But I don't. I don't think the same way at all.'

'Yes you do. You must do. Otherwise you wouldn't have given Seymour an interview.'

'No. You're wrong. That's not why I did it.'

She leant close to me across the arm of the sofa, lowering her voice as if to whisper a secret. 'I'm glad we're on the same side, Robin. I reckon we both need an ally. A friend we can turn to. I was very much afraid you were in on it. I can't tell you what a relief it is to know you weren't.'

'In on what?'

'I can see now I made too much of your . . . economy with the facts. But there was always a simpler explanation for that, wasn't there? Some girlfriend you wanted to protect. Some fiancée, perhaps. Has she fallen by the wayside since? Is that why you've risked putting your head above the parapet?'

'I don't know what you're talking about.'

'Yes you do. But have it your own way. I don't want to force you to admit anything.' She reached slowly out and traced a circle with her index finger on the back of my hand where it rested on the arm of the chair. 'Or to do anything. Unless you want to. Unless we both want to.'

I looked into her eyes and realized with a shock of sudden desire that we both wanted what was still – but only just – avertible. The reasons were sick and wrong. There'd be a third party to anything that happened. A rival. A substitute. A silent observer. And yet—

'Louise is gone, Robin. But you don't need to let go of her completely. People always said how alike we were.' I believed her. Even more than I wanted to believe her. The ghost I was chasing made flesh. Warm and close. The hem of the dress sliding up her thigh as she leant forward. The white lace bra glimpsed through its buttons. As once before. Pursuit, denial and temptation. Joined. 'In so many ways.'

She kissed me slowly and deliberately, giving me ample time to recoil, but sensing I wouldn't. Her eyes were closed at first. When they opened, I looked into them and knew we both meant to play this game to the end. From cool formality to burning intimacy. From lust to consummation.

And so we did. With eager abandon as she stretched like a cat beneath me across the hearthrug. And later, in the bed she led me to, again and again, with measured delight, as the sunlight mellowed and lengthened and passion curdled towards excess. As the afternoon faded towards evening and *her* urgings became *my* desires. I found her out in all her ways and wiles; her pains and her pleasures. What she wanted and how she wanted it, explored and refined with the heightened sense only long denial can breed. Mine *and* hers. From brutality to tenderness. And back again. Some of the way. But not quite all.

'What are you thinking, Robin?' she asked when the frenzy was finally spent and we lay motionless together, drained by what we'd done. 'Are you shocked? That a middle-aged married woman should be capable of such depravity?'

'No,' I murmured in reply. And it was true. Sophie hadn't shocked me. Nor had the things she'd let me do to her. Our shared and savoured spasms meant nothing. Compared with the dangerous fantasies that had coiled themselves around every moment of release – and all the moments after.

'My husband is my husband in name only, you know,' she went on, heedless of the ambiguity of my denial. 'We haven't made love in years. And even when we did . . .'

'Is there somebody else?'

'No. Nobody else. Not any more, anyway. Just as there isn't for you, is there? Nobody. Not a single person who can replace her.'

'I don't understand you.' It wasn't quite true, of course. I seemed to understand her only too well. As she did me. And there was the rub. She shouldn't have been able to. She shouldn't have been capable of prying so deeply and accurately into my thoughts. And yet she was. 'What do you mean, Sophie? What do you think you know about me and Louise?'

'We were each other's oldest friend, Robin. We were bound to share our secrets, even if we didn't intend to. Call it intuition if you like, though it was far more than that. She as good as told me who you were.'

'Told you? About me? You're crazy. How could she? She was dead within hours of our only meeting.'

Sophie chuckled. 'You can drop the pretence with me. After what we've done, I think you should, don't you? Louise meant to leave Keith. I know she did. I heard it from her own lips a few weeks before she died. She was going to leave him that summer. Quite possibly that very day. She was going to meet you in Kington, wasn't she? And you were going to carry her off.' She must have seen the stupefaction in my face. But what she read it as I can't imagine. 'What went wrong? Did you argue? Did you have second thoughts? You may as well tell me. Why didn't she leave with you?'

'Because we'd never met before. Because we were strangers.'

'Come on. She confessed to me. She talked to me about the man in her life. The one she'd met on Hergest Ridge that spring.

Mid-March, wasn't it? Just after Oscar's exhibition in Cambridge. So she said, anyway. And perhaps you know what else she said. Is that why you said you were strangers? Did she call you that to your face?'

'Call me what?' The grotesque fallacy at the heart of Sophie's reasoning no longer mattered as much as the need to hear it through to the end.

'"My perfect stranger." Her exact words. Her description. Of you.'

A long moment of silence followed in which time and my own thoughts seemed to stand still. It wasn't possible. It made no sense. It was pure madness to leave the idea unrefuted even for a second. Yet I did. And, for as long as that, I almost believed it myself.

'Don't worry. Nobody else knows. Only me.'

'Sophie—'

'Don't deny it. Don't underestimate me to the extent of thinking you *can* deny it.'

'But I have to. It isn't true.'

'She couldn't have made it up. The coincidence would have been too great. The man she met on Hergest Ridge and fell in love with was you. She never named you, of course. I wouldn't have expected her to. But what she did tell me was enough for me to suspect you the very first time we met. And after your interview with Seymour . . . I was certain.'

'You're wrong.'

'No. Why else should you still be trying to avenge her? Why – unless you loved her?'

'I didn't love her. I never had the chance.'

'That's not what Louise said.'

'What did she say, then? Tell me. Precisely.'

'All right. If that's what it'll take to convince you. I've nothing to hide. Louise and I went to a health farm near Malvern for a few days in the middle of June that year. It was a place we'd often used before. Somewhere we could relax and get into shape. Sarah's graduation ceremony was coming up and Louise wanted to look her best for it. Well, that was her story. But there was a glint in her eye I knew had nothing to do with her daughter's academic achievements. The last night we were there, she admitted she had a lover. A man she'd met by chance on Hergest Ridge. She'd gone to Kington to return some of Oscar's pictures after the exhibition in Cambridge. Oscar wasn't in. So she left the pictures in his studio and drove up to Hergest Ridge for a walk.

The weather was unusually warm for March. She wanted a breath of fresh air. You were there for the same reason. I suppose.'

'It wasn't me.'

'Whoever. She met him on the ridge. They fell into conversation. They left together. He took her to a hotel near Hereford. They stayed overnight. She told Keith she was staying with me. The same story she used in July. But a lie on both occasions. Instead . . . Well, you know what happened instead far better than I do. A one-night stand that turned into a passionate love affair. So passionate she was already determined to leave Keith when she told me about it. I'd never seen her that way before. So . . . overwhelmed. So . . . carried away. She was losing control. And control was what she'd always had in abundance. But not in those last weeks. Thanks to you.'

'Not me. Somebody else. If what you're saying is true.'

'You know it's true. And you know it's not somebody else. You can't forget her, can you? That's why you've stayed in touch with her family. Why you helped Seymour stir up interest in the case. Why you came here this afternoon. Why what we did was so . . .' We stared at each other, her belief and mine meeting but never joining. She wasn't lying. Louise had told her what she'd just told me. In every particular. 'I've worked it out, Robin. I've lain in wait and now I've found you. It has to be you. There's nobody else it can be. She was the love of your life. Wasn't she?'

I hardly remember now how I left the flat. Everything is clear in my mind. What we did. What we said. Except at the end. I was too confused by then to concentrate, too taken aback by Sophie's misapprehension to construct a response to it, let alone a rebuttal. She must have expected me to tell her everything. She must have hoped I'd share my secrets with her as I'd shared my desires. But her reasoning was as sound as her conclusion was false. There was nothing I could tell her. Beyond what she'd already refused to believe. And there was nothing I could tell myself. To stop the indefinable fears she'd planted in my mind growing and taking shape. Sophie was wrong. But in so many ways – too many to shake off or disregard – she was right. They'd met – as we'd met – on Hergest Ridge. By pure chance. As perfect strangers. Louise – and somebody else. Who was he? Who could he be? If not me?

'You can stay . . . if you like.'

'No. I must go.'

'When will we meet again?'

'I don't know. I'm not sure. I'm not . . . sure of anything.'

I fell asleep on the train and relived the afternoon in my dreams. Closing my eyes to forget, I only saw more clearly. Sophie and me. Every action. Every detail. Seen again, as if by an invisible observer.

It was dark when I reached Petersfield. A cool still night after the breathless day. I walked round to the factory, where I'd left my car. I was tired now, too weary to think it through any more. The answer would have to wait. At least until tomorrow.

My car was the only one left in the yard. It was on the far side, near the drying shed, an open-sided structure where the newly delivered clefts of willow were stacked and left to sweat out the last of their sap before they were moulded into blades. A security light came on as I approached, dazzling me for a moment. I shielded my eyes and went on to the car, fumbling in my pocket for the keys. As I rounded the boot and my vision adjusted to the glare, I looked up. To see a man standing a few yards ahead of me, silhouetted against the light. He stood quite still, his arms folded in front of him. He seemed to be waiting for something. Or for someone. Only when he spoke did I realize who he was.

'You've been a long time.'

'Paul?'

'But it doesn't matter. I'd have stayed as long as I had to.'

'What . . . what are you doing here?'

'I've come to speak to you.'

'But . . . we could have . . .'

'Worked something out? I don't think so. Maybe before. But not now. I had some news today, you see. About Rowena.'

'Rowena?'

'She was pregnant.'

'What?'

'Two months pregnant. She'd known for some time. Her doctor seemed surprised she hadn't told me. Well, maybe she was planning to make a special announcement. It's the anniversary of our engagement later this week. Maybe she was leaving it until then. We'll never know now, will we?'

'Paul, I—'

'We'll never know because you and that bitch Sophie Marsden did for her between you with your poisoned words and your evil little insinuations. Didn't you?'

'Look, I'm sorry for what happened. Sorrier than I can say. But I never—'

'I don't want your sorrow!' He was shouting now, his voice rising in a cracked crescendo, his arms swinging free. I suddenly saw he was holding a bat cleft in his hands, raising it like a club as he advanced towards me. 'I don't want anything from you!'

Before I could even turn to run he was on me, the cleft slamming into my midriff. I doubled up and fell back against the car door. He aimed a blow at my head which I managed to parry with my forearm, then another I barely beat off. I tried to rise, knowing I had to get past him if I was to stand a chance. But he saw me coming and shoulder-barged me to the ground. I sprawled across the tarmac and scrambled onto all fours. I remember trying to push myself upright as the first of the pain lanced through the shock. I remember seeing him out of the corner of my eyes, behind and above me. I even remember the whistle of the cleft through the air as it sliced down towards me. Then nothing. The night swallowed me whole. As if I'd never been.

CHAPTER TWELVE

Apparently I was conscious when the ambulance reached the scene. I don't remember it myself. Nor much else that night beyond a succession of blurred faces staring down at me and the unique disinfected smell of a hospital ward. I pieced together what had happened the following morning from the jumble of my own recollections and the puzzled questions of a staff nurse. The shock of seeing me lying stunned on the ground with blood oozing from my mouth and cheek must have stopped Paul in his tracks. Frightened by what he'd done, he rushed round to his car in Frenchman's Road and called an ambulance. He waited with me until it arrived, saw me aboard and promised to follow me to the hospital. But he didn't turn up. He hadn't been seen since. And nobody knew who he was.

I decided from the outset to play dumb. The tragedy I'd helped create would only be worsened and prolonged by Paul being charged with assault and battery. I didn't feel as if I was being a hero or a martyr. I didn't even feel I was doing Paul a favour. It just seemed the least painful way out for all of us. Shielded from the police on medical orders until the middle of the following day, I rehearsed a suitable story, then trotted it out to a gullible detective constable. I'd returned late from London, surprised somebody I took to be a burglar skulking around the factory and been beaten up for my pains. Since it had been pitch dark, I couldn't begin to describe my assailant. Nor, come to that, the Good Samaritan who'd found me and dialled 999. I was a victim of the rising crime rate who warranted nothing more than an obscure place in constabulary statistics.

Physically, I wasn't in bad shape. A broken rib, a fractured cheek-bone, two loose teeth, sundry cuts and bruises; and what the doctor called a 'straightforward' case of concussion. But that alone necessitated twenty-four hours of rest and observation. Which, in the end, turned out to be nearer forty-eight. Rushed in on Tuesday night, I wasn't released until Friday morning.

Jennifer, Simon, Adrian and Uncle Larry all trooped in to see me, plying me with fruit, magazines and sympathy. Adrian was full of plans to improve security at the factory and left me with the brochures of a couple of guard-dog patrol companies to leaf through. He even suggested I might like to convalesce at his house. Thankfully, he interpreted my refusal as a reflection of my independent spirit. This spared me the need to explain why a few days spent under the same roof as Wendy and the children – not to mention the dogs – would probably see me readmitted to hospital suffering from nervous exhaustion.

I heard nothing from Bella and assumed she didn't know of the incident. There was really no reason why she should, unless Paul had decided to come clean. And even if he had, who was going to blame him for what he'd done? He had a child now as well as a wife to mourn. Just as Sir Keith had lost a grandchild along with a daughter. The grief had spread like a stain across three generations. And I couldn't redeem or reduce it with a few broken bones.

I knew I'd hear from Bella eventually, of course. She'd be expecting me to report the outcome of my meeting with Sophie. But the longer that could be postponed the better. I felt as if I genuinely needed a spell of rest and recuperation before confronting her with whatever lies I decided to substitute for a truth even she would have found shocking. As for Sophie herself, each hour that passed made what we'd done seem not merely more remote but more unimaginable.

My dilemma hadn't diminished by Friday morning, when Jennifer came to collect me and drive me home. Indeed, it was because of it that I jumped to a false conclusion when, halfway up the A3 towards Petersfield, she suddenly said: 'Guess who was asking after you yesterday.'

'Bella?'

'No. Her stepdaughter. Sarah Paxton. She'd heard you were in hospital and—'

'How did she hear?'

'She didn't say. Does it matter?'

It mattered a good deal. But for reasons I was in no position to explain. 'Er . . . I suppose not.'

'Well, she seemed genuinely concerned about you. Quite touching really, in view of her recent bereavement and . . . well . . . how easy it would be for her to hold you at least partly to blame for her sister's suicide.'

'As I'm sure she does.'

'You could be wrong. She's going to look in on you at Greenhayes over the weekend, apparently. Check you're all right. She said she was going to be in Hindhead anyway and it'd be no trouble, but, you know, it sounded to me as if she might be making a special trip. Just to see you. *Very* solicitous, I'd say. There isn't something you want to tell me about the two of you, is there?'

'Nothing you want to hear, Jenny. Believe me.'

She arrived on Saturday afternoon. It was another in a succession of hot airless days. I was in the garden, dozing in a deckchair after too many cold beers, when I heard a car turn in from the lane. She must have guessed where I'd be, because, without pausing to try the doorbell, she walked straight round from the front of the house. I'd struggled to my feet by then and composed something close to a smile to greet her. But she wasn't smiling. She stopped as soon as she saw me and gazed at me expressionlessly. Only then, after a few seconds of deliberation, did she come closer.

'Hello, Robin.' Still there was no smile. And even the formal kiss she'd normally have bestowed was banished. She was wearing a straw hat, dark glasses she showed no sign of removing, an outsize white shirt over pale blue trousers and sandals. And she was carrying a video cassette in her hand. I didn't have to see the label on the cardboard case to know what it was.

'Hello, Sarah. I . . .'

'You look as if you've been through the mill.'

'A spot of bother at the factory. Did Jenny tell you how it happened?'

'She didn't need to. Paul told me.'

'Ah. I see.'

'He's been expecting to hear from the police. But I gather you've covered his tracks for him.'

'Well . . .' I shrugged. 'I don't think any useful purpose would have been served by bringing a complaint against him. Do you?'

'No. But it was good of you, even so.'

'Not really. Not after everything else.'

'Daddy doesn't know. Nor Bella. There seemed no point telling them.'

'About me, you mean? Or about . . .'

'About you.' She stretched out her hand, offering the video to me. I had the strange impression that if I didn't take it from her straightaway she'd drop it on the grass between us. I took it. 'They know about the baby, of course. Daddy's reacted badly. Paul too, I suppose. But he keeps his feelings bottled up. What happened with you . . . the loss of control . . . was unusual. Unprecedented in my experience.'

'I don't blame him.'

'Neither do I. But . . . on his behalf . . . and for Rowena's sake . . . thank you for not taking it further.'

Silence and distance crystallized in the still air. Her mouth didn't so much as quiver. And what there might be in her eyes to reveal her real opinion of me I couldn't see. 'Would you . . . like a drink?'

'No. I can't stay.'

'Not even for a few minutes?'

'What would be the point?'

'I don't know. I just . . .'

'Why did you say those things to Seymour, Robin? I'd like to know that much at least. I really would.' Even if her face remained a mask, her voice had now, at last, betrayed a hint of emotion. 'I mean, after making us think of you as a friend, after assuring us of your best intentions . . . After all that. Why?'

'What I said was true.'

'And that excuses everything, does it? That makes Rowena's death worthwhile?'

'No. Of course it doesn't.'

'What about Sophie? I gathered from Bella you'd undertaken to find out what she thought her few minutes of character assassination were likely to achieve. I can't believe *she* pretends to have been speaking the truth.'

'She does, as a matter of fact.'

'I see.' Sarah sighed and gazed past me up at the hills behind the house, their wooded slopes shimmering in the heat. 'Good old Sophie.'

'Sarah—' She looked round at me, daring me, I sensed, to make some attempt at mitigation or apology, almost craving the opportunity to reject whichever I offered. But I knew better than to try. Whatever blame attached to me for Rowena's death I meant to accept. It was my secret act of mourning. But blame for something even worse than a despairing dive from Clifton Suspension Bridge hovered at the margins of my thoughts. Which Sarah might just be able to help me corner at last. 'Sophie claims your mother told her a few weeks before her death that she was planning to leave your father.' No reaction. No response. Just the same blank grief-sapped stare. 'You once told me something similar yourself. As a theory. As a suspicion you'd formed. Sophie seemed rather more definite.'

'Did she?'

'But she didn't know who your mother was planning to leave your father *for*. Who the man in her life was. Nor did you, as I recall.'

'Why does there have to have been a man?'

'No reason, I suppose. Except . . . Lying in hospital most of this week's given me time to think. And to remember. Ten days after the murders, I drove up to Kington with Bella. We had lunch with Henley Bantock. He told you about it. You said so when you wrote to me in Brussels. You'd been there the same day.'

'What of it?'

'So had somebody else. He nearly drove into Bella and me in Butterbur Lane. Did Henley mention him to you? He did to us.'

'I don't think so. Why?'

'Because the driver of the car was obviously extremely upset. He might have been . . . well, he could have been . . .'

'The man in Mummy's life?'

'Well, he could, couldn't he?'

'Yes. I suppose he could. So, who was he?'

'I don't know. But it occurred to me you might. If I described him. As a friend or acquaintance of your mother. Of your father too, perhaps. A neighbour. A colleague. An art collector. Something like that. He was – let's see – a chap in his fifties, with thick silver-grey hair. Round face. Chubby. Well, more flabby really. As if he'd lost weight recently. Of course, it was only—' I stopped. Sarah's lips had parted in surprise. She plucked off her dark glasses and stared at me intently. 'You know him?'

'Maybe. What sort of car was he driving?'

'A Volvo estate.'

'Colour?'

'Maroon.'

'It has to be, then.'

'You *do* know him?'

'Yes. I think I do. But it can't be. Not really. Not him and Mummy.'

'Who is he?'

'I'm surprised neither you nor Bella's met him. But I suppose there's no reason why you should have. He didn't come to Rowena's wedding. Or to Mummy's funeral. That seemed odd at the time. Disrespectful almost. Even though you could say he was represented by Sophie. But perhaps he was afraid of—'

'What do you mean by *represented*?'

'She's married to him, Robin. The man you've described is Howard Marsden. Sophie's husband. To the life.'

It became clear to me in an instant. As if I'd crept into a darkened room and stumbled around in the gloom, navigating by touch and guesswork. Only for the light to be suddenly switched on. And for me to find myself not where I thought at all. Howard Marsden. Sophie's husband. And Louise's lover. Yes, of course. It made sense. Sophie must have known all along. So now she was taking her revenge. On Louise by tarnishing her reputation to the best of her ability. And on Howard by cuckolding him at the first opportunity. If I *was* the first. Her story about the 'perfect stranger'; her claim to believe I was the man in question; her expression of doubt about Naylor's guilt: all were artful pretences designed with a particular purpose in mind. And I didn't flatter myself that my seduction was it. No, no. Sophie was playing a deeper game, in which her husband's total humiliation was the goal. He couldn't object to her infidelity without being told that what was sauce for the gander . . .

'So that's why Sophie wants to hurt us,' murmured Sarah.

'Looks like it.'

'Oh God. What a mess.'

'I don't suppose she meant to harm Rowena. Your mother's good name was what she wanted to—'

'But you can't pick and choose when you start this sort of thing. You can't be sure of all the consequences.'

'No. As Rowena once told me, there are too many variables in life to predict any outcome with precision.'

Sarah shook her head and rubbed the sides of her nose where the dark glasses had been resting. She looked suddenly tired. 'Can I sit down, Robin? I think I would like a drink after all.'

I fetched another chair as well as a drink and we sat there in the garden together for an hour or more as the heat of afternoon turned towards the cool of evening. Our mutual dismay had lowered our defences. Allowing, if not a reconciliation between us, at least a *rapprochement.* As Sarah admitted, she'd made her own misjudgements. By trying to keep Rowena insulated from reality. By failing to foresee what she'd do if she found out she'd been deceived. The irony was that, even if I'd not given Sarah the video, she'd probably have recorded the programme herself while she was out with Paul and Rowena. Rowena had simply read her sister's mind more acutely than she'd been given credit for.

As for the act of suicide itself, maybe that didn't have the clear and simple motive it had comforted Sarah to believe. Why had Rowena not told Paul she was pregnant? Why had she seemed so depressed? Because motherhood wasn't necessarily the future she had in her sights? Yet it had been going to arrive whether she liked it or not. Until the shock of her mother's rewritten past had given her a way out. And she'd yielded to temptation.

'I wonder if that's why Paul lashed out at you. Because he's afraid that might be the truth of it. He won't admit it, of course. I wouldn't ask him to. But I think it may be there, even so.'

'How is he now?'

'Subdued. Self-controlled. A little remorseful, I think. A little ashamed of what he did. But don't expect an apology. Or any kind of thanks for not preferring charges. It isn't in his nature.'

'Will you tell him about Howard Marsden?'

'Oh yes. If Rowena's death has taught me anything, it's the danger of secrecy.'

'And your father?'

'He may already know. He may always have known. Maybe it's what was in the note he destroyed.'

'But if not?'

'I'll leave Bella to solve the problem. Isn't that what step-mothers are for?'

'Will you let Sophie know we've found out?'

'Only if she asks. Which is unlikely, since I don't intend to seek her company. Or her husband's.'

'What sort of a man is he?'

'Well, there's another irony. Cautious and conventional sums him up. Rather dull, I'd always thought. Not at all Mummy's type. So I'd have said, anyway. But what would I know? More and more, my mother seems like a stranger to me. Or an impostor. Somebody who was never what she came across as. But what she really was . . . I've no idea.'

'You're not saying you believe Naylor may be innocent?'

'Oh no. That's the worst of this. The very worst. Seymour and his kind will go on pressing for that bastard's release. And Rowena's suicide will only help them. They'll say she had a guilty conscience, won't they? They'll say it was her way of avoiding the truth.'

'Surely not.'

'I'm afraid so. The bandwagon's only just started rolling. There'll be more books. More programmes. More articles. There'll be a committee formed before long to coordinate the campaign for his release. Questions will be asked in the House. Pressure will mount for a re-trial. Or a reference to the Appeal Court at the very least. And they'll never stop. They'll never be satisfied. Until the day Naylor walks out of the Royal Courts of Justice a free man and is carried away down the Strand in the arms of his adoring supporters.'

'I can't believe that.'

'You'd better. Because it'll happen. Eventually. Inevitably. Whether we like it or not. There's nothing we can do to stop it. We can only . . .'

'Yes?'

'Lead our lives, Robin. What else?'

There was nothing else. No corner to turn. No redoubt to defend. No stand to take. Sarah would go on with her life. And so would I. When she drove away from Greenhayes that evening, I sensed it was a final parting whatever the technicalities of time and chance might subsequently dictate. She was heading into her future. And into my past.

I went down to the Cricketers after she'd gone and drank so much I had to be driven the short distance home by the landlord. And though I woke next morning with a thick head, my prospects were clearer in my mind than they'd been for weeks. If Bushranger Sports took over Timariot & Small, I'd quit before they could sack me and return to Brussels at the expiry of my *congé*. I'd turn my back on a disastrous diversion in my career. I'd give up chasing shadows and revert to the pursuit of wealth and leisure. I'd bid Louise Paxton an overdue farewell. I'd walk away. And forget. Even though

> Those two words shut a door
> Between me and the blessed rain
> That was never shut before
> And will not open again.

* * *

Rowena was buried in Sapperton on Monday the twenty-eighth of June. I stayed in Petersfield, putting in a gingerly half-day at the factory to keep myself occupied. But the media weren't about to let me off the hook. That night, on the television news, there was a filmed report from outside St Kenelm's Church, hymn-singing audible above the commentary. '*As speculation mounts that Rowena Bryant killed herself rather than face the thought that her testimony helped convict an innocent man, a spokesman for West Mercia Police insisted they had no intention of reopening their inquiries into the Kington killings.*' Before the scene switched to the cemetery I could picture so easily, I switched off.

Half an hour later, Sophie rang. I heard her voice purring from the answering machine. But I didn't pick up the receiver. And I didn't return her call. She'd made a fool of me once. And that was enough. I didn't mean to give her the slightest chance of doing so again.

Two days after the funeral, Bella paid me a visit. She and Sir Keith were returning to Biarritz the very next day, so this was in the nature of a goodbye. But not just for that reason.

'It'll take Keith a long time to recover from the loss he's suffered, Robin. If he ever does. And it'll take him a long time to forgive those he holds responsible for that loss.'

'Like me, you mean.'

'Yes. Like you.'

'You never were one to mince your words.'

'Would you want me to?'

'No. I wouldn't. Sarah told you about Howard Marsden, I suppose?'

'She told me.'

'Mentioned it to Keith, have you?'

'No.'

'So, it's time to sweep things under the carpet, is it? Time to batten down the hatches?'

'Time to go, Robin. That's all.'

'Without even a farewell drink?'

And at that she had the decency to smile.

We went out to the Red Lion at Chalton, where she'd taken me in July 1990 to pump me for information about the Kington killings. The three years that had passed since seemed more like ten when I looked at her across our table in the pub garden and saw her eyes drift to the field behind me. A blue drift of linseed, then as now. She too was remembering.

'You said I'd be making a mistake by going back into the company,' I remarked.

'And I was right. Wasn't I?'

'As it's turned out, I suppose you were. But you've been able to make sure you were right, haven't you?'

'It's Adrian's idea to accept the Bushranger offer. Not mine.'

'But without your support, he can't force it through, can he?'

'Technically, no. But I haven't the slightest intention of changing my mind. So don't waste your breath by—'

'I'm not about to. I've learnt my lesson. You see before you a man who isn't going to swim against the tide any longer. I've made a pact with the future. And you should be flattered, Bella, you really should. Because it's your example I'll be following.'

'In what sense?'

'I'm going to take the money and run.'

For a moment, I thought she meant to throw her lager in my face. But after staring at me for a few seconds, she merely shook her head and laughed. When all was said and done, she and I understood each other.

Two weeks passed. And the third anniversary of Louise's death approached. Since it fell on a Saturday, there was nothing to stop me driving up to Kington, as I'd long been tempted to, and walking out once more across Hergest Ridge. It was a day very like its well-remembered counterpart. Yet it could never be the same. And I didn't want it to be. What I wanted was the stony soil beneath my feet and the gorse-cleansed air in my face to assert the normality of the place. To convince me no magic or mystery was waiting for me there. Nor any perfect stranger. Only turf and sky and sheep. And nature's placid disregard for mankind's illusions.

I made my way down into Kington and called at the Swan for a drink, as I had three years before. This time, however, I struck up a conversation with one of the locals, who didn't seem to mind discussing the murders one little bit. Neither of the victims having been genuine Kingtonians, their memories evidently merited no special protection from outsiders. 'More about that to come out, you wait and see. Much more. From what I've heard, that Nick Seymour on the telly got it all wrong. Forgery weren't Oscar Bantock's game. Oh no. Satanism. That's what it was. Devil worship. His nephew rents Whistler's Cot out to holidaymakers, you know. But I wouldn't spend a night under that roof. Not after everything old Oscar got up to. Not me. No way. 'Course, there's a lot of it about round here. Black magic, I mean. It's the Dyke as gets 'em going. Covens. Sacrifices. Black masses. Midnight orgies. You wouldn't believe the half of it.' And on that last point at least he was absolutely right.

I left the Swan and drove straight out of the town. I'd thought I might take a look at Whistler's Cot, but, when it came to the point, I no longer needed to. An encounter with some exuberant family on a bargain break delighted to report they hadn't seen any ghosts would have constituted one dose of reality too many. I'd gone to Kington to close a chapter in my life. And I left confident of having done so.

I could have stopped in Sapperton on the way back to Petersfield and visited Rowena's grave as well as her mother's. It would only have been a few miles off my route if I'd gone through Gloucester. As in normal circumstances I would have done. But these weren't normal circumstances. So I headed south, through Monmouth and the Forest of Dean, joining the motorway at Chepstow. Crossing the Severn Bridge, I knew better than to glance to my left. Just in case I should see a lone figure standing on Sedbury Cliffs at the end – or the beginning – of a journey. Instead, I kept my eyes fixed on the road ahead. And didn't lift my foot from the accelerator.

Most of last summer appears now wholly inconsistent with everything that preceded it and was to follow. At the time, though, my life seemed set on a definite course which, if not ideal, was at least acceptable. Wrangling over small print delayed finalization of the Bushranger deal, but after Adrian and Jennifer had flown to Sydney twice and Harvey McGraw had dragged himself away from a hospitality tent at the Oval Test Match long enough to swagger round the factory with a retinue of financial advisers, the remaining difficulties were ironed out and a definitive set of terms put together. Adrian let it be known that we'd take a formal and final vote on the offer at a board meeting scheduled for the twenty-third of September.

Since there wasn't any doubt about the outcome, I laid my own plans. I spent a few days in Brussels early in September, treating various former colleagues to lunch. The consensus among them was that the Director-General could be induced to have me back on virtual parity with the post I'd left in 1990. The official line would be that I'd reluctantly done my bit for the family firm following my brother's death, but it was now back on its feet and I was therefore eager to return to the fold. As admissions of defeat went, mine seemed likely to be virtually painless.

And so no doubt it would have been. But for the intervention of events I could never have foreseen. From a quarter I thought I'd heard the last of. Even though the world hadn't. Sarah's predictions were already being borne out in one form or another. The victims of the Kington killings clearly weren't going to be allowed to rest in peace. An interview here. An article there. A slow drip-feed of curiosity and scepticism to keep the subject stubbornly alive. But not in *my* heart. I'd buried it. Beneath a dead weight of abandoned uncertainty. Yielded ground. Surrendered memory. The past sloughed off. Surely now I was beyond its reach. Safe and secure.

But no. I wasn't. Not at all. That wet Friday evening, the tenth of September, it stretched out its hand to tap me on the shoulder. I turned to meet it. And in that instant it reclaimed me.

'Paul?'

He was standing behind me, close enough to seem threatening. Yet in his rain-beaded face there was no hint of violence. Only sorrow and anguish. Previously he'd always been smartly turned out. Now his suit was drenched and crumpled. his shirt gaping at the neck, his tie askew. And there was at least two days' growth of stubble on his chin. His features were familiar yet not completely recognizable, as if he were some less favoured elder brother of the man Rowena had married, stern and prematurely aged, stooped beneath an unendurable burden.

'This is a surprise, I must say.'

We were in the factory yard, only a few yards from the spot where he'd waylaid me in June. The rain and low cloud were hastening the dusk, but it wasn't yet dark, as it had been then. And Paul's mood was utterly different. He moved and spoke slowly, as if his brain distrusted his commands and subjected each of them to scrutiny before putting it into effect.

'How are you?'

'As I am,' he mumbled.

'What can I do for you?'

'Listen to me. That's all. Somebody has to.'

'Well, I . . .'

'Can we go somewhere?'

'Er . . . Yes. Of course. Where would you—'

'Anywhere. It doesn't matter.'

'There's a pub down the road. We could—'

'No. Somewhere we can be alone.'

'All right. But—'

'Just drive me somewhere. Out of town. In the open. Where I can breathe.'

In view of what had happened the last time we met, I should have felt nervous about being alone with him. But his manner somehow overcame all such concerns. He seemed so weary, so utterly drained, that it wasn't possible to be afraid of him. Quite the reverse. I pitied him, sensing the grief and despair that had dragged him down to this shabby shuffling mockery of the confident young man I'd first encountered in Biarritz. I wanted to help him. And I knew I could trust him.

We drove out through Steep, past Greenhayes and up the zig-zag road to the top of Stoner Hill. Before we reached the summit, I pulled into one of the lay-bys beneath the trees, where the wooded depths of Lutcombe yawned beneath us through the branches. Night had all but fallen now. Only the dregs of daylight hovered above the hangers. Raindrops fell in random percussion on the roof of the car. Headlamps glared and slid across the windscreen as vehicles passed us. I watched Paul wind down his window, put out his hand to wet his palm, then rub the moisture across his face.

'Are you all right?' I asked.

'I haven't been *all right* in a long time. Years, I suppose.'

'Surely not years. When Rowena was alive—'

'It started before she died. Don't you understand?' He broke off, then resumed in a calmer vein. 'No. Of course you don't. That's why I came here. To make you understand. I'm sorry for what I did to you. I should have hurt myself, not you. But at least it solves the problem of who to tell. It means you deserve to hear it first.'

'To hear what?'

'The truth I've been dodging and evading all these years.'

'What do you mean?'

'I killed her, you see.'

'Nobody killed her, Paul. We can debate where the blame rests. But ultimately it was her decision.'

'I don't mean Rowena.' I sensed rather than saw him looking at me across the gloom of the car. 'I mean Louise.'

'Sorry?' I was instantly sure I'd misheard him. Or failed to comprehend some metaphor. Whatever he meant, it couldn't be literally *that*.

'I murdered Louise Paxton. And Oscar Bantock too. At Whistler's Cot. On the seventeenth of July, nineteen ninety.' An approaching pair of headlamps lit up his face in pale relief. He was staring straight at me. With a solemnity that somehow forced me to believe him. Even though I didn't want to. Even though I hardly dared to. 'I'm the man who should be serving the life sentence passed on Shaun Naylor. I'm the real murderer.'

'You can't be serious.'

'Oh yes. I'm serious. The lies are over now. I'm done with them. With Rowena dead, there's nothing worth lying *for*. So I may as well tell the truth. And face the consequences.'

'You really mean this?'

'Yes. I mean it. Shaun Naylor didn't murder Louise. Or old Oscar. I did.'

'But . . . you can't have.'

'How I wish you were right. But I did. Worse still, I let an innocent man go to prison in my place. I told myself he didn't matter. Some low-life petty criminal society was well rid of. My conscience was up to that. But Rowena was different. I married her because I thought, if I could take care of her, if I could make sure nothing bad ever happened to her again, that would somehow compensate for depriving her of her mother. But I didn't take care of her, did I? I just made it worse. So much worse she couldn't face the future shackled to me. And was prepared to go to any lengths to escape it. You said I didn't kill her and, technically, I didn't. But in every other sense I did. I should be grateful, really. It proves there *is* something my conscience can't bear. I've wrestled with it these past few months. I've lain awake night after night trying to find some other way out. But there isn't one. I'm certain I'll have no peace until I've confessed to the crimes I've committed. And paid the penalty. It's as simple as that.'

I couldn't find any words to express my reaction to what he'd said. Everything I'd assumed – everything I'd deduced – about Louise Paxton's death had been overturned in a matter of minutes. A man claiming to have killed her was sitting next to me on an isolated hillside as a wet September night closed about us. If I believed him, I should have been afraid for my own safety. And I did believe him. Not because of the note of sincerity in his voice. Rather because of the unmistakable impression of relief conveyed in his manner and bearing. And that's also why I wasn't afraid of him. He sat beside me, hunched and defeated, a man whose store of lies and evasions was long since exhausted. All he seemed to want to do now was speak freely about himself. He was no longer a threat to anyone.

'The police won't believe me at first, of course. They won't want to. I'll be an embarrassment to them. But they'll come round in the end. When I've told them the whole story, they'll realize it's true. But before I go to them, I'd like you to hear it. All of it. So you can tell Sarah and her father before they read about it in the newspapers or see it on television. I haven't the courage to face them myself. I thought I might have, but I've woken up every morning this week meaning to go to Sarah and then failing to. It can't go on. That's why I've turned to you. Not quite a friend. Not quite a stranger. Perhaps that makes you the perfect confessor. If you're willing to listen, that is.' He paused. I saw his head droop in the shadows. Then he pulled himself upright and sighed. 'Are you?' he asked huskily.

'Yes,' I replied. 'I'll listen.'

And so, as the rain spat at the windscreen and the dark damp smell of the night crept in around us, Paul Bryant began his story. I listened to him in silence. And long before he'd finished, I realized nothing would ever be the same. Now his confession had been heard.

CHAPTER

THIRTEEN

'My parents met in the bank where they both worked. Dull decent ordinary people. Never been abroad. Never committed adultery. Never sworn in public. Never dreamt of being more than they were. My sisters and I were all conceived in the same bed in the same room in the same semi-detached house in Surbiton. Made in our parents' unaspiring image. So they must have thought, anyway. If they ever did think about such things. And I suppose they were right about my sisters. A few holidays in Majorca and one divorce between them doesn't change an awful lot, does it?

'I always wanted more though. More travel. More culture. More company. More variety. And it turned out I had the brains to get what I wanted. Winning a place at Cambridge didn't just round off a good education and enhance my employment prospects. It got me out of the stifling tedium of my suburban adolescence. Cambridge had more than its fair share of poseurs and idiots, of course. But it gave me something I'd never had before. The conviction that life contained limitless possibilities. The belief not only that I could have whatever I desired if I put my mind to it, but that I deserved to have it. Elitism. Egotism. Supreme self-confidence. They came in the water. And I drank of them deeply.

'Too deeply, I suppose. I mean, it was all a charade. Of course it was. I know that now. A game of froth and gaud in which the key to winning was to take yourself deadly seriously while pretending to treat everything as a joke. I played the game. But I mistook it for the real thing. So the shallowness of the other players baffled and enraged me. They didn't seem to understand that arguing an academic point and appreciating a fine painting in the Fitzwilliam were the same thing: a celebration of individual superiority. I soon came to believe that I felt more, sensed more, understood more, grasped the essence of being and doing and thinking more, than the whole trivial pack of them put together.

'It started from that. My dissatisfaction with the people I got drunk with or went to bed with. It turned into contempt for their lack of maturity. I longed to escape their puking and prattling. I longed for older wiser friends to debate the virtues and vices of the world with. But they weren't to be found in Cambridge. I felt like a hungry man offered a shopful of candyfloss. Like a philosopher put to work as a baby-minder.

'Then, during the Lent term of my second year, I met Sarah. We went out a few times. It didn't come to much. Not even sex. But I happened to be the man she had in tow when she went along to the private view her mother had arranged to launch Oscar Bantock's exhibition. I nearly didn't go. She actually had to come and get me when I didn't show up at her room. Things were cooling off between us pretty rapidly by then. Besides, I hated Expressionism. I also had a fixed mental picture of the artist and his patroness. A raddled old bohemian running to fat and some horse-faced socialite offering cheap wine in exchange for cheap compliments. That's what I expected. And in Oscar Bantock it's more or less what I got. But Louise? She was a different story altogether.

'The gallery was a small but exclusive place. Crowded that night, of course. A grinning mob of so-called aesthetes expelling enough hot air to steam up the windows completely. We pushed our way in. Sarah made straight for her mother. To ensure her presence was noted, I suppose. That's when I first saw Louise. It was like an electric shock. I mean, it was instantaneous. She was so beautiful. She was so . . . mind-blowingly lovely. I just gaped at her. I remember thinking, "Why aren't these people looking at her? Can't they see? Don't they realize?" You met her once yourself, so maybe you understand. She was incredible. She was the woman I'd been longing to meet. And in that instant, before Sarah had even introduced us, I knew I'd have to have her. To possess her, body and soul. It was as simple as that. Over the top, of course. Absurdly unrealistic. Totally mad. But I never questioned the instinct for a moment. It was so strong I felt certain it had to be right.

'I only spoke to her for a few minutes. We didn't discuss anything profound or meaningful. But that didn't matter. The tone of her voice. The movement of her hair when she laughed. The haunting coolness in her eyes. It was as if they were branded on me. I'd have done anything for her. Gone anywhere to be with her. I was in her power. Except she didn't know it. Which left my infatuation to feed on itself. Outright rejection at the start might have nipped it in the bud. But she was too polite – too sensitive – for that. I managed to muscle in on a lunch she had with Sarah the next day. I contrived to be hanging around Sarah's staircase when Louise called on her to say goodbye the day after. I was the archetypal bad penny. Louise probably thought I was trailing after her daughter. That must be why she suggested I visit them in Sapperton during the Easter vacation. But Sarah was having none of it. After her mother had gone, she made it obvious she didn't want to see me there.

'I went home at the end of term assuming I'd soon forget about Louise. But the sterility of life in Surbiton only reinforced the yearning to be near her. I knew they had a town house in Holland Park. So I went up there one day and called round. To my surprise, Louise answered the door. She was alone. Sarah was out with friends. Rowena was at school. Sir Keith was at his surgery. I claimed to be in the area by chance. She invited me in. Offered me coffee. Said she didn't know how long Sarah would be. I said it didn't matter. And that was true. The longer the better, as far as I was concerned. Just to be with Louise, just to look at her across the room and listen to her speaking, just to feel her attention resting on me when I was speaking . . . It seemed like a glimpse of paradise. And having her to myself, however briefly, seemed like an opportunity I couldn't afford to let slip. When she went into the kitchen to fix me another coffee, I followed her. And that's where I told her. In the time it took the kettle to boil.

'I'd already imagined how she was going to react to my declaration of undying love. A hesitant admission that she felt the same way. Then a passionate surrender. She'd let me kiss her. Maybe even let me take her upstairs and make love to her. Or arrange to meet me next day at some classy hotel, where we'd spend the whole of the afternoon and evening in bed. Later, we'd start planning our future together. Discuss where we were going to run away to. All self-deluding nonsense, of course. All so much folly and arrogance. But I was so taken in by the fantasy

I'd created that it's actually what I expected to happen.

'Needless to say, it didn't. The first thing she said when I'd finished was, "Oh dear". She seemed more embarrassed than angry. Almost sorry for me. She tried to let me down lightly. She took me back into the lounge and gently explained the impossibility of what I'd suggested. She was a happily married middle-aged woman with a daughter my own age. There could be no question of her betraying her husband. With me or anyone else. Strangely enough, she didn't seem particularly shocked. Perhaps other men had poured out their hearts to her in similar circumstances. Perhaps she was used to being the object of hopeless adoration. "This is just a phase you're going through," she said. "A phase you'll soon grow out of." She spoke of it so lightly, so dismissively. As if I was some silly little boy with a crush on her. I could have hated her if I hadn't loved her. And in a sense I suppose that's when I started to. Hate as well as love, I mean.

'But love's the wrong word anyway, isn't it? It was an obsession amounting to mania. I loaded everything of meaning and significance in my life onto her. I made winning her a test of the very purpose of my existence. A test I was bound to fail. Because she wasn't interested. Not a bit. She wasn't even worried by me. Not then, anyway, though later . . . She didn't take me seriously, you see. That was the worst of it. I could have her pity. Even her scorn, if I persisted. But never what I wanted. Never, come to that, her respect, now I'd shown my hand.

'She very politely threw me out. Reckoned it would be best if I didn't wait for Sarah. But she promised not to tell her anything. "Let's forget this ever happened," she said. "Let's write it off as an unfortunate misunderstanding." I suppose that's what it was in a way. A misunderstanding. She just didn't understand that I really meant it. And I didn't understand how preposterous what I meant really was.

'But as for writing it off, that didn't seem possible. I called her several times over the next few days. Put the phone down if somebody else answered. Spoke if it was her. I begged her to reconsider. Pleaded with her to give me a chance. Just one meeting. Just a few minutes of her time. Eventually, she agreed. We met in a café in Covent Garden. Her mood had changed by then. If I persisted, she said, she'd inform the college authorities. So far, nobody else knew. But if I didn't stop now, everybody would know. Sarah. My parents. My fellow students. My director of studies. My tutor. In my own interest, I had to give up. Immediately. As she very much hoped I would.

'I hadn't promised anything when she left. But I did try. The disgrace and the mockery a formal complaint by her could bring down on me was a sobering thought. It made me see reason. For a while, anyway. I wrote her an apologetic letter, saying she wouldn't hear from me again. And I meant it. I really did. I went back to Cambridge after Easter determined to knuckle down to my studies and forget this ludicrous pursuit of an older woman.

'For a while, I almost thought it would work. But once my exams were over, I found myself with a lot of time on my hands. A bloke I shared a landing with, Peter Rossington, said he was looking for a partner for an inter-rail trip round Europe that summer. You know, the cheap rail pass tour most students do at least once. Well, it was either that or Surbiton. Not much of a contest. I said I'd go with him and we agreed to set off early in July. Until then, I had nothing to do but laze around Cambridge and think. About Louise. About how I might still make her change her mind. About how I might yet persuade her to give herself to me, even against her better judgement. I stayed on till the bitter end of full term and was still there when the third year students came back to graduate. Including Sarah. Which meant Louise was bound to come to Cambridge as well. I wheedled out of Sarah which hotel her parents would be staying in. The Garden House. A big modern place on the Cam, behind Peterhouse. The graduation ceremony was on the last Friday in June. They were to arrive on the Thursday and leave with Sarah on the Saturday.

'I should have left on the Wednesday, of course. Or sooner. But I didn't. I hung around, hoping for a glimpse of her. Maybe even the chance of a talk with her. Early on Friday morning, I started walking along the riverside path on the opposite side from the Garden House. Down past the hotel and back. Again and again. Hoping she might see me from her room, even though I didn't know if they had one facing the river. Well, she must have noticed me and walked round from the hotel to confront me, because suddenly she appeared on the path ahead, approaching from the Mill Lane end. And she was angry. "Are you mad?" she demanded. "You agreed to leave me alone. What do you mean by patrolling up and down like this?" I pretended it was all a big mistake. I just happened to be taking a stroll there, with no idea she was staying at the hotel. It was obvious she didn't believe me, but she couldn't prove me a liar either. In the end, she just walked away. I ran after her, begging her to stop and talk. But she wouldn't. I followed her all the way down Granta Place towards the hotel. Eventually, just inside the entrance, she stopped and rounded on me. "My husband's waiting to have breakfast with me in the restaurant," she said. "Do you want to join us, Paul? Do you want me to tell him what's going on? There'll be no going back if I do." Well, I wasn't ready to confront Sir Keith. Not then. Not just like that. Her bluntness shocked me. I mumbled some kind of apology and beat a retreat.

'But it could never be a permanent retreat. I hung about the streets, watching the procession to the Senate House. Then I slunk round to the Backs and spied on the lunch party at King's for graduates and parents. I caught a glimpse of Louise, looking radiantly lovely. Sir Keith was with her, of course. It was the first time I'd seen him. Naturally, he looked completely unworthy of her to me. I crept away and left them to it. I was utterly miserable by then. Depressed and disgusted with myself. Yet I was still so much in love with her I simply couldn't put her out of my mind.

'They left next morning. I spent the weekend drinking. And formulating a plan. I was due to meet Peter in London on Wednesday. That gave me two days when I might be able to get Louise on her own. I didn't know whether she'd be in Sapperton or London, so I decided to hedge my bets by going to Sapperton first, on Monday. I drove over there that morning. Arrived about eleven o'clock. Parked near the church. Spied out the land. Tried to think exactly how to approach her.

'I was sitting in my car at the end of the lane leading to The Old Parsonage when Sarah came past, returning from a stroll, I suppose. I didn't see her coming and she spotted me straightaway. I trotted out some story about visiting an aunt in Cirencester and diverting to Sapperton to see if Sarah was free for lunch. Well, she seemed to be taken in by it. Nobody else was at home, apparently. She suggested we drive to a nearby pub. And I had to go along with it now I'd started, so off we went. To the Daneway Inn, down in the valley below Sapperton. It wasn't exactly a relaxing occasion. I think Sarah was puzzled. Worried, perhaps, that I might want to start things up again between us. Maybe that made her nervous. And talkative as a result. Whatever the reason, she told me more about her family than she probably realized.

'Sir Keith was in London. But Louise had gone over to Kington to visit Oscar Bantock. "She sees quite a lot of him," Sarah said. "I suppose there's nobody else she can discuss Expressionism with." I didn't make anything of it at first. Sarah was going to Scotland at the end of the week for a holiday with some other lawyers from King's. Her parents were off to their villa in Biarritz at the same time. Rowena would join them there when her school broke up for the summer. All very cosy and convenient.

'We had some tea back at The Old Parsonage. Then I left, not sure what to do next. But, driving back to Cambridge, I suddenly saw the answer. Louise hadn't told anyone about me. Why? Because she felt sorry for me? Or because she was afraid her husband mightn't think she was a wholly innocent party? Maybe he already had grounds for suspicion. About Oscar Bantock, perhaps. Or somebody else. Maybe they weren't the devoted couple she'd claimed.

'It's strange, but I think I could have eventually accepted her rejection of me if I'd gone on believing she was a faithful wife. It was the idea she might not be that got to me. If she was going to betray her husband, the warped logic of my mind said it ought to be with me. Not with some derelict old painter or God knows who else. She wasn't being fair. She wasn't giving me a chance.

'I didn't go back to Sapperton. With Sarah there, it was just too risky. Besides, I didn't need to. She'd told me where I could find her mother. All summer long. I met up with Peter in London on Wednesday. We set off for Europe the following day. We spent a long weekend in Paris, then headed for Italy. I said I wanted to stop off in the French Alps, knowing Peter was champing at the bit to see Florence and Rome. After an argument in Lyon, we agreed to split up. He went on to Italy. I made for Chamonix. Well, that's where I told him I was going. Actually, I returned to Paris and caught a train to Biarritz.

'I arrived there late on Thursday the twelfth of July. Booked into a cheap *pension* near the station. Next day, I tracked down L'Hivernance and hung around, hoping to see Louise leaving on foot. Or Sir Keith leaving, so I'd know she was alone. Nothing. Except they drove out together in the early evening. Heading for some posh restaurant, I assumed. I gave up. But I was back the next day, determined to be more resourceful. After I was sure everything seemed quiet, I scaled a wall round the side and crept through the garden towards the house. There was nobody about. But, as I got closer, I heard voices coming from one of the open ground-floor windows. Closer still, I recognized one of them as Louise's. The other was Sir Keith's. They were arguing. I can't tell you what pleasure – what hope – that gave me. If they were going to split up, I might catch her on the rebound.

'I never did get close enough to hear exactly what was said. But it was obvious Sir Keith was angry. He mentioned Bantock. "That bloody dauber," he called him. And he said he was leaving next day. "So what you do is your affair, isn't it?" I couldn't catch Louise's answer. She spoke more softly than him. Kept her anger in check. Anyway, some gardener showed up then, so I had to run for it. By the time he spotted me, I was disappearing over the wall.

'But I'd found out what I wanted to know. They were at each other's throats. And Sir Keith was going away. Clearing the path for me. I was back early on Sunday, waiting to see him go. He was in no hurry. It was midday before he left. By taxi. With a couple of cases on board. I couldn't believe my luck. Louise would be vulnerable and upset, I reasoned. In need of sympathy. In need of love.

'I decided to wait until evening. Turning up straight after Sir Keith's departure might look suspicious. It was a sunny afternoon. The beaches were crowded. I shuffled around, kicking my heels and eating ice-creams. At one point, a girl tried to pick me up. All pout and swaying hips. I should have fancied her, I suppose. But she just seemed so pathetically immature compared with Louise. They all did then.

'By dusk, the beaches were empty. I started back for L'Hivernance. But, before I got there, I saw Louise. She was out by the waterline on the Plage Miramar, walking slowly, lost in thought it seemed. I went down to the sea wall and watched her from the covered alleyway beneath the terrace of the Hôtel du Palais. She just walked up and down the same length of sand as the breakers rolled in and night fell. I intended to intercept her on her way back to the villa. But when it was nearly dark and she still showed no sign of coming in, I decided to go out to her.

'She didn't notice me as I approached. She was looking out to sea, gazing at the last few streaks of sunset beyond the horizon. When I was only a few yards from her, she slipped her wedding ring from her finger, drew back her arm and threw it as far as she could out into the waves. I pulled up in amazement, unable to believe she'd done such a thing. Then she turned round. And saw me.

'"Paul!" she said. "What are you doing here?" It's funny. She didn't seem particularly surprised to see me. I made my prepared speech about being unable to stay away. About being deeply in love with her. And about being sure she needed a friend – perhaps more than a friend – now her marriage was failing. She must have realized then I'd been spying on her. But she wasn't angry. "I can't talk to you now, Paul," she said. "I have too much on my mind. But come to L'Hivernance tomorrow morning about eleven o'clock and we *will* talk. Properly." Then she kissed me.

Just a formal fleeting kiss on the cheek. But it was enough to make me think I was at long last breaking down her defences. I watched her walk away, my mind racing to imagine what would happen when we met again. This time at *her* instigation.

'I called at L'Hivernance on the dot of eleven the following morning, wearing a jacket and tie I'd bought less than an hour before and clutching a bunch of flowers. I was nervous and uncertain. But I was also excited and expectant. Not for long, though. The housekeeper who answered the door told me Louise had left for England early that morning, saying nothing about an appointment with me. I was dumbstruck. Too horrified to speak. I stumbled off in the direction of the lighthouse and took one of those narrow winding paths down towards the shore. At first, I didn't know what to think. Then it came to me. She'd tricked me. Fobbed me off for the short time it took to pack up and go. I hurled her flowers into the sea and wept. Then rage replaced despair. She'd trampled on my pride. She'd deceived me along with her husband. Well, I'd make her pay for that.

'I knew where she'd gone. Kington. To be with Bantock. By car and plane, she'd get there long before I could. But that didn't seem to matter. Just so long as I caught up with her in the end. I rushed back to my *pension*, packed, booked out and made for the station. Where I found I had more than two hours to wait for the next train to Paris.

'All the time I waited, my determination to confront Louise with the evidence of her treachery grew. Of course, the only thing she'd really betrayed was the fantasy I'd woven around her. Nothing else. She didn't owe me anything, least of all an explanation. Making an appointment with me she had no intention of keeping was just a sensible way of getting me off her back. And the state of her marriage was absolutely none of my business. I see that now very clearly. But back then I saw nothing clearly. Least of all what I'd do when I finally found her.

'It took me twenty-two hours to travel from Biarritz to Kington by train, ferry and bus. Paris. Dieppe. Newhaven. London. Newport. Hereford. I killed time in them all on the way. Eventually, at one o'clock the following afternoon – Tuesday the seventeenth of July – I clambered off a bus in the middle of Kington.

'I got Bantock's address from the telephone directory and a handy little free map showing where Butterbur Lane was from the tourist office. Half an hour later, I was at Whistler's Cot hammering on the door. I felt sure Louise was there, even though her car wasn't. But I was wrong. Bantock came round from the back, demanding to know what all the racket was for. He recognized me from the exhibition. I had the wit to claim I was on holiday in the area and was keen to see his work. He asked me in and showed me his studio. Work in progress. That sort of thing. Well, it was obvious Louise wasn't there. But I was still convinced she would be before long. Maybe she'd stopped in London. Whatever the reason, I'd somehow overtaken her en route.

'Bantock said he had to go out and I was glad of the excuse to cut my visit short. My imitation of an art buff was wearing pathetically thin by then. He offered me a lift, but I said I preferred to walk. I set off at a slow pace and he passed me halfway down the lane in his car. As soon as he was out of sight, I doubled back and followed the lane past Whistler's Cot out onto the common. Then I prowled around the fields above the lane until I found myself on the other side of the hedge opposite the cottage. I could see over the hedge well enough and the height of the bank below meant I was on a level with the bedroom windows. I settled down in the shade of a beech tree that overhung the hedge and waited for them to return. I was certain it would be *them*. Bantock had gone to meet her and would come back with her sooner or later. I had no doubt of it. When he did, I'd be ready.

'At about five o'clock, Louise arrived in her car. I was positively elated to be proved correct. But I'd got one thing wrong. Bantock wasn't with her. She knocked at the door, then went round the back. I thought she was going to wait for Bantock inside, but she came out a few minutes later and drove off again. I couldn't understand it. But I was still determined to stick it out. It could only be a matter of time.

'I had a couple of lagers in my rucksack. Drinking them was a mistake, because what with the heat and the stress and strain of the journey, I fell asleep. When I woke up, it was nearly dark and I was cold. There was no sign of life at Whistler's Cot. I began to feel a bit of a fool. My confidence began to drain away. Much longer and I'd have given up and gone. But just then, at about nine o'clock, Louise's Merc came back up the lane, followed closely by a yellow van. Both vehicles pulled in by the cottage. She had somebody with her this time. But it wasn't Bantock. Oh no. It was somebody I'd never seen before. I've seen photographs of him since, of course. It was Shaun Naylor. He looked what he is. A handsome young thug. The sort you'd expect to see selling bootleg perfume on a street-corner or prowling round a car park trying the locks. Rough and ready. Ready, in fact, for anything. With a narcissistic streak thrown in for good measure. What he was doing with Louise I just couldn't work out. He wasn't her type at all. So I'd have thought, anyway.

'But I didn't know what her type was, did I? All I knew was that she'd picked this piece of garbage up from somewhere. And not long ago, to judge by the few words they exchanged before going indoors. "You nearly lost me back there," he said to her in a cockney accent. "I wouldn't have let that happen," she replied. "Not when I've only just found you." Then he pulled her towards him and kissed her roughly. I couldn't believe what I was seeing – or hearing. She leant up and whispered something in his ear. "You're a real tease, aren't you?" he said in response. "Who's teasing?" she answered. "Shall we go in?"

'She led him round to the back. A few seconds later, some lights came on. Just downstairs at first, where I couldn't see much. Then, after about ten minutes, on the landing and in one of the bedrooms. I had a clear view straight in through the window. I saw Louise and Naylor walk into the room. Neither of them made a move for the curtains. Perhaps they didn't think there'd be anybody outside, watching them. Perhaps they just didn't care. At the time, I had the crazy idea Louise knew I was there and wanted me to see what she was capable of – with the right sort of man.

'I'm not going to dcscribe what she let him do to her. Well, there wasn't much she didn't let him do. She was a willing partner all right. Like Naylor said at his trial, it wasn't rape. If only it had been. I could have rushed in and tried to rescue her then. I could have been her white knight in shining armour. Instead, I just sat there and watched what would have been a Peeping Tom's dream come true. It was horrible. Not because of the sex itself. That was just two bodies moving together in a rectangle of light. Like a pornographic movie on a TV screen. No, it was the pleasure on her face, the leisurely expertise of her actions that so appalled me. It couldn't have been the first time she'd done such things. It was a practised performance. She did it well. As well as the most accomplished of whores. I could almost have believed that's what she was. A high-class tart for this . . . creature she'd found . . . to use and abuse. Anyone's. If the money was right. Or she took a fancy to you. Anyone's at all. But not mine. Never mine.

'He didn't stay long afterwards. Got dressed and walked out, leaving her in bed. Well, on the bed. She didn't even bother to cover herself. He came out and drove away. She didn't get up.

She must have fallen asleep. I went on watching her for a few minutes. Disbelief turned to jealousy. And jealousy became rage. I wanted to punish her for denying me everything she'd so casually given to a stranger. For shattering the image of her I'd built up in my mind. For not being the woman I'd dreamt she was.

'I scrambled through a gap in the hedge, dropped down the bank into the lane and crept round to the back of the cottage. The door wasn't locked, of course. I went in, moving as quietly as I could. I still didn't really know what I was going to do. The lights were on in the kitchen and the lounge. The studio door was open. I glanced in and noticed a coil of picture-hanging wire on a bench. I stood staring at the wire, until I'd convinced myself she deserved it. Until I'd committed myself to the act so completely it seemed inevitable. I picked up some pliers that were lying next to the wire and cut off a length. Then I put on an old pair of leather gloves I'd seen on a shelf near the back door. I wasn't thinking about fingerprints. It was just I didn't want the wire to cut into my hands. As I knew it would, when I drew it tight around her neck.

'I can't remember exactly what happened next. The surge of conflicting emotions blots out part of the memory, I suppose. I went up to the bedroom. But whether I tiptoed or ran I can't say. I was suddenly in the room, looking down at her, naked on the bed. She was lying on her side, her face averted. She heard something and stirred. "Shaun?" she said. "Is that—" Then I was on her, forcing her down against the mattress with the weight of my own body as I looped the wire over her head and pulled it taut around her throat. She gagged and tried to throw me off. But I was too strong for her. "It's me, you bitch," I shouted in her ear as I strained at the wire. "It's Paul." She choked and writhed and struggled. But there was no way out now. For either of us. It went on longer than I'd expected. So much longer. But, in the end, all the life was squeezed out. And she lay limp and still beneath me. No breath. No movement. No flicker of the eyes. She was dead.

'I stood up and looked down at her beautiful body, which I'd once longed to touch and caress. But now there was nothing there. Just her pale flesh, growing colder by the second. I turned round and saw a reflection of the scene in a large mirror that filled most of the wall facing me. Seeing myself, hollow-eyed and panting, with her body on the bed behind me, made it somehow even worse. I lashed out at the mirror with my boot, splintering one of the corners. Then I rushed out of the room.

'I'd got as far as the kitchen when I heard a car draw up

outside. It sounded like Bantock's. The creaking of the garage door confirmed my guess. I was about to run for it before he came in when I suddenly realized how disastrous that would be. If he saw me, he'd recognize me. Even if he didn't see me, he'd tell the police I'd called there on an unconvincing pretext earlier in the day. And my rucksack was on the other side of the hedge. If I left it there, there'd be no doubt of my guilt. What little I knew of forensics suggested that if they had cause to suspect me, they'd be able to prove I'd been there that night. A fingerprint. A fibre. A hair. God knows what. But they'd find it. And I'd be done for. Whereas if they had *no* cause to suspect me . . . if they had no reason even to think of me . . .

'I dodged into the studio and cut off another length of wire. I was planning to pounce on Bantock as he went through the kitchen. But when he opened the back door, shouted "Louise?" and got no answer, he stopped, then turned towards the studio, almost as if he sensed my presence there. I shrank back behind the door and, as he came in, leapt at his back, looping the wire over his head and tightening it around his neck in one movement. He yielded as I pulled, then fought back, hurling himself forward in an attempt to throw me off. We crashed to the floor and rolled over several times. I could hear and feel objects tumbling around us. He was a big strong man, but overweight and out of condition. I had the advantage of youth and determination. I couldn't afford to let him get the better of me. I forced him onto his stomach, managed to pin his arms with my knees and twisted at the wire in a frenzy. And that was how he died, a choking clawing heap on the floor of his studio, his face smeared with a fine multi-coloured dust formed of tiny flakes of paint shed over the years from his brushes and palettes.

'I struggled to my feet and tried to think clearly. With Bantock dead, there was nobody to connect me with what had happened. I was supposed to be abroad and, if I could get back to France without being seen by anybody who knew me, I was almost certainly safe from detection. The instinct for self-preservation erased the horror of what I'd done, at least for a while. I pocketed the coil of wire and the pliers, kept the gloves on and rushed out into the lane. There was nobody about. I was safe if I kept my nerve. I ran up the lane to the common and worked my way round to the beech tree where I'd left the rucksack. I took out my torch and checked the ground for things I might have dropped, gathered up the empty lager tins and stuffed them into the rucksack, then stumbled down across the field towards the road into Kington, navigating by the lights in the houses along Butterbur Lane.

'Once I was on the road, I reckoned I looked like any other hiker. I walked straight through the town, restraining my pace all the way, resisting the urge to break into a run, and out to the bypass. Then I started trying to hitch a lift. My luck was in. A lorry driver stopped for me after only a few minutes. He was heading for Coventry. Well, anywhere as long as it was far from Kington suited me. He dropped me at a motorway service area between Birmingham and Coventry in the small hours of the following morning. I managed to pick up another lift from there down to London. By the time the bodies were found at Whistler's Cot, I was on a ferry halfway across the Channel.

'I spent most of the next week drifting down through Germany, Austria and the Balkans, buying day-old English newspapers at every stop in search of information about what line the police were following, what clues they'd found at the scene. The panic attacks lessened. The fear of imminent arrest ebbed away. Then came creeping revulsion at what I'd done. An inability to *believe* I'd done it so strong I started quite genuinely to doubt I had. My geographical remoteness from the crime became a psychological remoteness as well. My memory told me what had happened, but my conscience refused to accept it. It was partly a survival mechanism, I suppose. A way of coping with the guilt. A method of evading responsibility for my actions. It was Louise's fault for provoking me beyond endurance. Bantock's for barging in when he did. Naylor's for grabbing and soiling what I'd not been allowed to touch. Anybody's fault. Except mine.

'I still didn't know who Naylor was then, of course. When I read of his arrest, I was briefly tempted to go to the nearest British Consulate and turn myself in. Then I thought I'd wait to see if he was charged. When he was – with rape as well as murder – I realized exactly who he must be and why the police were bound to think they'd found the culprit. I was in the clear. And suddenly it seemed not merely a matter of luck but of fate. Destiny had decreed I shouldn't be punished and Naylor should. Who was I to argue? It was only fair, after all. It was only as it should be. I hadn't known what I was doing. I'd lost control. In France, they'd have dismissed it as a crime of passion, an understandable and pardonable surrender to anger and jealousy. As for Naylor, well, there was an ironic form of justice in the likelihood that he'd suffer for what I'd done. Because he'd goaded me into doing it in the first place.

'So I told myself, anyway. It sounds contemptible, I know. It *is* contemptible. But you don't know what excuses and justifications the mind is capable of until you find yourself in such an extreme situation. Louise was dead. So was Bantock. I couldn't bring them back to life by confessing to their murders. And Naylor was nothing to me. He was nothing *compared* with me. I had a successful and worthwhile life ahead of me. I had the chance to redeem myself by hard work and respectability. Whereas he was just some sordid nonentity who'd be as happy in a prison cell as he would be on the streets. Sacrificing myself to save him would be a pointless waste. It would only make matters worse than they already were. I had endless conversations with myself on the subject, turning it round and round like a debating point. I even convinced myself Louise would have forgiven me and urged me not to confess. I saw her occasionally in my dreams. Even more beautiful than the reality had been. So serene. So understanding. And I kept hearing her voice. Speaking the words she'd used that afternoon in Holland Park. "*Let's forget this ever happened. Let's write it off as an unfortunate misunderstanding.*" In the end, it seemed to be her will I was yielding to, her last wish I was respecting. I'd murdered her, yes. But by letting Naylor take the blame, I was protecting her reputation. She could be remembered as a faithful wife and a devoted mother. So long as I held my tongue.

'I got home in late August, sure by then that nothing could implicate me in the murders and that my conscience, though it could never be clear, was at least secure. I wrote a letter of condolence to Sarah and got a polite but guarded reply. I decided to leave it at that. Our paths had divided and I was confident they'd never cross again. I went back to Cambridge in October determined to start my life over again. To recreate myself and in the process cast aside forever the memory of the things I'd done that night at Whistler's Cot.

'I succeeded. I made new friends and threw myself into new activities. By the time the trial started, I was beyond its reach, so safe in my busy self-regarding world that I didn't even read the newspaper reports of its progress. It was only thanks to another student who'd known Sarah that I learnt of Naylor's conviction. And do you know what I felt when I heard the sentence? Relieved. That's what. Just relieved it was over. Just glad he was going to be locked away for twenty years. Just happy to know I could forget all about him.

'But I couldn't, could I? Not as it turned out. Because after graduation I toyed with several job offers, thinking one wasn't much different from another, and accepted a post with Metropolitan Mutual Insurance. A fatal mistake, I suppose you could say. Because it meant moving to Bristol. Where Sarah had gone to take her articles. And Rowena had also gone, to study mathematics. I didn't know they were living there, of course. I had absolutely no idea. Until the day I bumped into Sarah in Park Street.

'It seemed no big deal at the time. A coincidence I could simply brush off. But Sarah invited me to dinner and I could hardly refuse. So I went out to Clifton one night and met Rowena for the first time. Early January of last year. Not long ago really. Not long at all. Yet in other ways it seems . . . Sarah admitted later that she was keen for Rowena to meet as many new people as possible. It was only six weeks or so since she'd tried to commit suicide. Sarah thought varied company might take her out of herself. That's really why she invited me.

'It started slowly. As an attraction to the things in Rowena that reminded me of Louise. A rapport developed between us, based on a subconscious awareness that we were both suppressing something. In Rowena's case, doubts about her mother's death. In my case, the knowledge of what really lay behind those doubts. She was lovely as well, of course. Lovely *and* vulnerable. Right from the beginning, I wanted to protect her. To shield her from a truth I thought she'd be unable to bear. And to shield myself at the same time. Chance had given me the opportunity to repair some of the damage I'd done and to silence the voice that still whispered reproaches to me in the long watches of the night. It seemed as if fate had taken a hand in my life once more.

'And so it had. But not in the way I thought. I married Rowena and for a while everything seemed perfect. Loving her made me see my obsession with Louise for what it had truly been: a shallow delusion. But its consequences endured. Whether the secret I always had to keep ate away at Rowena's trust in me or whether she just wasn't quite capable of abandoning her doubts I'm not sure, but something was wrong even before the book appeared, let alone the TV programme. And then there was the pregnancy, of course. How that affected her I don't know. But she didn't tell me about it, did she? So maybe it wasn't good news as far as she was concerned. Maybe it just added to her problems. Made her future seem as doubt-ridden as her past. And just as intolerable.

'I shouldn't have tried to keep her in the dark. That's obvious now. But I was afraid that facing up to the rumours and speculation would eventually oblige me to tell her the whole truth. Secrecy becomes a habit, you see. More than a necessity. A way of life, almost. It can't just be shrugged off. It doesn't work like that. So my response to the growing interest in the case was to block it off and pretend it didn't exist. It was all grotesquely misplaced anyway. Oscar Bantock may or may not have been a forger. But I knew better than anyone why he'd died. And forgery didn't come into it.

'Except in the sense that my whole life had become a forgery. A convincing but counterfeit piece of work. A sham based on a lie. The only genuine thing in it was my love for Rowena. When she threw herself from the bridge, she took the purpose of my deception with her. She exposed my forgery. For the world to see.

'But it didn't see, did it? It never does. It never wants to. It has to be forced to open its eyes. The righting of wrongs is a deeply uncomfortable experience. Admitting to a mistake is much more difficult than concealing it. And usually there are so many ways to dodge the issue. To avoid the admission. But not this time. Not now. Because I intend to be seen *and* heard. I intend to set the record straight. And to face the consequences. Along with everyone else.'

CHAPTER FOURTEEN

Listening to Paul Bryant's confession made me realize how little I'd really known about the Paxton family and the events of July 1990. I'd mistaken glimpses of the truth for insight and understanding. I'd constructed a whole version of reality from the constituents of my limited knowledge. And now, suddenly, I saw it for the travesty it had always been. The past was as fluid and uncertain as the future.

I was too shocked at first to react to what Paul had said. So much was altered by it, so much thrown into disarray. Louise hadn't been what I or others had thought she was. She hadn't been prepared to be what we wanted her to be, even in death. Everything we'd believed about her had been a lie. And the one thing said about her that we were sure was a lie turned out to be true. Naylor wasn't guilty. But almost everyone else was. Of deceiving others. Or of deceiving themselves. It hardly mattered which.

Except in Paul's case, of course. He'd lived the grossest lie of all. He'd murdered two people and let an innocent man go to prison in his place. I should have felt angry. And so, eventually, I did. But not because of the hideous crime he was at long last owning up to. Oh no. What really angered me was the revelation of so much falsehood, so much shared credulity. It had just been too pat and convenient to resist, I suppose. Naylor locked away. And our doubts with him. But now he – and they – were going to be released. The villain of the piece was going to be revealed as the ultimate victim. History was about to be rewritten. And everyone who'd subscribed to the version I knew now to be false would be exposed as at best a fool, at worst several different kinds of scoundrel.

I suppose the unavoidable acknowledgement of my own gullibility explains the muted dismay with which I finally responded. I was horrified, of course. But horror loses its edge at three years' remove from the deed. The satisfaction with which I'd greeted Naylor's twenty-year sentence could never be renewed. Paul's guilt was somehow diminished by the injustice I'd participated in. And by the shame I felt at its realization. There was a moment when I was tempted to urge silence on him, to whisper some weaselly platitude about letting sleeping dogs lie. Then I faced down the thought. There had to be an end of evasion and collusion. And this was it.

'What you did, Paul – what you freely admit you did – was terrible. Awful. Unpardonable. I believe murderers should be executed. Hanged by the neck until dead. You understand me? Done away with.'

'I understand you, Robin. I hear what you're saying. I actually agree with you. A life should be repaid with a life. But the law says otherwise. So . . .'

'What will you do now? Go to the police?'

'Not directly. I've an appointment with Naylor's solicitor in Worcester tomorrow morning. I'll tell him exactly what I've told you. Then it'll be up to him to decide what to do. I'll be glad when it is, to be honest. Grateful to let him set the wheels in motion. Besides, going to him avoids any possibility of the police turning a deaf ear.'

'You think they'd try to?'

'Who knows? This way, they won't have the option, will they?'

'And Sarah? When will you tell her?'

He sighed. 'I'm not sure I can face her with it. Confessing to you or Naylor's solicitor or the police or whoever is one thing. But standing in front of Sarah and explaining what I did – when and why – to her own mother . . . her own flesh and blood . . .' He shook his head. 'That's too much.'

'She has to be told.'

'Of course. Otherwise the first she'll know of it will be when the police come to her for corroboration of my statement. That's partly why . . .' I sensed him staring at me in the darkness. 'I came to you.'

'You want me to tell her?'

'If you will. If you can. As a favour, perhaps.'

I hesitated, torn between the wish to refuse and the knowledge that it would be better for her to hear it from me first. In the end, it wasn't a difficult choice to make, however hard it was likely to be to act on. 'Very well. I'll tell Sarah. But I'll do it as a favour to *her*, Paul. Not to you.'

A few minutes passed in silence, during which he may have reflected on the many rejections and condemnations he'd soon be laying himself open to. Then he said simply: 'Thank you.'

'Why did you do it?' I asked, the wish that he would suddenly say no, it was all a joke really, buried beneath the question. 'I mean, in God's name, why?'

'I don't know, Robin. I remember the actions, not the reasons. She cast a spell on me that was only broken by her death. And now it seems as inexplicable to me as it does to you.'

'All those lies you told. How could you sustain them?'

'Necessity. Fear. Practice. And a morsel of pride, I suppose, at not being found out. They were enough. Until Rowena took their place. But now she's gone, there's nothing. No reason. No purpose. No point to the deception. I've been going to church these past few weeks, you know. Praying for guidance. Preparing to confess, I suppose you could say. In one of the readings, there was a verse from St John's Gospel that stuck in my mind. Six words that gave me more courage than all the rest put together. And just enough for me to be able to do this. "The truth will make you free." I've thought of it a lot. The hope, I mean. It's easy to say. Not so easy to believe. But I've started to believe it. I really have. Just in the time I've been talking to you. I haven't felt free since the night I killed her. But now there's a chance. That the truth *will* make me free. At last. All over again. Truly free.'

If anyone had told me I'd one day entertain Louise Paxton's murderer as an overnight guest in my home, I'd have thought them mad. But Paul Bryant *did* spend that night at Greenhayes. When it came to the point, there was really nowhere else for him to go. He admitted he'd be grateful for company on the road to Worcester next morning and I suppose part of me wanted to be certain he meant to go through with his confession before I started throwing pebbles into the same pond.

We set out at dawn, Paul looking as if he'd slept considerably better than me. Perhaps the longed for freedom was already making itself felt. He said little as we drove north, leaning back in the seat with his eyes closed, an expression close to contentment on his face. He smiled occasionally and muttered to himself. But whenever I asked him what he'd said, he only replied, 'It's not important.' Nothing *was*, I suppose, compared with the story he had to tell. Nothing counted at all – except his fierce determination to set the record straight.

We reached Worcester in good time for his ten o'clock appointment. Cordwainer, Murray & Co occupied modest first-floor premises near Foregate Street railway station. I dropped him at the door and watched him go in before driving away. He didn't look back as he entered. He didn't even hesitate. It seemed as much as he could do not to break into a run as he took the irrevocable step.

I was in a hurry too, knowing delay would only breed prevarication. There was no easy way to tell Sarah all her worst fears about her mother were justified. But there was no way to avoid it either. I drove straight down the motorway to Bristol and made for Caledonia Place.

But she wasn't in. Well, why should she have been? It was an ordinary Saturday morning as far as she was concerned. I should have phoned ahead. I should have planned my tactics. But Paul's confession had made tactics seem futile and ridiculous. What was there to cling to in its wake but instinct?

I waited for twenty minutes that seemed like an hour. Then she pulled up in her car, unloaded some shopping and carried it to her door. I went to meet her, felt the normal greetings die on my lips and finished up making her start with surprise when she fished her keys from her handbag and looked up to find me waiting.

'Robin! What are you doing here?'

'I've some news for you, Sarah. Let's go inside.'

Her reaction was similar to mine. I could read in the alterations of her expression the same stages I'd gone through myself. Confusion. Disbelief. Slowly growing conviction. Then horror. At what Paul had done. And at what it meant. About Naylor. About Louise. About all of us. Finally came anger. Directed firstly at Paul. Then at the swathe his confession was bound to cut through all our comfortable assumptions and convenient interpretations. Nothing was going to be comfortable or convenient again. And Sarah knew that now. As well as I did.

'I never thought,' she said, 'never imagined . . . When he turned up that day at Sapperton . . . When I found he was still hanging around Cambridge during my graduation . . . I never had any idea what was really going on.'

'How could you?'

'Mummy should have told me. Then I could have put a stop to it before she left for Biarritz.'

'You can't be sure. He was completely obsessed with her. I don't think anything would have stopped him.'

'Don't you? Well, maybe you're right.' She crossed to the window and stared out at the damp grey roofs of Clifton, turning her back as if she was afraid to look at me while she said what I'd already thought. 'But it wouldn't have ended in murder, would it? Not if Mummy had been the faithful wife she wanted us to think she was. Not if she hadn't picked up Naylor, just like he always said she did, on a whim, on an off-chance, for no reason except . . .' She bowed her head and I thought she was about to cry. But there were no tears in her eyes when she turned round. 'It's stupid, isn't it? But somehow what this tells us about Mummy seems even worse than what it tells us about Paul.'

'You mustn't say that. He murdered her. And Bantock. There can be no excuses. Whatever problems there may have been in your parents' marriage—'

'They didn't have a marriage, did they?' Her anger was finding a new target now. Her mother was dead. And the man responsible was willing at last to face the consequences. Only her father's lies remained to be nailed. 'It was all a sham, wasn't it? A put-up job. She *was* leaving him. Just as I always thought. But not for Howard Marsden or some other well-groomed middle-aged lover. She was leaving him for anyone she could get. And Daddy must have known that all along. He must have known she was capable of what Naylor claimed she did.'

'You can't blame your father. He probably wanted to shield you and Rowena from—'

'Where's *shielding* got us? Your sister-in-law foisted on us as a stepmother. Rowena forced into saying things in court she didn't really believe. Then married to her own mother's murderer.' She stared at me, horrified into silence by the extra dimension of reality her words had somehow conferred on the facts. Then she added in an undertone: 'And finally driven to suicide.'

'Sarah, I—'

'Aren't you pleased, Robin? You always said we shouldn't keep so many secrets in our family. Well, this certainly proves you right, doesn't it?'

'You can't think I take any—'

'No!' She held up her hands as she spoke in a gesture of conciliation, then frowned, as if puzzled by the violence of her reaction. 'I'm sorry. I didn't mean . . . Besides, it does prove you right. I should have listened to you sooner.'

'It wouldn't have made any difference.'

'Maybe not.' She lowered herself slowly onto the sofa and shook her head in weary dismay. 'It's all a bloody shambles, isn't it?' I sat down next to her. She let me hold her hand for a moment, no more, then gently shook me off. The way she braced her shoulders and took a deep determined breath declared her intention clearly. Consolation would only hinder her. She'd find the strength to face this alone. Self-reliance would be her guarantee against the betrayals that had dragged her sister down. 'Where's Paul now?'

'In Worcester. With Naylor's solicitor.'

'So it's begun already. He'll prepare a formal affidavit and submit it to the Crown Prosecution Service as grounds for an appeal. They'll ask the police to verify Paul's statement. And assuming they do . . .'

'Paul seemed to think they might try to ignore him.'

'I doubt they'll be able to. I can confirm part of his story myself. So can Peter Rossington, I imagine. Then there'll be a lot of details that didn't come out at the trial. Stuff only the real murderer could know. They always keep a few things back as a safeguard against nutcase confessions. If some of them tie up with Paul's statement, the statement of a man who's never even supposed to have visited Whistler's Cot . . .'

'I think we both know they will tie up.'

'Yes. In which case . . .'

'How long before it becomes public?'

'Your guess is as good as mine. Strictly speaking, there's no necessity for it to become public until Naylor's been granted leave to appeal. And that won't be until the police have finished their investigation. Even then, the grounds for the appeal needn't be disclosed – or Paul named – until the appeal's actually heard. But most police forces leak like a sieve. This is sensational stuff. Sooner or later, the press will get wind of it. And my bet would be sooner.'

'But we have a few weeks at least?'

'Oh yes. A few weeks. The police will probably drag their feet. They're going to look pretty stupid when this comes out. But then who won't? Nobody can crow about it, can they? Not even Nick Seymour. He turned out to be right for the wrong reason. The only one who'll end up smelling of roses is . . .'

'Naylor.'

'Yes. Some randy little housebreaker who happened to . . .' Another deep breath. Another summoning of inner reserves. 'But he *is* innocent, isn't he? He's spent three years in prison for a crime he didn't commit. We owe him an apology, don't we? We who went to such lengths to ensure he'd bc convicted.'

'We thought he was guilty.'

'Yes. We thought. But now we have to think again.'

'Witnesses said they heard him confess.'

'Police stooges. I knew that's what they were even if you didn't.'

'What?'

She smiled at me, as if pitying my naïvety. 'A part-time barman at a Bermondsey pub who probably had a record as long as your arm and a remand prisoner hoping for a light sentence. They weren't exactly disinterested. I'm afraid the police have a tendency to improve on reality in cases like this. It catches up with them, of course, when it turns out they fitted up the wrong man. But I doubt either witness will ever be charged with perjury. That could get very messy.'

'You're saying some of the evidence against Naylor was fabricated?'

'It must have been. For the best possible reason, of course. To ensure he didn't get away with murder. The only snag is . . . he wasn't the murderer.'

'Good God. And I . . .' My mind was a jumble of all the things I could have said in court that might have altered the outcome of the trial. The guilt spread thin and far. And now it lapped at my feet.

'Don't reproach yourself, Robin. Maybe you could have been more forthcoming. But I didn't want you to be, did I? I as good as asked you not to be.' We looked at each other and seemed to acknowledge, without the need of words, the waste and folly we'd both been lured into. Paul had lived a lie for three years. And to greater or lesser extents, we'd lived it with him. 'It would have been justified – it would have been right – if Naylor had been guilty. But he wasn't.'

'What can we do?'

'Nothing. We must let the law run its course. It could be six months or more before an appeal's heard. Until then, Paul can't be charged with anything. He can't even be held in custody.'

'You're not suggesting he might make a run for it?'

'No. I can't believe he would have confessed in the first place if he didn't intend to go through with it. But he's got a long gruelling wait ahead of him. And then there's Naylor to consider.'

'What do you mean?'

'Well, if the police can't pick any holes in Paul's confession, the prosecution will have to accept that Naylor's innocent. Which means they'll offer no evidence at the appeal. If they declare that as their intention, Naylor may be released on parole before the appeal's heard. If I were his solicitor, it's what I'd be pressing for.'

'So?'

'Think about it. Naylor set free. And Paul not yet arrested. It sounds like a dangerous situation to me.'

'Surely Naylor wouldn't be so stupid as to take revenge on him.'

'I hope not. Though why I should . . .' Whatever she'd been about to say, she evidently thought better of it. She looked away and shook her head. 'We don't know Shaun Naylor at all, do we? We don't know a single thing about him. He's a total stranger to us. Yet there's no part of our lives he hasn't touched. Or ruined.'

'But he didn't murder your mother. Paul Bryant did that.'

'Yes. And when I think of how charming he always seemed . . . How smart and respectable . . . Worming his way into our lives. Flattering us into *such* a high opinion of him. I was glad – I was *grateful* – when Rowena said she wanted to marry him. Can you imagine? I was actually pleased for her. And all the time . . .'

'I think he really did love her.'

'Good. Then I hope he misses her as much as I do. I hope the damage he's done hurts him as deeply as it hurt her. And I hope it goes on hurting him. For the rest of his life.'

She pressed her fingers to her forehead and sighed. I wanted to put my arm around her then and offer her what comfort I could. But I sensed she wouldn't welcome it. Nor did I expect her to take up the suggestion I was about to make. But still it needed to be made. 'Sarah, if you'd like me to . . . break the news . . . to your father . . .'

'No. You've done enough already.' She meant it appreciatively, I think. Yet still, despite everything, there was a hint of accusation in the remark. And an echo of the temptation I'd briefly felt myself. '*Couldn't you have persuaded him to keep his mouth shut*?' she seemed to want to say. '*For all our sakes*.' But it was a pointless game to play. Like an exile's nostalgia for his homeland, its lure was also its torment. There could be no going back. 'I'll phone Daddy myself,' she said in dismal finality. 'As soon as you've gone.'

It was strange, I reflected as I drove back to Petersfield, how time alters the way we feel. If Paul Bryant had turned himself in to the police before Naylor's arrest in July 1990, his prompt surrender wouldn't have deflected our wrath. We'd have wanted him punished to the limit of the law. Waiting three years while an innocent man languished in prison should have magnified his offence. Yet instead it had somehow mitigated it. There was a tendency, which Sarah and I had both displayed, to blame Paul's victims for the delusion he'd let us labour under. It was absurd and contemptible, of course. As if Louise had invited her murder. Or Naylor his wrongful conviction. And yet it squirmed there, at the back of the mind, seducing us in moments of weakness with the promise that our responsibility for a monstrous miscarriage of justice could be passed off onto others.

But it wasn't the worst evasion we could be reduced to. There was something more desperate still. The thought that could never be spoken but was bound to be shared. It would have been better if Paul had owned up straightaway. Obviously. Self-evidently. But since he hadn't, since every solution to the problem he'd handed us was now second best, mightn't it have been preferable – or at least less awful – if he'd never confessed at all?

It reminded me of an apocryphal tale I'd once heard, based on the famous massacre of the three hundred Spartans at Thermopylae. The people of Sparta took such pride in their soldiers' self-sacrifice – '*Go tell the Lacedaemonians that we die here, obedient to their wishes*' – that when one of them who'd survived the massacre by an honourable fluke returned to his wife and children, he was turned away and cast out as a stranger. His failure to have died was an embarrassment to them. Just as Louise Paxton's and Shaun Naylor's failure to have played the parts allotted to them was an embarrassment to us. But, unlike the Spartans, we couldn't pretend it didn't exist. Paul Bryant wasn't going to let us.

Three days passed without news of any kind. My determination to let the Paxtons confront their difficulties without interference from me was sorely tested, but it held. Even though the silence from Bella in particular assumed an ominous significance in my mind. Then, on Wednesday afternoon, Sarah phoned me at the office.

'I'm at The Hurdles, Robin. With Daddy and Bella. Can you join us?'

'Er . . . yes. I suppose so. I take it . . . they both . . .'

'They know everything. Daddy spoke to Paul this morning. He wants . . . Well, *I'd* be grateful, too . . . if you could talk to Daddy. It might help him understand.'

'All right. I'll be there in an hour.'

It was Sarah who opened the door to me, which I thought odd until I followed her into the lounge and found Sir Keith pacing up and down by the fireplace while Bella sat stiffly in an armchair, smoking a cigarette. She didn't even get up to greet me and I recognized her mood at once. This was one bolt from the blue too many for her tolerance. She was opting out of the whole ghastly affair. Leaving her husband to repair the damage she no doubt held him responsible for. I couldn't blame her, really. Scandal had nowhere featured in her understanding of their marriage settlement. But now here it was. A codicil that didn't need her consent. And therefore wouldn't be honoured with her attention.

I hadn't seen Sir Keith since Rowena's death. It was immediately obvious that the tragedy had aged him. His hair hadn't been as white before, or his shoulders as rounded. His complexion was as ruddy as ever, but there was an unmistakable haggardness to his features. He looked like a man driving himself – or being driven – too hard. But not by the cares of a career. I'd dreaded meeting him because I'd thought he was bound to blame me for his daughter's suicide. Yet suddenly that was no longer an issue between us. It had been overtaken by events. As we all had.

'I'm sorry to have dragged you up here, Robin,' he said, shaking my hand distractedly. 'This is a God awful business.'

'There's no need to apologize. If there's anything—'

'Sarah tells me it was you Paul first came to.'

'Yes. It was.'

'I saw him this morning. In Bristol.'

'How did he seem?'

'In a trance, if you really want to know. Like a man in a bloody trance.'

I looked at Sarah in search of clarification. She shrugged and said: 'He's resigned from Metropolitan Mutual. As of last Friday. Now he's just sitting in that little house at Bathurst Wharf waiting for them to come for him.'

'But . . . you said it could be months before . . .'

'It will be. But he doesn't seem to care. It's like he's ceased functioning. For any purpose other than seeing his confession through to the end.'

'If it goes that far,' put in Sir Keith.

'Isn't it bound to?' I said. 'As soon as the police have verified his account—'

'But will they verify it?' he snapped. 'That's the question.'

'They won't have any choice, surely?'

'You're assuming he's telling the truth.'

'Well, isn't he?'

'I don't know.' He stopped and cast a strangely suspicious glance at Bella and Sarah. 'Unlike everyone else, I'm keeping an open mind on the subject.'

'Daddy thinks Paul may have made it all up,' said Sarah, her tone not quite concealing her exasperation. 'As some sort of self-imposed punishment for failing to prevent Rowena's suicide.'

'Well, it's possible, isn't it?' he responded, as much to me as to Sarah. 'None of us knows what's been going on in his head these past few months. He's taken to going to church, you know.'

'That settles it, then,' Bella remarked through a cloud of cigarette smoke. 'He can't be telling the truth.'

Sir Keith rounded on her and opened his mouth to speak. I thought for a moment his patience with her had finally snapped. And I couldn't help feeling pleased if it had. But he swallowed the rebuke before it was uttered, slumped back against the mantelpiece and frowned sulkily. 'He *isn't* telling the truth,' he growled. 'Not about Louise, anyway. She was my wife, for God's sake. I ought to know.'

'*Yes*,' Bella's fleeting glare announced. '*You ought to. But it seems you don't*.' Sir Keith didn't catch her look. He wasn't meant to. Not yet.

I felt sorry for him then, ground between the millstones of his first wife's fickle memory and his second wife's failing sympathy. Perhaps he felt he had no alternative but to go down fighting for his edited version of the past. Perhaps he'd rehearsed it so many times he really believed it. But if so, he was the only one who did. 'Isn't the truth really only a matter of our point of view?' I ventured. 'I mean, what we believe *is* the truth. Until it's shown not to be.'

'Until it's *proved* not to be, you mean,' muttered Sir Keith.

'Well, yes. But the police will do their damnedest to disprove Paul's story. If they fail, we have to accept it.'

'*If* they fail,' he said stubbornly.

'They won't,' said Sarah from behind me. 'You know they

won't, Daddy. It's ridiculous to suppose he could have invented such a story. That weekend in Cambridge after the exhibition when he pestered me and Mummy. That day he came to Sapperton and took me out to lunch at the Daneway. I know he did those things because I witnessed them. I just didn't see the pattern they were part of. When he visited Mummy in Holland Park. When he met her in Covent Garden. When he lay in wait for her at the Garden House Hotel. How could he make those events up? He couldn't have been sure we wouldn't be able to rule them out, could he? To say "No, actually, we know for a fact she was elsewhere the day you claim to have seen her in London." The chances of him getting away with such a deception would be astronomical.'

'She'd have told me,' he insisted hoarsely. 'That morning in Cambridge . . . She just went for a walk before breakfast, for God's sake.'

'But how could he have known she went for a walk unless he was there?'

'I don't know, God damn it. Luck. Guesswork. Something like that.'

'He must have been phenomenally lucky', Bella said slowly and coolly, 'to guess that you had a . . . disagreement . . . with Louise the day before you left Biarritz.'

'I didn't. Not as such. Not a row on the scale he describes. He's distorted everything. He says I called Bantock a – what was it? – a "bloody dauber". Well, I never used the phrase. Not then. Not later. I never said it.'

Silence loomed between us. Bella drew on her cigarette. Sarah shrugged her shoulders. Sir Keith pulled out a handkerchief and dabbed at the side of his mouth. He must have known we wouldn't believe him. There was something of the cornered fox in his crouched stance, something of the last resort in his pointless denial. He should have said there'd been no row at all, no walk-out, no discarded ring, no dismissive note. But he couldn't. So he offered instead a futile quibble about a single phrase. And an imploring gaze in my direction.

'Surely you share my misgivings to some extent, Robin?'

'Not really. It seemed clear to me Paul was telling the truth. Whether his memory of every single detail is absolutely correct can't alter that. Besides, as Sarah said, he simply couldn't have made it all up.'

'I see. So you're not even willing to suspend judgement until the police complete their investigation?'

'My judgement's only an opinion. What good would it do for me to pretend I didn't have one? The police aren't going to be swayed by what I think anyway.'

'No. Nor by what anybody else thinks either, I dare say.' He pulled himself upright and stuffed his handkerchief back into his pocket. 'Well,' he said, 'perhaps you'll excuse me. I need a breath of air.' Then he made for the door, head bowed, without even so much as glancing at Bella.

'Daddy!' Sarah called after him, filial pity flashing in her eyes. 'Can't we just—' But he didn't stop. He didn't even slow down. The door closed behind him with a click that was more eloquent that any slam would have been. Then we heard the front door open and close. And a few seconds later the sound of the Daimler starting and crunching away down the drive.

'Don't worry,' said Bella. 'He'll be back soon enough.' It was as if she was presenting a dispassionate assessment of human behaviour with no particular interest in its accuracy. I felt sure she was right. But I didn't envy Sir Keith the welcome he'd get from his wife when he returned. She'd given him unstinting support in crises that were none of his making. But this crisis was different. And so was Bella's response. I wish I'd had the courage to ask her there and then: *'When are you going to ditch him, Bella? Before Paul's trial? Or after?'* But I'd already done enough looking forward to be heartily sick of the view. And, besides, Bella gave a kind of answer to my unspoken question in what she said next. 'Tell me, Sarah. As a lawyer, how long do you reckon it will take for this business to be settled?'

'Longer than any of us would like,' Sarah replied. 'A police investigation. An appeal. A trial. It could take a year or more.'

Bella's eyes briefly closed, as if to ward off a spasm of pain. Then she said: 'And for it to be forgotten?'

'Oh, I don't think it'll ever be forgotten.' Sarah looked at both of us in turn before adding: 'Do you?'

CHAPTER FIFTEEN

The mind is master of its own defences. There's always one more drawbridge to raise, one more portcullis to lower. There was nothing I could do to block or blunt the consequences of Paul Bryant's confession. And so, without admitting what I was doing even to myself, I began to prepare my retreat from them. The Paxtons would have to face their future without me. I'd tried before to detach myself from them and failed. This time I had to make the break. I'd told Bella I meant to take the money and run. And now I had an even more compelling reason than when I'd said it to do precisely that.

It wasn't just that the tidy self-contained life of a Eurocrat suddenly seemed like a haven from scandal and recrimination. It also seemed like a refuge from my own broken dreams. What some people might have found wholly incomprehensible about Paul's behaviour in July 1990 – his infatuation with Louise Paxton – was to me only too credible. A single encounter with her of a few minutes' duration had left me with a trace of sympathy for Paul's inability to defeat his obsession. And for the violence of his reaction when he glimpsed the true nature of the woman he'd idolized and idealized. There but for the grace of God – or the mercy of chance – went I.

It was easy to maintain my detached pose. Until the police investigation began – and for some time after that – only a handful of people would know what was happening. Bella urged me to be reticent: '*Do please try to keep your mouth shut about this, Robin.*' But she needn't have bothered. I had no intention of telling anyone, least of all members of my own family, whom Bella imagined crowing at her discomfiture. Even if I'd wanted to confide in them, the acrimony that grew between us as the climactic board meeting approached would have ruled the idea out. Confidence had long since gone the same way as our profits.

I was still determined to resist the Bushranger bid, of course, futile as doing so was bound to be. But even futility can serve a purpose. My opposition to the future Adrian had mapped out for Timariot & Small gave me an honourable reason for refusing to participate in it. And for scuttling back to Brussels long before the Kington killings returned to the headlines. My fall-back position was ready. And there seemed no reason why my retreat to it shouldn't have at least the appearance of an orderly withdrawal. Except that, not for the first time, I'd reckoned without Bella's unpredictable ways.

A week had passed since my visit to The Hurdles. Sarah had gone back to Bristol, while Bella and Sir Keith had returned to Biarritz. So Bella had led me to assume anyway. Having given her proxy vote to Adrian, there was certainly no need for her to hang around for the board meeting. So I was surprised when she phoned me at home early on Wednesday the twenty-second, the day before the meeting. Eight o'clock was an hour I didn't think she knew much about. And the clarity of the line made it seem as if she was in Hindhead rather than Biarritz. Which, as a matter of fact, she was.

'Can we meet for lunch, Robin?'

'Today?'

'Yes. My treat.'

'I'm not sure. I've got a lot—'

'It's really important.'

'In what way?'

'In almost every way. I'll explain over lunch.'

'Yes, but as I've just—'

'The Angel at Midhurst. Twelve thirty. Don't be late.'

I drove across to Midhurst at noon through the sunshine and showers. The trees were turning, the first leaves of autumn beginning to fall. This time next year, I remember thinking, it'll all be out in the open. Not over. Not even then. But no longer hidden. No longer my secret. Or anyone else's. And I'll be out of it. Out altogether.

The Angel was busy, but Bella had booked one of the more secluded tables. I was early and she, naturally, was late. Having pressed me to be punctual, that was only to be expected. But still, in my present mood, it grated. After twenty minutes of toying with a mineral water while eavesdropping on nearby conversations about school fees and racing form, I was seriously considering walking out, when, as if timing her arrival by intuition, Bella strolled unhurriedly into view. She was wearing a startlingly well-cut red suit that drew admiring glances from men and women alike, though for very different reasons. I couldn't help returning her smile as I rose to greet her.

'I expect you're wondering why I'm still in the country,' she said after ordering a drink.

'I assumed you were going to tell me.'

'I am. But first I must apologize for the . . . atmosphere . . . last time we met. Partly my fault, I expect. Paul's . . . news . . . was a terrible shock.'

'Yes. Of course. How's Keith been since?'

'Better. He's come to terms with it, I think.'

'And have you?'

'Not exactly.' But she didn't light up when her drink arrived. That alone signalled some kind of adjustment. 'Keith's eager to go back to Biarritz. He thinks we can weather the storm better there.'

'What's stopping you?'

'Unfinished business.' Seeing me frown, she said: 'Tell me why you oppose the Bushranger bid, Robin.'

'You've been thinking about that? At a time like—'

'Just tell me. There's a good boy.'

The phrase reminded me, as perhaps it was meant to, of times past. Our secret times together of which we'd tacitly agreed never to speak. It had only ever been an affair of the flesh. With Bella, I suppose, nothing more was possible. Yet a little frail mental bond remained. She'd never tried to exploit it. She'd never needed to. Till now. I didn't mind rehearsing my objections to surrendering a hundred and fifty-seven years of English tradition to the Ned Kelly of Australian bat making. I was actually pleased to be asked to. But I never for a single moment thought Bella was really interested in hearing them. Around the time her salmon in sorrel sauce arrived and my diatribe against smash-and-grab commercial raiding wound to a close, she began to reveal her true concerns.

'So you still intend to vote against the bid?'

'Certainly.'

'Along with Uncle Larry?'

'He won't change his mind. Neither will I.'

'But you'll lose.'

'It seems so.'

'Unless somebody else changes their mind.'

'True. But I'm not holding my breath.'

'Perhaps you should. You can have my vote if you want it.'

I stared at her in amazement, a fork-pronged potato stalled halfway to my mouth. 'You're not serious.'

'I am. I can go to Adrian this afternoon and withdraw my proxy. Uncle Larry and I hold twenty thousand shares each. That's forty per cent of the total. With your twelve and half per cent stake . . .'

'It would be fifty-two and a half per cent. A slim but decisive majority. I can do the maths, Bella.' I put down my fork and sipped some wine. 'But not the guesswork. Why would you vote with us?'

'Because the outcome doesn't matter to me anything like as much as it matters to you. I can turn down Bushranger's offer without a second thought. Whether Timariot & Small make a profit or a loss doesn't make a lot of difference to me. I'd prefer a profit, of course. Who wouldn't? I'd prefer twenty per cent of two and a half million pounds. Naturally. But I don't need it. Not as much as I need something else.'

'And that is?'

'Your help.'

'With what?'

She leant across the table and lowered her voice. 'Proving Paul Bryant didn't murder Louise Paxton and Oscar Bantock.'

'What?' I found myself whispering as well.

'I want you to help me break his story. Find the flaw that's got to be there. Prove he couldn't have done it.'

'But he did do it. You know that as well as I do. Last week, you virtually said as much.'

'Last week was last week. As Keith pointed out, there are inaccuracies in his account. Suspicious ambiguities.'

'No there aren't.'

'There are grounds for doubt,' she persisted. 'Enough to warrant close scrutiny.'

'Well, they'll get close scrutiny. From the police.'

'Naylor's solicitor has only just submitted Paul's affidavit to the Crown Prosecution Service. It could be weeks before the police investigation gets underway. And very messy when it does. In the meantime, there's a chance to forestall it. To make it unnecessary. To spare ourselves a great deal of agony.'

'How do you know what Naylor's solicitor's been up to?'

'I asked him, of course. He didn't seem to mind telling me. Well, why should he? He's feeling very pleased with himself. For the moment.'

I sat back in my chair and shook my head. 'Bella, this is ridiculous. You know Paul's telling the truth. How can you—'

'I know no such thing. I've come round to Keith's point of view. That it's possible Paul's loading all this guilt onto himself to compensate for the guilt he feels about Rowena. That he wants to be punished. And has made up this story to ensure he will be.'

'You don't believe that. You can't.'

'Maybe not. But I don't disbelieve it either. I simply want to test the possibility.'

'Before your husband – and you – get a lot of unwelcome publicity?'

'Well? What if that is my motive? I'm sure I've never claimed to be a humble seeker after truth. If posing as one pleases you, be my guest.'

'Bella, you advised me a couple of months ago to take the money and run. Now you're proposing to turn your back on half a million pounds.'

'Yes. But some things are more important than money. You want to save Timariot and Small from the barbarians. I want to save Keith from having his first wife portrayed as a nymphomaniac.'

'And how do you propose to do that?'

'By checking Paul's story. If he's lying, he can't have been in Kington the day of the murders. Or Biarritz a few days beforehand. He must have been somewhere else. So, there'll be an alibi, won't there? An alibi he's doing his best to conceal. Possibly more than one. Start with his family. They might know something. It can't be anything obvious, or they'd have mentioned it. Paul *has* told them, by the way. Keith had a phone call from Mr Bryant. The man was barely coherent, but he should have calmed down by now. He might be able to put you on the right track. Then there's this friend Paul went round Europe with, Peter—'

'You expect me to cross-question these people?'

'Yes, Robin. I most certainly do. And anyone else who might lead us to the truth.'

'In exchange for voting down the Bushranger bid?'

'Exactly. A generous offer, don't you think?'

But much of what I thought I couldn't afford to express. My glorious defeat was in danger of becoming a Pyrrhic victory. Yet I couldn't help wanting it. Harvey McGraw's millions thrown back in his face. Adrian's self-serving plans spectacularly sabotaged. And Timariot & Small's independent status dramatically saved. It was an alluring prospect. And yet – 'Why not do it yourself? You don't need me to turn over the stones.'

'I do, actually.' She fiddled with the stem of her wine glass and licked her lips nervously. Her gaze slipped to the plate in front of her. 'You see, Keith's forbidden me to approach anyone. He's afraid that if it got to be known I'd been digging around . . . Well, he's concerned people might think he was trying to prevent a miscarriage of justice coming to light simply to protect his good name.'

'And they'd be right. His good name – and yours. Aren't they what all this is about?' As I said it, the incredulity hit me. Marrying a knight couldn't have made Bella *that* conscious of her reputation. There were too many skeletons in her cupboard for her to think half a million pounds worth staking on the slim chance of keeping just this one under lock and key. There had to be more to it. 'Or is there something else you haven't let slip yet? Something more important than being able to hold your head high in the thalassotherapy clinic?'

'I just want to do what can be done. Before it's too late.'

'But the police have as good a reason as you to want to discredit Paul's story. And they have the resources and the expertise to do it. If it's possible. What do you seriously think *I* can achieve?'

'I don't know. Until you've tried.'

'But Bella—'

'Will you do it?'

It was a small price to pay, I reasoned. I needn't do much more than go through the motions. A few uncomfortable and inconclusive conversations would be the end of it. I could still take my escape route to Brussels, of course. But just the thought of the expression on Adrian's face when he realized he'd lost was enough to ensure I wouldn't. Along with the niggling doubt I'd cornered but still not crushed. The truth never seemed to be complete. Even Paul's confession left several questions unanswered. Now I had the perfect incentive to ask them. And nothing to lose in the process. So far as I could see. 'I could say

I'd do it, Bella, and change my mind after tomorrow's meeting. What then?'

She smiled. 'You wouldn't do that.'

'How can you be sure I wouldn't?'

'Because, in your own mixed up kind of way, Robin, you're an honourable man. Quite possibly the only one I know. You really believe the claptrap you spouted about Timariot and Small embodying certain values that are worth defending at all costs. And I imagine honouring a bargain is one of those values.'

I shrugged, unsure how to respond to such a backhanded compliment. 'Maybe it is, at that.'

'Which also makes me confident you'll abide by the one condition I have to impose.' She waited for me to look quizzically across at her before continuing. 'Whatever you find out about Paul, good or bad, you'll bring to me first. Before you tell anyone else.' She paused, then added with solemn emphasis: '*Whatever* it might be.'

'Won't that be difficult, if Keith's to go on thinking you'll comply with his request not to interfere?'

'Keith needn't know anything about it. We can communicate by telephone under the guise of business discussions. Some may genuinely be necessary after tomorrow's meeting. Adrian won't take defeat lying down. Of course, I can always pop back here if things become . . . urgent.'

'How will you explain your change of mind to Keith?'

'The same way I'll explain it to Adrian, Simon and Jennifer. I'll say you've persuaded me we can do better in the long run as an independent company. It might even be true for all I know.'

'I believe it is.'

'There you are, then. In a sense, you *have* persuaded me.'

Silence fell while a waitress cleared our plates and placed dessert menus in front of us. Bella emptied the bottle of wine into our glasses, lit a cigarette and sat back to study me across the table.

'Deal?'

'You're not going to get anything out of it, Bella. All I can do is confirm Paul's story. He's telling the truth. You know that, don't you?'

'No, I don't.'

'You think he's lying?'

'I think he may be.'

'The police will find out if he is.'

'But they won't forewarn me, will they, if the truth turns out to be even more scandalous than the lie? Whereas you will.'

So that was to be my role. Bella's scout into uncharted territory. But she wasn't telling me all she knew. That was certain. And it was just as certain she never would. If I wanted to discover what it was, I'd have to go in search of it myself. Which was precisely what Bella wanted me to do. She'd dangled the carrot in front of me. And now she was showing me the stick. I should have been warier than I felt. I should have haggled for more information. But I doubt I'd have got it. And in the end it would have made no difference. I was curious now as well as suspicious. And curiosity always wins.

'Deal?' Bella repeated.

Nothing ever does turn out quite as you expect. I'd thought Bella was handing me victory on a plate. Actually, she was only giving me her vote, which amounted to the same thing in my mind but fell crucially short of it in reality. Adrian's response to a challenge was the element I'd omitted from my calculations. He'd underestimated me often enough before. Now I underestimated him. I realized he'd guess something was up as soon as Bella notified him she was withdrawing her proxy and attending the meeting to vote in person. But I assumed he'd be powerless to do anything about it even if he deduced what Bella's change of plan signified. And there I was wrong.

I phoned Uncle Larry that night to tell him I'd won Bella over to our side. He was as delighted as he was surprised. But by the following morning, when we all assembled in the boardroom, his mood seemed to have altered. He was still visibly pleased at the turn of events, but there was a sheepishness about his manner when I took him aside beforehand that puzzled me. I hadn't had a chance to find out what lay behind it, however, before Simon sidled over and asked why we thought Bella had put in an appearance. She was looking unwontedly serious in a black suit and purple blouse, to Simon's evident dismay. And she contrived, in mid-conversation with Jennifer, to glance across and catch my eye as I muttered a non-committal answer. Fortunately, before I could be backed into a lie, Adrian called us to order.

'You've all received details of the Bushranger bid,' he began, when we'd settled round the table. 'Jenny's worked very hard securing as many safeguards for us as possible and I'd like to pay particular tribute to her efforts. I'm sure we're all very grateful to her.' There were murmurs of assent. Jennifer smiled in acknowledgement. 'The offer document before you is now in its final and definitive form. The lawyers have been through it thoroughly and I take it there are no outstanding questions about its terms.' A mutual nodding of heads. 'Very well. Before I put the offer to the vote, there's only one other thing I wish to say.' He paused and glanced down the table at me, then went on. 'If this board decides to reject the Bushranger offer, I shall resign, both as chairman *and* managing director.'

Jennifer and Simon turned and stared at him in astonishment. The meeting wasn't going as they'd expected. 'We aren't going to reject it, Ade,' Simon put in with cheerful bafflement. 'I should save your ultimatum for another day.' But when he looked round at the rest of us and saw only shifty unsmiling faces, his tone altered. 'Well, we aren't going to, are we?'

'That depends, doesn't it?' said Adrian, 'on why Bella's joined us today.'

'Turn up for the books, certainly,' said Simon, still hoping he'd misunderstood. 'Though always a pleasant one.' He treated Bella to a leery grin, which she conspicuously ignored.

'Why *are* you here, Bella?' Jennifer asked pointedly.

'To vote, of course. Like the rest of you. I do have a substantial stake in this company, even if I don't work in it.'

'To vote which way?' enquired Adrian, looking her squarely in the face.

'Against acceptance,' she coolly replied.

'Bloody hell,' said Simon in surprise.

'Why?' asked Jennifer, rounding on her. 'After clearly indicating your approval for so long.'

'I've changed my mind.'

'Or had it changed,' suggested Adrian.

'You can put it that way if you like. The fact is that Robin's persuaded me we'll do better in the long run as an independent company.'

'The long run?' Simon gaped at her. 'What about the short run? The quick bucks? The two and a half million quid?'

'Money isn't everything.'

'I can't believe you just said that. It's like the Archbishop of Canterbury announcing he's turned atheist.' Bella arched her neck and looked down her nose at him. She didn't seem to be amused. 'What about the losses we've been making?'

'We'll have to ride them out.'

'But we'll go bust.'

'Not in my opinion,' I intervened, trying to sound as reasonable as possible. 'By divesting ourselves of Viburna straightaway and concentrating on our traditional—'

'Let me get this straight,' Jennifer interjected. 'You three' – she glanced at Bella, Uncle Larry and me – 'mean to vote against the offer?'

'Yes,' I said. At which Uncle Larry nodded and Bella straightened her neck in a graceful gesture of assent.

'Then the sale can't proceed. The motion's lost.'

'The motion's not yet been put,' said Adrian. At once, the absence of panic in his voice sounded a worrying note in my mind. 'As I've indicated, I'd have to resign if the offer was rejected out of hand. In view of the concerns that have been expressed, however, I'm willing to suggest a compromise. It would appear the bid as it stands is unacceptable to three members of the board. I'm therefore prepared to seek an improvement of the terms. More money up front, perhaps. More guarantees for the workforce. Whatever I can squeeze out of Bushranger.'

'That'll be sod all,' said Simon. 'You've got nothing to negotiate with.'

'I'm willing to try.'

He was playing for time. I knew as well as he did that Harvey McGraw wouldn't give another inch. But if Adrian could persuade us to postpone a final decision, he might hope to lure Bella back to his side of the argument before the extension expired. No doubt he thought he could top my offer if he could only find out what she wanted. Which would have been sound reasoning, but for circumstances he had no inkling of. I almost admired his acumen. But I had no intention of allowing admiration to stand in my way. 'The terms aren't the problem,' I said calmly. 'No offer from Bushranger is acceptable to me.'

'What about you, Uncle?' asked Adrian, smiling indulgently.

'Well, I . . .'

'I'm just asking for a little time.'

'Yes, but—'

'If I can't get anywhere with Bushranger or if such improvements as I obtain aren't sufficient to sway you, I'll accept your decision as final.'

Uncle Larry stared fixedly at the papers in front of him and pursed his lips. 'Well, that would avoid a . . . regrettable split . . . wouldn't it?' He looked round at me, pleading for my agreement. 'No sense forcing Adrian to resign, is there? Not when we can all . . . emerge from this with dignity.' He'd been nobbled. I could tell as much from his crumpled frown and his refusal to meet my gaze. Adrian had got to him before the meeting and forced him to choose between a family rift and a fallacious compromise. Fallacious because Adrian intended to use whatever breathing space he was granted to negotiate with Bella, not Harvey McGraw. And because his threat to resign would never have been carried out. With a wife, four children, two dogs and a mortgage to support, he couldn't afford to pick up his ball and go home.

'I suggest we review the situation in a month's time,' Adrian continued. 'And leave the offer on the table until then.'

'That sounds reasonable to me,' said Jennifer.

'And me,' mumbled Simon.

Adrian looked at Uncle Larry with raised eyebrows. The old fellow cleared his throat and adjusted the knot of his tie. 'Fair enough,' he said at last.

Bella looked across at me and made a mocking little circle of her mouth, as if to say, '*Oh dear*'. But what she actually said was: 'Well, why not?'

'Because this should be settled now,' I said, trying hard not to shout. 'Once and for all.'

'But that's not the sentiment of the meeting,' said Adrian, goading me with the placidity of his expression. 'Is it?'

'Apparently not.'

'Very well, then.' He smiled and flicked open his diary. 'I suggest we hold a special meeting to discuss progress on, let me see, Thursday the twenty-eighth of October.'

'No good,' objected Simon gloomily. 'You and me are going up to Lancashire, remember? To persuade a certain rising star to flash a T and S bat in front of the TV cameras.'

'Of course. The following Thursday, then. The fourth of November.'

'That's six weeks away,' I protested.

'Well, we're all busy people, Robin,' Adrian replied. 'Especially me, now I have to go to Sydney at short notice.'

'Yes, but you only asked for—' I gave up, sensing hostility growing around me. It was bad enough for me to have opposed what Simon, Jennifer and Uncle Larry all obviously considered to be a sensible compromise. I was now in danger of looking petty-minded into the bargain. 'Oh, forget it,' I concluded impatiently. 'The fourth of November it is.'

'Good,' said Adrian, so affably you might have thought an unfortunate clash of dates was all he was trying to resolve. 'Will you be able to join us then, Bella?'

'I'll be able to, certainly,' she replied. 'As to whether I will . . .' She glanced across at me and shook her head faintly, as if to disclaim responsibility for the way things had gone. 'That depends.'

Bella and I had agreed beforehand to leave Frenchman's Road at different times, in order to avoid stoking up suspicion, and to rendezvous at the Five Bells in Buriton. I'd expected to feel in a celebratory mood, tolerant of her vagaries. Instead, I was angry and resentful. Angry with myself for not having foreseen what might happen at the meeting. And resentful of the enviable position events had placed her in. Instead of having to fulfil her half of our bargain first, then trust me to fulfil mine, she could now sit back and await the results of my efforts on her behalf, knowing it would be six weeks before I could call in her debt. By which time, if I'd achieved nothing of value, she could go back on our agreement, secure in the knowledge that there wasn't a single thing I could do about it. There was no way I could stretch my enquiries out to fill six weeks. Long before the fourth of November, I'd have to come up with the goods. Or admit my failure. And the latter seemed much the likelier outcome. Which left me with no alternative but to seek a promise from her I knew she wouldn't feel bound to keep.

'I'll do what I can, Bella. But if I end up even more certain than I am now that Paul's telling the truth . . .'

'Can you rely on me to vote with you on the fourth of November?'

'Exactly.'

'Don't worry about it. Just find out what Paul's up to.'

'Yes, but—'

'You should be glad things turned out as they did, really.'

'Why?'

'Because this gives you just the incentive you need.' She smiled disingenuously. 'I don't know why you're glowering at me like that. Anyone would think what happened was my fault.' It was a thought that until then hadn't occurred to me. But now it had been planted in my mind, I knew it wouldn't go away. Was it possible she'd tipped Adrian off in some way, foreseeing how he'd react? Was it conceivable she'd set me up from the start? 'I'm going back to Biarritz tomorrow, Robin. I'll phone you early next week to see how you're getting on. And remember . . .' There was a twinkle in her eyes as she sipped her drink and looked up at me across the rim of her glass. 'There's no time to be lost.'

CHAPTER

SIXTEEN

I phoned the Bryants that night and asked if we could meet to discuss the implications of Paul's confession. It was his father I spoke to and he seemed quite touched that a member of the Paxton family – as my connection with Bella somehow made him regard me – should want to see them at all in the circumstances. It was also clear that any help I could offer them would be gratefully received. 'I don't mind telling you, Mr Timariot,' he said, 'Dot and I have been beside ourselves with worry this past week. We just don't know which way to turn.' I was obviously going to be greeted as a welcome visitor in Surbiton on Saturday afternoon. Though whether I'd be remembered as such was altogether less certain.

I didn't know whether to be glad or sorry when the weekend came. By then, I'd had a bellyful of the recriminations at Timariot & Small that had followed Thursday's board meeting. Adrian and I said nothing to each other, biding our time for our own particular reasons. But Simon and Jennifer more than compensated for that with endless dissections of a situation both confessed they couldn't understand. 'What's Bella up to?' demanded Jennifer. 'The game you've persuaded her to play could lose us this offer, you know.' She treated me to more of the same, in innumerable variations. While Simon veered from bemusement to paranoia. From 'Adrian can't seriously think he's going to get anything out of Harvey McGraw,' to 'You've cooked this up with Joan, haven't you, to stop me buying my way out of her clutches?' But however wild his theories became, they could never match the truth. I felt I was almost doing him a favour by keeping him in the dark where that was concerned.

The Bryants lived in Skylark Avenue, a long curving road of identical pebble-dashed mock Tudor semis on the Berrylands side of Surbiton. I knew from Paul, of course, that they'd lived there all their married life. Driving along it on a mild grey Saturday afternoon of lawnmowing and car cleaning, I sensed the stultifying predictability he'd rebelled against in his teens. Yet I couldn't help identifying with it at the same time. The scrawny youth tinkering with his rust-patched car while a football commentator lisped at him from a badly tuned radio. The overweight commuter working up a weekly sweat by trimming his hedge to geometric perfection. They were each in their own frustrated way part of the fabric of life. Which Paul had ripped to shreds in a single night.

The first sign of which was the lack of outdoor activity at number 34. The silence and stillness of mourning reigned. And Norman Bryant invited me in with the subdued politeness of the recently bereaved. What I'd called to discuss was worse than a death, though. Paul's mere extinction wouldn't have left his father's shoulders bent with shame as well as sadness. It would in fact, his bearing implied, have been preferable to the blow he'd suffered. He was a thin stooped timid-looking man in his early sixties, the tie beneath his pullover a testimony to forty years of dressing for the bank. His skin and hair were grey, his clothes brown, his mind set in ways not designed to meet their present challenge. 'It'll be a relief just to be able to talk about it to somebody else,' he admitted. 'Bottling this up isn't doing Dot any good.' Nor him, I strongly suspected. 'Thank God at least we've both retired. How I'd have faced them at the bank . . .' He shook his head at the unthinkability of such a prospect, then showed me into the lounge.

Mrs Bryant was waiting there with one of her daughters. I recognized them from the wedding, doleful though the contrast was. Mrs Bryant was a small round pink-faced woman whose dimpled smile had been my clearest memory of her. But there was no sign of that now. She was trembling and fidgeting like a startled dormouse, her eyes alternately staring and darting. And her handshake was so limp I expected her arm to drop to her side the moment I let go. 'You're . . . Lady Paxton's brother?' she said, so hesitantly I hadn't the heart to correct her. 'This is . . . our daughter . . . Cheryl.'

'Hi,' said Cheryl, smiling faintly. 'We met last year.' She was a tall slim fashionably casual woman of thirty or so, not quite as smart and self-confident as Paul but nearly so, with short dark hair, a direct gaze and a hint somewhere at the back of her eyes that she was on her best behaviour for her parents' sake.

'We told Cheryl you were coming,' said Mr Bryant. 'I hope you don't mind.'

'Not at all. I'm glad you did. Will your other daughter be—'

'Ally lives in Canada,' said Cheryl. 'Well out of it.'

There was an edge to the remark her father seemed to feel he couldn't ignore. 'We haven't told Allison, Mr Timariot. There seemed no point burdening her with it. Not before we have to, anyway.'

'We're forgetting our manners,' said Mrs Bryant abruptly. 'Please sit down, Mr Timariot. Would you like some tea?'

'Thanks. That would be nice.'

'I'll make it,' said Cheryl, heading for the kitchen with the eagerness of somebody glad of any excuse to leave the room.

'Use the cups and saucers,' her mother cried after her, before turning to me with a blush. 'I do so hate mugs. Don't you?'

'Well, I . . .'

'Mr Timariot hasn't come here to talk about crockery, love,' said Mr Bryant, patting his wife's hand. They sat on the sofa facing me, a pitiful optimism blooming in their expressions. Could I somehow, they seemed to be wondering, put matters right? Could I turn the clock back to their son's blameless childhood and correct the fault before it was too late? 'It goes without saying that we're . . . very sorry . . . very sorry indeed . . . about all this . . .'

'It's not your fault.'

'You wonder if it is, though,' he said, frowning down at the carpet between us. 'You bring them up as best you can. You give them so many things you never had yourself. So many advantages. And then . . .'

'He was such a good-natured baby,' Mrs Bryant remarked. Then, as if aware how irrelevant the observation was, she launched herself on another tangent. 'Sir Keith must feel this dreadfully, he really must. My heart goes out to him.'

'It must be just as bad for you,' I said.

Mr Bryant nodded and flexed his hands. 'He came here last weekend. Paul, I mean. Sat us down and told us. From the chair you're sitting in now. Calm as you like. Poured it all out.'

'Awful,' murmured Mrs Bryant.

'Said he hoped we'd understand. But how can you understand *that*?' He sat forward and stared at me. 'I'm afraid I lost my rag. I hit him, you know. For the first time in his life, I actually hit him. I was angry, you see. But he wasn't. Even then. He was so . . . controlled. I hardly recognized him as my son.'

'He was never a violent boy,' said Mrs Bryant. 'Secretive. But never violent. That's why I can't believe it.'

Mr Bryant gave me a confidential smile, as if to say: '*That's motherhood for you*.' But fatherhood, apparently, wasn't quite so blinkered. 'He didn't make it up, love. We're going to have to accept it. At least he's owned up. Better late than never.'

'Why do you think he's owned up now?' I asked.

'He said it was because of Rowena,' answered Cheryl as she bustled into the room with the tea tray. 'Said he couldn't stand it any longer.'

'So some good's come out of poor Rowena's . . .' Mr Bryant adjusted his glasses and looked at me as Cheryl moved between us with the cups. *Suicide* was the word. But he couldn't bring himself to pronounce it. Or *murder*, come to that. The truth could only be approached obliquely. 'At least an innocent man won't be kept in prison much longer,' he concluded with a sigh.

'You're sure he is innocent?' I said at once, seizing the opportunity now it had been presented to me.

'Well . . . aren't you?'

'Not entirely. Bella . . . Lady Paxton, I mean . . . and I have considered the possibility that Paul might be confessing to the murders in order to punish himself for Rowena's suicide.'

'You mean . . .' Mr Bryant's brow furrowed. He looked round at his wife and daughter. 'You mean he might . . .'

'Not have done it?' put in Mrs Bryant, her eyes wide with sudden hope.

But Cheryl was too realistic to be taken in. And in no hurry to let her parents be. 'That's crazy,' she said, looking straight at me.

'Not necessarily.'

'I heard him say it, Mr Timariot. All of it. And it was all true.'

'I heard him myself. And it was convincing, certainly. But there's a possibility – no more, I grant you – that he might be lying.'

'Because he feels responsible for Rowena's death? Come on.'

'It's true he's never got over it,' said Mr Bryant. 'But I can't believe—'

'What about the postcard?' His wife had seized her husband's elbow and jerked forward in her chair, spilling tea into her saucer. 'I told you I didn't imagine it.'

Mr Bryant sighed. 'Not that again.' He shook his head and looked across at me. 'You know Paul went round Europe by train that summer, Mr Timariot?'

'Yes, of course.'

'Well, he sent us several postcards. Half a dozen all told, I should think. Just tourist stuff. The Eiffel Tower. The Acropolis. That sort of thing. I can't remember much about them. But Dot seems to think—'

'One of them was of Mount Blank, Mr Timariot,' his wife put in. 'And that place he told his friend he was going to when they split up . . .'

'Chamonix?'

'Yes. It's right underneath Mount Blank, isn't it? I looked it up in the atlas.'

'Are you saying the card was posted in Chamonix?'

'Well . . . Not exactly. I don't recall where . . .'

'And she's thrown it away since,' Mr Bryant explained.

'I thought I'd kept them,' Mrs Bryant said stubbornly. 'For the stamps. I can't think how they came to be—'

'Dot's a great one for clear-outs,' said her husband, with a rueful smile.

'It must have been some peak in the Austrian Alps, Mum,' said Cheryl, her tone suggesting she'd already heard enough of the topic.

But Mrs Bryant wasn't to be moved, even though her excruciating mispronunciation of Mont Blanc only underlined her capacity for error – as well as self-delusion. 'It was Mount Blank,' she insisted.

'Maybe it was,' said Cheryl, glancing at me as she spoke. 'Maybe Paul sent it specifically to make us think he'd been to Chamonix. But when and where was it posted? That's the question.'

'I don't know.' Her mother was becoming irritated now. 'I didn't take down the details of the postmark.'

'What does Paul say?' I asked, anxious to calm the waters.

'We haven't asked him,' Mr Bryant replied. 'He'd gone by the time Dot thought of it.'

'And the card's gone too,' said Cheryl. 'So there's not really much point talking about it, is there?'

'Perhaps not,' I said, still trying to sound like the embodiment of sweet reason. 'But it's the sort of thing that could be helpful. If Paul *is* lying, some little slip he's made is what will find him out. I mean, if he wasn't in Kington on the night in question, he must have been somewhere else, mustn't he? And somebody must have seen him there.'

Cheryl sighed 'He wasn't anywhere else.'

'But supposing he was . . . for the sake of argument . . . Then – and on those other occasions. In Cambridge and—'

'He did stay up there after the end of term,' tolled Mrs Bryant's mournful voice. 'I remember that.'

'During the Easter vacation that year, then. Did he seem . . . in a strange mood?'

'He was always in a strange mood,' said Cheryl. 'From birth, as far as I could tell.'

Mr Bryant looked round sharply at her, then said: 'Paul's never been what you'd call open. It's never been easy to know what's going on inside his head.'

'We know now,' murmured Cheryl.

Her mother, meanwhile, had been casting her mind back to April 1990. 'He seemed the same as usual, Mr Timariot. Like Norman says, he's always had a . . . private nature. Never one to make friends easily, our Paul.'

'Or at all,' Cheryl threw in.

'What about Peter Rossington?'

'We've never met him,' Mr Bryant replied. 'I think they were just travelling companions.'

'Paul must have *some* friends.'

Mr Bryant shrugged. 'Not really. The boy's always been a bit of a lone wolf.' He seemed to wince, as if suddenly struck by the predatory connotations of the description. 'That's why we were so pleased when he and Rowena . . .' He tailed off into silence, realizing every word only took him in deeper.

'Somebody ought to check with that Peter Rossington,' his wife resumed. 'He might know when Paul was in . . . what do you call it? . . . Chamonicks.'

'He was never in Chamonicks,' snapped Cheryl. She took a deep breath and pressed a hand to her forehead before quietly correcting herself. 'Chamonix.'

'The police *will* check with him, love,' Mr Bryant consoled his wife.

'I'd be happy to speak to him myself,' I said, coming rapidly to terms with the likelihood that my visit was going to leave me with no other avenue to explore. 'Do you know where he can be contacted?'

'Paul said he worked for some big advertising agency in London,' Mrs Bryant replied. 'But I can't quite . . .'

'Schneider Mackintosh,' said Cheryl, smiling coolly at me. 'You know? The people we can thank for the result of the last election.'

'Ah yes. Of course.'

'Are you going to see him?' asked Mrs Bryant.

'If he'll see me, certainly.'

'Good.' She risked a sidelong glance at her husband. 'I'm glad somebody's doing something.'

'You're wasting your time,' said Cheryl. 'He'll only confirm what Paul's already told us.'

'Perhaps. But—'

'And do you know why? Because it's the truth.'

'How can you be so sure?'

'Because he's my brother, Mr Timariot. I've known him all his life. I've watched him grow up. But I've never really understood him. Until now. He's always been hiding something before. Keeping something back. But not any more. It's all out in the open now. I wish it wasn't. But it is. And the sooner we face up to it, the better.'

'Cheryl's right,' said Mr Bryant as he walked me to my car. 'We have to accept what Paul did as best we can. There's no sense in . . . blocking our ears to it.'

'I just want to be sure, Mr Bryant. Only your wife doesn't seem to be.'

'She's his mother. What else would you expect? She can't bring herself to believe he could commit murder.'

'But you can?'

We reached the car and stopped. He didn't look directly at me or answer my question specifically. But a shuffle of his feet and a droop of his chin gave me some kind of response. 'It was good of you to call, Mr Timariot. I appreciate it. But I have to think of Dot, you see. I have to help her come to terms with what's happened. And what's going to happen. Raising her hopes will only make her feel worse when they're dashed.' Now he did look at me. 'As you and I both know they will be.'

'I'm trying to keep an open mind on the subject. I think you should do the same.'

'Paul's walked out on his job, you know. It was a good job too. The basis of a fine career.'

'You think that proves something?'

'I think it proves he's preparing for the worst. That's why we have to do the same.' He frowned. 'I'd be grateful, Mr Timariot . . . for Dot's sake . . . if you didn't come to see us again . . . in the circumstances.' Then he sighed and added: 'Sorry.'

'What if I learn something useful from Peter Rossington?'

A car drove past us and Mr Bryant waved over my shoulder to the driver, a smile coming instantly to his lips – and leaving as quickly. His eyes followed the vehicle for a moment, as if he were wondering how many neighbourly waves he'd have to do without, once Paul's guilt became widely known. Then he looked back at me. 'You won't,' he said, without the least hint of animosity.

'I might.'

An expression of politely restrained scepticism crossed his face, such as I could imagine him having worn when a heavily overdrawn customer of the bank sought an extension of credit on the flimsiest of grounds. 'Goodbye, Mr Timariot,' he said, shaking my hand and turning dolefully back towards the house.

I phoned Schneider Mackintosh from my office first thing Monday morning. Peter Rossington proved elusive, being out of the room or on another line each time I tried and showing no inclination to return my call. Eventually, around four o'clock, I struck lucky and was rewarded with a brief conversation. He sounded young, cocksure and faintly patronizing. He also sounded distinctly suspicious when I said I wanted to talk to him about Paul Bryant. Well, I couldn't blame him for that. But jumping to the conclusion that I was some kind of headhunter keen to check Paul's suitability for prestigious employment was quite another matter. Since it was an idea I'd done nothing to plant in his mind, it seemed only fair to make the most of it. Especially since lunch at my expense in a restaurant of his choice was the fancy price I had to pay for whatever information he was prepared to dispense. I suggested the following day, but he pleaded pressure of other commitments and we finally settled on Thursday.

By then, Bella had been in touch, eager for news of my progress. But a description of my visit to the Bryants didn't seem to qualify under that heading. 'You didn't get anything out of them at all?' she complained, contriving to imply the reason lay in some deficiency on my part rather than the dismal truth that there was nothing to be got. 'Well, you'd better be more persistent when you meet Peter Rossington, hadn't you?'

But I doubted if persistence – or any other kind of interrogative ingenuity – was going to reveal a flaw in Paul's account of his activities in the summer of 1990. Cheryl Bryant had told me I was wasting my time and, as far as I could see, she was absolutely right. But Bella wouldn't be satisfied until I'd wasted a good deal more of it.

Another difficulty weighing on my mind when I travelled up to London on Thursday morning was how to question Peter Rossington about Paul without revealing the real reason. Posing as a headhunter was only going to carry me so far. And it was a pose I knew an astute young advertising executive would see through in pretty short order.

It transpired I needn't have worried. Not about that, anyway. Rossington was waiting for me when I reached The Square, a light, airy and punctiliously staffed establishment in the heart of St James's. He was a pencil-thin pasty-faced fellow with haircut and suit so abreast with the fashions that he looked even younger than I reckoned he was. More like nineteen than twenty-five. His smile was broad but cool, his eyes frankly appraising. A keen brain was apparent behind the braying voice and sneering air. I disliked him at once. And I had the distinct impression that the feeling was mutual. But neither of us was there to indulge our feelings. Though the senses were evidently a different matter, as his call for a second glass of champagne immediately revealed.

'Cards on the table, Mr Timariot,' he said straightaway. 'There was something ever so slightly fishy about your invitation. So I decided to check with Paul. One of the reasons I put off meeting you until today. I wanted time to take the temperature.' He raised his eyebrows and lowered his voice. 'Turned out to be a lot hotter than I'd ever have imagined.'

'Right,' I said, my mind racing to accommodate the consequences of what he'd said. My cover was blown, of course. But worse still, Paul now knew I was digging around in his past. It was something I might have avoided if I'd been honest with Rossington from the outset. But it was too late to repair the damage. 'So . . . You know what this is about, do you?'

''Fraid so. Wish I didn't, as a matter of fact. Sounds hideously messy. But that's Paul's problem, isn't it? And yours, apparently.'

'Have you seen Paul?'

'Yeh. We met yesterday. He told me the lot. It was a real shaker. I mean, we were never close friends. Never friends at all, come to that. Paul wasn't the matey type. He didn't let you see inside his head. And now I know what was going on inside it, I can understand why. But even so . . .' He lit a cigarette, without troubling to offer me one. 'Even so, it takes some getting used to, doesn't it? Being acquainted with somebody capable of . . .' He shook his head and sent up a plume of smoke. 'Bloody hell.'

I smiled awkwardly. 'Sorry to have misled you.'

His eyes narrowed. 'Yeh. Well, so you should be. Perhaps you'd like to explain why you did. It's the one thing Paul couldn't enlighten me about.'

'I'm simply trying to confirm his story before the police become involved.'

'They already are, according to Paul. He warned me to expect a visit. Can't say I'm looking forward to it.'

'Why not?'

He frowned. 'Because nobody likes being mixed up in something like this. Murder's bad enough. Especially with a sex angle. But . . .' He made another effort to speak softly. Clearly, it didn't come naturally to him. 'But a miscarriage of justice makes it worse, doesn't it? Big headlines. Mega-coverage. And my name in there somewhere. Where colleagues are bound to notice it.'

'So you're worried about a little . . . professional embarrassment?'

'You bet I am. Some swine's going to suggest I should have tumbled what Paul was up to, aren't they?'

'And should you have?'

'Of course not. He never gave me any hint—' He broke off to order his meal. Unprepared, I ordered the same. Wine wasn't mentioned. Something rather stiffer might have hit the mark. But that wasn't mentioned either. 'Like I told you,' Rossington resumed, 'Paul was and is a closed book to me. I suggested we tag along together on the trip to Europe because I didn't fancy going alone. Simple as that. He gave me no inkling of an ulterior motive. Well, I suppose there wasn't one at the time. That came later, didn't it?'

'Did you notice a change in him between fixing up the trip and setting off?'

'I've *never* noticed a change in him. He seems the same to me now as he did then. Cool, calm and collected. Absolutely his own man.'

'And you split up in Lyon?'

'That's right. Because he wanted to spend a week in the Alps and I was keen to press on to Italy before my money ran out. I didn't have a lot of it then. I had no idea he meant to go to

Biarritz. How could I have? Paul isn't the sort to drop clues in your lap.'

'But what would he have done if you'd agreed to divert to Chamonix?'

'How the f—' Rossington calmed his irritation with a long draw on his cigarette. 'How would I know? He'd have dreamt up some other excuse, I suppose. He was always good at thinking on his feet. I actually saw him off at the station in Lyon, you know. On the train to bloody Chamonix. My train left later, you see. Do you know what he did, the cunning bastard? Got off at the next stop down the line, waited till he could be sure I'd be on my way, then doubled back to Lyon and caught the next train to Paris. Simple, really.'

'On what day did this happen?'

'Can't remember. Paul told me yesterday it was Wednesday the eleventh of July. Well, that sounds right to me. It was certainly towards the end of the week when I hit Rome.'

'And the next time you saw Paul?'

'Was back at Cambridge in October. I'd heard about the Kington murders by then. Knew Sarah Paxton's mother was one of the victims. Well, everybody was talking about it. Even Paul. But he played it bloody cool, I can tell you. You'd never have guessed. Not in a million years. He even set up a sort of alibi for himself with me. Boasted about some Swedish sex-bomb he'd picked up in Chamonix. Made her sound so real he had me drooling with envy. But it was all a lie. He admitted as much yesterday. A lie to stop me thinking he might have been somewhere else. Like Biarritz, for instance. Or Kington.'

Our meals arrived, leaving us to contemplate each other across the same succulent dishes neither of us had an appetite for. Rossington extinguished his cigarette and cocked his head, examining me critically.

'You do realize, don't you, Mr Timariot? He did it. Trying to trip him up over dates and places isn't going to work.'

'You may be right. I just want to be sure.'

'Who are you doing this for? Paul said you had only the most tenuous connection with the case. And with the family.'

'Maybe I'm doing it for him.'

'He doesn't seem to think so.'

'For myself, then.'

'But you already believe he's telling the truth. You told him so, apparently.'

'I'm just double-checking, that's all.'

'And what's your double-checking turned up so far? Any doubts or discrepancies?'

I smiled in spite of myself. 'Not one.'

'There you are, then.' He picked up his knife and cut off a yielding slice of duckling. 'Seems to me you'd do better following my example.'

'And what is your example, Mr Rossington?'

'Look after number one.' A pink morsel of flesh slipped between his polished teeth. 'And let Paul Bryant look after himself.'

Rossington's advice was sound but impractical. Paul knew I was up to something and the least I owed him now was a prompt if necessarily incomplete explanation. When I left the restaurant, I hopped into a taxi and went not to Waterloo but to Paddington. From there I caught the next train to Bristol. And by four o'clock I was standing outside the chic little town house on Bathurst Wharf that Rowena had been walking towards the last time I'd ever seen her.

Paul answered the door quickly, as if he'd seen me approaching. He was looking smarter than when he'd come to Petersfield, but Sir Keith's description of him – '*like a man in a trance*' – held good. His self-control had become so total, his sense of purpose so dominant, that a calmness amounting almost to blankness had descended on him. He gazed at me as a committed member of some closed religious order might gaze at a hapless stranger who'd knocked at their gate. With disdain and pity equally mingled. 'Hello, Robin,' he said quietly. 'Come on in.'

I followed him along a short passage past a dining-room and kitchen, brushing against a coat hanging on a hook that had surely belonged to Rowena. I glanced into the kitchen and glimpsed other traces of her presence. A casserole dish moulded and painted to look like a broody hen. A calendar above the sink illustrated with Beatrix Potter characters. I couldn't make out which month it was, but the word was too short to be September. It could easily have been June, though – the month of her death.

The thought stayed with me as we climbed the stairs to the first-floor lounge. And there it was strengthened. The curtains and carpets, the upholstery of the sofa, the oval rug in the centre of the room, the bowl of pot-pourri, the vase of dried flowers: she'd chosen them all. And there was a scent in the air reminiscent of the delicate floral perfumes she'd worn. So reminiscent, in fact, that I was tempted to ask Paul if the pot-pourri had the same aroma. But a sudden fear that he might tell me I was imagining it got the better of me. I went to the window and looked down at the yachts moored along the wharf, at the swing-bridge across the harbour that I'd watched her cross that day in June. Craning forward, I could even make out the floating pub on the other side of St Augustine's Reach I'd watched her from. Everything was the same. Everything was exactly as I remembered. But no lone figure with flowing hair was approaching. Nor ever would be.

'Looking for something?' asked Paul from the other side of the room.

'No.' I turned round to meet his gaze. 'Nothing.'

'Like me, then. I stand there and stare out at nothing quite a lot. It helps me think.' He slowly rounded the sofa as he spoke. Then he stopped, propped himself against its back, folded his arms and frowned at me with mild curiosity. 'What's all this about, Robin? I take it you did have lunch with Peter Rossington today.'

'Yes. I did.'

'Is he the only person you've been questioning about me?'

'Actually, no. I spoke to your family.'

'Did you? They haven't mentioned it.'

'Perhaps they didn't think there was any need to.'

'Perhaps not. Mind explaining why you went to them?'

'Not at all. It's why I came. To explain.' I tried to smile, but only succeeded in producing a tight-lipped grimace. 'I just wanted to confirm your story . . . to check some of the details . . . before the police became involved.'

'Why? Don't you think they'll do a thorough job?'

'It's not that. I . . .'

'You don't doubt the truth of what I told you?'

'No.' I said, happy to be able to answer honestly. 'I don't.'

'Then what are you trying to accomplish?'

I shrugged. 'Absolute certainty, I suppose.'

He pushed himself upright, walked to the window where I was standing and leant against the sill. He rested his head against the glass and looked at me thoughtfully. 'Who put you up to this, Robin?'

'Nobody.'

'Sir Keith?'

'I told you. Nobody.'

'Sarah, then. If so, she's disappointed me. I should have thought a lawyer would prefer to handle such things personally.'

'Sarah has no idea what I've been doing.'

'It must be Bella in that case.' He raised his head from the glass and clicked his tongue. 'Yes. On reflection, it has to be Bella. She'd always ask whether something was deniable before she wondered whether it was true. What does she have on you that obliges you to act as her errand-boy?' Before I could reply, he'd moved back across the room and slumped down into an armchair, his arms still firmly crossed, his brow still quizzically furrowed. 'Don't bother to answer. It's really none of my business. Besides, I don't mind you questioning whoever you please. I've nothing to hide. If you can persuade my mother to face the truth about me, or Sir Keith the truth about Louise, so much the better. They'll have to do so eventually. As for Bella, she can do as she pleases as far as I'm concerned. So can you. The police will subject my statement to far closer and more critical scrutiny than you'll be able to. But the result will be the same. In a few months from now, you'll have what you claim to want. Absolute certainty.'

'Perhaps I can have it now.'

'Be my guest.'

'Your mother thinks you sent her a postcard of Mont Blanc. From Chamonix.'

'Mum remembers that, does she? Well, well, well. I did, as it happens. But not from Chamonix. I bought it in Chambéry, where I got off the train from Lyon. Posted it before getting the next train back. Thought it might help to cover my tracks. *Said* I was in Chamonix, of course. "A few lines as I sit in a cable-car being winched up Mont Blanc." That sort of thing. Dated it the following day. There was no chance of Mum making much sense of a blurred French postmark. I thought it might come in useful. Hasn't she got it, then?'

'No.'

'Well, it doesn't make much difference. It's just another of those little details. The police will go through them all with a fine-tooth comb.'

'It can't do any harm for me to check a few of them myself, can it?'

'None whatever.' He shook his head and looked at me intently. 'But do me a favour, will you? Tell Bella it won't work. I've set my course and nothing's going to blow me off it. The sooner you and she and everyone else involved confronts what that means for them, the less painful it will be when the truth comes out. As I mean to make sure it does.'

* * *

I'd intended to set off back to Petersfield as soon as I left Bathurst Wharf. But when it came to the point, a long and solitary rail journey, with an empty house waiting at the end of it, didn't appeal. Whereas a walk out to Clifton and an impromptu visit to Sarah did. I badly needed to discuss my difficulties with somebody and she was about the only person I could rely on being at all sympathetic.

There was another reason for seeing her, as I admitted to myself over a pint in a pub just round the corner from her flat, where I stopped off to give her time to get home from work. Sooner or later, she was going to find out what I'd been up to. Paul would probably tell her the next time they met, whenever that might be. It was even possible his parents might contact her, or she them. Either way, I couldn't take the risk of her alerting Sir Keith to my activities on Bella's behalf. It seemed altogether wiser to enlist her in our conspiracy of silence without delay.

I waited until I was confident she'd be back before leaving the pub. In the event, I nearly waited too long, because, when I arrived, she was clearly preparing to go out for the evening. She was looking unusually glamorous, in a short black dress adorned with discreet jewellery. And her hair had a lustre to it that suggested it had been professionally styled that very day.

'Robin! What brings you here?'

'It's a long story. Do you have time to hear it?'

'I'm afraid not. Rodney's picking me up in about twenty minutes.' The news that Rodney was still on the scene set my teeth on edge. 'He's taking me to a party. And since it's being thrown in my honour, I can't really arrive late, can I?'

'In your honour? What's the occasion?'

I was momentarily afraid Rodney's persistence might have lured Sarah into an engagement to marry him. So I was mightily relieved when she replied: 'This is the last day of my articles. As of tomorrow, I shall be a fully fledged lawyer.'

'Really? Well, congratulations.'

'Thanks.'

'Will you be staying on at Anstey's?'

'For the time being. Until something better turns up, anyway. *If* it turns up. To be honest, I can't help wondering whether my connection with a miscarriage of justice, however remote it may be, will have some effect on my career prospects. Learning the truth from Paul was like grasping a cactus. You just can't tell how deep some of the spines may sink.'

I smiled consolingly. 'You could say that's why I'm here.'

'I thought it probably was.' She glanced at her watch. 'Look, twenty minutes *is* twenty minutes. Do you want a drink?'
'Thanks. I think I do.'

Perhaps the constraint on time made it easier. Obliged to be swift, I was also succinct, holding back none of the discreditable aspects of my dilemma. What would have been the point? Sarah knew Bella's nature as well as I did. And she also knew how insoluble my problem was.

'Well,' she said when I'd finished, 'I certainly won't say anything to Daddy. But I still don't understand what Bella's trying to achieve. She doesn't seriously think Paul's lying, does she?'

'No. I don't believe she does.'

'Then what's she hoping you'll turn up?'

'Grounds for legitimate doubt, I suppose.'

'But so far you've drawn a blank?'

'Yes. As complete as it was predictable.'

'Which leaves you in a genuine quandary. How to let Bella down without provoking her into a breach of your agreement.'

'Exactly.'

'That's tough.' She crossed to the window and looked down into the darkening street. But there was evidently no sign of Rodney. 'As a lawyer, I ought to be able to give you some good advice. I'm not sure I can, though.' She turned round and shrugged. 'I'm sorry you should have been dragged into this, Robin. You don't deserve to have been.'

'It's not your fault.'

'Maybe not. But I'm still sorry.'

'Sounds as if you think I should just give up.'

'I suppose I do. The police will take a microscope to every detail of Paul's story. If there's a flaw to be found, they'll find it.'

'But Bella's not prepared to wait for them. Which would be *her* problem, except . . .'

'It's yours.' Sarah shook her head and sighed. She seemed about to speak when a car drew up outside and sounded its horn. She glanced out, smiled and waved. 'That's Rodney,' she said to me over her shoulder. 'I must go.'

'Of course. I'll come out with you.'

She crossed to where I was standing, grinned awkwardly and clutched my hand, willing me, it seemed, to accept what she was about to say. 'Actually, why don't you wait till I've gone, then let yourself out? Rodney doesn't know anything about this. And I don't want to have to . . . Well, you understand, I'm sure.'

'Yes.' I looked at her and nodded in explicit agreement. 'I understand.'

Then she frowned, as if some point had just occurred to her. 'If you feel you have to go on with this . . .'

'I don't have much choice, do I?'

'Then there is one angle you could try approaching it from the police may ignore. They'll try to find witnesses who saw Paul somewhere else when he claims to have been in Kington. You could look for a witness to *Mummy's* whereabouts – or *Naylor's* – at the time Paul says he was spying on them at Whistler's Cot.'

'But there aren't any witnesses. If there were, they'd have come forward at the trial.'

The car horn sounded again, an impatient triple beep. 'What about Howard Marsden? If he knew Mummy as well as we think . . .'

I frowned, then broke into a smile. 'That's inspired.'

'No,' she said, kissing me briskly and hurrying towards the door. 'That's legal training.' She pulled the door open, then paused on the threshold and looked back at me. 'I don't suppose you'll get anything of value out of him. But if you do . . . learn something about Mummy I mean . . . you will tell me, won't you?'

'Of course. It's a promise.'

But it was a promise too quickly given. Only after I'd heard Rodney's car accelerate away along Caledonia Place did I realize how easily it could conflict with my obligations to Bella. In the circumstances, it was to be hoped Sarah's supposition about Howard Marsden proved to be correct. Otherwise, I might find myself trying to keep two promises – and breaking both.

CHAPTER SEVENTEEN

Sophie Marsden had told me her husband was in the agricultural machinery business and I knew from their telephone number that they lived in or near Ludlow. That led me, without the need of much deduction, to Salop Agritechnics Ltd of Weeping Cross Lane, Ludlow. And a telephone conversation on Friday morning with its managing director, Howard Marsden.

'What can I do for you, Mr Timariot? We spoke at the time of that blasted *Benefit of the Doubt* programme, I remember, but—'

'I'm hoping you'll agree to meet me, Mr Marsden. To discuss a matter of considerable urgency. It concerns your relationship with Louise Paxton.'

'I beg your pardon?'

'I'm sorry to be so blunt, but I really have no alternative. And I'm sure you'd agree it's a subject best discussed face to face.'

'I don't know what you mean. Louise Paxton was a friend of my wife. That's the only basis on which I knew her.' But there was an undertone of defeatism in his voice. He must already have despaired of seeing me off with a blustering denial.

'In that case, your display of grief last time we met was rather excessive, wasn't it?' I waited for him to reply. But he said nothing. Several silent moments passed. Then I pressed on. 'Butterbur Lane, Kington, Mr Marsden. Twenty-seventh of July, nineteen ninety. You nearly drove into me.'

There was a heavily pregnant pause. Eventually, he said: 'What's this about, Mr Timariot?'

'It's about Louise.'

'I can't help you. You'd do better speaking to my wife. She—'

'I've already spoken to your wife. Now I need to speak to you.'

Another pause, perhaps the longest. Then he gritted out the words I wanted to hear. 'Very well.'

'I can come to Ludlow, if that suits you. I imagine you're a busy man. I also imagine you'd prefer to leave it until after the weekend.' He didn't query the remark. We both knew what I meant. A discreet slot in his working day didn't require explaining to Sophie, whereas . . . 'What about Monday?'

'Impossible.'

'Surely not. Name a time.'

'Well . . . it would have to be very early.'

'No problem. I'll drive up the night before.'

'You'll stay at the Feathers?'

'If you recommend it.'

'It's the best you'll find. All right, Mr Timariot. I'll call at the Feathers at eight o'clock on Monday morning. Not *too* early for you, I hope?'

'Not at all,' I replied, determined to give no ground. 'See you then.'

Manoeuvring Howard Marsden into meeting me was one thing. Gaining something of value from such a meeting was, of course, a different matter. I spent most of the long drive up to Ludlow on Sunday turning over in my mind how best to approach the subject of his affair with Louise. That they'd had an affair I didn't seriously doubt. The tears I'd seen streaming down his face in Butterbur Lane hadn't been the tears of a platonic friend. And Sophie's story about Louise's 'perfect stranger' made no sense in any other context. The real question was: had the affair still been going on in July 1990? If not, Howard wasn't going to be much help to Bella. Fortunately, though, she hadn't been in touch with me since my return from Bristol. So, if it turned out I was wasting my time, at least she needn't know.

Not that it was destined to be a complete waste, whatever happened. These days away from the office, arranged at short notice and without explanation, were beginning to prey on Adrian's mind. He clearly suspected I was playing a deep and devious game. And with his trip to Sydney looming on the horizon, it was no bad thing to let him go on doing so. I felt he richly deserved just as much anxiety as I could contrive to generate for him.

* * *

The deep silence of a windless Sunday night was settling on Ludlow when I arrived. I instantly warmed to its steepling streets and cobbled alleys, its timber-framed jumble of old houses and ancient inns. The Feathers was an ideally if not idyllically comfortable hotel of the kind I'd thought English market towns long since bereft. If I'd been looking for a rest cure in a soothing backwater, I'd have chanced on the perfect location. Unfortunately, that wasn't why I was there.

To prove it, I was still munching a slice of toast and sipping coffee next morning after an early enough breakfast to have caught the kitchen on the hop when word came that a visitor was waiting for me in reception. Howard Marsden evidently hadn't got wherever he was in the world of agricultural machinery by being late for an appointment.

He didn't look anything like as forlorn as I remembered. He'd put on a bit of weight and gone magisterially white at the temples. He was on his home ground too, which always bolsters self-confidence. Altogether, in his pin-stripe suit, cashmere overcoat and battered racing felt, he looked about as easy to move to tears as one of the wooden faces carved beneath the gables at the front of the hotel. But what I'd seen I'd seen.

'Shall we take a stroll?' I asked, donning my coat. He nodded in agreement. Neither of us seriously thought we'd do any talking where we could be overheard.

We went out into the empty street and headed towards the centre of town. It was a chill bright autumn morning, a sharp breeze blowing trails of leaves across the pavements in front of us, sunlight glinting and glaring at us between the rooftops. A butcher arranging sausages in his window looked up and touched his boater at the sight of my companion. 'Good morning, Mr Marsden,' he called, getting little more than a grunt in response.

'You're well known hereabouts?'

'It's a small town. And we're a big employer.'

'Have you always lived here?'

'No. I was in the Navy for twenty years before—' He broke off and looked round at me. 'You're not interested in my autobiography, Mr Timariot. Why don't you come to the point?'

'All right. I will. You know quite a lot of people think Shaun Naylor didn't murder Louise?'

He snorted. 'People like Nick Seymour, you mean. Mountebanks, the lot of them.'

'Perhaps. But it seems they may be right. A man's come forward and confessed.'

'What?'

'The real murderer's owned up – three years late.'

'Good God.' He pulled up sharply and turned to stare at me. 'Surely not.'

'I'm afraid so.'

'Who is he?'

'It wouldn't be fair to name him until the police have investigated his claim.'

'His *claim*? You mean there's some doubt about it?'

'Not much. But we'd all like to disbelieve it, wouldn't we? If we could.'

His frown of astonishment melted slowly into one of utter confusion. 'You're saying Naylor's innocent? And this . . . other man . . . committed the murders?'

'Apparently so.'

'My God.' He plucked thoughtfully at his lower lip, then squinted at me suspiciously. 'Why are you telling me this?'

'Because I think you may be holding back valuable information about Louise's movements that day. Information the police have no cause to suspect you possess. They don't know you were in love with her, you see. But I do.' He flinched and took half a pace back, as if I'd made to strike him. 'You had an affair with Louise Paxton, didn't you?'

'I most certainly did not.'

'Come on. You nearly drove into me that day because you were so upset. And your wife more or less admitted—'

'What? What did she admit?'

'That she knew something was going on between you and Louise. But the state of your marriage is none of my concern. I'm only—'

'Damn right it's none of your concern!'

'Listen,' I said, holding up my hands to placate him. 'I'm not here to judge or condemn anybody. I simply want to know whether you met Louise in Kington the day she died.'

His anger seemed to subside. His hostile glare crumpled into an exasperated scowl. 'You think she went there to meet *me*?'

'She'd walked out on her husband. Who else would she have been meeting?'

'She'd left Keith?'

'It seems likely.'

'Oh, bloody hell.' He sighed and started walking again, more slowly than before. 'If only you were right,' he muttered. 'If only I'd known.'

'Didn't you?'

He shook his head. 'Of course not.'

'But—'

'There was nothing between us. Never had been. She wouldn't let there be. Sophie's well aware of that, damn her.'

We came to the market-place, where traders were already erecting their stalls and setting out their wares amidst a cacophony of clattering poles, flapping tarpaulins and good-humoured banter. Marsden trudged gloomily down one side of the square, oblivious to the bustling scene. And I tagged along.

'Since you seem to know so much, you might as well know it all. At least then you'll get it right. I *was* in love with Louise. Still am, in a way. She never gave me any encouragement, though. Nothing *ever* happened. I wanted it to, God knows. I'd have walked out on Sophie without a backward glance if only—' He sighed. 'She'd have preferred that, I sometimes think. Louise's rejection of me was more of a blow to Sophie's pride than an affair or even a divorce would have been. The knowledge that her best friend had turned her nose up at me – at *her* husband – and must have realized as a result what a sick joke our marriage was . . .' A weary shake of the head seemed to sum up more years of discontent and dissatisfaction than he cared to count. 'I worshipped Louise. I would have done anything for her. But she didn't want to know. I was an embarrassment to her. Sophie found that humiliating and unforgivable. Which I suppose it was.'

As one piece of the puzzle fell into place, another fell out. If Howard Marsden was telling the truth – as I felt sure he was – then he'd played no part whatever in Louise's decision to leave Sir Keith. But somebody must have done. Not Oscar Bantock, as Paul had initially suspected. He seemed more likely to have been her pander than her lover. Nor Naylor, since she'd only met him when she had by chance. Who, then? There was no answer. But hovering at the margin of my thoughts was the 'perfect stranger' Sophie had spoken of. I'd never quite convinced myself she'd invented him. And now my willingness to do Bella's bidding revealed itself in my mind for what it truly was. Not an attempt to prove or disprove Paul's confession. But a pursuit of the most elusive figure in Louise's life. Who was straying more and more into mine.

'You know as much about Louise's movements the day she died as I do, Mr Timariot. Perhaps more. You met her, after all, I didn't. I have no information – for you or the police.'

'No. I see that now.'

'I'm afraid you've had a wasted journey.'

'It doesn't matter.'

We'd reached the other side of the square and were standing at the top of a wide street that led down towards the river. Marsden surveyed the view for a moment, then turned to me and said: 'The man who's confessed. Is there *any* doubt of his guilt?'

'Not really.'

'Which means Naylor was telling the truth all along?'

'Yes.'

'About Louise? About how they met? And why?'

I didn't need to answer. The look we exchanged said it all. Each of us wanted to cling to our own memory of Louise. But neither of us was going to be allowed to.

'This will destroy her reputation,' he murmured.

'Yes,' I said, unable to offer him the slightest comfort. 'I'm very much afraid it will.'

I was careful to leave Howard Marsden with the impression that I'd be heading back to Petersfield straightaway. But I had no intention of quitting Ludlow without running Sophie to earth first. For reasons I certainly couldn't explain to her husband.

I'd got their address from the telephone directory at the hotel. Frith's End, Ashford Carbonell, turned out to be an impressively appointed black-and-white house in a well-to-do village a few miles south of Ludlow. The overall effect was one of prosperity neither flaunted nor hidden, but robustly declared. I arrived just after half past nine, reckoning Sophie would be up but not yet out by then. And so she was, though the pink silk bathrobe, casually sashed over not very much, suggested I could safely have delayed my visit by another hour at least.

She must have been surprised to see me, but only a momentary widening of her eyes revealed the fact. 'Robin!' she said with a flashing smile. 'Won't you come in?'

I followed her into a large and elegantly furnished drawing-room, parts of which seemed familiar from her *Benefit of the Doubt* interview – or else from glossy interior design magazines leafed through over the years in dentists' waiting-rooms. French windows gave onto a gently sloping lawn, recently mown and sparkling with dew. Beyond, trees turning to varying shades of gold lined a long curving reach of the river. While indoors everything was tastefully immaculate: a soothing mix of gleaming walnut and glittering brass; plump-cushioned sofas and thick-piled rugs; fat-bellied urns and slim-stemmed vases.

I watched Sophie as she crossed the room in front of me, the inviting lines and soft folds of the bathrobe drawing half-forgotten images to the surface of my thoughts. She knew I was watching her, of course. The knowledge pleased her. Her movements were probably designed for an audience even when she was alone. A newspaper, some letters and an empty breakfast cup stood on a low table by an armchair that faced the television, on which two figures mouthed silently to each other in a studio. Sophie must have zeroed the sound when she heard the doorbell. Now, stooping to tap a key on the remote control that lay ready on the arm of the chair, she switched off the picture as well – and turned to face me.

'I don't like being pestered, Robin. But I don't like to be neglected, either. I think you might have been in touch before now.'

'What happened in London—' I began, eager to erect a line of defence before it could be crossed.

'Was a mistake? A misunderstanding? An unfortunate and never to be repeated lapse?' Her eyes mocked me. 'You can do better than that. You did at the time, as I recall.'

'It isn't going to happen again.'

'You think I want it to?' She sat down in the chair and studied me with a puzzled frown. 'You're no different from most men, you know. Arrogant enough to believe that what you want is all-important. Pusillanimous enough to deny what it is you really want.'

'What I want is the truth about Louise Paxton.'

'No it isn't. It's the exact reverse. You want me to validate your fantasies about her. To say "Yes, what you wish she'd been is what she truly was." Well, I can do that.' She crossed her legs, artfully judging just how much thigh the bathrobe would fall open to reveal. 'If you think it'll add to the excitement.'

'I'm not here for excitement.'

'Really? All this way for a dry debate about verity and falsity? You disappoint me. You also fail to convince me.'

'Why did you make up that story about Louise meeting a man on Hergest Ridge and planning to run away with him?'

'I didn't. I'd hardly have suggested you were the secret man in her life if I'd invented him in the first place, would I? That would have been absurd.'

So it would. Which left room for only one conclusion. That

there had indeed been such a man. And Sophie had mistaken me for him. 'It wasn't me, Sophie. As God's my witness, it wasn't me.'

'No?' Her frown softened. 'Well, perhaps not. Even I can make mistakes. Though one I never make is to regret them. But if it wasn't you . . .'

'Who was it?'

'I don't know. I felt so sure at first. I felt so certain the mystery of her death would draw him out. That's why half of me still suspects you, Robin. Still fears you could be cleverer than you seem. There's something about you. Some impression she left on you, that's too strong and enduring to explain. Unless you *were* her lover.'

'I wasn't.'

'So you say. So you say.' She rose, moved to the window and gazed out for a moment. I saw her flex her shoulders and arch her neck. She tightened the sash around her waist, then turned and walked slowly across to where I stood. 'But I don't quite believe it. And neither do you.'

'It was somebody else.'

'Or nobody else.'

'It wasn't me.'

'Just like the man who was so . . . insatiable . . . that afternoon in Bayswater . . . wasn't you?' Her eyes took their measure of me. As the mind behind them judged whether the distance between us could or should be bridged. 'Is that what you mean?'

'No. It isn't.'

'Then why do you keep coming back?'

'I won't. This will be the last time.'

'I don't think so. I'm the closest you can get to Louise now. And you just can't leave her alone, can you? Even in death. Now why should that be? Unless I was right all along.'

'I don't know. But you're *not* right.'

'And not entirely wrong?' She moved closer, smiled and raised one hand to her mouth, slipping first one finger, then two, between her teeth. She bit down gently, then slowly removed them. 'Do you want to stay? Or go?'

I wanted to do both, of course. But I knew I couldn't. If I succumbed a second time, there'd be a third and a fourth and a fifth. Her claws would sink into me, deeper and deeper. Her lies would become mine, her husband my victim as well as hers. How like her had Louise really been? I wondered. Much more so than I could bring myself to admit? Or much less than Sophie cared to pretend? There had to be an answer. But I'd never find it in Sophie's arms. 'I must go,' I said, taking half a step backwards.

'Must and will aren't the same.'

'This time they are.'

'And next time?'

'Like I told you. There won't be one.'

But she didn't believe me. Or perhaps she just wasn't prepared to let me have the last word. As I walked from the room, she flung a parting remark at me with the conviction of a prophetess. 'Be seeing you, Robin.'

I drove south down the A49 to Leominster. As far as Leominster, I could tell myself I meant to keep to the homeward route. But must and will, as Sophie had said, aren't the same. From Leominster I took the Kington road and saw the hills I'd walked along more than three years before rising slowly on the horizon, darkened by shower-cloud and the massing of memories. Always I was drawn back, it seemed. To the point of intersection. The place of meeting and parting. The ridge of no return. But swifter now than before. For now I had a quarry as well as a quest.

I travelled fast, in hopes I should
Outrun that other. What to do
When caught, I planned not. I pursued
To prove the likeness, and, if true,
To watch until myself I knew.

Who was he? There was no way to tell. He wasn't waiting at the Harp Inn, where I lunched alone and watched a rainbow form beyond the squall-line over Radnor Forest. He didn't tap me on the shoulder as I stood by the cairn on Hergest Ridge where Louise and I had sat together that lost summer's evening of long ago. I came and I went. But nobody joined me. The sun shone feebly as the wind honed its solitary edge. And the rain came in hastening gusts, blurring the edges of sight, smearing the margins of perception. There was nothing to give him a name. Or to deny him mine. There was only the doubt, as there had always been. And the still unanswered question. '*Can we really change anything, do you think? Can any of us ever stop being what we are and become something else?*' Or some*one* else. Perhaps that's what she'd really meant. Perhaps that's what she'd been trying to tell me. All along.

* * *

I'm not sure what stopped me driving up to Whistler's Cot. Stealth? Caution? A touch of dread? Something of all three, perhaps. Something, at all events, that made me park at the bottom of the lane and walk up from there.

Rainwater draining from the fields ran in curling rivulets down to meet me as I went. Sunlight glistened on moisture-beaded leaves and wet slate roofs. The truth, I sensed, retreated ahead of me, out of sight though never far off. Over the hedge, perhaps, where Paul had hidden that day. Or round the corner. Always just beyond the next encounter. Like the one awaiting me at Whistler's Cot.

A car stood half in and half out of the garage, its boot raised on several box-loads of mops, brushes, soapflake cartons, polish tins and aerosol cans. Just about every window in the house was open, red-and-white check curtains billowing out in the breeze. And the frantic whirr of a washing machine in its spin cycle could be heard from within above the growl of a vacuum cleaner.

If I'd realized what all this activity implied, I think I'd have turned and fled. But I was so distracted by the half-grasped meanings of other less commonplace occurrences that I simply stared in bemusement. And then it was too late. Because Henley Bantock had emerged from the rear of the house clutching a well-filled black plastic refuse sack – and pulled up at the sight of me.

'Mr Timariot!' He peered at me round the tuft his fastening of the sack had created. 'Good heavens, it *is* you. What an unexpected pleasure.'

'I'm sorry,' I said. 'I didn't know . . . That is . . .'

'Don't be sorry. This is just the excuse Muriel and I need to take a break. You find us in the midst of the end-of-season clear-out. The last of the holidaymakers left at the weekend. But they didn't take all their rubbish with them.' He grinned and plonked the sack down in front of him. 'Why don't you step in and have a cup of tea?'

Tea with the Bantocks in a sitting-room smelling of beeswax and air freshener was a salutary if depressing experience. Muriel was a twitteringly attentive hostess full of apologies for her house-keeping kit of tennis shirt and tracksuit bottoms. She was also an alarmingly affectionate wife, given to squeezing Henley's knee in mid-conversation and casting him long and loving looks. Henley, meanwhile, coped with the antagonism he must have detected in me by pretending we were the most civilized of rival theorists, who'd simply agreed to disagree. It was as if the angry letter I'd sent him after the publication of *Fakes and Ale* and his sarcastic reply to it had never been written.

It might have been different if Whistler's Cot had still resembled Oscar Bantock's home in anything more than the dimensions of its rooms. But it didn't. Everything from those years had been swept away. Along with any ghosts that might have lingered. In the studio, where Oscar had lain dead beneath his easels, a pool table stood, flanked by conservatory chairs. The walls around us, where his pictures had hung thick and vibrantly, were filled with insipid hunting prints and reproduction maps of Olde Herefordshire. While in the bedroom . . . I didn't like to ask. But even there, I felt sure, the process would have been the same. It was exorcism by disinfection. And its effectiveness was undeniable.

'*Fakes and Ale* will be coming out in paperback next spring,' Henley announced through a mouthful of custard cream. 'We're very pleased, of course.' For some reason he seemed to think I'd also be pleased. 'And the hardback should do well over Christmas, I think, don't you, Muriel?'

'Oh yes, dear.'

'What happens,' I couldn't stop myself saying, 'if it's overtaken by events?'

Henley frowned. 'How do you mean?'

'Well, the book follows a certain line about the murders, doesn't it? Ties them in with your uncle's art fraud. What would you do if that was shown to be incorrect?'

'But it's not incorrect, Mr Timariot. It's clearly what happened.'

'Mr Maitland went into it very thoroughly,' said Muriel in a tone of deep awe.

'No doubt he did. But it doesn't amount to proof positive, does it?'

'Not legally, perhaps,' said Henley. 'But we can't expect it to, can we? Not at this late date.'

'I wouldn't be so sure. You never know what might come to light.'

My persistence was beginning to worry Henley – as it was meant to. 'You have . . . something specific in mind?'

'No, no. Just . . . stray thoughts. For instance . . . have you ever wondered whether there might have been something between Oscar and Lady Paxton?'

It was a queston designed as much to mislead as to goad. I never expected any useful information to come my way as a result. But, as so often, my expectations were to be confounded.

'No need to wonder,' said Henley with a chortle. 'I can absolutely rule it out.'

'But your uncle's reputation as a ladies' man surely—'

'Led me to assume something of the kind long ago. But when I was rash enough to hint at it to Uncle Oscar, he nearly boxed my ears for my trouble. "She's far too good for me, boy," I remember him saying. "And far too good a patron to risk losing for half a chance of some slap and tickle."'

'Well, you wouldn't expect him to admit it, would you?'

'Oh, but I would. Uncle Oscar never stopped boasting about his conquests. If Lady Paxton had been one of them, I'd have heard about it, you can be sure.'

'It was purely a business relationship, then?'

'I didn't say that. He relied on her support. What she asked for in return may not have been so businesslike. I believe she brought Naylor here that night. So do Barnaby Maitland and Nick Seymour, for that matter. The queston is: why? In its way, it's an ideal place . . . for what she seems to have planned. And perhaps the night of the murders wasn't the first time she'd done it. Perhaps Uncle Oscar regularly absented himself when she required him to. He may have thought it was a price worth paying.'

Yes. That was what they *would* say. It was what Seymour had implied in his TV programme. And it fitted the facts. Better than Seymour or Henley yet knew.

'Unless you think that theory too might be . . . overtaken by events?'

'No,' I said, resisting the impulse to tell him that very soon it would not be overtaken but vindicated by events. Events that would nevertheless scupper the paperback edition of *Fakes and Ale*. But it seemed only fair *not* to forewarn him of his modest share in the disaster to come. After all, he'd done as much as I had to bring it about. 'I shouldn't think so,' I concluded with a smile. 'Like you say, it's probably too late for anything of the kind.'

'More tea, Mr Timariot?' asked Muriel.

'Thank you, but no. I think it's probably too late for that as well.'

'Off so soon?' said Henley as I rose from my chair.

'I'm afraid I must be.'

'But you haven't explained yet what brought you here.'

'Goodbye,' I said, smiling broadly and ignoring Henley's remark too brazenly for him to protest. 'It's been a pleasure.'

The showers blew themselves out as I drove east. Hergest Ridge and its surrounding peaks fell away behind in the rear-view mirror. The truth drew back to watch me from its hidden vantage-ground. The stranger merged with the twilight. His unseen face dissolved into the dusk. And only my reflection looked back at me. I travelled alone. But in company.

I reached Bristol at nightfall, diverted to Clifton and found Sarah at home. It was a relief to have someone to share my unguarded thoughts with. A friend to see and set them in proportion. I was beginning to curse Bella for starting me down this road. The road back into a mystery I'd walked away from. But couldn't escape.

'It seems Howard Marsden harboured an unrequited passion for your mother for many years,' I explained. 'She and Sophie both knew that. It's what Sophie most keenly resented: the fact that it *was* unrequited.'

'Hence her eagerness to blacken Mummy's character.' Sarah shook her head in dismal recognition of Sophie's motives. 'What a sad petty-minded woman she must be. To think I've known her all these years without realizing that. I can't help feeling sorry for Howard. She must make his life hell.'

'Yes,' I said, careful not to imply I had any specific knowledge of the subject. 'I think she may do.'

'But you believe her about this . . . other man . . . in Mummy's life?'

'It sounded like the truth. The question is . . .'

'Who was he?'

'Who *is* he?'

'I don't know.' Sarah rose and crossed to the mantelpiece, returning with the framed photograph of her and Rowena with their mother. 'Taken on her fortieth birthday. She was beautiful, wasn't she?'

'She certainly was.' Louise Paxton smiled delphically at me from the faintly blurred snapshot. Her beauty was preserved in the developer's emulsion, but something else was lost. Like the sepia smear left by a moving figure on an early Victorian photograph, the secret of her soul had bequeathed an unfocused ambiguity to her gaze, a perpetual uncertainty about what or who beyond the camera she was really looking at.

'The further into the past her death slips,' said Sarah, 'the more mysterious her life seems to become. I've wondered if this man, whoever he was, deserted her at the last moment. Didn't turn up where he was supposed to be. Left her in the lurch. I've wondered if that's why she encouraged Naylor. But unless you find him, we'll never know, will we?'

'How can I find him? There are no clues left to follow.'

'I know. That's why I think the question will never be answered. Unless Naylor knows. I mean, she may have said something to him. Given *him* a clue. Nobody's ever asked him, have they? Nobody's ever thought to. But we'll get the chance soon enough.'

'When he's released, you mean?'

'Yes. When he's released.' The words were spoken almost as a sigh. She took the photograph back to the mantelpiece, positioned it carefully between a carriage clock and a china rabbit, then looked round and smiled wryly at me. 'None of which helps get you off the hook with Bella, of course.'

I shrugged. 'Can anything do that?'

'I doubt it. She wants you to disprove something you and I – and probably she – believe to be true. And that's a game you can't win, isn't it?'

'Yes. It is.'

'But one you'll go on playing?'

'I'm afraid I have to.' Now I too summoned a smile. 'At least for a little longer.'

Sarah offered me a bed for the night, but I insisted I'd better press on home. It occurred to me, flogging across Salisbury Plain through the inky blackness as rain spat at the windscreen, that the offer might just possibly have been more than a friendly gesture. But then I dismissed the thought. In the prevailing circumstances, Sarah needed a friend far more than she needed an aspiring lover. And so did I.

Besides, my relations with the Paxton family were already quite complicated enough. As the three recorded messages from Bella on my answering machine testified. Each one ended with the same promise: '*I'll call again.*' Early the following morning, when I was still only half awake, she did so. And it was immediately obvious the hour didn't agree with her temper.

'You've turned up *nothing*?'

'It's not for the want of trying, Bella.'

'Then you'll just have to try harder.'

'But how? There's nobody left to ask.'

'This postcard Mrs Bryant remembers . . .'

'*Thinks* she remembers.'

'And *thinks* was sent from Chamonix. Where Paul claims he never went.'

'Not from Chamonix, according to Paul. Chambéry. A station on the main line from Lyon. It was a ruse. A deliberate blind.'

'Or else his explanation's the blind. I went to the *pension* he says he stayed in here in Biarritz yesterday. Showed his photograph to the landlady. She's never seen him before in her life.'

'You mean she didn't recognize him.'

'Same difference.'

'No it isn't, Bella. He spent a few days there more than three years ago. Did you seriously expect her to remember him?'

'The fact is she didn't. But maybe somebody in Chamonix does.' I knew at once what she was going to say next. And I also knew what my answer was bound to be. 'So you're going to have to go there, Robin. Aren't you?'

CHAPTER

EIGHTEEN

I flew out to Chamonix the following Friday, telling Adrian, Simon and Jennifer that a friend in Brussels needed helping out of an emotional crisis and I was going to see what I could do for him in the course of a long weekend. God knows what Adrian made of it, since he was due to have left for Sydney by the time I got back. Simon suggested I was hoping to discover an EC regulation that the Bushranger bid could be said to contravene. But I don't *think* he was serious.

In the event, I might have been better employed on just such an errand. Several days of trekking round the hotels, restaurants, cafés and boarding-houses of an out-of-season Alpine skiing resort from which the vast shadow of the Mont Blanc massif seemed never to lift proved as futile as I'd anticipated – and even more frustrating. Nobody remembered the name Paul Bryant. Nobody recognized the bridegroom's face in the photograph I'd brought with me of his and Rowena's wedding. And nobody thought it remotely likely that anybody else would. '*Un étudiant, monsieur? Il y a plus de trois ans? Vous plaisantez, non*?'

I wasn't joking, of course. But I might as well have been. I'd had enough by the end of the first day, but felt obliged to plug on. Come the third day, however, I called a halt at lunchtime and rode the cable-car – as Paul had told his mother he'd done – up the mountainside to the Aiguille du Midi. I stared out from the observation platform at the dazzling snowfields that stretched as far as Italy, breathed the clear cold air and reflected on the pointlessness of my journey. Paul had never been there. His footprints were nowhere to be found. But somehow I didn't think that conclusion was going to satisfy Bella.

Answering to Bella, however, wasn't the first problem to confront me when I flew home on Tuesday. Liz had left a recorded message saying that Detective Inspector David Joyce of West Mercia CID would be coming down to see me the following afternoon. And she'd added a disturbing rider. '*I tried to tell him I couldn't confirm the appointment until I'd spoken to you, but he told me he wasn't asking for an appointment; he was making one.*'

He looked as irksomely youthful as he had three years before. I congratulated him on his promotion, which his desultory thanks implied was old news. He enquired after my mother and seemed genuinely sorry to hear of her death. And then, when Liz had delivered the tea and gone again, he weighed in.

'As you may know, sir, we've been asked to investigate Paul Bryant's confession to the murders of Louise Paxton and Oscar Bantock.'

'I knew it was likely to come to that, Inspector, of course. But I didn't know your investigation was actually under way.'

'Well under way. And already we've learnt from Mr Bryant's family and from a Mr Peter Rossington that somebody else seems to be engaged on what you might call a parallel inquiry.'

'Ah. I see.'

'But I don't, sir. What exactly are you trying to accomplish?'

'The same as you, I imagine. I simply wanted to check Paul's story before it became public. To spare the family any unnecessary—'

'The Paxton family, you mean?'

'Well, yes, of course.'

'Of which you're not a member.'

'Not directly, no. More a friend. Although my sister-in-law—'

'Ah yes, the present Lady Paxton. With you. More complicated than the Borgias, isn't it?' His smile would have been no more than irritating had I thought sarcasm his sole object. But I detected an implication that my connection with Sir Keith's second wife had aroused his suspicion. Which I doubted could be dispelled by a simple explanation of how such a state of affairs had come about. 'Do I take it you're unconvinced of Mr Bryant's guilt?'

'No. But there must be a remote possibility he's lying.'

'Why would he be lying?'

'I don't know. But his wife killed herself only four months ago. A thing like that could . . . well . . . lead to irrational behaviour.'

'We've had a psychiatrist give him the once over. He's pronounced Mr Bryant as sane as you or me.'

'Really?'

Joyce's smile took on a weary edge. 'The point is, Mr Timariot, we're paid and equipped to enquire into all these matters. And we're doing so. Thoroughly and expeditiously. Interference from amateurs, however well-meaning, is only likely to obstruct our efforts.' So we'd arrived where I'd assumed we would from the start. The warning off.

'I didn't realize asking a few questions constituted interference.'

'Well, it does. Raking over the ashes of a dead case is disagreeable enough at the best of times.'

'Especially when you may have to admit you got the wrong man.'

It was a dig I'd been unable to resist. But the flush of anger in Joyce's face and the steely hint of a threat in his voice made me regret it at once. 'Exactly, sir. It could prove very embarrassing. For us – *and* the witnesses at Naylor's trial who helped send him down.' He cleared his throat. 'I have with me a copy of a statement you signed on the twenty-fifth of July, nineteen ninety.' He pulled the document out of his pocket and held it out. 'Do you want to refresh your memory of what you said?'

'I can remember perfectly well, thank you.'

'And is there anything you want to add to it?'

'No.'

'Despite what you said on TV earlier this year?'

'I was the victim of selective editing.'

He treated me to a long sceptical frown, then took another piece of paper from his pocket and read my own recorded words back at me. '"When she offered me a lift, I thought it was just a kindly gesture. Now I'm not so sure. I think she must have wanted me – wanted somebody – to stay with her."' He looked up at me. 'Not quite the same as your statement, is it?'

'What I said to Seymour was an impression, nothing more. But I certainly mentioned the offer of a lift in my statement. And in court.'

'Indeed you did, sir. I remember it well. I also remember your answer when I asked why you hadn't accepted the lift. You said it was because you were planning to walk the whole of Offa's Dyke eventually and didn't want a gap left in the southern half of the route.'

I smiled. 'You have a good memory, Inspector.'

'Finish it the following year, did you? Dabble your toes in the sea at Prestatyn, like me?'

'No. I didn't. And I haven't.'

'I see. So you might just as well have taken the ride.'

'Yes. And then everything might have turned out differently. You think I haven't thought of that?'

'Difficult not to, I imagine.'

'Very. Just as it's difficult not to wonder about other things.'

'Such as?'

He'd had his fun at my expense. It seemed only fair to respond in kind. 'A solicitor I know tells me you keep back a certain amount of information in cases like this as a sort of litmus test for compulsive confessors.'

'What if we do?'

'Well, I assume Paul Bryant's already passed the test. Otherwise you wouldn't be going on with your inquiries, would you?'

He shifted uncomfortably in his chair. 'I can't comment on that.'

'Which means you must already realize Shaun Naylor's innocent.'

'Is that what you think, sir?'

'What I think is that, if he is, those two witnesses who testified they'd heard him admit to the murders have a great deal of explaining to do. Unless, of course, you already know what their explanation's going to be.'

He looked at me levelly. 'You have one in mind, sir?'

'No. But it's an anomaly, isn't it?'

'Perhaps you think we put them up to it. Is that what you're getting at?' His gaze was direct and challenging. He knew as well as I did it was what people would say. And already he felt compelled to present his rebuttal. 'They both came forward of their own volition. Their statements were completely unsolicited.'

'And completely false.'

'That remains to be seen.'

'Have you spoken to them yet?'

A recital of the 'no comment' formula seemed to be on the edge of his lips. Then he evidently thought better of it. 'Jason Bledlow, the witness who said Naylor confessed to him while they were sharing a cell on remand, is out of our reach, Mr Timariot.

He was shot dead while taking part in an armed raid on a bullion warehouse in September of last year.'

'Good God.'

'And Vincent Cassidy, the barman at Naylor's local pub who said Naylor had boasted to him about committing the murders, has disappeared. Vanished without trace. Very recently, at that. As if he knew we'd be wanting to talk to him.'

'But he can't have done.'

'No. Unless somebody forewarned him. Inadvertently, I mean. By asking him the sort of questions we want to ask him.' His stare grew cold and contemptuous. 'I'm thinking of some well-meaning but interfering amateur. Know one, do you?'

'I haven't spoken to Cassidy.'

'I really do hope that's true, sir. For your sake.'

'Inspector, I can assure you—'

'Don't say anything you might come to regret.' He smiled knowingly at me, softening and relaxing as he did so, a pose I somehow found more disturbing than open hostility. 'We'll find Cassidy sooner or later. He hasn't the wit to stay hidden for long. When we do, we'll also find out who tipped him off. Intentionally *or* unintentionally.'

'It wasn't me.'

'In that case, you've nothing to worry about.' He finished his tea and craned towards me across my desk. 'Either way, Mr Timariot, please stay out of this from now on. It's much the wisest thing for you to do.'

Joyce's attempt to intimidate me would probably have been successful but for a single wholly understandable flaw in his logic. I knew what he couldn't know: I *wasn't* Cassidy's informant. So the question I was left asking myself was unlikely even to have occurred to Joyce. If I hadn't tipped Cassidy off, who had?

There seemed only one credible answer. And only one way to confirm it. I telephoned Cordwainer, Murray & Co in Worcester straightaway and demanded to speak to Shaun Naylor's solicitor. I was angry at the injustice of Joyce's accusation and impatient to pin the blame where I thought it belonged: on Vijay Sarwate.

But Sarwate proved to be both quick-witted and emollient. 'Your reaction is quite understandable, Mr Timariot. Let me assure you, however, that I have had no contact, direct or indirect, with Vincent Cassidy. I entirely accept you did not alert him to the police inquiry but I must point out I did not do so either.'

'Who did, then?'

'I cannot say. But look here, would it not be helpful for us to meet in order to discuss this unfortunate misunderstanding? There are, as a matter of fact, several related issues I would value exploring with you.'

'I really don't—'

'As it happens, I am travelling down to the Isle of Wight tomorrow to visit my client. It would be a simple matter to call on you afterwards. Would four o'clock suit you?'

It wasn't just my inability to justify a refusal that made me agree to meet Sarwate. I also saw it as a sop to Bella; a demonstration that I was leaving no stone unturned on her behalf. In view of the blank I'd drawn in Chamonix, I reckoned it would be as well to have something else to report when she called. As it turned out, though, she hadn't been in touch by the time I drove down to the Southampton Hilton for our appointment.

The venue was my suggestion, for which Sarwate had been effusively grateful, since it spared him a diversion from his route back to Worcester. Naturally, his convenience hadn't been in my mind. But the advantages of an anonymous hotel in which one pair of dark-suited businessmen blended forgettably with the rest certainly had.

We recognized each other from the *Benefit of the Doubt* broadcast. Sarwate didn't know, of course, how Seymour had stitched me up. Nor was he aware of the real reason for my double-checking Paul's confession. As a result, a degree of bewilderment about my motives was at once detectable behind the Indian courtesy and professional reticence. I was a puzzle he could probably have done without. And a puzzle he was poorly placed to solve.

'Mr Bryant told me he had unburdened himself to you before coming to me. He gave me no indication that you harboured any doubts about his confession, however. Am I to take it they have only recently developed?'

'I'm just trying to be healthily sceptical.'

'The police will be that, Mr Timariot. Perhaps even *un*healthily sceptical. They need neither your assistance nor your encouragement.'

'So they said.'

'Then why not leave them to it?'

'Because I like to see and hear things for myself, I suppose. To be sure in my own mind.'

'And you are not?'

'Not completely. Not *absolutely*.'

'But Mr Bryant has vindicated the misgivings you expressed in your television interview. He has revealed what you, I think, suspected all along. That my client is the victim of a miscarriage of justice.'

'Maybe.'

'How can you doubt it?'

'I'm not saying I do.'

'Dear me, this is most perplexing.' Sarwate sipped his tea and studied me over the rim of the cup, then said: 'Shaun – Mr Naylor – was disappointed to hear of your . . . equivocation. I had held out the hope to him that you would be prepared to expand on the testimony you gave at his trial. To revise your original statement in the light of your televised comments. Am I to understand—'

'I've told the police I don't wish to alter my statement.'

'Oh dear.' He looked genuinely crestfallen. 'I am sorry to hear that.'

'Quite possibly. But—'

'Shaun *is* innocent, Mr Timariot. I have known so from the beginning. He has consistently proclaimed his innocence, even when he might have made life easier for himself by admitting his guilt. He has spent more than three years in prison for a crime he did not commit. A category of crime, moreover, for which prisoners with wives and daughters of their own exact penalties undreamt of by the law. He has suffered much.'

'I'm sure he has.'

'But he has not deserved to. That is my point.'

'A point you haven't yet proved, Mr Sarwate.'

'If you could only meet him, I believe you would agree with me.'

'Perhaps. But since I can't—'

'But you can. I could arrange a visit very easily.'

Sarwate's smile gave me the queasy feeling I'd walked into a trap. From which the only way out was backwards. 'I've nothing to say to your client.'

'But he may have something to say to you.' Sarwate's eyes twinkled. 'Are you not seeking to identify Vincent Cassidy's informant?'

'You know I am,' I said, crushing all curiosity out of my voice.

'I raised the question with Shaun. It seems he is able to take an educated guess.'

'He named the person?'

'He named the person he thinks it almost certainly must have been.'

'Then who was it?'

'Ask him yourself, Mr Timariot.' Sarwate beamed at me with the proud delight of a conjurer who's just pulled off a particularly demanding sleight of hand. 'When you visit him.'

Bella phoned that night, while I was still smarting at the thought of how adroitly Sarwate had outwitted me. A face-to-face encounter with Shaun Naylor was the last thing I needed. But it was something I'd evidently have to endure if I wanted to get Joyce off my back. Which only made Bella's sneering displeasure at my lack of success in Chamonix the more unbearable.

'I might as well have gone tiger-hunting in Africa, Bella. Paul's never been to Chamonix.'

'You didn't look hard enough, Robin. That's the truth.'

'No. The truth is you've sent me on one wild goose chase after another. With the same result every time. Surbiton or Chamonix, it makes no bloody difference.'

'Don't take that tone with me.'

'I'll take any tone I like. Thanks to you, I've got to visit Shaun Naylor in prison. You remember him, I assume?'

'What are you talking about?'

With irritable brevity, I explained why I was soon likely to find myself queueing up with the wives and girlfriends outside Albany Prison. I hadn't expected any sympathy, of course. It was more likely Bella would welcome the opportunity this gave us to quiz the man she still preferred to believe had murdered Louise Paxton. Strangely however, that wasn't her reaction.

'There's nothing to be gained by seeing Naylor,' she said, much of the sharpness gone from her voice, along with all the pleasure she'd derived from my discomfiture. 'Call the visit off.'

'Why?' I was suspicious now, my mind casting back to our lunch in Midhurst and the niggling dissatisfaction I'd felt since then about her motives.

'Because it's a waste of time and effort. Concentrate on Paul.'

'I have done. To no effect.'

'He must have had friends at Cambridge besides Peter Rossington. We need to—'

'*I* need to convince the police I'm not obstructing their inquiries. And Naylor may be able to help me do so.'

'That's your problem, not mine. I don't care who tipped off Cassidy. I only care about—'

'Why don't you want to know?' I wasn't ready to let her off the hook yet. There was something almost desperate about her eagerness to ignore Cassidy. 'In fact, why aren't you encouraging me to go looking for him in case he was telling the truth about Naylor's confession? With Bledlow dead, he's the only one who can—'

'Forget Cassidy!'

'Why?'

'Because he's *irrelevant.*'

'All right, all right.' It wasn't all right, of course. My contrary nature was urging me to do what Bella had forbidden me to do precisely for that reason. But I knew it would be as pointless to confront her with my suspicions as it would be disastrous to inform her of my intentions. She was always at her least dangerous when she believed she was getting her own way. So I decided to say what she wanted to hear – while meaning none of it. 'Let's cross Cassidy off the list. And Naylor too. Let's go back to Paul. What exactly would you like me to try next?'

Bella's tactics sounded like barrel-scraping to me. I was to contact the best man at Paul and Rowena's wedding – Martin Hill, a colleague of Paul's from Metropolitan Mutual – and see what he knew. I was to question Sarah – without telling her why – about Paul's friendships at Cambridge. Then I was to go to Cambridge and speak to his old tutor, along with any students who might remember him. I assured Bella I'd make a start that weekend.

Which I duly did, travelling up to Bristol on Saturday for lunch with Martin Hill and tea with Sarah. Hill was an amiable and talkative fellow, but he could only tell me what he'd already told the police. He'd shared an office with Paul, but no secrets. The invitation to act as his best man had come as a surprise. 'To be perfectly frank, I don't think he had any real friends he could ask. I was a last resort.' This picture of a friendless and withdrawn individual tallied with Cheryl Bryant's account of her brother's childhood. And so did Sarah's description of his years at Cambridge. 'You know what Paul's like, Robin. Easy to get on with. Hard to fathom. He was no different at Cambridge. I suppose that's why he and I drifted apart. Nobody ever got close to Paul . . . except Rowena. I can tell you who his tutor was. She was mine as well. Doctor Olive Meyer. See her by all means. I'll even phone her and arrange an appointment if you like. But I don't think you'll get anything out of her. Not what Bella's hoping for, anyway. I'm afraid she has you looking for something that simply doesn't exist.'

* * *

Sarah was right, of course. With the board meeting less than three weeks away, it was a fact Bella and I would soon have to face. But there was still time to jump through a few more hoops in the hope of persuading her to honour our bargain. And there was definitely time to start down the one path she'd tried to stop me following, working on the basis that what she didn't know couldn't harm her – even if what I might find out could.

On Sunday morning, I drove up to London. It was a pluperfect autumn day, the sky a flawless blue, the fallen leaves gleaming in golden patches along the pavements and across the parks. But the beauties of nature couldn't do much for Jamaica Road, Bermondsey. Or for the vomit-stained frontage of the Greyhound Inn, most of whose customers looked as if they'd have difficulty remembering how much they'd drunk the previous night, let alone when Vincent Cassidy last pulled a pint for them.

Not so the stern tattooed landlord, however. His memories of Cassidy were clear. But he had no intention of sharing them with me. 'Vince Cassidy hasn't worked here in over a year. But I make a point of respecting the privacy of my employees – past *and* present.'

'He has nothing to fear from me.'

'Maybe not. But how do I know that?'

'I'm only asking if you might know his present whereabouts.'

'Last I *heard*, he was working for Dave Gormley. He runs a tyre-and-exhaust place down Raymouth Road.'

With that, he moved off to serve another customer. Freeing a paunchy greasy-haired man on the bar-stool next to me to snigger at my expense. 'Syd's short-changing you,' he muttered. 'Don't take it personal. He does it to his regulars as well.'

'You mean Vince doesn't work for Dave Gormley?'

'Not any more. Done a runner about a fortnight ago. Dropped out of sight like a rabbit down his burrow. Only in Vince's case even his burrow's empty. The Old Bill have been after him. Don't know what for. Wouldn't be the same reason you're looking for him, would it?'

'I shouldn't think so.'

'Makes no difference either way. Vince has turned into the Invisible Man.'

'Doesn't anybody know where he is?'

'I didn't say that, did I?' He winked, swallowed the last of his beer and frowned at the empty glass. Subtlety wasn't his stock-in-trade. But a fresh pint and a double whisky chaser revealed that information was. Vince Cassidy had a sister. And my thirsty acquaintance knew her address.

Sharon Peters, née Cassidy, lived in one of the crumbling yellow-brick tenement blocks wedged between Jamaica Road and the main railway line out of Charing Cross. To the east, the Canary Wharf tower shimmered in the sunshine, a perpetual reminder to the residents of how worthwhile the economies were that deprived them of adequately lit stairways and an occasional dab of fresh paint. They were the slums of a future that was very nearly the present, as unnerving a place for somebody like me to visit as it was no doubt depressing for somebody like Sharon Peters to inhabit.

She was a busty bottle-blonde in her late twenties, dressed in grubby grey leggings and an orange T-shirt, cleaning away the remnants of a junk-food lunch left behind by her children. They might have been among the jeering group that had jostled past me on the stairs and I couldn't help wondering if they were even now opening my car door with a bent coat-hanger prior to a Sunday afternoon joy-ride round the estate. Either way, there was no sign of them. Nor of their father, assuming he still lived with them. Sharon Peters was alone. And she looked as if she preferred it that way. The omnibus edition of *EastEnders* was playing on the television, though not loudly enough to blot out the beat of the reggae music from a neighbouring flat. The door had been ajar and she'd shouted for me to enter when I'd rung the bell, assuming I was somebody else, I suppose. Now she stared at me across her toy-strewn lounge as if I were an alien from another planet. Which in a sense I was.

'Christ! Who are you?'

'Robin Timariot, Mrs Peters. I believe you're Vince Cassidy's sister.'

'So what?'

'I'm looking for him.'

'Oh yeh?'

'And I was hoping you might be able to—'

'Like I told the fuzz, I haven't a clue where he is.'

'Naturally you'd say that to the police, Mrs Peters. But I'm not the police.'

'No? Well, maybe there's worse than them looking for our Vince. Even if I knew where he was – which I don't – I wouldn't tell the likes of you. What are you? Debt collector? Private detective? Bit of both?'

'Nothing of the kind. I was a witness at Shaun Naylor's trial and this latest turn of events has put me in a difficult position. Just like Vince.'

'I don't know what you're talking about.'

'Come on, Mrs Peters. Why has Vince gone to ground? If he was telling the truth at the trial, he has nothing to fear. And if the police put words into his mouth, he wouldn't be running away from them, would he? So, somebody else must have put him up to it. I'd like to find out who that was.'

'I still don't know what you're talking about.'

'I think you do. But never mind. Just tell Vince—'

'I can't tell him anything. I don't know where he is.'

'I might be able to help him.'

'Pull the other one.'

'All right. I might be able to *reward* him. If he turns out to have some valuable information. I gather he's out of a job at the moment. Maybe he needs some spare cash.'

'Don't we all?'

'Quite.' The hostility in her gaze had fractionally diminished, allowing the hint of a proposition to emerge. 'Well, if a little . . . money . . . would help you remember where Vince said he was going . . .'

'You have a bloody nerve, you do.' Her face flushed red with rage. 'If I was ready to sell my own brother down the river for a few quid, I'd be up Soho, wouldn't I, waggling my tits at men like you, not stuck here, working my fingers to the bone just so—' She broke off and turned away, leaning against the kitchen doorway for support as she chewed at her thumbnail. She was angry at Vince as well as me, I sensed. Maybe she was even angry at her own loyalty. 'Why don't you just piss off?' she murmured.

'All right. I'll go. But here's my card.' I took one from my pocket, wrote my home telephone number on the back and slid it towards her across the table that stood between us. 'Tell Vince what I said . . . if you see him.' She glanced down at the card, but made no move to pick it up. My impression was that when she did, it would only be to throw it in the bin. But at least I'd given her the option. In the circumstances, it was the most I could hope to achieve.

Sharon Peters' flat was at the far end of a second-floor walkway. As I retraced my steps along it, I glanced down into the courtyard below, noting with some relief that my car was still where I'd left it, complete with four wheels.

A young woman emerged from the stairwell ahead of me as I looked up and strode swiftly towards me, high heels clacking. She was thin and slightly stooped, with dark curly hair framing a pale gaunt-featured face. Her clothes were market-stall *haute couture*: a black imitation leather coat several sizes too big for her over a striped sweater and red mini-skirt. Her eyes met mine for a fraction of a second as we passed. Something close to recognition flickered in her gaze and stirred in my mind. Then both of us seemed to dismiss the thought and hurry on.

But by the time I'd reached the head of the stairs, the faint impression of familiarity had revived. I stopped and looked back along the walkway. She was standing outside Sharon Peters' door, staring at me over her shoulder as she rang the bell. She frowned. I could sense her thinking what I was thinking: who *is* that? Then the door opened and she stepped inside, smiling briskly. The door closed. And I was alone. With the answer slipping from my grasp.

CHAPTER NINETEEN

I combined my visit to Cambridge with a long-overdue tour of willow suppliers in Suffolk and Essex. This kept me away from the office for most of the following week, which was something of a bonus, since Adrian was due back from Australia halfway through my absence and was sure to think I was deliberately avoiding him.

Cambridge turned out to hold no more clues than Chamonix to the secrets of Paul Bryant's soul. Even if he'd revealed anything of himself to Doctor Olive Meyer, I doubt she'd have noticed. She wasn't exactly the sensitive type. Largely as a favour to Sarah, however, she did give me the name of a third-year student who'd roomed next to Paul in his first year. But Jake Hobson, when I finally tracked him down in the college bar after a lengthy vigil outside his Romsey Town lodgings, had difficulty even remembering what Paul looked like. 'Hardly said two words to him all year, mate. He was a closed book to me.' In that, I reckoned, Paul was unlikely to have been alone.

So, once more, like a laboratory mouse in a maze, I was back where I'd begun. I stood on the riverside path opposite the Garden House Hotel, imagining Louise walking towards me through the chill October mist as she'd walked towards Paul through the warm June sunshine. I went to the gallery where they'd met that momentous March night and strolled past the pale still lives that had succeeded Bantock's blood-bright daubings. I paced the courts of King's College and wondered why I couldn't see her, as Paul had, rounding a corner or looking down, half in fear and half in temptation, from a high window. But the past didn't lie like the yellowing leaves about me, waiting to be gathered. It kept its distance. One step behind. Or ahead.

I got back to Greenhayes on Thursday night, at a loss to know what I should do next. But there, obligingly, the answer was waiting, among the bills and junk mail on the doormat. A visiting order from Albany Prison, authorizing me to pay a call on Shaun Andrew Naylor of E Wing any afternoon during the next four weeks. There and then I decided to go the following day. Delay wasn't going to make the encounter any easier. Urgency just might.

It was another apple-crisp autumn day, with the Solent like a millpond and the cosy countryside of the Island bathed in golden light. But Albany was still a prison with a high wall and a locked gate. And the cramped foyer I waited in with the other visitors still contrived to preserve, like an essence in the air, the closeness of confinement, the claustrophobic reality of long-term imprisonment. Naylor had served just over three years of a twenty-year sentence. Standing there with the wives, girlfriends, mothers and children, I began to wonder, for the very first time, what it was like to face such a future when you knew – as nobody else did – that you were innocent, not guilty, not the right man; that you were going to spend a third or more of your life rotting in this place or some place like it as a punishment for something you hadn't done.

Two o'clock came and the other visitors went in. There was a delay, they told me. Naylor hadn't known I was coming and had to be fetched from the gymnasium. I read the signposted Home Office prohibitions for the nth time, stared out at the blue sky and the traffic moving on the Cowes to Newport road, struggled to remember what Naylor looked like and tried to decide what to say to him. Then, after twenty minutes that had seemed like hours, I was called.

A prison officer took me through two time-locked sliding doors, up a flight of steps, through a metal detector and into the visiting room. Which, to my surprise, was comfortably furnished and pleasantly decorated, with potted plants and pictures on the walls that somehow made you forget the bars on the windows. Family groups sat at well-spaced tables in peach-upholstered chairs, drinking tea and smoking cigarettes, chatting and smiling.

While in the farthest corner from the supervising officers' desk sat one man without companions. And he was staring straight at me.

A stone heavier perhaps and longer-haired than when I'd studied him in the dock at his trial, Shaun Naylor looked bemusingly fit and well, his eyes clear and intense, his gaze direct and mildly challenging. He was wearing the regulation outfit of blue denim trousers and striped shirt, cuffs rolled high above the elbows to reveal gym-honed biceps and forearms. He finished a cigarette as I approached and stubbed it out in the ashtray without taking his eyes off me. He didn't smile or get up or even uncross his legs. He just waited, like a man who'd learnt the necessity of patience, like a man with time to spare – even for me.

'You came, then,' he said quietly as I sat down. 'Didn't think you would.'

'Didn't Mr Sarwate explain? I—'

'Oh, he explained. Still didn't think you'd show up, though. These places put people off.'

'Well . . .' I glanced around. 'Facilities here seem quite . . . reasonable.'

'Yeh. Well, they would, wouldn't they? Different story back there.' He nodded towards a door behind him, the door to the rest of the prison.

'Yes. I imagine it is.'

'That's all you have to do, though, ain't it? Imagine. You don't have to live it.'

'No. Well, of cour—'

'Get us a cup of tea, will you?' He pointed over my shoulder to a serving hatch. 'Two sugars.' Obediently, I went and bought him a cup. When I brought it back to him, he uttered no word of thanks, merely took a gulp and said: 'It ain't so bad here. I don't get as much harassment as . . . other places. My first night at Winson Green, well, I thought it was going to be my last. Anywhere. They beat the shit out of me. Literally. Cons don't like nonces, see.'

'Nonces?'

'Sex offenders. We have to be segregated. That's why I'm here in the VPU. Vulnerable Prisoner Unit. Locked away with the child molesters. You know? Really nice people. But I can't complain, can I? Being a rapist and a murderer. I'm getting off lightly. Don't you reckon?'

'It's not for me to—'

'You know I didn't do it. You met her that day. You must have known what she wanted. Is that it? Have you got it in for me because you missed out on a sure thing?'

It was the tiny fragment of truth in his question that angered me more than the suggestion itself. 'If you're trying to antagonize me, Mr Naylor, you're going the right way about it.'

'That right?' A sneer quivered across his lips. 'Well, if you came here expecting me to beg, you've had a wasted journey.'

'I came here at your solicitor's suggestion, in the hope you might be able to—'

'Tell you who tipped off Vince? Yeh, he said. He also said the police think you did.'

'Yes. They do. But I'm sure you don't.'

He lit another cigarette and took a long draw on it, then said: 'Tell you what. Agree to alter your statement. Agree to say you knew all along she was on the pull that day. Then I'll give you what you want.'

'Are you trying to blackmail me?'

'Nah. You'd know if I was. That's just an offer. A fair offer. Causes you no grief. It's only the truth anyway.'

'No it isn't.'

'Come on. You know what she was after. I could tell when I heard you give evidence. You'd seen the signs. Like me. Oh, you hadn't done anything about it. Too well-bred, I suppose. But you knew what her game was, didn't you?'

'No. I didn't. What *was* her game?'

'You want me to tell you? You want to hear me say it? OK. She was seeing how far she could go. Seeing how far she *enjoyed* going. And that was quite a way. She wanted a stranger to do the things to her she'd never dared ask her husband to do. Or her lovers. She was after some rough trade. And I gave it to her. You bet I did. A classy lady, no holds barred. Too good to refuse. A real bargain, I reckoned. But it didn't turn out to be much of one, did it?'

'Obviously not.' Remembering Sarah's suggestion, I added: 'Tell me, did she mention anybody else to you that day?'

'No.'

'Some man in her life who'd ditched her or . . . let her down in some way?'

He looked nonplussed. 'She didn't say nothing like that.' And it was clear to me he didn't have a clue what I was getting at.

'Never mind, then,' I concluded lamely.

He grinned cockily. 'I'm going to get out, y'know. Never

thought I would. Never thought the bastard who croaked them would cough. But he has, hasn't he? Pretty soon, everybody's going to know I didn't do it.'

'You don't need me to change my statement, then.'

'It ain't vital, if that's what you mean. But Sarwate thinks it'll help, so . . . I said I'd talk to you.'

'Who tipped off Cassidy?'

Naylor smirked and picked a flake of tobacco from his tongue. 'Not so fast. You going to change your statement?'

'Perhaps.'

'I need a promise.'

'They come cheap. What if I gave you one, then broke it?'

'I'd bear it in mind. For when I get out. I'll have some scores to settle then. You wouldn't want to be one of them.' He took another gulp of tea and eyed me knowingly. 'What you said on the telly would be good enough.'

And what I'd said on the television had been truer than I'd realized at the time. To resist the conclusion was to cling stubbornly to a memory every fresh discovery showed up as a lie. And stubbornness was a luxury I couldn't afford. He was going to get out. He knew it. So did I. There would be other settlements – other surrenders – more painful than this one. 'All right. I'll make a fresh statement. Along the same lines as my interview on *Benefit of the Doubt*. You have my word.'

He chuckled. 'The word of a gentleman?'

'If it amuses you to say so.'

'Yeh. It does. But, then, the whole thing's a bit of a joke, ain't it? All that effort – all that closing of ranks – to get me put away. And the real murderer turns out to be one of your own. I've heard of keeping it in the family, but—'

'Who was Cassidy's informant?'

'Ain't it obvious?'

'Not to me.'

'I'm only entitled to a couple of visits a month, mate. Why d'you think I'd waste one on you?'

'Because Sarwate advised you it was—'

'Sarwate? I don't take orders from some—' He broke off and smiled grimly. 'Truth is, I got visits to spare. The missus don't come to see me no more. Says it's bad for the kids. But that's bullshit.'

'Why doesn't she come, then?'

'Because she's got somebody else. Simple as that. Can't blame her, really. I mean, twenty years is a long time, ain't it? Must have come as a bit of a shock to hear I was going to be out in less than four. Like I say, I can't blame her. Leastways, I *wouldn't*. If it had been anybody else but Vince Cassidy.'

'You're saying . . .'

'My wife tipped off Vince. Nobody else it could be. Sarwate told her about Bryant. She told Vince. And Vince scarpered. What else could he do? Hang around till the police came for him, then explain he helped have me sent down just so he and Carol could . . .' He shook his head. 'Don't think so, do you?'

'Why didn't you say this at your trial?'

'Didn't know, did I? Not then. Carol talked me into believing he'd done it to get the Drugs Squad to drop some charges against him. But I've heard since he was having it away with her long before . . .' He swirled the tea glumly in his cup and drained it. 'Should have guessed. She was always thick with that tart Vince had for a sister.'

Then it came to me. The girl on the walkway outside Sharon Peters' flat. The faint but mutual recognition. We'd seen each other on the same videotape. Carol Naylor and me. Carol Naylor, calling on Vince Cassidy's sister. *She'd* tipped him off. There was treachery everywhere. Even, perhaps especially, for Shaun Naylor.

'You look more shocked than I was at the time, mate. Not the answer you was expecting?'

'Not exactly.'

'Sorry to disappoint you. But it's the oldest story in the book.'

'You're certain of this?'

'Oh yeh. I'm certain.'

'And Bledlow? Why should he have testified against you?'

Naylor shrugged. 'Christ knows. He hated my guts, but . . . maybe he'd have done some deal even if he hadn't. He got a light sentence, y'know. Must have thought he'd played it real sweet. Funny how it goes, ain't it? If he'd kept his mouth shut and copped the usual, he wouldn't have been out in time to get his head blown off in that bullion raid. I have a laugh about that sometimes.'

The trail ended here, I suddenly realized. The mystery of Vincent Cassidy's motive – and his foreknowledge – dissolved into the sordid normality of adultery and deceit. And the enigma of Louise Paxton vanished with it. I hadn't found what Bella wanted. Instead, at every turn, I'd been met by something much less palatable: the truth; the whole unquenchable insistent truth.

'What you going to do now?'

'Alter my statement. As promised. I'll have to tell the police about Cassidy and your wife, of course.'

'Be my guest. They probably already know. Probably just *said* they blamed you. To frighten you off. Sounds like their style.'

'You may be right.'

'What about this digging around Sarwate said you been doing? Going on with that?'

'I don't think so.'

'Why not?'

'Because there's nowhere left to dig.'

'Meaning you'll have to admit Bryant did the murders?'

'Oh, I'll leave that to the proper authorities. Time I dropped out of the picture, I think.'

'You're lucky you can,' he said, apparently without rancour.

'Quite.' I pushed my chair back and stood up. 'Well, I must be going. Thank you . . . for seeing me.'

He made no move, merely raised his eyes fractionally to meet mine. 'No problem.'

'I'm sorry . . . about your wife.'

'Not half as sorry as you are I didn't do it, I bet. Galling, ain't it?'

He was smiling now, already savouring the foretaste of his ultimate victory, already planning the humiliation he'd heap on those who'd wronged him. I should have counted myself lucky to face mine behind closed doors, with ample warning; to be baited by this loathsome man to the point where I could tell myself he didn't deserve to hear the apology he was owed. But I didn't feel lucky at all. Only eager beyond reason to be out of his sight.

'This guy Bryant . . .' he began, his smile fading into a thoughtful frown.

'What about him?'

Several silent seconds passed as Naylor looked up at me. Then he said: 'Nothing. It don't matter.'

'Very well. I—'

'Best be on your way, eh?' The smile returned as he raised the cigarette to his lips.

'Goodbye, Mr Naylor,' I said through gritted teeth. I waited for him to respond, but all I got was a cool stare through a veil of smoke. Then I turned and walked slowly towards the exit, catching the eye of one of the prison officers as I passed their desk.

'Leaving so soon, sir?'

'Yes.'

But it didn't seem soon to me. Steeling myself not to glance back at Naylor as I waited for the door to be unlocked, it seemed, in fact, all too late.

Sitting in the passenger lounge on the car ferry back to Portsmouth an hour later, I confronted and took the decisions I could no longer delay. Whatever Bella might say, this *was* the end. She'd be outraged as soon as she heard I'd changed my statement, so I might as well cut my losses and tell her I wouldn't be doing her bidding from now on. She'd probably retaliate by giving her vote to Adrian, unless I could persuade her I really had done all she could expect of me. And even then . . . But it couldn't be helped. I'd plead my case as forcefully as I was able. In the end, though, it wasn't up to me. My visit to Naylor had made me almost glad of that. Suddenly, I didn't want to be involved any more, whatever the cost.

Determined to act on my decision at once, I telephoned Bella that evening. She seemed irritated I'd made contact and insisted on calling me back later, 'when it'll be easier to talk'. This turned out to be near midnight, one of her most alert and active hours. On other occasions, she might have found me sluggish and slow-thinking. But on this occasion I was ready for her.

'I have to see you straightaway, Bella. There's been a development.'

'What sort of development?'

'I can't discuss it over the phone. We have to meet.'

'Well, I can't come to England at the moment.'

'Then I'll come to you.'

'No. Things are fraught enough here without you turning up out of the blue. Keith's in no mood to entertain unexpected guests.'

'Then what do you suggest?'

'Let me think,' she snapped. A few moments passed. Then she said: 'We could meet in Bordeaux.'

'All right. But how does that—'

'Get a flight out on Tuesday. I'll drive up the same day. A shopping trip with an overnight stay won't sound suspicious to Keith. I've done it before. I'll stay at the Burdigala, as usual. You'd better stay somewhere else. Meet me in the hotel bar at six o'clock.'

'OK. I'll be there.'

'And Robin—'

'Yes?'
'This had better be worth it.'

My absences from the office had become so conspicuous and commented on that I gave no warning of the next one. Monday elapsed with merciful swiftness, Adrian proving as reticent about his trip to Sydney as I was forced to be about my tour of East Anglian willow plantations. The board meeting was ten days away, its imminence spreading apprehensiveness and suspicion among the entire staff, let alone my siblings. Our futures are always in the balance, of course. But usually we manage to ignore the fact. At Timariot & Small, during the last week of October, that simply wasn't possible. As for the consternation my phone call to Liz from Gatwick on Tuesday morning was likely to cause, I'd ceased by then to give a damn.

The Hotel Burdigala was a stylish *grand luxe* establishment close to the fashionable stores and restaurants in the centre of Bordeaux. Bella always insisted on the best, which the soulless low-rise joint I'd booked into out at the airport certainly wasn't. But her standards had slipped in one respect at least. This time, she didn't keep me waiting. Or guessing long about her response when I told her what I meant to do – and why.

'So, you're giving up on me, Robin.'

'I don't have any choice.'

'That's ridiculous. I don't accept we've exhausted all the possibilities yet.'

'*I've* exhausted them. And myself in the process. Naylor was set up. Deservedly so, you could say. But that's supposed to be the acid test of justice, isn't it? Doing right by the innocent, even when you can't stand the sight of them.'

'And Paul?'

'Is facing up to what he did. I suggest you find the decency to do the same.'

She might have bristled at that. Instead, she treated me to a soulful stare. 'You don't know what you're asking, Robin. This business is tearing Keith apart. And our marriage with it.'

'I'm sorry, Bella. That's not my problem. You have my sympathy, but . . .'

'Not your help?'

'I've done all I can.'

'I don't agree.'

'Meaning you'll break your promise and vote with Adrian?'

'I didn't say so.' She lit a cigarette, her hand shaking faintly as she did so. Was she really upset? I wondered. Or just seeking another route round my defences? 'Won't you reconsider? I genuinely believe Paul's made all this up. There has to be some way of—'

'For God's sake!' I'd spoken loudly enough to turn heads elsewhere in the bar. Now I leant forward across the table and softened my tone. 'I've spoken to everyone who knew him three years ago. I've been everywhere he went. And some places he never went. I've tried everything. And ended up where I knew I would all along. I don't want him to have done it. I wish he hadn't done it. But he did. And you have to accept it.'

She raised her left hand to her face and covered her mouth, her thumb pressing against one cheekbone, her forefinger against the other. Her engagement ring glittered in the lamplight. Smoke climbed in a gentle plume from the cigarette in her right hand. And in her eyes there was such brilliantly simulated agony that I could almost have believed it was what she truly felt. But when she took her hand away, her mouth was set in a firm determined line. 'I have to think of myself now, Robin. You do understand that, don't you?'

'I've always understood that.'

'I have to prepare for an independent future.'

'You'll ditch Keith, then?'

'It's not a question of ditching. It's a matter of necessity.' She saw me raise my eyebrows in doubt, but carried on unabashed. 'And it's not the only one. I shan't vote with Adrian. I'll vote with you. But we'll lose.'

'What do you mean?'

'Adrian's made me an offer, you see. One that's too good to refuse. Especially now.'

'What offer?'

'He's willing to buy five thousand of my shares. At a substantial premium over the Bushranger price.'

I almost smiled in spite of myself. And so, I think, did Bella. Five thousand shares would exactly invert the voting ratio, giving Adrian a 52½ per cent majority in favour of acceptance. Bella would vote on the losing side, but end up even better off than if the offer had gone through unopposed. She'd make a fool of me *and* Adrian. And then she'd walk away with the money she needed to rid herself of a husband who was about to become an embarrassment to her. Farewell, Timariot & Small. *Adieu L'Hivernance*. They'd been pleasant enough while they lasted.

But Bella had decided it was time to leave. And time for them to go.

We walked out into the mild Bordelaise dusk. Bella looked and sounded genuinely sorry for me as she stood beside me in front of the hotel. But her sorrow came cheaper than her vote. Much cheaper. 'I booked a table for two at Le Chapon Fin,' she said. 'It's an excellent restaurant.'

'You'll have to dine alone. I know I shall prefer to.' It wasn't meant as bitterly as it may have been taken. But I hadn't the energy to pull my punches, even the unintentional ones.

'As you please,' said Bella. 'I suppose it's an arrangement I may have to get used to.'

'Not for long, if I know anything about it.'

She frowned slightly, as if struggling to construct an explanation of her motives. I thought I understood them well enough already. And the task was an unfamiliar one for her. With a toss of the head, she abandoned it. 'What will you do, Robin?' she asked with amiable curiosity. 'Go back to Brussels?'

'Which you said I should never have left? I don't think so. There's such a thing as too much security.'

'What, then?'

'I'll resign from the company, of course. Before Harvey McGraw gets a chance to fire me. Then, well, I don't know. I'm a free agent. I'll have three hundred thousand pounds burning a hole in my pocket thanks to you and Adrian. I think I may do some travelling. See the world. Get away from it all. Get a very long way away – before friend Naylor comes out of prison.'

'And Paul goes in?'

'That too, of course.' I raised a hand as a taxi pulled into the hotel lay-by. The driver nodded and drew up beside me. 'That too.'

'Good luck,' said Bella.

'I'd wish you the same,' I responded, 'but the words might stick in my throat. Besides, you've never needed luck to get what you want, have you? I don't suppose that's about to change.'

'But it is,' she said, so softly I only half-heard the words as I climbed into the taxi. 'Believe me, it is.'

I flew home to England the following morning and was back in the office before the end of the day, dodging Simon's ever more frantic questions and acting dumb for Adrian's benefit. He'd made it known in my absence that McGraw had refused to budge on the offer price. This didn't surprise me, but it worried Simon and Jennifer considerably, since Adrian had said nothing to them about his alternative method of winning the board over. Accordingly, I said nothing either, preferring to let matters take their course. A letter from Bella reached me before the end of the week, appointing me her proxy for the meeting. But it was the key to an empty cage, as Adrian's smug cat-who's-dined-on-a-canary expression confirmed. The game was up. But both of us meant to play it to the end.

I contacted Inspector Joyce around the same time and made an appointment to see him in Worcester the day before the board meeting for the purposes of making a new and revised statement about my encounter with Louise Paxton on 17 July 1990. Our telephone conversation, like my exchanges with Adrian, embraced a fair amount of shadow-boxing, since we were both aware how big a climb-down this represented. In an attempt to preserve some self-respect, I put it to him that Naylor's wife might be the person who'd tipped off Vince Cassidy. And something in his tight-lipped demurral told me Naylor had guessed right. They'd known all along.

I turned to Sarah, as so often before, for sympathy and advice. She was naturally curious about the sour and sudden end my enquiries on Bella's behalf had come to and suggested we meet at Sapperton, where she had to go on Sunday to do some 'clearing out' at The Old Parsonage.

It was the last day of October, mild, dank and breathlessly still. I stopped at the cemetery on my way into the village and visited Rowena's grave for the first time. It stood beside her mother's, with fresh flowers in both urns, matching headstones and echoing inscriptions. I remembered Louise's well enough: *First Known When Lost*. But now the words seemed dense with bitter unintended irony. Which only heightened the poignancy of the phrase of Thomas's Sarah had found to commemorate her sister.

ROWENA CLAUDETTE BRYANT, NÉE PAXTON
23 MAY 1971 – 17 JUNE 1993
THE SUN USED TO SHINE

In my mind, I was on Hergest Ridge again, turning slowly, like a teetotum about to fall. Take all, half or nothing. The chances were always as slender, the mathematics of unpredictability as unyielding. I walked back to the gate, my shoes crunching in the gravel, an illusion of some fainter step behind me garlanding itself around the surrounding silence. The wrought-iron railings of the gate met my hand as the balustrade of the bridge must have met Rowena's. For an instant, I could see the abyss and sense its appeal, its strange gaping allure. To jump. And leave it all behind. But I couldn't. There was only the ground beneath my feet. Only the close grey sky above my head. Only the future to face.

And Sarah, of course. She was the one among us who seemed the most resilient as well as the most perceptive. She didn't ignore reality or buckle under it. She defied it to do its worst, then retaliated by leading a normal well-balanced life. Not for her Rowena's despair or Sir Keith's refusal to recognize the truth or even Bella's eagerness to subvert it. I knew I could rely on Sarah to do what had to be done. I knew I could look to her for answers as well as questions.

The 'clearing out' she'd mentioned on the phone turned out to be rather more than that. She was removing all the family's personal possessions prior to the arrival of tenants on a six-month lease. As she explained, Sir Keith had only kept the place as a weekend retreat for her and Rowena, then for Rowena and Paul. They had no use for it now. It was time to close another chapter.

We went down to the Daneway Inn for lunch and sat outside, scarfed and sweatered against the chill. I described my trips to Cambridge, Albany and Bordeaux. I left nothing out, reckoning Sarah if anyone deserved to hear it all. After the reappraisal she'd been forced to make of her mother's character, the extent of her stepmother's selfishness was no big deal. Besides, Bella's desertion of her father was something Sarah had already anticipated.

'The sooner she goes the better. Perhaps then Daddy will be able to come to terms with what's happened.'

'You think he will?'

'Eventually. There's still quite a lot of time for all of us to prepare ourselves.'

'Is that what you're doing?'

'I'm trying to. So's Paul, I suppose.'

'Have you seen him recently?'

'No. I have nothing to say to him. But I met Martin Hill the other day. He'd been round to see Paul.'

'Did he say how he seemed?'

'Yes. Martin was expecting some histrionics, I think. But instead he got what you got. This immense chilling calm. Paul's reading the Bible, apparently. I don't mean he's dipping into it. I mean he's reading it from cover to cover, memorizing whole chunks. Can you believe it? He sits in that house, with Rowena's possessions – Rowena's memories – thick about him, *reading the Bible*. All day every day as far as I know.'

I shook my head, admitting my unwillingness as well as my inability to guess the state of his mind. I'd start feeling sorry for him, I knew, if I tried to imagine his plight. And I didn't want to feel anything for him, even contempt. I didn't want to share Nayor's innocence or Paul's guilt. I didn't want to rail against an injustice or rejoice at its correction. All I craved now was what I could only have had if I'd read the newspaper articles and watched the television reports back in July 1990 – and said absolutely nothing. Uninvolvement. Indifference. The stranger's sanctuary. Which for better or worse I'd turned my back on.

'I came across something this morning that might interest you,' Sarah said suddenly, reaching into her handbag and taking out a pocket diary, which she laid on the table in front of me. The red leather cover had the year embossed on it in gold. 1990. 'It's Mummy's. Returned by the police at some stage, I suppose. Daddy must have hung on to it, then forgotten he had it.'

I reached out and picked the diary up, turning it over in my hand. I wanted to open it at once, to rifle its secrets. But I needed Sarah's permission to camouflage my desire. 'May I?' I said.

'Of course. There's not much. Mummy was no diarist. Just the usual. Hair appointments. Telephone numbers. Flight times. Birthdays. Anniversaries. Dinner dates. Deadlines. What you'd expect. The normal everyday fixtures of life.'

Already I was flicking through the pages, seeing her handwriting for the first time, sensing her fingers close to mine as she penned the entries. Sarah was right. There was nothing unusual. But even mundanity can be portentous. *Wednesday March 7: Oscar's Private View. Allinson Gallery, Cambridge, 6.30*. I turned on. *Friday March 16: Collect pictures from Allinson p.m.* My gaze flicked to the next day. *Saturday March 17: Take pictures to Kington*. There it was, then. Confirmation of Sophie's claim. According to her, that was the day Louise had met her 'perfect stranger' on Hergest Ridge. '*The weather was unusually warm for March. She wanted a breath of fresh air. You were there for the same reason, I suppose.*' But it wasn't me. It never had been.

'Look at the entry for April the fifth, though,' said Sarah. 'That's not quite so normal.'

Thursday April 5: Atascadero, 3.30. I frowned. 'What does it mean?'

'It was just a hunch, but when I checked with directory enquiries and phoned the place, it turned out to be right. Atascadero is a café in Covent Garden. The one where Mummy met Paul to give him his marching orders.'

'So this corroborates his confession.'

'Yes. I suppose I shall have to bring it to the attention of the police. But there's something else. Something much more significant to my mind, though I doubt they'll agree.'

'What?'

'Turn to the week of her death.'

I leafed through to the week containing 17 July. There was only one entry. An Air France flight number and departure time for the morning of Monday 16 July. Nothing else. But why should there be? By 18 July, she was dead. 'What of it?' I said.

'Turn on.'

I did so. But there were only blank weeks, their days and dates printed on empty uncreased pages. No trips. No appointments. No *aides-mémoires*. Nothing.

'Don't you see? There should be something. I don't know. A dental check-up. A hotel booking. Some trivial commitment. But there isn't a single one. It's as if—'

'She knew she was going to die.'

'I remember Rowena saying that. I remember telling her not to be so absurd. And now there it is, in Mummy's handwriting. A full stop. An end. A void.'

'That she chose to step into.'

'But she can't have done, can she? I mean, it doesn't make any sense.'

'It could simply have been a precaution,' I suggested. 'She might have refrained from putting her plans for the rest of the summer down on paper in case your father got hold of the diary and deduced from the entries that she was planning to leave him.'

'Wouldn't a total blank look even more suspicious?'

'I suppose it might, but . . . what other explanation can there be?' I gazed across at Sarah and saw my own incomprehension reflected in her face. There was never going to be an answer. There never could be. Rowena had known as much without the need of a diary to prove it. Her mother's life had reached a turning point. And become her death.

CHAPTER TWENTY

As I've grown older, I've learned to analyse my own behaviour as well as other people's. I've come to understand that just as every mood is temporary, so is every triumph and every disappointment. It isn't much of a consolation, but it's an effective antidote to despair. One day, I suppose, it'll make even death seem an acceptable trade-off with reality.

Meanwhile, as November advanced, there were surrenders to be negotiated and escape routes plotted. On the third, I drove up to Worcester and made my promised statement to Inspector Joyce, admitting Louise Paxton could well have been actively seeking male company when I met her during the evening of 17 July 1990. On the fourth, I attended the last board meeting of Timariot & Small as an independent company, made an impassioned speech urging Simon and Jennifer to change their minds, then lost the vote by a slim – but for Adrian expensive – margin. Uncle Larry entered a plea for family unity; Adrian tried and failed to be more gracious in victory than he'd been in defeat; Simon burbled contentedly; and Jennifer twittered about completion dates. None of which prevented me minuting a formal protest at what they'd done and resigning with immediate effect.

My strategy was clear in my mind. And though I gave my fellow directors no hint of it, the future I'd mapped out for myself was in many ways preferable to leading a long struggle for commercial survival at Timariot & Small. More or less by default, I'd been granted another twelve-month extension to my *congé de convenance personelle*. So, until November 1994 at the earliest, I was a free and unfettered man. I was also about to become a moderately wealthy one, thanks to Bushranger Sports. And since it was wealth I'd tried hard to resist acquiring, I'd decided I might as well enjoy disposing of it.

For a variety of reasons, I didn't walk out there and then, despite implying I meant to. It took several weeks for the sale to be finalized and I eventually agreed to stay on until a Bushranger apparatchik could be flown in from Sydney to take over my duties. I tried to reassure the staff about the new régime, but felt rather like Kerensky explaining how wonderful life was going to be under Lenin. Nobody believed me, any more than I believed myself. And they all knew I had something they didn't. A way out.

It wasn't just a way out of the barbarization of Timariot & Small, though. What sweetened the pill for me was knowing I could bc bcachcombing on some South Sea island by the time the news broke of Shaun Naylor's innocence and Paul Bryant's guilt. The press hadn't got wind of the story yet and until they did an eerie calm seemed likely to prevail. Files and reports shuttled back and forth between the police and the Crown Prosecution Service, between Sarwate and the Criminal Appeal Office, between the servants of the law and its dispensers. Shaun Naylor counted the days in his cell at Albany Prison. Paul Bryant read the Bible in his house beside the water. And we all waited.

But some weren't prepared to wait. It was the last Saturday in November when Jennifer telephoned me in considerable excitement to report an encounter with Bella during a Christmas shopping trip to Farnham. 'She's left her husband, Robin. Told me so quite bluntly over a cup of coffee. Back here for good and contemplating divorce. I didn't know what to say. I mean, they've only been married a couple of years. But she doesn't seem to have any compunction about it at all. As for sympathy, forget it. She doesn't need any. Do you know what she said when I asked, as tactfully as I could, why it had come to this? "You wouldn't understand, my dear." How patronizing can you get?'

I thought I understood perfectly well, of course. As I made clear when I called at The Hurdles the following morning, to find Bella reluctantly reacquainting herself with the dullness of an English Sunday. 'I didn't think you'd move as quickly as this, Bella. Aren't you in danger of jumping the gun?'

'Not at all. Keith's solicitor has been monitoring developments on our behalf and reckons Naylor will be released on bail before

Christmas. The police have caved in, apparently, and the prosecution won't be offering any evidence when the case comes to appeal. So, I've been left with no choice in the matter.'

'You could have *chosen* to stand by your husband.'

'You wouldn't say that if you knew how he's been behaving lately.'

'I imagine he's been under a lot of strain.'

'*I've* been under a lot, as well.'

'Of course. But—'

'You wait and see, Robin,' she said with sudden intensity, stabbing out her cigarette in an ashtray littered with the broken-backed corpses of several others. 'When all this comes out, you won't think so badly of me.' But that I found hard to believe.

As family ruptures go, ours was a pretty cordial affair. There didn't seem much point bearing grudges now everything was settled. And the wanderlust that grew in me as the final break approached drained the event, if not the experience, of much of its bitterness. Merv Gibson, my successor, turned out to be a milder and more sensitive soul than any I'd thought could thrive in Harvey McGraw's empire. It was almost possible to persuade myself nothing much was going to change at Frenchman's Road under the Bushranger umbrella. Almost, but not quite. The fact was that however dexterously appearances were managed, an era had ended.

At least I didn't have to stay and watch the start of a new one, though. Timariot & Small and I came to the parting of the ways on Friday the seventeenth of December. The staff gave me a more rousing send-off than a mere three years as works director really justified. I think they were saying goodbye to their past along with mine, as their farewell gift to me – a watercolour of Broadhalfpenny Down commissioned from a competent local artist – tended to confirm.

That day also saw the appearance of the first newspaper articles heralding Naylor's release from prison. They struck a cautious note for the most part, referring to '*indications that Shaun Naylor may be set free following an appeal hearing next Wednesday*' and '*speculation which a police spokesman failed to deny that an as yet unidentified person has confessed to the murders for which Naylor was sentenced to life imprisonment in May 1991*'. But if the press were being uncharacteristically diffident, my brother Simon wasn't, especially after several drinks at my leaving party. 'What the bloody hell's all this about, Rob? And don't try to tell me you don't know, because I'm bloody certain you do.' Playing a dead bat to Simon when he was cruising towards inebriation being out of the question, I tried bafflement instead, which worked a treat. 'My lips are sealed, Sime. Ask Bella, though. She might be able to enlighten you.'

By the weekend, a little more had seeped into the public domain. West Mercia Police and the Crown Prosecution Service were still being tight-lipped, but Vijay Sarwate had given an interview and said as much as he evidently felt he could. '*I can confirm we will be applying for leave to appeal against Mr Naylor's convictions at a hearing on the twenty-second of this month and that the basis for the application is a full and voluntary confession of guilt by the real murderer of Oscar Bantock and Lady Paxton. I understand the police have satisfied themselves as to the accuracy and veracity of this confession and the prosecution will therefore not only be raising no objection to the appeal going ahead but also offering no evidence when it does so. In those circumstances, I anticipate that an application for Mr Naylor's release on bail pending the appeal will be favourably received. You will appreciate I am anxious to do all I can to reunite Mr Naylor with his wife and children so they can celebrate a family Christmas together for the first time in four years.*'

Sarwate must have found it difficult to keep a straight face while painting this Cratchit-like portrait of the Naylors, but, as an embellishment of the case for bail, I suppose seasonal sentiment was too good to resist. The newspapers were evidently confused by the turn of events. It didn't suit either lobby in the affair to have Naylor acquitted for reasons unconnected with the only coherent argument the media had ever advanced for his innocence. Yet since a contract killer hired by Oscar Bantock's accomplices in the forgery game was hardly likely to want to clear his conscience at this late date, it must have been obvious to all concerned that they'd got it badly wrong. Their unanimous response to which was a retreat behind *sub judice* reticence. This definitely wasn't the stuff of outraged leader columns.

Nor was it going to be the stuff of my future, however near or far I looked. I'd booked a Christmas Eve flight to Rio de Janeiro at the start of what I intended to be a slow and utterly relaxing meander through the Americas, finishing – according to my hazy estimate of a schedule – amidst the blazing foliage of a New England fall. I didn't anticipate meeting anyone on the way who'd ever heard of Shaun Naylor. And I didn't anticipate wanting to.

A week of solid packing still lay between me and the footloose life, however. I'd agreed to let Jennifer, Simon and Adrian put Greenhayes on the market in the New Year, so all my possessions had to go into store. There were actually precious few of them compared with what remained from my mother's day. But the exercise still turned into an exhausting chore, as I'd known it would. Which wasn't the only reason I'd left it as late as I could. I'd also dreaded the psychological effect of sifting through the detritus of mine and my parents' lives. It drew my thoughts back to my childhood, when Hugh used to take me for hair-raising rides round the lanes on his motorbike and Jennifer's boyfriends all dressed like Frank Zappa, when Simon's laugh never needed to be rueful and Adrian was the master of nobody's destiny, even his own. It lured me, as I'd feared it was bound to, into introspection and nostalgia. And it left me ill-prepared for the reminder that came my way on Monday of how much easier it is to get into something than it is to get out.

'Hello?'

'Is that Robin Timariot?' The voice on the other end of the telephone was guttural and unfamiliar.

'Speaking.'

'You on your own?'

'Who is this?'

'Vince Cassidy.'

'I'm sorry?'

'You know who I am. Sharon said you wanted to talk to me.'

'There must be some misunderstanding.'

'No there ain't. The message was clear. You wanted to know who paid me to fit up Shaun Naylor.'

'That was two months ago, Mr Cassidy. I'm no longer interested.'

'You don't mean that.'

'I'm afraid I do. Besides, I've found out since why you did it.'

'The fuck you have.'

'Shaun told me about you and his wife, Mr Cassidy. Is that why you're phoning? In the hope of extracting some money from me with which to put yourself out of Shaun's reach when he's released? If so, I—'

'This ain't nothing to do with Carol.'

'Then go to the police. They may be prepared to listen to you, but certainly not to pay you. For myself, I'm willing to do neither.'

'Hold on. You don't—'

I put the phone down and switched on the answering machine to ensure I didn't have to talk to him again. The newspaper articles had panicked him. That was as obvious as it was understandable. But it was far too late for him to tap me for help. A few minutes later, somebody rang, but failed to speak after the beep. Cassidy? It had to be. And even if he hadn't left a message, he'd evidently got one. Because he didn't ring again. Then or later.

Tuesday was the first bright day in what seemed like weeks, so I treated myself to a lengthy tramp round the hangers after lunch. It was something of a farewell tour of the countryside I'd grown up in, left, returned to and now was leaving again. I didn't turn for home until it was nearly dark and, in the event, never made it to Greenhayes on foot. A car passed me in the lane beneath Shoulder of Mutton Hill, pulled up a short distance ahead, then reversed to meet me. And only when the driver wound down her window did I realize whose car it was.

'Sarah! What are you doing here?'

'Offering you a lift home,' she said with a smile. I climbed in and we set off. 'Actually, I've just finished a two-day refresher course back at the College of Law in Guildford, so I thought I'd see how you were.'

'You're lucky to have caught me. I leave for Brazil on Friday.'

'I wish I could do the same.' She sounded genuinely envious. 'I really do.'

'Come with me,' I said frivolously.

'You don't know how tempting the suggestion is.'

'Because of tomorrow's appeal hearing, you mean?'

'Yes.' I watched her as she concentrated on a sharp bend. She was looking tired and careworn, sapped by her expert foreknowledge of the legal convolutions that lay ahead. 'That and everything it entails.'

Over tea at Greenhayes amidst the book-stacks and packing-cases, Sarah described the nagging pressure of events, the pitiless predictability of all that had happened since Paul's confession and all that was still bound to happen. Her father's refusal to face the reality of the situation had led to his virtual estrangement from her as well as his actual estrangement from Bella. 'I can't talk to him, Robin. He won't let me help him through this. And he's not prepared to help me through it. So, we have to endure it as best we can in our separate ways. But it isn't easy. And it's only going to become more difficult.'

'If there's anything I can—'

'No, no. You're right to get out of it. Go and enjoy yourself. And don't worry about me while you're at it.' She grinned gamely, as reluctant, it seemed to me, to admit her need of comfort as she was to acknowledge her own unspoken wish: that Paul should have let the truth die with Rowena. It was different now from when she'd come to me in Brussels. We were both older and wiser and sadder. Yet it was also the same. We represented to each other a link with Louise as she'd been that last day of her life. We embodied the failing hope that something could be salvaged from the wreckage of facts to ennoble her death. But in our sombre faces and subdued words we detected the same creeping awareness that nothing ever would be. 'When did you say you're leaving?'

'Friday.'

'Friday,' she repeated musingly, gazing past me to the dusk-shuttered window. 'A lot will have happened by then.'

'You mean the hearing?'

She didn't answer. And the distant look in her eyes deterred me from pressing her to. Besides, there seemed no need. What else could she mean?

We went down to the Cricketers for a drink as soon as it opened. Sarah's periodic distraction became as pronounced as her occasional outbursts of gaiety. She talked about Rowena and her mother with rambling fondness, recalling childhood scenes and adolescent incidents. They'd been an ordinary affectionate family then, untouched by tragedy, unmarked by notoriety. 'I didn't see it coming, Robin. I never had a clue. I never felt the future coiling its tentacles around us. I just thought we'd go on in the same serenely happy way.' How I wished then I could have seized the chance Louise had given me of making sure they would. Even though I hadn't known that's what it was.

At half past seven, she said she ought to start back for Bristol. When I assured her she was welcome to stay at Greenhayes, her refusal took a long time to come. But I suppose we both knew she had to refuse. This was an end, not a beginning. This was a stepping apart, a turning away. Only the last lingering looks back remained.

'I'll miss you,' she said, her breath clouding in the frosty air as we stood beside her car in the pool of yellow light cast from the windows of the pub. 'There doesn't seem to be anyone else who understands.'

'You must have better friends than me, Sarah.'

'As a matter of fact, I don't think I have.'

'What about Rodney? Aren't you going to make him a happy man one day soon?'

'No. Since you ask, I'm not.'

'Really? You almost make me wish—'

'Don't say it.' She put her gloved hand to my mouth to stop me speaking, then smiled at the extravagance of the precaution. 'Sorry. I don't know what I'm doing.'

'Saying goodbye?'

'Yes. I suppose that's it.' She frowned. 'Don't let anything make you postpone your flight, will you?'

'Why should it?'

'No reason. It's just . . . I think it'll do you good to go. And I wouldn't want newspaper talk about Mummy . . . or Daddy, come to that . . . to make you think you had to stay.'

'There'll be some hard things said.'

'I know. But none of them will be your fault. So promise me you'll leave on Friday. Whatever happens.'

'All right. It's a promise.'

'Good.' She brightened. 'And now you'd better kiss me. And let me wish you *bon voyage*.'

A few minutes later, I was standing at the side of the road, watching the lights of her car vanish from sight. She'd offered me a ride back to Greenhayes, of course, but I'd declined, preferring a solitary walk up the hill through the cold night air. The stars were scattered brightly across the sky, a sickle moon riding high and clear among them. 'When first I came here I had hope,' I recited under my breath as I went. 'Hope for I knew not what.' And now, just when I thought I might know . . . 'I'm bound away for ever. Away somewhere, away for ever.'

Wednesday the twenty-second of December. The clouds had rolled in from the west and it had been raining all morning, in London as well as Steep. There was the sheen of it on the pavement behind the trench-coated correspondent as he gave his report in front of the Law Courts in the Strand for the one o'clock television news. And there was the steely tap of it at the window behind me as I sat and listened to his words.

'Shaun Naylor will be released from prison later today following an hour-long hearing before Lord Justice Sir John Smedley at the Court of Appeal this morning. He was granted bail pending a full appeal next March against his convictions for the murders of Oscar Bantock and the rape and murder of Lady Louise Paxton in July nineteen ninety: the so-called Kington killings. The judge at his trial ten months later described him as 'a depraved and dangerous individual' and recommended that he serve at least twenty years in prison. But Naylor has consistently protested his innocence since then and it was confirmed here in court this morning that a person identified only as Mr A has confessed to the murders and that the police now believe he, not Naylor, carried out the killings. Naylor has always admitted having sexual intercourse with Lady Paxton on the night in question, but has denied rape. The implication of his release on bail is that the prosecution accepts all three convictions will be quashed at the full appeal. Until then, the person referred to as Mr A cannot be charged with any offence. Lord Justice Smedley said the prospect of a fair trial would be prejudiced if the suspect was identified at this stage and urged the media to exercise restraint in the matter. Shaun Naylor's wife Carol was not in court to hear the ruling. It is believed she is planning to rendezvous with her husband at an undisclosed address later today.'

So he was free. Or soon would be. What his wife would say to him about Vince Cassidy if and when they met 'at an undisclosed address' I couldn't imagine. And what Shaun planned to do when she'd said it I didn't want to imagine. It wasn't over for them. And it wasn't over for Paul Bryant. Or Sarah. But, for me, it very nearly was. In two days' time, I'd be flying away from all of it.

Jennifer entertained me to dinner that evening as her way of saying goodbye. Thursday, my last night in England, was ear-marked for a drinking session with Simon, who I knew would be full of questions about Naylor's release. But Jennifer was as yet unaware of the event, for which I was grateful. The less I had to talk about it, the easier it was to avoid thinking about it. Deflecting Jennifer's suggestions of ways to patch things up between Adrian and me was child's play by comparison. In the end, she agreed my absence in itself would probably do the trick. 'Time's a great healer,' she observed. And I refrained from pointing out that the example of Louise Paxton proved the exact reverse.

*   *   *

It was nearly midnight when I got back to Greenhayes. To say the sight of Bella's BMW parked in front of the garage was a surprise would be a considerable understatement. As I pulled up behind it and climbed out of my car, the unlikely idea occurred to me that she'd decided I shouldn't be allowed to leave without some parting words of advice. But the expression on her face when she opened the window of the BMW and gazed up at me suggested an altogether more serious purpose.

'God, I thought you were never coming back,' she said. And somehow the lack of reproachfulness in her voice heightened my concern.

'I've been at Jenny's.'

'Yes. I guessed you were probably with her.'

'Then why didn't you call round – or phone?'

'Because the fewer people who know what's happened the better.'

'What *has* happened?'

She peered past me, as if fearing I mightn't be alone, before answering. And when she did, it was no answer at all. 'Can we go inside?'

I led the way indoors, busying myself with keys, light switches and heating controls while Bella went into the sitting-room. She'd already lit a cigarette by the time I joined her and was standing by the fireplace, flicking ash into the empty grate. I'd stripped the walls of pictures and plates and shrouded the furniture in dust-sheets in preparation for the redecoration Jennifer had insisted would be necessary to attract a buyer. What with that and the half dozen tea-chests standing ready in one corner, the room had already lost most of its homely atmosphere. Which only seemed to accentuate Bella's uncharacteristic restlessness. She paced the stretch of carpet where the outline of the hearthrug was still visible, her raincoat collar turned up and her shoulders hunched as if to ward off the cold. As I entered the room and glanced across at her, I thought I saw a shiver run through her.

She was wearing no make-up beyond a smear of lipstick and looked pale and haggard as a result. Her eyes were red with fatigue, her hair in need of brushing and there was that faint tremor in her hands I'd noticed in Bordeaux. It was hard to imagine what could have had such an effect on her. I'd seen her ride out the loss of a husband and a stepdaughter without batting a tinted eyelid. But now—

'What's wrong, Bella?'

'Keith's dead,' she said abruptly.

'*What?*'

'My husband is dead.'

'But . . . how?'

'His body was found yesterday at the foot of some cliffs in southern Portugal. They seem to think it must have been there since the weekend.'

'Portugal? I don't understand. What was—'

'They have no idea why he should have gone there.'

'But . . . was this . . . an accident?'

'That's what the Portuguese police seem to think. His car was parked near the top of the cliff. It's something of a tourist attraction apparently, not far from Cape Saint Vincent.'

'It couldn't have been . . .'

'Suicide?' She stopped pacing up and down and looked straight at me. 'Well, it could have been, of course. There's no way to tell. Nobody's going to believe Keith went there to admire the view, are they? So I suppose suicide is what most people will assume, whatever the official verdict.'

'Good God. Did you have any inkling he might do such a thing?'

'They've asked me to fly out to Portugal as soon as possible to identify the body and make the necessary arrangements,' she said, so matter-of-factly it seemed she simply hadn't heard my question. 'I leave first thing in the morning.'

'Can I help in any way?'

'Yes. That's why I'm here. I've been trying to contact Sarah all day without success. She's not answering her phone at home and she's not been at work today. Off sick with flu, apparently.'

'Really? She seemed all right last night.'

'Last night?'

'She called in. On her way back to Bristol from some course or other in Guildford.'

Bella shook her head in weary puzzlement. 'I don't know anything about that. The point is she has to be told. I'd ask that gormless boyfriend of hers, but I don't have his number. I can't even remember his surname, for God's sake! Could you go up there tomorrow morning and break the news to her? At least I can rely on you to make a sensitive job of it. First her mother. Then her sister. Now her father. It's going to hit her hard, isn't it?'

The mounting tally of Sarah's bereavements suddenly came home to me. They were all gone now but her. All that serene normality she'd described growing up in had been pared down by different kinds of self-destruction till only she remained. Explaining it to her would be bad enough. But to live with it, as she'd have to, on into middle age and beyond . . .

'You will go, won't you?'

'Of course.'

'It doesn't interfere with your travel plans, does it?'

'No.' Sarah's words of twenty-four hours before bubbled into my mind. '*Promise me you'll leave on Friday. Whatever happens.*' It was almost as if she'd foreseen the catastrophe. As if she'd known what her father meant to do. 'But my plans don't matter anyway. Not now.'

'I'm only asking you to see Sarah, not to cancel your trip.'

'In the circumstances—'

'Catch your plane on Friday, Robin.' Bella had moved closer and lowered her voice. Her eyes seemed to urge me to accept her advice. 'Get out while you can.'

'Get out of what?'

'All of this.'

There was something beyond her words and looks, some message she wanted to convey without declaring what it was. 'Sarah's bound to ask whether her father's death was an accident or suicide. What do I tell her?'

'What I've told you. Nobody knows.'

'She may want to follow you to Portugal.'

'Try to discourage her. There'd be no point.'

'How can you be so sure?' Bella's strength was failing. Her will to keep whatever it was to herself was ebbing. Even her self-reliance had its limits. And now we'd reached them. 'What the hell is all this about, Bella?'

'I don't know.'

'I think you do. It wasn't an accident, was it?'

'I doubt it.'

'Then he must have killed himself?'

'Not necessarily.'

'You're not suggesting he was murdered?' She didn't reply, merely swallowed hard and took a drag on her cigarette. But her eyes remained fixed on me. And in them there was no longer much attempt at concealment. 'Why would anybody kill Keith?'

'There's a reason. A very good reason.'

'What is it?'

'It would explain why he went to Portugal. And why he never left.'

'Tell me what it is.'

'I can't.'

'If you want me to go and see Sarah, you must.' It was a bluff. I think we both knew that. We were beyond such bargaining now. But still Bella hesitated, weighing some other issue in her mind. The need to guard her secret against the desire to share it.

'All right.' She moved back to the fireplace and tossed the remnant of her cigarette into the grate, then leant against the mantelpiece, slowly arched her neck as if it were aching and turned her head to look at me. 'Keith knew Paul was lying, Robin. Paul couldn't have murdered Louise *or* Oscar Bantock.'

'What are you saying?'

'I'm saying Keith knew Paul's confession to be a pack of lies from start to finish.'

'You mean he hoped it was.'

'No. He *knew*. For a fact.'

'How could he?'

'By being responsible for the murders himself.' She studied the shocked expression on my face for a moment, then said: 'Keith paid Shaun Naylor to kill Oscar Bantock. He commissioned the crime. And unintentionally brought about his wife's murder as a result.'

'That can't be true.'

'Yes it can. He told me so himself when he realized there was no other way to convince me Paul was lying.'

'But . . . why should Paul have lied?'

'That hardly matters now, does it? Don't you see? Keith wasn't prepared to let Louise's murderer get away with it. He was going to intervene to prevent Naylor's release. He was going to admit his part in the crime. That's why he's been killed. To stop him confessing.'

'I . . . I don't understand. If Keith hired Naylor . . . who killed Keith?'

'There were intermediaries. Keith never met Naylor. The whole thing was arranged for him by somebody else. And I'm pretty sure it's that somebody who murdered Keith – or had him murdered.'

'If this is true—'

'It's true.'

'Then we must go to the police. Without delay. Naylor isn't innocent after all. A guilty man's just been set free.'

'Perhaps you'd like to explain what we'd go to them *with*.' There was more pity than scorn in her expression as she stared at me. 'Keith's dead. And I can't prove a single thing he told me.' She sighed and looked away, motioning dismissively at me with her palm. Only to abandon the gesture halfway through and slowly lower her hand to her side. 'Get me some gin, Robin,' she said wearily. 'I think it's time you heard the whole story.'

CHAPTER

TWENTY-ONE

Bella took a deep swallow from the very large gin and tonic she'd just poured herself, lit another cigarette and crouched forward across the coffee-table between us. The central heating had already taken the edge off the chill, but Bella, whose preferred temperature was five degrees above most people's, hadn't even turned down the collar of her raincoat, let alone taken it off.

'You'll say I mishandled it from the start,' she began. 'You'll say I shouldn't have kept you in the dark or tried to solve the problem without forcing Keith to own up to what he'd done. Well, you can say what you damn well please. I was actually trying to spare everyone a lot of unnecessary suffering. I might even have succeeded if you'd been just a bit more—' She broke off and gave me a little head-shaking smile. 'Sorry. Recriminations won't get us anywhere, will they? And nor will being wise after the event. You remember coming to The Hurdles a few days after Paul had confessed to you? You remember Keith insisting Paul had made it all up? Well, I didn't believe him any more than you did. But the following day, after Sarah had gone back to Bristol, Keith told me how he could be so sure. And then I did believe him.

'It seems Keith became convinced during the spring of nineteen ninety that Louise meant to leave him for Oscar Bantock. He accused her of having an affair with Bantock and she neither admitted it nor denied it. She said he had to make up his own mind about her fidelity. As for leaving him, she wouldn't promise not to do that either. He'd always been a possessive husband. Sometimes an irrationally jealous one as well. I've seen that side of him myself. And ours was never exactly a love match. Whereas he really did love Louise. Too much for her peace of mind, I suppose. She wanted the freedom to do as she pleased. And if leaving Keith was what it took to find it, that's what she was willing to do.

'I don't blame her. In fact, I'm sorry never to have known her. She sounds like a woman after my own heart, though you probably think I'm flattering myself. But, reasonable or not, it was a dangerous line to take with Keith. He'd always suspected there was something going on between Louise and Howard Marsden, despite Louise telling him how unwelcome Howard's attentions were. Perhaps he suspected it just *because* she told him. In his mind there were lots of other men she didn't tell him about.'

'He can't have believed that,' I put in. 'The idea's absurd.'

'How would you know?' Bella eyed me curiously for a moment, then said: 'Anyway, jealousy *is* absurd. It's also destructive when left to fester. The point is that Keith couldn't prevent himself believing his own fantasies, couldn't help interpreting every gesture of independence by Louise as an act of infidelity. To him, her interest in art had always seemed like perfect cover for an affair. Her friendship with Oscar Bantock was the last straw. Keith simply couldn't bear the thought of Louise letting a man like Bantock touch her. As for the possibility of them running away together, well, that was too much for him to take.

'He'd probably have done nothing about it even so, except that he happened to know somebody who could have Bantock taken out of Louise's life on a permanent basis. Keith never told me his name. Said it'd be safer for me not to know. Let's call him Smith. About fifteen years ago, Keith treated Smith's wife for infertility. Carried out some tricky operation that enabled the poor cow to have children. Smith's one of those men who thinks life isn't complete without a son and heir. He was very grateful to Keith. I mean, *extremely* grateful. Said if there was ever anything he could do for him, any favour, however small or large, Keith had only to ask. And Smith, behind the respectable lifestyle – big house in the suburbs, golf club membership and so on – was actually a full-time professional criminal. A crook. A gangster. One of those Mr Big types you read about who never go to prison even when their capers go wrong. He never said that's what he was, of course. But

Keith had got the message clearly enough. So now he decided to contact Smith and call in the debt. By asking him to have Bantock killed.'

'Just like that?'

'Well, I wouldn't think you'd need to dress things up for a man like Smith, would you? You just put it to him and he says, "Sure, no problem. Leave it to me." It's the kind of thing he does, after all. Kill people. For money, usually. But in this case as a favour.'

'Good God.'

'The plan was to wait until Keith and Louise left for Biarritz after Sarah's graduation, then take out poor old Oscar. That's all Keith knew and all he wanted to know. Smith was to handle the details. Keith didn't have to worry about a thing. But he should have worried. Because Smith was semi-retired by then. Spent most of his time at his villa in the Algarve.'

'The Algarve?'

She nodded. 'That's right. Southern Portugal. Well, it seems Smith's contacts weren't as numerous – or as reliable – as they had been. But he hadn't wanted to disappoint Keith, so he contracted the job out to somebody more active – let's call him Brown – who sub-contracted it to a man called Vince Cassidy. Remember him? He was a prosecution witness at Naylor's trial.'

'I remember.' Bella could have no idea just *how* memorable Cassidy was to me. Instantly, I wished I hadn't refused to listen to him when I'd had the chance.

'Cassidy took the job, but at the last moment got Naylor to do it for him. Brown would never willingly have used Naylor, apparently. He had a reputation for carelessness. And for mixing business with pleasure if women were involved. But women weren't involved. Or weren't supposed to be. The trouble was Louise chose the same weekend to walk out on Keith as Naylor chose to raid a few houses in Herefordshire, adding Bantock's murder onto the list. The prosecution got it right. Louise must have walked in on Naylor just after he throttled Oscar. And Naylor must have decided he couldn't afford to let her live.'

'He'd have had no idea who originally commissioned the murder, would he?' I asked, picking up the thread of Bella's reasoning. 'Or why?'

'Exactly. To his warped mind, she must have seemed like an unexpected bonus. So he raped her – and then he strangled her.'

'When did Keith find out?'

'When he got back to Biarritz from his conference in Madrid. He found Louise had gone, leaving a note for him. It didn't say she'd dashed back to England on impulse to buy one of Bantock's paintings, as he claimed later. It said she'd left him for good. And it also said she hadn't left him *for* anybody, least of all Oscar Bantock. She'd simply had enough of his possessive ways and meant to start a new life on her own. Then, almost immediately, Keith heard the news of her death and realized what must have happened. By setting out to do everything in his power to keep her, he'd only succeeded in destroying her.'

'What did he do?'

'He was horrified, gripped by guilt as well as grief. And frightened into the bargain. He had to think quickly. He had to decide what he was going to do before he went back to England. Tell the police everything, with no guarantee they'd ever catch Louise's murderer but an absolute guarantee he'd be charged with conspiracy to bring her murder about. Or suppress his part in the whole ghastly business and strike a deal with Smith to have the culprit brought to book. Not a difficult choice, really, was it? Keith excused himself on the grounds that his confession would only increase Sarah and Rowena's suffering and deny them his help and support in coming to terms with their mother's violent death. A handy piece of reasoning from his point of view, but I suppose we should give him the benefit of the doubt.'

I said nothing, some vestigial reluctance to speak ill of the dead reining in my tongue.

'Keith contacted Smith straightaway. Smith had met Louise a few times and was almost as horrified as Keith by what had happened. He flew up from Faro to meet Keith at Bordeaux. Then they flew on to England together, agreeing a strategy on the way. The man who'd raped and murdered Louise would be made to answer for it, but their connection with the crime would be kept out of it. Not difficult, since Naylor didn't know who'd hired Cassidy and Cassidy didn't know who'd hired Brown. While Keith went to comfort his daughters and pose as the baffled and bereaved husband, Smith went to sort things out with Brown. Brown hauled in Cassidy and told him he had to inform on Naylor to make up for using him in the first place and take his chances if Naylor told the police he'd put him up to it. Once Naylor was charged and put away, Brown would pull a few strings to supply another witness in case Cassidy botched it up.'

'You mean Bledlow?'

'Presumably. Though, as it turned out, Naylor never named Cassidy as an accomplice because he decided to plead not guilty. A risky thing to do, since it committed him to portraying Louise as a scarlet woman. Distasteful stuff, which probably added a few years onto his sentence. But at least Keith could console himself he'd been properly punished. As for his indirect responsibility for Louise's death, he tried to put that out of his mind completely. And he didn't do a bad job, because I never had the slightest suspicion. His grief seemed genuine to me, which it was of course, and uncomplicated – which it wasn't.

'I know you think I set out to marry him for his money. But there was more to it than that. I couldn't just hang around here after Hugh's death. I needed a complete change of scene. Well, Keith gave me that. And he gave me a lot of fun too. As I did him. At least at first. But Louise just wouldn't go away. His memory of her, sharpened by guilt. And the mystery of how she'd died, sustained by Naylor's refusal to admit killing her. Then there was Henley Bantock and his bloody book. That started them all sniffing around, didn't it? The scandalmongers and mischief-makers. Nick Seymour and his ego-trip of a TV programme. Which *you* helped him out with. Along with the Marsden bitch.'

Again, I held my tongue. There seemed no point reminding Bella that I'd been taken for a ride by Seymour. She knew, anyway. Pretending she didn't was merely an attempt to forestall some of the condemnation she'd earned.

'Rowena committed suicide because of the doubts about her mother Seymour planted in her mind with all his prying and probing. But Paul must have blamed himself for her death and decided he deserved to be punished for it. Why else would he confess to a crime he hadn't committed? He's obviously unhinged. I suppose his attack on you was the first sign of that. And his confession was the second. How he convinced the police it was true – how he put together his story without making some vital slip – is quite simply beyond me. He must be extremely clever as well as seriously insane.

'Keith didn't think he *would* convince the police. He was sure they'd find some flaw in his account. But what if they didn't? What if somehow, by some uncanny fluke, Paul was believed? Keith said he'd have no choice. Weak and frightened as he was, he'd own up rather than let Naylor walk free. I could see he meant it. And that meant I might find myself married to a known murderer, with everybody suspecting I'd gone along with his attempt to cheat justice. Can you blame me for doing everything in my power to prevent that happening?'

'No. But I can blame you for setting about it the way you did.'

'Yes, well . . .' She gave a faintly contrite toss of the head. 'It stood to reason there had to be a weak spot in Paul's story. It was a lie, after all. And lies are never perfect. But I didn't trust the police to search it out. And I wasn't prepared to wait while they tried. I reckoned the sooner we put a stop to Paul's madness the better. Since Keith forbade me to take a hand myself, I had to persuade somebody to do it for me, somebody intelligent and reliable who might be willing to help me out for old times' sake.'

'Old times' sake? Come off it, Bella. Thanks to the Bushranger row, you had me over a barrel. And you never let me forget it.'

'Does it make you feel better if I say I'm sorry?'

'Not much.'

'Well I am, anyway. Especially since it was all for nothing. He'd covered his tracks well, hadn't he? So well you became even more convinced than when you started that there were none to follow. What's worse, you began to chase clues I'd have preferred you to leave alone. Naturally, I didn't want you to go after Cassidy. There was a faint chance you might learn the truth that way. By the end, when you finally threw in the towel, I was almost grateful. At least it made up my mind for me. If Paul's story was watertight, the chances were Keith would be forced to confess. Well, I had to be out of it before then, so I capitalized my assets as best I could – Adrian was a real help there with his money-no-object determination to get the better of you – and told Keith I couldn't live with a man who was capable of commissioning a murder. He took it more calmly than I'd have expected. I suppose he thought divorce would be the least of his problems if it came to the crunch.

'There was still a chance it wouldn't come to the crunch, of course. But once the police had said they were satisfied Paul was telling the truth, that chance dwindled to virtually nothing. When I last spoke to Keith, about a fortnight ago, he was clinging to the hope that Paul might lose his nerve and withdraw his confession. I never thought he would, though. He'd already gone too far by then to turn back.'

'Couldn't you have tried to talk him out of it? If you could have convinced him you were absolutely certain he was lying—'

'How could I have done, without telling him why I was certain?' Bella frowned thoughtfully. 'Besides, it had crossed my mind by then that Paul might have suspected the truth for some time. It would make sense, wouldn't it? He might have confessed in order to smoke Keith out.' She sighed. 'If so, it's rebounded on both of them, hasn't it?'

'When did Keith hear Naylor was going to be released?'

'I don't know exactly. My guess would be a couple of days before the papers broke the news. His solicitor was keeping him in touch. The rest is guesswork on my part too. I think Keith went to Portugal in order to warn Smith he was about to blow the whistle on all of them. And I think Smith decided to stop him. I suppose he felt he didn't have much choice. It was either that or face the prospect of extradition on a conspiracy to murder charge. So he took Keith for a one-way trip along the coast.'

'Will you tell the Portuguese police any of this?'

'Certainly not,' she replied, arching her eyebrows at me. 'There'd be no point. I don't know who Smith is. Or Brown, come to that. I haven't a shred of evidence. And now Keith's dead, I'm unlikely to get any. I shan't be looking anyway. These people are dangerous, Robin. They stick at nothing. I won't be making any waves. It wouldn't be wise – or healthy. And you'd do well to follow my example. Just tell Sarah her father's dead, make sure she's all right and leave it at that. As for Paul, he's made his bed-of-nails and must lie on it. What he does now is up to him. What I shall do is my duty as Keith's widow. That and nothing more.'

Bella had always possessed the ability to disarm me with her breathtaking combination of frankness and duplicity. Somehow, despite admitting to deceit and downright callousness, she'd almost managed to convince me she deserved my pity for becoming caught up in all this. She might even have succeeded, but for one awkward fact. I knew – and she knew I knew – that she'd willingly have colluded in her husband's evasion of justice if I'd been able to pick a hole in Paul's mesh of lies for her.

But for the moment there were more important things to consider. There was the stinging realization that Naylor had been guilty all along. And there was the bewildering discovery that Paul's confession had been false in every detail.

'I left several messages on Sarah's answering machine,' said Bella. 'But she hasn't phoned back. So, either she's too sick to pick the damn thing up, which I doubt, or she's off playing hooky somewhere. Maybe Rodney knows where she is. Or a neighbour. Either way, I can't hang around to find out. You do see that, don't you?'

'Oh yes. I see it.'

'I even tried phoning Paul, but he wasn't answering either. I suppose he'll have to be told eventually. How do you think he'll react? I mean, if he really did suspect Keith, he'll also suspect his death wasn't an accident, won't he?'

'Perhaps you want me to break the news to him as well.'

'No, no.' Bella frowned at me, immune in her current mood to sarcasm. 'The police would think it very odd if we contacted him before they did. As far as they're concerned we still believe he murdered Louise. It's best if they think we're not even on speaking terms with him. Surely you can appreciate that.'

'Of course. Stupid of me.'

Her frown darkened, but she decided not to pursue the point. 'I happen to have a set of keys to Sarah's flat. They belonged to Rowena originally. Keith left them at The Hurdles. Use them if all else fails.' She fished two keys on a ring from her handbag and plonked them on the table in front of me. 'One's for the street door. The other's for the flat itself.' I stared down at them, but made no move to pick them up. 'You are listening to me, aren't you, Robin?'

'Intently.'

'Much the best thing for her to do is simply to sit by the phone and wait for some news. I shall arrange for the body to be flown home as soon as possible, though Christmas could complicate matters, I suppose. What a time for this to happen.' She clicked her tongue, apparently in irritation at her late husband's lack of consideration. Perhaps she thought he should have waited until the holidays were over before getting himself thrown off a Portuguese cliff. 'The Consulate have booked me into a hotel in Portimão. The Globo. I'll leave you the number. Get Sarah to call me there as soon as she can. Or she can call the Consulate direct if she prefers. Either way, get her to make contact.'

'I'll do my best.'

'I'm relying on you to. Handle Sarah as delicately as you can. She's strong. But whether she's strong enough for this . . .' She glanced at her watch. 'I ought to go home and pack. I'm booked on a horribly early flight.' She rose to her feet and looked down at me, suspicion tainting her concern. 'Are you all right?'

I stared up at her, too confused by the blizzard of consequences her revelations had whipped up in my mind to conceal my distaste for the motives she'd so blithely admitted. 'What do you think?' I asked, daring her to define how I ought to react to what she'd said.

'I don't have time for this,' she snapped, letting anger get the better of her candour. 'I've told you everything I know. And I've apologized for misleading you. What more can I say?'

'Why *did* you tell me everything?'

'Because I thought you had a right to know the truth. And

because I thought I could rely on you to give Sarah the support she'll need once you'd understood the seriousness of the situation.'

'You can. But I wonder if *you* understand the seriousness of the situation.'

'Of course I do.'

'I'm not sure. You've known Paul to be lying for the past three months. But you've done nothing about it. Now Louise's killer's been set free. And your husband's been murdered. Some might hold you to blame for that.'

'Rubbish. Nobody can prove I knew anything.'

'No. But they can go a long way to proving I did, can't they? Thanks to the enquiries you got me to make on your behalf. Which I suppose you could deny asking me to make. If it suited your purpose.'

'I wouldn't do that.' But smiling as she spoke gave the game away. We both knew she would do it – if she thought she had to. Was this, then, why she'd chosen to enlighten me? So I'd be in no doubt how much I stood to lose along with her? So I'd refrain from telling Sarah the truth for fear she'd blame me, not Bella, for trying to suppress it? 'Just find Sarah for me, Robin,' Bella concluded in her most mellifluous tone. 'Then fly away from all this. And count yourself lucky you can.'

Bella probably read into my subdued farewell a reluctant agreement to do what she'd more or less instructed me to do: break the news to Sarah of her father's death without challenging the official view that it was a tragic accident; leave Paul well alone; and view subsequent developments, whatever they might be, from a safe distance.

But that was her way, not mine. And no amount of pressure, whether subtle or overt, was going to force me to follow it. There was something she'd overlooked, something she'd never have been capable of understanding. The truth was shocking and appalling. Of course it was. But it was also immensely uplifting. Because suddenly Louise Paxton was free of all suspicion. She hadn't led Naylor on. She hadn't been having a secret affair with anyone. Her 'perfect stranger' had been an invention, designed to deflect Sophie's curiosity. Or else some kind of joke at Sophie's expense. Either way, Louise had met nobody on Hergest Ridge until the day she'd met me there. And that was the day she'd died. She was an innocent victim. Not only of a brutal rapist, but of a jealous husband, a treacherous friend and a self-serving pack of doubters and deceivers.

After Bella had gone, I lay on the dust-sheeted sofa in the sitting-room, an alarm-clock stationed on the floor beside me. It was set to go off at half past five. If I was on the road by six, I could be in Clifton by eight. Not that I expected to need an alarm to wake me. Tired though I was, sleep seemed a remote contingency. Fear and elation stalked my thoughts, stretching my weary nerves. I felt if I could only rest and reflect on what Bella had told me, the answer would emerge, as logical as it was obvious. What was the final link in the chain connecting Sir Keith Paxton's hidden jealousy with Paul Bryant's manufactured guilt? What purpose could be served by setting a murderer free?

I did fall asleep, of course, though not for much more than an hour. But that was time enough to dream of Louise. She was waiting to meet me as I walked along Offa's Dyke. The sun was setting behind her and I couldn't see her face clearly. She was standing a few yards beyond an artist's easel, set up directly in my path, with a canvas ready for use on its frame. But the canvas was blank, save for the tentative pencilled outline of a figure that seemed to dissolve as I approached. I tried to speak, but couldn't seem to. I knew I had to warn her of something, but what it was I couldn't remember. Then she turned and walked away down the slope. I ran after her, but the gap between us only widened. There was a line of trees at the foot of the slope. I sensed I had to overtake her before she reached them in order to avert a catastrophe. But there was nothing I could do to stop her. She entered the trees without looking back. And vanished from my sight.

Then the alarm was buzzing angrily close to my ear. With a jolt, I sat up and stabbed at its button until silence returned. The trees were still visible to my mind's eye, the patch of shadow she'd stepped into still tantalizingly close. But as the ghostly shapes of the shrouded furniture emerged from the darkness around me, the trees slipped away, until only the faintest trace of a memory – the lightest breath of a breeze between their leaves – remained.

A blank canvas. Ready to picture the future she'd never lived to shape. Like her diary. An empty space that would never be filled. '*Can we really change anything, do you think?*' I could remember the words, but couldn't recreate the voice. There seemed to be nothing I— Then it came to me, so suddenly and forcefully it was as if somebody had struck me in the face. The diary. Of course. If Paul was lying, then every detail of his obsessive pursuit of Louise was also a lie. Even his meeting with her in the Covent Garden café. It hadn't happened. Yet Sarah had shown me the proof that it *had* happened. In her mother's own handwriting. *Thursday April 5: Atascadero, 3.30.* A forged entry? Or a clever manipulation of a genuine one? Either way, Paul couldn't have had access to Louise's diary without— 'Sarah.' I spoke her name aloud as I rose from the sofa and headed for the door.

CHAPTER

TWENTY-TWO

It was a cold wet dawn in Bristol, too bleak and early, I'd have guessed, for Sarah to have gone out. But there was no response to my persistent prods at her bell in Caledonia Place. And only a recorded answer when I tried her number on my car-phone. I went back to the door, intending to use the keys Bella had given me to go in, but a well-dressed middle-aged woman emerged as I approached and fixed me with a suspicious glare.

'Are you the person who's just been ringing Sarah Paxton's bell? I live in the flat below and couldn't help wondering when you were going to give up.'

'Well, it *was* me, actually, yes. I'm a friend of Sarah's.'

'Really? Well, I know for a fact that she's gone away. So you're wasting your time, aren't you?'

'Apparently so.' I smiled uneasily. 'Any idea where she's gone? Or for how long?'

'None at all, I'm afraid. Excuse me.'

She bustled off to her car, but lingered ostentatiously after opening the boot, clearly reluctant to leave while I was lurking around her front door. In the circumstances, there was nothing for it but to retreat to my own car and drive away.

I could have doubled back straightaway of course, but I decided to wait and see what I could glean from Anstey's first. I parked on the circular road round Clifton Down and gazed along the gorge at the suspension bridge, its familiar shape blurred and distorted by the runnels of rainwater on the windscreen. How often did Sarah come up here, I wondered, and study the same view? How often did she imagine she could see Rowena leaning against the railings in the middle of the bridge and staring back at her? As now I almost did myself.

By nine o'clock, I was at Anstey's offices in Trinity Street, explaining to a bemused secretary that I was a friend of the Paxton family, trying to contact Sarah on a matter of extreme urgency. The news that Sarah wasn't at home clearly embarrassed the poor woman, who until now had been happy to believe her absence was due to flu. 'She phoned in sick on Monday morning. As far as I know, we haven't heard from her since.' She wanted me to wait for the senior partner, who usually arrived by nine thirty, but her confirmation that Sarah had lied to me about the course in Guildford made such a delay unthinkable. Did she know where I could find Sarah's boyfriend? Yes, she did. 'You mean Rodney Gardner. He's a solicitor too. But not with this firm. Haynes, Palfreyman and Fyfe. In Corn Street.'

I'd met Rodney just once, at The Hurdles a year before. He remembered me as well as I remembered him: not very. Which turned his natural caution into acute wariness when he received me in his office at ten o'clock that morning.

'Why exactly are you looking for Sarah?'

'A family matter.'

'But you're not family, are you?'

'Does that make a difference?'

'I don't know.'

'Look, I may as well tell you. Her father's died.'

'Good Lord. How?'

'Do you know where she is?'

'Well, not really, no.'

'She's not been at work since Monday. She told them she had flu. But she's not at home either. So, where could she be?'

'I've no idea.' He fiddled with the ribbon marker of his desk diary for a moment, then said: 'To be honest, I'm the last person you should be asking. Sarah and I had a . . . disagreement . . . about a month ago. We haven't spoken since.'

'What did you disagree about?'

'It was a stupid business really. But . . . baffling. I'd been getting a bit resentful of the number of times she couldn't see me. She always seemed to be working. Even at the weekends. Well, the parents-in-law of one of the partners here, Clive Palfreyman, have retired to the Isle of Wight. Clive and his wife went to see them one weekend and met Sarah on the car ferry back. When they asked what had taken her to the Island, she said she'd been visiting a client in Parkhurst Prison. Clive mentioned it to me and asked if the client was some local villain we might have heard of. Sarah had been pretty tight-lipped, apparently. Well, she'd said nothing to me about it. Not a thing. And when I raised it with her, she was too quick to plead confidentiality for my liking. I had a quiet word with one of her colleagues later. We play a weekly game of squash. He was more or less adamant that Anstey's had no client banged up in Parkhurst. She had to be lying. But why? When I confronted her, she flew completely off the handle. Accused me of spying on her and God knows what. Said if that was how I was going to behave, it'd be best if we stopped seeing each other. And that's what we did.'

'You haven't seen her since?'

'No. As a matter of fact, I was going to try and patch things up this week. I'd bought her some rather expensive earrings for Christmas. But then I heard about Shaun Naylor's appeal. And something clicked. I remembered which prison they'd said he was in. Albany. On the Isle of Wight. Just down the road from Parkhurst. And I wondered if . . .'

'That's who she'd been to see.'

'Yes. That's exactly what I wondered. Which would be weird, wouldn't it? I mean . . . why should she?'

If Sarah had helped Paul concoct his confession, as I was beginning to think she must have done, maybe she was hiding – though what from I couldn't imagine – at his house on Bathurst Wharf. I walked from Corn Street back through the unrelenting rain to Queen Square, where I'd parked the car, then on to the quay where I'd seen Rowena for the last time six months before and across the swing-bridge to her former home.

By the time I reached the door I was sure something must be wrong. It stood open to the wind and wet and a grey-haired woman in housecoat and wellingtons was peering in over the threshold. As I approached, a man appeared beyond her in the hallway: Inspector Joyce.

'Mr Timariot,' he said, spotting me immediately over the woman's shoulder. 'What brings you here?'

'Well, I . . .'

'Looking for Mr Bryant?'

'Er . . . yes. Obviously.'

'You're out of luck.' He stepped onto the pavement and erected an umbrella. 'My sergeant will lock up, luv,' he said to the woman. 'He'll drop the key back to you. Thanks for your cooperation.' Then he moved past her and walked slowly towards me, frowning suspiciously. Until the brim of his brolly snagged on mine and he pulled up abruptly. 'That's the next-door neighbour,' he said. 'Bryant leaves a key with her. When we couldn't raise him, we thought we'd better take a peek inside.'

'What did you find?'

'Nothing. He's not there. But it doesn't look as if he's gone for long. Anxious to contact him, are you?'

'Not exactly.'

'Heard about his father-in-law?'

'Yes. As a matter of fact, I have. That's why I'm in Bristol. To offer Sarah my condolences.'

'You mean she's still here? I should have thought she'd be in Portugal by now, trying to find out what happened. I wouldn't mind knowing myself.'

'An accident, I believe.' Grateful for the excuse he'd unwittingly supplied me with, I added: 'But you're probably right. Sarah must already be on her way to Portugal. Stupid of me to expect to find her at home, really. I only came on here in case—'

'She was with Bryant? Not very likely, is it?'

'Probably not.' Irritated by his habit of interrupting me, I made an attempt to put him on the defensive. 'And why are you looking for Paul, Inspector?'

'Because Naylor's release on bail seems to have coincided with a crop of fatal accidents. And coincidences make me twitchy. I just wanted to make sure Bryant hadn't met with one.'

'I don't follow. Sir Keith's death hardly constitutes a crop.'

'No. But there's been another since then.' He paused, relishing, it seemed, the chance to study my expression while I waited for him to continue. 'Vincent Cassidy's surfaced. Literally. In the Thames, night before last. Dead as most of the fish.'

I could have told him all I knew then. And perhaps I should have done. But I was determined to find Sarah and demand an explanation from her before I carried tales about her to the police. 'An accident, you say?'

'It's what the coroner will probably say. No fixed abode. Plenty of drink and drugs in the bloodstream. Sounds a simple case of drowning, doesn't it? He could have got the head wound hitting a bridge pier on the way in. Naylor was still in custody at the time, so we can't go accusing him of anything. I expect we'll have to settle for accidental death. Same as Sir Keith.'

'And this happened on Tuesday?'

'Monday, more likely. The pathologist reckons he'd been in the water about twenty-four hours.' Monday was the day Cassidy had phoned me. He'd sounded desperate. And now it seemed he'd had good reason to be. Smith and Brown were covering their tracks – with merciless efficiency. 'Why do you ask?'

'Oh . . . no reason.'

'I generally find there's a reason for everything.'

'Do you? Tell me, Inspector, you are absolutely certain Paul Bryant murdered Oscar Bantock and Louise Paxton, aren't you?'

'We'd hardly have let Naylor go if we weren't, would we, sir?' He looked at me scornfully. 'And you wouldn't have changed your statement if you had any doubts.'

'But what convinced *you*?'

'The accumulation of detailed knowledge. As you once pointed out, we always keep a few things back. And Bryant knew what a lot of them were.'

'Such as?'

'I can't go into that.'

'Just give me one example. I know about the diary. There must have been more.'

'Of course there was, sir.'

'Like what?'

'Oh, all right,' he said impatiently. 'Bryant knew what Lady Paxton was wearing. I mean every single garment. He described them accurately. Colour, fabric, the lot. Now how could he – unless he really did watch her take them off?'

'I suppose he couldn't.' But my mind was already pursuing a different answer. Louise's clothes would have been returned to her family at some point. Sarah would probably have looked after that. She'd have wanted to spare Rowena and her father the task. So, she'd have known exactly what her mother had been wearing.

'Then there was his description of Bantock's face after he'd killed him,' said Joyce, warming to his theme. '"Smeared in multi-coloured flakes of paint." Well, that's just how it was. It's what Jones said – the postman who found him. "Like it was covered in hundreds and thousands." But it was never mentioned in court.'

'Surely Jones might have talked about it subsequently.'

'Of course. We thought of that. We had Jones in to take a look at Bryant. He'd never set eyes on him before in his life.'

'I see.' And so I did. I saw precisely how it could have been managed. Jones had never met Paul. But he might have met Sarah. And she might have persuaded him to reminisce about the scene at Whistler's Cot. But Joyce wouldn't have asked him if she had. The idea would never have crossed his mind.

'Besides, those meetings with Lady Paxton he listed – complete with dates, times and places. There were too many to fake. Far too many. And every single one checked out.'

'Did it?' Sarah had been ideally placed to supply dates, times and places, of course. Even corroborate some of them herself. And she'd have realized they could risk inventing a few incidents that a living person would know to be untrue – so long as that person was sure to be disbelieved. 'Not *every* one, surely. I thought Sir Keith denied having the row with Lady Paxton Paul claims to have overheard in Biarritz.'

'Well, he would, wouldn't he?' Joyce said with a cynical smile. He looked round. The door to number thirteen was closed now and a bedraggled figure I took to be his sergeant was sheltering from the rain beneath the first-floor bay. 'OK, Mike. Go back to the car. I'll join you there.' The sergeant nodded and hurried away.

'Where do you think Paul's gone, Inspector?'

Joyce shrugged. 'Christmas shopping, for all I know. He's free to go wherever he likes. Until Naylor's been acquitted. The neighbour's going to ask him to phone me as soon as he gets back, though. Just to put my mind at rest.'

'They said on television Naylor's appeal wouldn't come to court until March.'

'That's right.'

'It's a long time to wait.'

'For Bryant, you mean?' Joyce glanced over his shoulder at the empty rain-streaked windows of number thirteen. 'Oh, he'll sit it out patiently enough, I reckon.' Then his brow creased into a frown. 'That's not what's worrying me.'

'What is, then?'

He shook his head. 'To be frank, Mr Timariot, I'm not quite sure. There's something wrong here. But I can't for the life of me work out what it is.'

Why had they done it? The question circled giddily in my mind as I ran back to Queen Square, jumped into the car and started for Clifton. Why should they have wanted to do it? It made no sense. Yet clearly, to them, it did. They'd planned this. They'd plotted and prepared it. Every step of the way. But I had no more inkling than Joyce of what they were trying to achieve.

I was already pursuing them, though. Whereas he didn't even know they'd fled. At Caledonia Place, I let myself in without bothering to try the bell again and went straight up to the second-floor flat.

Then nothing. As I closed the door behind me, only the motionless air of unventilated normality revealed itself. The flat was clean and tidy. But there was clearly nobody at home. I moved slowly from room to room, half-expecting something to happen, some meaning or significance to spring out at me from Sarah's domestic orderliness. But it didn't. Her pictures were still on the walls. Her saucepans still hung in line on the hooks above the kitchen worktop. Her coats and dresses still filled the wardrobes. She could have walked in at any moment and it would have seemed no different from all the other times she'd walked in at the end of a working day.

Except she wasn't going to. The certainty grew as the silence encroached. She wasn't coming back. Wherever she'd gone – why ever she'd gone there – retreat wasn't possible. I stood in the lounge, staring at the photograph of her and Rowena with their mother that was still in its place on the mantelpiece between the carriage clock and the china rabbit. Louise's gaze seemed to be directed at me now, not some indefinable point beyond the camera. It hadn't changed, of course. But I had. She'd invented the stranger on Hergest Ridge for Sophie's benefit, because she'd known Sophie would believe a fictitious affair more readily than the truth. What must she have thought, then, when she met me there? What must have gone through her mind?

Suddenly, the telephone rang, making me jump with surprise. As I moved towards it, the answering machine cut in and I heard Sarah's recorded voice addressing the caller. '*This is Bristol 847269. I'm afraid I can't take your call at the moment, but if you'd like to leave a message, I'll get back to you as soon as possible. Please speak after the tone.*'

It was the secretary I'd talked to at Anstey's. I recognized her at once. '*This is Dorothy Gibbons here, Sarah. Mr Anstey's most anxious to speak to you. Please contact him the minute you return. You can phone him at home if necessary. Thank you.*'

The machine clicked off and silence resumed. Then I pressed the replay button, waited for the tape to wind back and listened as the accumulated messages replayed themselves in sequence. A girl called Fiona, inviting Sarah to a New Year's Eve party. A bookshop, reporting the arrival of some paperback she'd ordered. Bella, sounding suitably urgent. Bella again, after drawing a blank at Anstey's. Then, something odd.

'*Katy Travers here, Miss Paxton. Hewitson Residential. I'm sorry to bother you, but Mrs Simpson – I think you've met her – keeps badgering me about her mail. She seems to think some of it may have gone astray. Perhaps you could give her a call on 071 624–8488. I'd have phoned you at Braybourne Court, but apparently the line's been disconnected and I didn't think you'd want me to give her your Bristol number. I'd be most grateful if you could have a word with her. I'm sure there's been some simple misunderstanding. Thanks a lot. 'Bye.*'

There were a few more messages after that, including a third from Bella, but I paid them little attention. Instead, I rewound the tape and listened to Katy Travers again. What the devil was she talking about? Who was Mrs Simpson? Where – and what – was Braybourne Court?

I switched off the tape, picked up the telephone and dialled Mrs Simpson's number.

'Hello?' She sounded well-bred, elderly and potentially tetchy.

'Mrs Simpson?'

'Yes.'

'I'm a friend of Sarah Paxton's. I—'

'Oh, good. I want to speak to Miss Paxton. I've been trying to contact her for several days, but she seems distinctly elusive. The agency refused to give me her telephone number, you know. Extraordinary behaviour.'

'Yes. That's why—'

'I have friends and relatives all over the world. Many of them will have sent me a Christmas card. But to my old address. That's the point. A substantial quantity must have arrived, but I've seen nothing of them. It really is too bad. It was distressing enough to have to leave my lovely flat without this. After that exorbitant rent increase, it's adding insult to injury to find that my successor can't even take the trouble to forward my mail. Don't you agree?'

'Well, I—'

'I called round the other day, which I found a most upsetting experience in view of all the happy times my late husband and I enjoyed there, but Miss Paxton wasn't in. Of course, I suppose she uses the flat merely as a *pied-à-terre*. And very agreeable too. But for those of us on fixed incomes—'

'Mrs Simpson!' I shouted.

'Yes?' she responded, briefly cowed.

'Are you saying Sarah's taken over the lease of a flat you used to occupy?'

'I don't understand. Surely you must know she has. Ah, Braybourne Court.' Her tone became wistful. 'Such a charming corner of Chelsea.'

'Chelsea, you say?'

'Certainly.'

'Where *exactly* in Chelsea?'

'What an extraordinary question. Surely Miss Paxton's told you.'

'No. As a matter of fact, she hasn't. She, er, neglected to give me the address. Which is awkward, since I've promised to visit her there. So, could you enlighten me?'

She didn't reply at once. I could almost feel her suspicion coursing down the line. 'How did you say you got my number, Mr . . . ?'

'Timariot. Robin Timariot. I'd be happy to discuss your forwarding problems with Sarah, Mrs Simpson. More than happy. I'm sure I could sort something out on your behalf. I can also give you her Bristol address and telephone number, which you might find helpful.'

'Hmm. Miss Paxton doesn't seem to be a very well-organized young lady, I must say.'

'Quite so.'

'Very well, Mr . . . er . . . Marriott. Braybourne Court is an apartment block in Old Brompton Road. My flat – Miss Paxton's, that is – is number two hundred and twenty-eight. Though what kind of a friend you count her as if she can't be bothered to supply you with such information herself I really can't imagine.'

'No, Mrs Simpson. Neither can I.'

The rain was unceasing, drifting in sheets across the dank green fields of Wiltshire and Berkshire as I drove towards London. I cursed the traffic and spray that slowed my progress, watched the clock tick round and the meagre light drain from the louring sky . . . and wondered. What would I find at 228 Braybourne Court? Why the secrecy? Why the cunning manipulation of events? What was it leading to? They'd been so clever I still couldn't see beyond the ruse itself. But for Sir Keith's death, of course, they'd still be safe from detection. And but for Mrs Simpson's obsession with some allegedly missing mail that could just as easily be caught up in the Christmas rush, there'd be no trail to follow. Only bad luck – only the unforeseeable intervention of the unpredictable – had defeated their precautions. Or had given me the chance of defeating them. For that's all it was. An outside chance. One I had to take.

It was the last full shopping day before Christmas and London was at its clogged and crowded worst. Wearying of the crawl in from the M4 that had stretched the journey from Clifton to nearly four hours, I abandoned the car near Baron's Court tube station and started walking through the deepening twilight. Red lights bleared at me from winding rows of cars and glimmered on Christmas trees in drawing-room windows. Danger winked out its warning as darkness gathered its strength. But I hurried on, following Louise into the forest even as night began to fall.

Braybourne Court was a large red-brick Edwardian mansion block near Brompton Cemetery, with separate security-locked entrances, each serving a dozen or so flats, spaced around its four sides. The entrance leading to flats numbered between 225 and 237 was in a quiet side-street. All I could see through the double glass doors was a plushly carpeted hallway, dividing discreetly after twenty feet or so. If I moved back to the steps spanning the basement area, I could catch a glimpse through the lofty ground-floor windows of corniced ceilings and flock-papered walls. An entry-phone system was in place to ensure this was as much of a view as unwelcome visitors ever got of the interior. Braybourne Court evidently placed a premium on privacy. And charged accordingly, I had no doubt. Sarah could easily be paying seven or eight hundred pounds a week for a *pied-à-terre* here. Which would have seemed absurdly extravagant – if that's what I'd believed she wanted it for.

But it wasn't, as the blank name-panel next to the buzzer for flat 228 somehow confirmed. Privacy wasn't the point. Secrecy was nearer the mark. Absolute secrecy. Which I was about to penetrate.

I pressed the buzzer, got no response and pressed it again with the same result. I waited a few moments, then tried three short sharp rings. Still nothing. But somehow I wasn't discouraged. She was there. And so was Paul. Why I didn't know and couldn't guess, but the intricacy of their deception convinced me of their presence. They might hope I'd give up and go away, but they'd be hoping in vain.

I pressed the buzzer again and this time kept my finger on it, counting the seconds under my breath. Before I'd reached forty, there was a click from the speaking grille and a voice I recognized with a surge of relief said: 'Yes?'

'Sarah? It's Robin. Can I come in?'

'*Robin?*' She sounded horrified as well as amazed.

'Yes. Can I come in?'

'What . . . How did you get here?'

'I'll explain inside. It's pretty cold and wet out here.'

'No. I . . . I can't see you, Robin.'

'Don't be ridiculous.'

'I'm not being. Please . . . Please go away.'

'You don't mean that.'

'Please, Robin. Leave. It's best, believe me. Goodbye.' There was another click as she put the phone down. I pressed the buzzer instantly, reckoning she couldn't just walk away while it rang. Sure enough, she picked up the phone again. 'There's nothing more to be said, Robin. I want you to—'

'Paul's with you, isn't he? I know he is, so don't bother to deny it. The police are looking for him.'

'What? Why?'

'Let me in and I'll explain.'

'Do they . . . have this address?'

'No. But if I have to walk away from here, they will have it.'

'Don't do this, Robin.' Her tone had altered. She seemed to be pleading with me – as much for my sake as hers. 'You have no idea what you're getting involved in.'

'Open the door, Sarah.'

'Please, I—'

'Open it.'

Several long speechless moments passed, during which a faint buzz from the grille assured me she was still on the line. Then there was a much louder buzz from the lock on the doors. And when I pushed against them they yielded.

I stepped inside. The doors swung shut behind me. Warm air and insulated silence wrapped themselves around me. I walked down the hall to the point where it divided, glanced left and saw a brass plaque on the wall inscribed 225–226; LIFT TO 229–237. Glancing right, I saw another plaque, inscribed 227–228. I headed that way, turned left, passed flat 227, rounded a bend in the corridor and saw the door to flat 228 at the far end.

It was fitted with a viewing lens, through which Sarah must have been watching out for me. The handle turned as I approached and the door slowly opened. But she didn't move into view. All I could see inside was a stretch of carpet and a bare wall, dimly lit. I called her name, but she didn't answer. I hesitated for a moment and called again. Still she didn't respond. Not that it made any difference. I knew what I was bound to do. It was too late to turn back now. I reached out and touched the door. It creaked slightly on its hinges. Then I stepped forward and crossed the threshold.

CHAPTER TWENTY-THREE

There was a window to my left, admitting some grey remnants of daylight. Ahead, the entrance hall narrowed into a passage, lit by two bare bulbs and the glare from a third beyond the right-angled corner at its end. Three or four doors stood open along the passage, but the rooms they led to were in darkness. The flat looked what I sensed it to be – carpeted and curtained, but otherwise unfurnished.

I heard the front door click shut behind me and turned to find Sarah looking straight at me. She was dressed all in black – pumps, tights, mini-skirt and polo-neck sweater. Her eyes were wide and staring. She was breathing with audible rapidity. And she was holding her right arm behind her back at an awkward angle, bizarrely reminiscent of a suitor concealing a bunch of flowers from his beloved.

'Hello, Sarah,' I ventured. 'Where's Paul?'

'Never mind Paul,' she replied breathlessly. 'How did you get here? And why did you come?'

The *how* was easy to explain. And I did. But the *why*? Something in her manner – something in her dilated eyes – stopped me telling her there and then that her father was dead.

'Mrs Simpson,' Sarah muttered when I'd finished. 'The stupid stupid woman. What do her bloody Christmas cards matter compared with—' She broke off and her tone became more controlled. 'Why was Bella so anxious to contact me? Why isn't she with you?'

'It's your father. He's . . . not well. Bella is . . . with him.'
'In Biarritz?'
'Look, can we—'
'What's wrong with him?'
'Why don't we go somewhere more comfortable?'
'No. Tell me now. Tell me here.'
'I'm sure it would be better if—'
'*Tell me!*' Her cry – of pain as much as impatience – echoed in the empty hallway.
'All right. Calm down.' I moved towards her, but she stepped smartly back, bumping against the wall behind her. I saw a muscle tighten in her cheek. Her gaze narrowed.
'He's dead, isn't he?'
'I'm sorry, Sarah. Really I am. But the answer's yes. Your father's dead.'
She half-closed her eyes and tears sprang into them. Her head drooped. Her voice faltered. 'How? How did it happen?'
'It's not entirely clear. Some kind of—' I stopped as her right arm slipped from behind her back and fell to her side. Then I saw what she was holding in her hand. A snub-nosed revolver, its barrel and chambers glistening in the cold electric light. 'Sarah! What in God's name—'
There was a movement – a shadow across my sight – further down the passage. I whirled round and saw Paul standing at the end. He was wearing jeans, trainers and a dark green sweat-shirt. And he too was holding a gun.
'Paul?'
'Leave now, Robin,' he called to me. 'Walk out and forget you were ever here.'
'I'll do no such thing.'
'This isn't your affair. Don't get involved.'
'Involved in what?'
'Just go. While you still can.'
'Sarah?' I turned and looked at her. She raised her head and dabbed away her tears with the knuckles of her left hand. She was holding the gun firmly, her forefinger curled round the trigger. And her jaw was set in a determined line. '*Sarah?*'
'You don't understand, Robin. But you will. Later. Just tell me how Daddy died. Then go.'
'I'm telling nothing and going nowhere until you two tell *me* what the hell's going on here.'
'It's best if you don't know. Believe me.'
'That's right,' Paul cut in. 'Believe her.'

'Why should I?'

'Just do it!' He leant against the wall behind him, glanced along the passage to his right, then looked back at us. 'I'll give you five minutes to get rid of him, Sarah.' With that he pushed himself upright and moved out of sight.

'Where's he gone?' I demanded, turning to Sarah.

'Don't ask.'

'But I am asking.'

'This is nothing to do with you.'

'Oh, but it is. I've seen through your deception, you know. Paul's confession. The faked corroboration. The whole elaborate game you've been playing.'

She stared at me incredulously, something in her expression signalling that she didn't intend to deny it. 'How?' she murmured.

'Never mind. What I want to know is: why did you do it? Why the secret address? Why the guns, for God's sake?'

'Can't you guess?'

'No. I can't.' I peered down the passage. There was no sign of Paul. But there'd been a sound – a groan and a chink of metal. 'Paul?' I called. There was no response. Except the same faint metallic rattle. I started towards it.

'Robin!' Sarah cried after me. 'Stop!' But I didn't stop. I don't think I could have done. The passage drew me on down its carpeted length, dream-like and surreal in the low-wattage light, with the black gulfs of empty rooms to either side. I had to know now. I had to see for myself.

I reached the corner and looked to my left. At the far end of the passage, bright light spilt from an open doorway. A shadow moved across it. I glanced round at Sarah, who was slowly following me, shaking her head, as if to urge me even at this stage to turn back, to reconsider, to leave well alone. Then I walked on.

It was a bathroom, blue-walled and chill. The view through the doorway was of a wash-hand basin and a frosted sash window. Propped incongruously on the window-sill was a bulky black tape recorder. As I stepped into the room, my view broadened to encompass a half-open door in the far corner, a wooden-seated loo visible in the gloom beyond. The bath was to my left, an old roll-top cast-iron tub with ball-and-claw feet. The tap end was out of my sight for the moment, behind the wide-open door. Paul was leaning against the wall near the other end, his right arm crossed over his chest, his left hand supporting his elbow while he nestled the gun against his cheek. I didn't know what to make of his narrow-lidded stare, but a phrase of Bella's came into my mind – '*extremely clever as well as seriously insane*' – and fear suddenly descended on me, like some unseen and unsuspected creature leaping onto my back.

'You shouldn't have come down here,' he said matter-of-factly. There was a moan and a rattle from behind the door. I stepped forward and turned my head. And then I saw.

Shaun Naylor, dressed in jeans, T-shirt and a denim jacket, was on his knees in the bath. His wrists and ankles were shackled together behind him, the shackles held fast by a chain tied round the tap mountings and stretched taut to eliminate all freedom of movement. His arms were bound so tightly that his shoulders had been dragged back and his chest pushed forward. His chin was lolling against his chest, but he raised it to look at me. One of his eyes was swollen to the point of closure. There was a gash on his forehead and drops of congealed blood round the neck of his T-shirt. A broad strip of adhesive brown sealing tape had been stuck across his mouth. He was breathing hard through his nose and sweating profusely, either from panic or the vain struggle to escape. He strained at the chain as I watched, his brow creasing with the effort, his eyes swivelling up to meet mine. The hollow noise of metal on pipework was what I'd heard from the hall. But his knees slid no more than an inch forward or sideways and he gave up, slumping against the wall of the bath and groaning in protest.

'He thinks he can fight his way out of this,' said Paul with a snigger. 'But he can't. Hear that, Naylor? There's no way out this time, you stinking bastard.'

'For God's sake!' I shouted, horrified more by Paul's gloating tone than the ugly weals on Naylor's face.

'But that's right,' said Paul. 'It is for God's sake. And Rowena's. And her mother's. And Oscar Bantock's. We're doing it for all their sakes.'

'That's your justification for torture?'

'It isn't torture,' said Sarah, stepping into the room behind me. I swung round to look at her. There was no hint of shame in her expression – or in her voice. 'It's justice.'

'*What?*'

'You wanted to know why. Well, this is why. When Rowena died, Paul and I agreed we had to put an end to the evil and suffering this man' – she pointed at Naylor – '*chose* to inflict on those we'd loved. We agreed to do what everybody seemed so anxious to do. Prove him innocent. Get him released from prison. Set him free. And then . . .'

'Take his freedom away again,' Paul concluded with a quivering smile.

'This doesn't make any sense.' I looked at each of them in turn and could see in their eyes the proof that it did make sense. To them.

'They'd never have given up, Robin,' said Sarah. 'I told you that. They'd have gone on and on and on. Until they'd turned Nayor into some kind of folk hero. Well, he's no kind of hero. And we're going to prove that.'

'How?'

'We've tape-recorded his confession. That's why we had to get him out of prison. So we could make him answer for what he'd done. And why we had to lure him here. So we could have him all to ourselves. It's thanks to you we worked out how to pull it off. You went to see him in Albany and told me afterwards about his marital problems. So, I went to see him myself. I've been every other week since. Assuring him how sorry I am he should have been wrongly imprisoned. Offering him whatever . . . consolation . . . he might need after his release. I was there on Tuesday, urging him to come round here as soon as he could. Didn't take him long, did it? I think he was expecting me to drop my knickers for him the moment he stepped through the door. I'd promised him a surprise Christmas present, you see. Well, I've kept my word, haven't I?'

'Not about this place you haven't,' complained Paul. Instantly, I was alert to the hint of friction between them. 'It was supposed to be impossible for anyone to trace the address.'

'Yes.' Sarah frowned in disappointment, as if somebody had just pointed out a trivial flaw in a legal argument. 'It was. But I suppose something was bound to go wrong eventually. We've been lucky to get as far as we have. There were times I thought we were certain to be found out.' She raised her head defiantly – almost proudly – as she looked at me. 'But you believed Paul's confession, didn't you, Robin, when we tried it out on you? And so did the police. They never dreamt I was feeding Paul the information they couldn't account for him possessing. Sarwate let me examine his files on the murders when I went to him and said I was beginning to have doubts about his client's guilt following the *Benefit of the Doubt* broadcast. That's how I got the facts right. By combing through all the statements from witnesses and speaking to one or two of them myself – without telling them who I was, of course. Sarwate had copies of just about everything. Even the scene-of-crime photographs. I asked him not to tell anybody about my enquiries to spare me family and professional embarrassment. And he agreed. From his point of view, it would have been advantageous to have me on his side. I don't suppose it ever occurred to him that Paul and I were conspiring together. He was hardly likely to look a gift horse in the mouth, was he?'

'You talk about this as if it were some kind of game.'

'It's no game,' said Paul.

I turned on him, stupefaction swamping my fear of what they meant to do. 'Whose idea was it? Which of you suggested it to the other?'

'It doesn't matter,' said Sarah.

Paul smirked grimly at me. 'It matters to you, though, doesn't it, Robin? Well, for what it's worth, *I* suggested it. I'd spent weeks mourning Rowena and our unborn child and the ache of it – the anger I couldn't vent – only got worse. I started looking back on our life together, trying to see how I could have prevented her death. It always came back to her mother's death. And to this worthless bastard.' He waved his gun at Naylor, who seemed hardly to notice. 'It started as an idle thought. Where was I the night Louise died? The answer was so banal. In bed in a cheap *pension* in Chamonix with some Swedish girl whose name I couldn't even remember. But then it came to me. How easily I could pretend I'd been somewhere else. How easily I could claim to have committed the murders. Then they'd have to let Naylor go. Well, he couldn't argue, could he? He couldn't change his mind and say he was guilty after all. And he wouldn't want to. Freedom's worth any amount of bewilderment. But once he *was* free . . . he was at our mercy.' He sniggered. 'I couldn't have done it without Sarah's help, of course. She had her mother's diary and her trained memory of what happened and when. She also had the forensic skill to put the whole thing together. All I had to do was act the part she wrote for me. Christ, it was a demanding performance, though. Three months of twisting my mind to fit the past we'd invented. Three months pretty close to hell. But they were worth it. For this moment.'

I turned back to Sarah, my gaze telegraphing the question it was hardly necessary for me to ask. 'Why did you go along with it?'

'Because Rowena's death was one death too many. I'd just about succeeded in putting what happened to Mummy behind me. In ceasing to imagine what it must have been like for her. Then Rowena threw herself off that bloody bridge. How I wished and wished I could have stopped her. But there was nothing I could do. She was dead and so was the baby I hadn't even known she was carrying. That made a third generation touched by murder. I wanted to strike back, to retaliate. But I couldn't see any way to. Until Paul told me what he'd been thinking and I saw there was a way to avenge them all.'

'And in the process portray your mother as some sort of nymphomaniac? What kind of revenge is that?'

Sarah bit her lip. 'We had no choice. The record will soon be set straight. I only wish Daddy had lived to—' She broke off, grief washing back over her. 'Tell me how he died, Robin. Was it his heart? He had a coronary about twelve years ago and ever since the murders I've been afraid—'

'He fell from a cliff, Sarah.'

'What? In Biarritz? Surely—'

'In Portugal.'

'I don't understand. What was he doing in Portugal?'

'Nobody seems to know. The authorities think it was an accident.'

'But you don't, do you?' She seemed oblivious to the tears glistening in her eyes. 'You're implying he killed himself. Like Rowena. And for the same reason. You're trying to blame me, aren't you? You're trying to suggest the things Paul said about Mummy drove him to suicide.' She swayed slightly on her feet and raised a hand to her forehead. 'God, if that's true, we've—'

'It *isn't* true,' shouted Paul. He rushed forward, pushing me aside and taking a stand directly in front of Sarah. His gaze was fixed so firmly on her – and hers on him – that I wondered for a moment if I should try to grab one of the guns. But as soon as the thought formed, I dismissed it. The only hope of a peaceful outcome was to reason with them. 'Listen to me, Sarah,' Paul continued. 'Do you want to waste all these months of planning and preparing? That's what it'll mean if you start blaming yourself for your father's death. We don't know the circumstances. You can't trust a one-sided account of them. For Christ's sake, if anyone *is* to blame, it's Naylor, isn't it? He started this. But we're going to finish it.'

'Yes.' Every muscle in Sarah's body tensed. Her knuckles blanched with the ferocity of her grip on the gun. 'You're right. It's too late to stop now.' She glanced down at Naylor. 'I'd have liked to get more from him on tape, but what we have will suffice.'

'For what purpose?' I put in, desperate to plant as many doubts in her mind as I could. 'A confession extracted in these circumstances surely carries no legal weight.'

'None whatever.' She sounded calm again, but I knew she wasn't. Her empty left hand was clasped as tightly as her right to stop it shaking. 'This isn't about the law,' she declared. 'It's about morality. It's about making Naylor pay for what he did to my mother and indirectly to my sister. And from the sound of it to my father as well. He's destroyed them all, hasn't he? So now . . .'

'You mean to kill him?'

'No,' said Paul emphatically. 'We mean to execute him.'

'You wouldn't.' I looked at Sarah as I spoke, silently urging her to see reason. 'You couldn't.'

'Why not?' Her gaze challenged me as much as the question itself. 'A bullet through the brain's more merciful than rape and strangulation, isn't it? Much more.'

'Maybe. But it would still be murder.'

'Only in the eyes of the law.'

'And doesn't that matter? You're a solicitor, for God's sake. You're supposed to *believe* in the law.'

'I did once. But not any more. Not since I've seen how powerless it is to draw the poison from the wounds people like Naylor inflict – on the living as well as the dead.'

'But if you kill him, you'll only end up where he belongs. Behind bars.'

'So be it. Don't you understand, Robin? What's right can't be made wrong by fear of the consequences.' I saw her certainty gleam like religious fervour in her eyes. And I saw beyond it the futility of debate. Part of me agreed with her. And the other part wouldn't be able to talk her out of it. Only the truth – only the one discovery she hadn't made – could sway her. 'He deserves to die.'

'Why?'

'You know why. Because he murdered two people and wrecked the lives of several others.'

'He's solely responsible for that, is he?'

'Of course he is.'

'What are you getting at?' Paul fired the question at me over his shoulder.

'I'm getting at the truth. Which is more complicated than you think.'

'What do you mean?' asked Sarah, staring at me intently.

'Has he said why he went to Whistler's Cot that night?'

'Some crap about being paid to kill Bantock,' snorted Paul.

'It's not crap. He *was* paid. Or would have been. By a man

called Vince Cassidy. Who later testified against him at his trial.'

Sarah blinked in surprise. 'How could you know he told us that?'

'Because it's the truth. Somebody hired Cassidy to kill Bantock. And Cassidy sub-contracted the job to Naylor. Your mother simply got in the way.'

'You can't know that for a fact.'

'I can. Because that somebody was your father.'

'No. It's not possible.'

'I'm afraid it is. He was convinced your mother meant to leave him for Oscar Bantock. And he was prepared to commission Bantock's murder to prevent her. It was to be dressed up as a burglary that went wrong. And it did go wrong. But not in the way he or any—'

'Shut up!' Paul rounded on me, raising the gun as he did so. His mouth was twisted into a snarl and his eyes were bulging. The mania I'd glimpsed in him before – the capacity for violence he probably didn't know the full extent of himself – drove me back across the room until I collided with the wash-hand basin. 'Do you think I don't know what you're trying to do?' he raged. 'Do you think I can't guess the way your mind's working?'

'Daddy?' Sarah murmured behind him. 'Daddy . . . started all this?'

'He's lying,' Paul shouted at her. 'He'll say anything to talk us out of what we agreed we had to do.'

'But that was before . . .' She looked past him at me, insisting I return her gaze. 'How can you know? How can you be sure?'

'He told Bella, to convince her Paul's confession was false. Remember his certainty, Sarah. Remember his insistence that it couldn't be true. All because he *knew* it wasn't.'

'But . . . he let Paul go on.'

'He couldn't stop him without admitting to complicity in his own wife's murder. But that's what he decided he had to do when he heard Naylor was to be released. He was going to make a clean breast of the whole thing. A former patient of his with underworld connections who'd retired to the sun was the man who'd set it up for him. That's why your father went to Portugal. To warn the man what he meant to do. But he wasn't allowed to do it. His death wasn't an accident *or* suicide. He was murdered. To protect the people who'd hired Cassidy on his behalf. Ring any bells, does it? A faintly shady acquaintance living in the Algarve? You may have met him a few times in the past.'

Sarah stared at me without speaking for several seconds while a host of puzzling recollections and unanswered questions must have assembled themselves in her mind and assumed the unmistakable symmetry of truth. Then she murmured 'Oh my God' under her breath and leant slowly back against the wall behind her. 'Ronny Dugdale.'

'Surely you don't believe him?' demanded Paul, stepping across to Sarah and shaking her by the shoulder. 'He's making the whole thing up.'

'I thought Daddy's reaction was just a different kind of grief,' she said quietly, almost reflectively, as if unaware of Paul's words ringing in her ears. 'I thought he just couldn't bring himself to think ill of Mummy and *that's* why he refused to accept our story. But I was wrong. It wasn't grief. It was guilt.'

'Jesus Christ, Sarah, concentrate on what we're here to do. You're letting it all slip away.'

'I was doing this for him. I was trying to take away his pain as well as mine. And now I discover . . . *he* was ultimately responsible for everything Naylor did.'

'Snap out of it.' Paul slapped her cheek and glared into her eyes. I moved cautiously towards them. 'Robin's lying to you.'

Sarah frowned pityingly at him. 'No, Paul. He isn't. Naylor named Cassidy as his accomplice when we held a gun to his head and gave him no choice but to tell as much of the truth as he knew. We just didn't want to listen. Because blame is so much easier to deal with when it's indivisible. Now it has to be shared out among God knows how many people, some of whom we've never even heard of. And my own father has to take the largest portion.'

'Only Naylor raped your mother. Only Naylor strangled her.'

'That's not good enough any more.'

'*Not good enough?*'

'No.' Her cheek had reddened where he'd slapped her. She cast me a fleeting look of conviction mingled with resignation. In it I felt I could read her exact state of mind. The justification she'd prepared for her actions had lost its purity. If she went on, its debasement would become all-consuming. Slowly and carefully, she opened the chambers of the revolver and slid the bullets out one by one into her palm.

'What are you doing?'

'I'm giving up. I have to. *We* have to.' She reached past him, dangling the empty gun by its trigger-guard from her forefinger, offering it to me while she kept her eyes fixed on Paul, so intently

– so imploringly – that he seemed unaware of what was happening. I stretched forward, lifted the gun from her finger and slipped it into my raincoat pocket. Unloaded, it didn't feel like a real weapon at all, merely a weight dragging at my coat, an encumbrance we'd all be well rid of. But I knew there was a second gun, clutched in Paul's right hand. And that was still very much a weapon. 'It's over, Paul,' Sarah said gently. 'We can't go on with it. Not now.'

'*You* can't, you mean.'

'It amounts to the same thing. We're in this together or not at all.'

'And at your say-so I have to write off three months of making people think I'm a murderer? I sometimes thought I'd be driven mad by the contradictions and convolutions of what you said I had to do to convince them. I only survived because I believed in what we'd set out to do. And now you're telling me to forget it. Dismiss it from my life. Well, I can't. And I won't.' The pitch of his voice had been rising as he spoke. Now something like a convulsion seemed to grip him. He took a step towards Sarah, then swung round and stared at me. 'You bastard!' he roared. 'You may have got to her, but you won't get to me.' He raised the gun and for a heart-stopping second I thought he was actually going to shoot me. Sarah must have thought the same because she rushed forward and grabbed his arm, the bullets she'd taken from the other gun spilling out of her hand and clattering to the floor.

'Paul! Listen to me.'

But Paul wasn't about to listen to anyone. He flung Sarah off, span round, leant over the bath, grasped Naylor by the collar and clapped the gun to his head. Naylor winced and squirmed, but was unable to resist. With the tape sealing his mouth, he couldn't even try to reason with the man who had it in his power to destroy him with one squeeze of his forefinger. The fragility of life – ours as well as his – was suddenly and horribly clear. Sarah and I stood stock still, both of us paralysed by the ease and imminence of the act. Perhaps Sarah hadn't imagined what it might mean until now; hadn't envisaged the smashed bone and spattered blood. If so, the images swarming in my head hadn't entered hers until this moment. It was a harsh awakening that might soon become a gory reality.

'Don't do it,' she said hoarsely.

'Why shouldn't I?' Paul looked round at us, his eyes blazing. 'I haven't forgotten Rowena, even if you have.'

'It's for her sake I'm asking. She wouldn't want you to do this.'

He hesitated. His grip slackened. The barrel of the gun eased back from Naylor's temple, leaving its circular imprint on his flesh. Paul began to tremble. He seemed to be holding tears only just at bay. Tears of anger and frustration and grief. 'We can't just . . . give up,' he sobbed.

'We must,' said Sarah.

'He deserves to die. You said so yourself.'

'Not this way. Not now.'

'It would be murder, Paul,' I said as calmly as I could. 'And Sarah would be an accessory. You'd be condemning her to prison along with yourself.' Whether this was legally true or not I had no idea. I could only hope Paul had none either. 'Do you want to do that? Do you *really* want to do that?'

'I want . . . justice.'

'Then let him live. There can't be any further doubts about his guilt. He'll go back to prison and rot there. You've made sure of that. You have his confession on tape. And we know the truth. Once that's out in the open, nobody's going to lift a finger to help him.'

'Aren't they?'

'You know they aren't.'

I could sense him longing to hear us say his efforts hadn't all been in vain. He'd risked his sanity, his liberty and his future to make amends to Rowena for not saving her. And they were still in the balance. But tilting even as we watched. Towards life. Towards hope. Towards some kind of dignity.

'You'll have stopped the tongues wagging, Paul. You'll have nailed the lies. Isn't that enough?'

It should have been. Paul should have said 'I suppose it'll have to be' and handed me the gun, reluctantly but conclusively. Then it would have been over. Finished. With no permanent damage done. We could all have breathed again. And lived.

But it wasn't over. And it was far from finished. Because Paul didn't respond to reason and logic the way I'd expected. I'd made the oldest mistake in the book. I'd calculated what I would do in his shoes. I'd imagined how I could best be talked into surrender and assumed it would work with him. But we never really know what's going on inside another person's head. We never have the faintest clue. Which words will douse the flame? Which words will fan it into a blaze that can become in a second a raging conflagration? We have no idea. We can only guess. Right or wrong.

'*Isn't that enough?*' No. It wasn't. Not nearly.

Paul stood upright and swung round, his eyes fixed unblinkingly on me. He put his left hand into the hip pocket of his jeans, pulled out a small key and held it in front of him, cupped in his palm. 'Take it,' he said quietly.

'What is it?'

'The key to the shackles. You want to let Naylor go, don't you? Well, do it.'

'Hold on. I'm not sure we should just—'

'Do it!' He raised the gun and pointed it straight at me, his finger still curled around the trigger, just as it had been when he'd held the weapon to Naylor's head.

'This isn't necessary, Paul,' put in Sarah. 'We can leave him where he is until the police arrive.'

'The police? Yes. I suppose they'll have to be called. To clear up the mess. That's about all they've ever done.'

'Why don't we—'

'Take the key and release him, Robin!' Paul's voice was unsteady and his hands were shaking enough to joggle the key in his palm.

'OK, OK. Whatever you say.' I reached out and took the key. Then Paul moved smartly aside and waved me past. I stepped over to the bath and glanced down into Naylor's eyes. Fear and pleading were swirling there. He knew how much was hanging by a thread. But he'd also heard me assure Paul that, whatever happened, his guilt was now incontestable.

'Go on,' said Paul from behind me.

I stooped over the bath and saw the twin keyholes on the shackles. I smelt Naylor's sweat, souring in the chill air. He was trembling too. And so was I. I looked back at Paul. 'We don't have to do this,' I pleaded. 'We really don't have to.'

'I say we do. Release him. Now.' He moved to the end of the bath and raised the gun again.

'All right.' I held up the key for him to see. 'I'm not arguing.' I leant into the bath, steadying the wrist manacles with one hand while I slid the key into the slot with the other. One turn and they snapped open. Naylor shuddered and parted his arms, allowing me to reach the other set and release his ankles. The shackles clanged hollowly against the enamel as they swung free at the end of their chain. I stood up and watched Naylor fall against the side of the bath, then straighten slowly out along it, his limbs uncoiling stiffly, his face grimacing as blood surged back into constricted joints and stretched muscles.

'Satisfied?' Paul asked bitterly. He leant forward and ripped off the strip of tape sealing Naylor's mouth in a single sweep of the arm. Naylor gave a cry of pain and squeezed his eyes tightly shut, rolling over as if to hide from his torturer. 'I hope you are. I hope you all are.' Paul's voice cracked as he spoke. He stood up, holding the gun oddly in front of him, as if he'd never seen it before, glancing quizzically at it and Naylor and us in turn.

'We should call the police,' said Sarah, fear writhing beneath the superficial logic of her words. 'Without delay.' She must have sensed by now what I too had sensed. That madness was streaming in around us like wolves into an undefended camp. None of us was going to get out of this unscathed.

'You disconnected the phone,' said Paul with a strange mirthless chuckle.

'We can use a neighbour's. It won't take long.'

'No hurry, then, is there?' He took a deep breath. 'Plenty of time, in fact.' Another breath, deeper still. 'You left and I should have followed. But I didn't have the courage.' Tears began to stream down his face. He wasn't talking to us any more. He wasn't talking to anyone we could see. But he could see her. Clearly and distinctly. 'I've found it now, though. This is the only way, isn't it?' He opened his mouth wide, pushed the barrel of the gun between his jaws, hesitated for a fraction of a second, then pulled the trigger.

The force of the shot blew Paul back against the loo door, which flew wide open. He fell onto his back in the doorway and the gun clattered to the floor at his feet. Blood trickled down the panelling of the door as it creaked back from its stop and came to rest against his shoulder. And more blood – much more – pumped out behind him in a spreading pool. Silence and immobility closed around us – a long frozen moment of jarred senses and delayed reactions.

Followed by the sound of Sarah sobbing. Then movement, rustling and gathering like reality breaking into a dream. I saw Naylor levering himself up and over the rim of the bath, head bowed, eyes trained on Paul's body. Time stretched elastically in my mind. And Naylor's intention burst into a realization. We'd told him his release from prison was an illusion we had the means to shatter. But Paul had been alive then. Now he was dead. If his co-conspirator were to die as well, along with the only other first-hand witness to what they'd done and why, then Naylor might – just might – walk free.

And even if he didn't, what did two more murders matter to

him? They were a risk well worth taking. We'd made him more dangerous than he'd ever been before. We'd turned him into a man with nothing to lose.

I launched myself across the room as he stepped out of the bath and shoulder-barged him with all my weight. Taken off balance with his limbs still rubbery, he fell towards the wall. I raised an arm to help him on his way, but he had the wit to grab my wrist and take me with him. Then his foot slipped on the enamel and I was free of him for as long as it took to drop to my knees and grab the gun from the floor.

I swung round, the gun in my right hand, my forefinger tracing the trigger-guard and sliding towards the trigger itself. Naylor was above me, one leg out of the bath and one in. He stopped when he saw what I was holding, freezing in mid-movement. His face, distorted by the gashes and bruises Paul had inflicted, knotted into a frown. To lunge at me. Or not. To go for broke. Or play for time. The calculations traced their pictograms across his features as I stared up into them.

'Don't move,' I said hoarsely, rising slowly and carefully to my feet, with the gun pointing straight at him all the time. And he didn't move. Not so much as a muscle. 'Sarah!' I called without taking my eyes from his. I could just make her out at the edge of my sight, a crouched figure in the doorway, arms clasped defensively around her shoulders. But I knew better than to look directly at her. Naylor would seize any chance I gave him, however slight. 'Sarah!'

'Y-Yes?'

'Go and call the police.'

'But—'

'Go!'

'All . . . All right. I'll be . . . as quick as I can.'

'Don't come back here. Wait for them outside. They'll need directions.'

'Outside? Surely—'

'Get out, Sarah. Get out now.'

She went without another word, perhaps guessing more of my meaning than I'd intended her to. I listened – and watched Naylor listening – to her footfalls as she ran down the passage. We heard the front door of the flat open and shut behind her. Then silence flooded through the empty rooms around us. It was just the two of us now. Just the confrontation – the decisive moment – we'd spent three and a half years feinting and circling and inching towards.

Naylor slowly lifted his other foot out of the bath and lowered it to the floor, his eyes daring me to tell him to stop. But if I told him and he didn't stop, I had only one sanction. He was testing my resolve, judging what I did – or didn't – have the nerve for. He didn't know. He wasn't sure. And neither was I.

'What happens now?' he asked, the challenge mounting as he spoke.

'We wait for the police.'

He shook his head. 'Don't think so.'

'I say we do. And I have the gun.'

'But you won't use it. You haven't got the bottle.'

'Can you be sure of that?'

His gaze narrowed. For a second or two, he weighed the question in his mind, seeking the certainty he needed. Then he said: 'Tell you what. I'll make a deal with you.'

'A *deal*?'

'Yeh. You let me climb through the window, with the tape in my pocket, before the Old Bill turn up . . . and we'll call it quits.'

'Why should I?'

' 'Cos if you don't, when they *do* turn up, I'll say you were in on it. I'll say *three* people took me prisoner and tortured me and threatened to kill me – and *you* were one of 'em. Abduction. Assault. Conspiracy. Christ knows what. You could be looking at quite a few years inside.'

'They wouldn't believe you.'

'Can you be sure of that?' He smirked. 'Look at it this way. Why risk it? What's it to you? The girl's mother. This bloke's wife. Some poxy old painter. What did they ever mean to you? Nothing, right?'

I almost wanted to smile. Naylor had just repeated my mistake. He'd fallen into the same fatal error. And taken my decision for me. 'You're right, of course,' I said. 'They were nothing to me but strangers. Perfect strangers.'

'There you are, then.'

'Do you know why I told Sarah to wait outside? I didn't. Until now.' I raised the gun and pressed the barrel against his forehead. His eyes widened. His mouth dropped open. He tried to step back, but, with the rim of the bath behind his knees, there was nowhere for him to go. '*Can we really change anything, do you think?*' Maybe we can, Louise. Maybe we can't. I don't know. I'm still not sure. But finishing things? That's different. When the moment comes and you recognize it for what it is, that's completely different. 'There's been a change of plan, Naylor. We aren't going to wait for the police after all. Or, rather, *you* aren't.'

'What?'

'You should be grateful. I'm actually doing you a favour. This way you don't have to go back to prison. *And* you find out how Louise Paxton felt when she realized you weren't going to spare her life.'

'Hold on, mate. You can't be—'

'Serious? Oh yes. I'm serious.' The trees thinned before me as I ran. There was a clearing ahead, a sun-filled glade where Louise was waiting. And this time I knew she wouldn't walk away. 'Never more so.'

'Yeh, but—'

He didn't finish his sentence. Although, in another sense, I suppose you could say he did. He paid the overdue penalty for what he'd done. There and then.

EPILOGUE

It began more than three [illegible] commenced, and it [illegible] another, at least to me. Was I only [illegible] so much longer ago and [illegible] [illegible] But I've nearly [illegible] have your [illegible]. Then you'll [illegible] and draw your own conclusions. [illegible]

[illegible] to identify [illegible] stood with the gun in my [illegible] in the [illegible] listening [illegible] [illegible] I wasn't [illegible] [illegible] he. But there were [illegible] [illegible] [illegible] in the [illegible] from the gun and recoil [illegible] [illegible] Horror made me [illegible] [illegible] in a vain effort to [illegible] [illegible] against the [illegible] wave of nausea swept over me. [illegible] the reflection of my face in the [illegible]

And only then did I [illegible] me. She came forward and [illegible] head against my shoulder. We [illegible] neither of us speaking. [illegible] [illegible] by the glow from [illegible] [illegible] the window. We [illegible]

EPILOGUE

It began more than three years ago, on a golden evening of high summer. And it ended yesterday, as a winter's night closed its shutters around me. Was it only yesterday? Sitting here, it seems so much longer ago and farther away. Time has stretched in the telling. But I've nearly finished now. Soon, you'll have your statement. Then you'll be free to type up your reports and draw your official conclusions. Then you really will know it all.

It's hard to believe, but it's true. Just twenty-four hours ago, I stood with the gun in my hand and stared down at Naylor's body in the bath, listening to his blood slowly trickle away. I wasn't sorry I'd killed him. I'm not sorry now. I don't think I ever will be. But there were more powerful emotions than sorrow to contend with in the aftermath of what I'd done. Shock made me drop the gun and recoil as it clanged against the enamel of the bath. Horror made me smear the bloodstains across my shirt and coat in a vain effort to wipe them away. Fear made me lean helplessly against the hand-basin, trembling and panting as a wave of nausea swept over me. Disbelief made me gape at the reflection of my face in the mirror above the basin.

And only then did I see Sarah, standing in the doorway behind me. She came forward and put her arms around me, resting her head against my shoulder. We stood like that for several minutes, neither of us speaking. Then we made our way to another room, faintly lit by the glow from a lamp in the communal garden beyond the window. We sat on the floor near the door, our backs to the wall. Still we said nothing. I supposed – when I became capable of supposing anything – that we were waiting to hear a police siren wail towards us through the distant hum of the traffic. But when Sarah broke the silence between us, I realized we weren't.

'I haven't called the police, Robin. I never left the flat. When it came to the point, I couldn't bring myself to. There was something strange in your voice when you told me to get out. Something . . . ominous. I stood in the hallway, trying to work out what it was, waiting and listening, quite what for I didn't know. Then I heard the gunshot.'

'Well, you'd better call the police now, hadn't you?'

'Are you sure you want me to? There'll be no going back if I do.'

'There's no going back anyway.'

'But there is. For you. If you left before I called the police, there'd be no need for them ever to know you'd been here. I could tell them Paul had shot Naylor, then himself. And I could tell them why.'

'It wouldn't work. My fingerprints are on the gun.'

'We could wipe them off. And off anything else you've touched. Besides, they wouldn't be looking for *your* fingerprints.'

'It still wouldn't work.'

'As a matter of fact, I think it would. I think you could leave here now and fly out to Rio tomorrow with no questions asked.' She slipped her hand into mine. 'Why not go, Robin? This was my idea, not yours. Why should you have to answer for it?'

I stared into the darkness around us, tempted by the thought of being able to walk away, untouched and unsuspected. The chance was there for the taking, a chance very close to a certainty.

But, if I'd gone, who would have told you she didn't want it to end as it did? You'd hardly have taken her word for it, would you? She knew that, of course. She knew it very well. So did I. That's why I had to refuse. Because two people can only cease to be strangers to each other once. From then on, there really is no going back. The only mistake is to believe there may be. But we're supposed to learn from our mistakes, aren't we? I walked away once and lived to regret it. This time, I'll stand my ground.